Coming Home

Fern Britton is the highly acclaimed author of six *Sunday Times* bestselling novels. Her books are cherished for their warmth, wit and wisdom, and have won Fern legions of loyal readers.

Fern is a judge for the Costa Book of the Year Award and is a supporter of the Reading Agency, promoting literacy and reading. Fern is deeply committed to a number of charities.

A hugely popular household name through iconic shows such as *This Morning* and *Fern Britton Meets...*, Fern is also a much sought-after presenter and radio host. She lives with her husband, Phil Vickery, and her four children in Buckinghamshire and Cornwall.

To find out more about Fern's books and upcoming projects, visit:

 /officialfernbritton

 @Fern_Britton

www.fern-britton.com

By the same author:

Fern: My Story

New Beginnings
Hidden Treasures
The Holiday Home
A Seaside Affair
A Good Catch
The Postcard

Short stories

The Stolen Weekend
A Cornish Carol
The Beach Cabin

Published in one collection as

A Cornish Gift

Fern Britton

Coming Home

HarperCollins*Publishers*

HarperCollins*Publishers* Ltd
1 London Bridge Street,
London SE1 9GF

www.harpercollins.co.uk

HarperCollins*Publishers*
1st Floor, Watermarque Building, Ringsend Road,
Dublin 4, Ireland

First published by HarperCollins*Publishers* 2018
8

A catalogue record for this book is available from the British Library

ISBN: 978-0-00-756302-9

Set in Birka by Palimpsest Book Production Limited, Falkirk, Stirlingshire

Printed and bound in the UK using 100% renewable electricity at
CPI Group (UK) Ltd

MIX
Paper from
responsible sources
FSC www.fsc.org   FSC™ C007454

This book is produced from independently certified FSC™ paper
to ensure responsible forest management.
For more information visit: www.harpercollins.co.uk/green

'A mother is always the beginning. She is how things begin.'

Amy Tan

ACKNOWLEDGEMENTS

I am so grateful to many people who have really believed in this book.

Firstly Kimberley Young, my editor, who has given me so much faith and support over wine and the kitchen table.

Secondly John Rush and Luigi Bonomi who have tirelessly guided my writing life with infinite kindness and generosity. You are the men I trust and turn to.

Liz Dawson, professionally the finest publicist and personally a great fairy lights arranger.

My dear husband Phil who doesn't have to read the books because he lives them every day for nine months.

My children who constantly smile and nod and put the kettle on when I need it.

The cats for keeping me company.

And you for reading my books. I hope this one is okay.

With love
Fern xx

PROLOGUE

Trevay, 1993

The house was still.

Her heart was hammering – she could hear it in her ears, hear her breath whistle in her nostrils.

She tried to quieten both.

In the dark of her bedroom, she strained her ears to listen for any noise in the house.

The church bell rang the half hour. Half past eleven.

She'd gone up to bed early, her mother asking her if she was feeling all right.

'Yeah. I'm fine.' She'd shrugged off the caring hand her mother had placed in the small of her back.

'If you're sure?' Her mother let her hand rest by her hip. 'Is it your period?'

She had hunched her shoulders and scowled at that. 'I'm just tired.'

'Ella and Henry had a lovely day with you on the beach,'

1

said her mother, bending her head to look up into her daughter's downcast eyes. 'You're doing so well.'

Sennen shrugged and turned to head for the stairs. Her father came out of the kitchen. 'Those little 'uns of yours asleep, are they?'

'She's tired, Bill,' replied her mother.

'An early night.' Her father smiled. 'Good for you.' She could feel her father's loving gaze on her back, as she ascended the stairs. She wouldn't turn around.

'Goodnight, Sennen,' chirped her mother. 'Sleep tight.'

Her parents had finally gone to bed almost an hour ago and now she picked up the heavy rucksack she'd got for her fifteenth birthday. It had been used once, on a disastrous first weekend of camping for the Duke of Edinburgh Bronze award. Even now the bone-numbing cold of one night in a tent and the penetrating rain of the twenty-mile hike the following day made her stomach clench. Back home she refused to complete any more challenges and dropped out. She used Henry as an excuse. He had just started to walk and her mother expected her to come home from school every weekend and do the things a mother should do for her child. On top of that she was expected to work hard for her exams. Why the hell would she want to learn how to read a map and cook a chicken over a campfire as well?

And then Ella came along.

Sennen had sat in the summer heat of the exam hall, six weeks from her due date, hating the kicks of her unborn child, hating being pitied by her teachers.

She rubbed a hand across her eyes and tightened the straps on the rucksack. What a model daughter she had been. Two babies by a father unknown and now she was leaving. Leaving them, her A levels, her over-indulgent liberal leftie parents who had supported her through it all – and leaving Cornwall.

She hovered on the landing outside Henry and Ella's room. She didn't go in. She knew she would never leave if she saw them, smelt them . . . She kissed her hand and placed it on their nameplates on the door. Downstairs, she tiptoed through the hall. Bertie the cat ran from under the hall table with a mew. She put her hand to her mouth to stop her startled cry then bent down to tickle him. 'Bye, Bert. Have a nice life.'

Slowly she turned the handle of the downstairs loo and edged in carefully, making sure that the rucksack didn't knock over the earthenware plant pot with its flourishing spider plant. Bert came with her and she had to nudge him out with her boot before closing the door behind him. The front door was too noisy to leave by.

The loo window always stuck a little and the trick was to give it a little thump with your palm. She held her breath, listened for any noise from upstairs. Nothing. She wound the small linen hand towel around her fist. It took three good pushes, each stronger than the last before the window swung open, noiselessly.

She threw the rucksack out first and then carefully climbed out after it.

She pushed the window shut and stood in the moonlit, tiled courtyard. In a corner was Henry's little trike and in another, Ella's beach pushchair. She had meant to take both in in case of rain, but had forgotten. She looked up to the night sky. Cloudless. It would be a dry night.

She picked her way over the sandpit, held in a wooden box that her father had made for her when she was little and now given fresh life to with a coat of scarlet paint, and made her way to the gate. The hinge creaked a little, but before it had shut itself she was already gone. Around the corner, down the lane and out to the bus stop by the harbour.

PART ONE
Adela's Only Love

1

Pendruggan, 2018

Kit Beauchamp stirred the tomato soup in front of him. 'When will your brother get here?'

Ella put her bowl down on the kitchen table and sat opposite him. 'Why? Nervous?'

Kit looked up into Ella's golden eyes. 'Should I be?'

'He'll adore you,' she reassured him. 'And if he doesn't, you'll know about it pretty quickly.'

'Oh blimey.' Kit really was nervous.

Ella loved that her boyfriend was taking this meeting seriously. Her brother was the only family she had left. His opinion counted for everything. She picked up her spoon and replied, 'Tomorrow lunchtime. He's getting the early train down from Paddington. Should be at Bodmin by about one.' Ella pushed curls the same colour as her soup behind her ears and dipped her spoon into the steaming bowl. She sipped and burnt her top lip. 'Ow.'

'Careful,' Kit said, blowing on his own spoon.

Freckles bounced across her face as she opened her mouth to fan cool air onto her burning tongue.

Kit tore at the centre of his crusty French roll and handed her some. 'It'll cool you down.' She took it gratefully.

For a couple of minutes neither spoke, quietly enjoying their simple lunch.

'I suppose,' frowned Kit, 'I don't want to make a bad impression.'

Ella giggled. 'I think Henry is the one who needs to be more worried. He can be a total arse.' She pulled Kit's hand over the table and rubbed it against her cheek. 'You'll be the brother he never had.'

Kit let his hand trail her cheek and chin. 'He's very important to you, isn't he?'

She blew on another spoonful of soup and nodded. 'We are the last of the Tallons.'

Kit wiped the final crust of bread around his bowl. 'Why do you think the solicitor wants to see you both?'

'The usual, I expect. Mum has either hidden herself so well that she doesn't want to be found, or she's dead.' Ella put her spoon down. Kit saw the lost child in the woman in front of him.

'He'll find her,' he said with a certainty he didn't feel.

'I don't know.' Ella sighed. 'Pass me your bowl.'

'I'll wash up,' he said glancing out of the window and looking at the sky. 'Fancy a walk? The dogs could do with one. Or are you too tired after all that vacuuming for your brother?'

Ella looked over at Terry and Celia who were lounging in their separate beds looking as disdainful as only Afghan hounds can.

'Well, Doggies? Fancy a walk?'

Terry managed a discreet waft of his feathery tail while

Celia sighed and raised an eyebrow. 'What a pair of lazy gits,' laughed Ella. She put her arm out to Kit as he passed on his way to the sink. 'But can it be to Trevay? I need to pick up some steak to make pasties for Henry tomorrow.'

Henry couldn't wait to get out of London. When the most recent solicitor's letter had arrived last week he had managed to wangle a decent chunk of leave in Cornwall. He wasn't too bothered about the letter. Another routine meeting. He and Ella had had so many since their grandmother had died. The problem lay with his unreliable, irresponsible mother who had left him and Ella when they were just tiny. He had been about two and Ella just over one. She'd disappeared to God knew where for God knew what whim and never come back. It had left Granny and Poppa heartbroken. Not to mention Henry, who still had vague memories of his mother. Sitting on her lap, being folded into her arms . . . *Stop it*, he told himself. *Hopefully the solicitor would tell him and Ella that his mother was lost forever, or dead. Either would be fine with him. Then at last they could sort out Granny's estate and move on with their lives.*

He returned his attention to the work on his desk. Two reports to finish, three phone calls to make and a handover to his colleague on how to deal with any issues that might arise in his absence and then – he rubbed his hands gleefully – Cornwall here he came.

Ella and Kit closed the door of Marguerite Cottage and waved at their nearest neighbour, Simon Canter, the vicar of Holy Trinity Church.

'Good afternoon,' Simon greeted them as he walked through the churchyard. 'Beautiful day. Enjoy it.'

'We will,' Ella called back.

He was right. It was a lovely day and as she waited for Kit to open up the car and load the dogs, Ella took time to absorb the moment. The Pendruggan village green with its cluster of old and new homes around it. Above her, tiny white cloud puffs floated in the bluest of skies. The smell of gorse on the wind, bringing with it the light rumble of surf on Shellsand Beach.

'Come on. Jump in,' said Kit, jangling the keys of his slightly aged car.

She climbed in. 'It's a day to be happy.'

'It's always a day to be happy for me,' he replied reversing out of the short drive.

She laughed. 'You're always so bloody happy. It's exhausting.'

'I'm a glass half-full man.'

'Don't I know it. My healthy scepticism, hoping for the best expecting the worst, balances us perfectly.' She waved and smiled as she spotted Queenie, owner of the village store and harbinger of all news, taking a quick fag break outside her shop. 'Queenie, however, is on permanent standby for disaster. Like Henry.'

Kit shoved the car into first gear and set off around the village green towards Trevay. 'So your brother's a miserable sod, then?'

'Yep. But he cheers up when he has beer inside him.'

'I'm the man for that job.'

They drove in friendly silence up the dappled lane that took them past their local, the Dolphin Pub and out to the top road headed towards Trevay.

Ella had always loved this road, even as a child living in Trevay with her brother and grandparents. She unwound the window and watched as the trees and small cottages gave way to high hedges with gateways offering tantalising vistas of the sea beyond. As the road reached its highest point the trees and farms opened to acres of green fields, with the glittering Atlantic below, crashing onto the rocks of the headland that sheltered her childhood village.

The final descent into Trevay revealed the busy harbour with its working fishing fleet tied up on the low tide. How she loved this place. How she had missed it when her old family home had been sold as a bed and breakfast business.

'Which way?' asked Kit as they got out of the car.

'Over to the headland?' Ella was opening the hatchback boot and putting Celia and Terry on their leads. 'These two can run around safely over there.'

The walk took them up the steep hill to the left of the harbour, past the Pavilions Theatre and onto the coastal path. The view from here was breathtaking. Jagged, slate-layered cliffs fell to the rolling boil of a gentle sea. Celia and Terry were unleashed and ran like cheetahs through the gold and purple of gorse and heather, forcing the shy skylarks to take to the wing and sing their beautiful song.

Kit pulled Ella towards him by the collar of her jacket and kissed her. 'Happy anniversary,' he said.

'Happy anniversary, my love.' She kissed him back. 'How many months is it now?'

'Five.'

She sighed. 'Five months. The best five months of my life.'

'And mine, sweetheart.' He kissed her nose and they walked on hand in hand. 'Fancy dinner out tonight? I mean five months is a hell of an anniversary, isn't it?'

'I've got to make the pasties for tomorrow. Henry will be disappointed if I don't.'

'Okay. How about coffee and a cake when we get back to Trevay?'

'Done.'

They walked and talked and threw Celia and Terry their balls until all four of them were ready to go back to the car.

'They'll sleep well tonight,' said Kit, shutting them in the boot.

'We all will.' Ella took off her jacket. 'I'm ready for that cake too.'

The Foc'sle was an old-fashioned teashop on the quay, two doors down from the Golden Hind pub.

'We could have a quick pint if you want?' said Ella.

'Much rather have a pot of tea.' Kit perused the slightly sticky, laminated menu. 'How about a cream tea? You need fattening up.'

'Do I?' She fluttered her eyelashes winsomely.

'Yes, indeed,' he said seriously. 'Being as lovely as you takes up many more calories than the average person. Fact. All that smiling and thinking kind thoughts is almost aerobic.'

'Well, in that case . . .' She nudged his knee under the table with her own. 'I can always do some exercise . . . at bedtime. You could join me if you wanted.'

'Oh, Miss Tallon,' he shrieked, pretending to be shocked, 'Just because you are a blazing firework of a woman with marmalade curls, you think you can do what you want with me?'

Ella giggled, 'Yes.'

'Then I am helpless, pulled by a current so strong I can't resist. Do what you will, but . . .'

She raised an eyebrow and in a deep voice said, 'Yes?'

'Be gentle with me.'

'Can I help you?' asked the middle-aged waitress with a name badge saying Sheree, who was standing over them.

Without missing a beat, Kit said, 'Two cream teas, please.'

The pasties didn't get made that night after all. When Ella came down in the morning the remnants of a chicken salad and a bottle and a half of wine were winking at her from the coffee table in the sitting room, reminding her of the evening they had spent curled up together, talking about everything and anything.

As she collected up the plates and stubs of candles she thought back to what they had talked about last night.

Ella wanted to talk about her plan to offer short painting courses for locals and holidaymakers. 'The cliffs, the harbour, the church. There's so much here for little children. We could go to the beach and find shells to paint or pebbles to paint on. That would be fun.'

'Like your granny did for you? Revisiting your childhood?'

'Oh.' Ella was anxious. 'Is that a bad thing?'

'Not at all,' Kit reassured her. 'It's lovely, and I think taking the little darlings from their parents for a couple of hours is a wonderful thing – for the parents.'

She flapped her hand and took another sip of wine. 'What about you? When are you going to get on the cliffs and paint?'

'I've got that portrait of Lindsay Cowan to finish, with her cat, dog and horse.' He rubbed his eyes. 'She's lovely, but what she sees as handsome, intelligent companions, I see as bloody pains in the arse. The cat is a toothless bag of bones, the dog stinks and growls at me and the horse farts and tries to bite me. But,' he topped up his glass, 'she pays well.'

'When you're done with her,' Ella lifted her hands and began to draw in the air, 'I want you to paint a huge canvas of a darkly rolling sea with stars twinkling and a lighthouse flashing across the waves. It'll be perfect above the fireplace.'

'One day,' he put his glass down and kissed her knee, 'that's exactly what I shall paint for you.'

Ella's hand was around his shoulders as he lay his head in her lap. The candlelight flickered warmly creating a cosy cocoon. 'This is nice,' she said sleepily.

'We won't be able to do this tomorrow. Your brother will be here and Adam will be back.'

'Oh yes.'

'And the day after, you might find out what happened to your mum.'

'Yes.'

'What do you think happened to her?'

'A million things. I have spent my whole life thinking about her and why she left. Sometimes I want her to come back and other times I hope she's dead. It would be easier. I could build a picture of a mum I want. Not a phantom built from questions.'

Ella wondered if what she had said last night was true. She felt no anger towards her missing mother. Just a need to know why. She took the dirty plates and glasses from last night and stacked them into the dishwasher before putting the kettle on for a pot of morning tea. As she waited for it to boil, she tidied the rest of the sitting room, plumping cushions, opening the curtains to the early sun and picking up a chewed slipper and a rubber chicken, both toys left by Celia and Terry.

She heard both dogs yawning from their room next to the kitchen and went to let them out. Terry came out, then sat scratching like any human man under his armpits and Celia strode out as if she was wearing thigh-high boots.

'Good morning,' said Ella.

The Afghan hounds ignored her and, pushing through her legs towards the kitchen door, took themselves into the garden.

Leaving the back door open, knowing there were no escape routes from the garden, she took a tray of tea up to Kit.

He was propped up against his pillows, waiting for her.

'And how is the mistress of the house today?'

Ella gave a little bob of a curtsey, and as she put the tray down and went to climb into bed, the phone rang.

'Leave it,' said Kit.

Ella picked it up. 'Hello? Henry, where are you? Okay. Lovely. Can't wait to see you.' She smiled at a scowling Kit. 'And Kit can't wait, either! Bye. Love you.'

Kit watched her as she put the phone down. 'I suppose this means I'm not going to see your ankles, Ruby?'

She grinned at him. 'There's always time for ankles, m'lord.'

'Ow!' Ella squeaked, putting the hot baking tray down quickly.

Kit, coming downstairs freshly shaved and smelling delicious, popped his head into the kitchen. 'You okay?'

'The tea towel was a bit thin and I burnt myself on the pasty tin.' She ran her fingers under the cold tap. 'I'm fine.'

'They smell good,' said Kit checking his watch. 'Anything I can do?'

She looked at him over her shoulder. 'I just want you and my brother to get on well. It would mean so much to me.'

She looked so anxious, cheeks pink from cooking, hair caught up in a bun with a pencil allowing curls to escape over her ears, and her singed fingers under the tap. Kit got a clean tea towel and went to her. 'Here, let me dry your hand.' He turned the tap off and gently wrapped her hand, kissing the tips of her fingers as he did so. 'Of course I'll like your brother. But will he like me?'

Ella began to laugh. 'Well, he will if you take him to the pub!'

'I think I can manage that.'

The rattle of a taxi in the drive heralded Henry's arrival.

'He's here!' Ella ran to the front door and opened it. 'Henry!' She charged out of the house and ran at him, smothering him in a hug and kisses. 'I've missed my bro.'

'Whoa, let me pay the driver,' he said, disentangling himself as best he could.

As he got his bag from the back seat and handed the driver his fare, he saw a man he assumed must be Kit. He gave him a quick scan. Thirtyish. Checked shirt and shorts. Nice tan. Looked okay.

He put his bag into his left hand and extended his right. 'You must be Kit. Henry.'

'Henry. Good to meet you.' It was Kit's turn to run a discerning assessment of Henry.

Long legs. Expensive jeans and jacket. White open-necked shirt. Flash watch. But he looked okay.

Ella looped her arms through each of the boys' and dragged them into the house. 'Welcome to Marguerite Cottage.'

Inside the hall, Henry dropped his bag on the flagstones and looked around him. 'Very nice, Ell's Bell's.'

'Come into the garden. Tea? Coffee? I could make a jug of Pimm's?'

Henry followed her through the lounge with Kit, and out through the double doors into the pretty garden. 'You have landed with your bum in butter, haven't you, Ellie? Very nice.'

'Yes, I have.' Ella replied, squeezing her shoulders to her

ears and grinning in delight. 'And I've got pasties for you. Homemade.'

'Fancy a pint?' asked Kit.

'Do I?' Henry smiled. 'With an offer like that, if Ella doesn't marry you, I will.'

Ella was mortified and dug Henry in the ribs. 'Shut up.'

'Just saying,' he said, clutching his side. 'Will the pasties keep for an hour?'

'Yes. Go on. They'll keep. I'll take your bag up to your room. You're in Kit's studio. For now.'

'I'll take it up later. It's heavy.' He opened it and hauled a bulging carrier bag out. 'Here, take this bag – it's got a huge pile of post for you. When you left me in London I didn't think you'd be falling in love and not coming back.'

Ella couldn't keep a blush from her cheeks. 'God, you are so embarrassing.'

Kit saved her. 'Neither of us expected to fall in love, but we did. I love your sister very much.'

Henry half closed his eyes and weighed up this open declaration. 'Good on you. Don't muck her about or I'll flatten you.'

'Fair enough.' Kit smiled. 'Now, how about that pint? Ella, do you want to come?"

'No thanks. You two go and get to know each other. I'll make myself a Pimm's and have a look through the post Henry's brought.'

She waved the boys off with their promise to be only an hour, or so, and took the Waitrose bag of post to the garden.

Getting a glass of Pimm's, she settled herself at the garden table and sifted through the mail.

The piles in front of her grew tediously. Catalogues. Charity requests. Bank statements. A postcard from an old school friend now living in Peru. Pension firms. Insurance firms. Funeral savings plan. And, a letter from a publisher. Months before she had written and illustrated a children's book called *Hedgerow Adventures*. She had hoped that her departed granny would guide her to a fruitful contract. She opened the envelope.

Dear Miss Tallon,
Re Hedgerow Adventures
   Thank you for your submission. Unfortunately this is not the sort of book we would publish. We will return the manuscript under separate cover,
   Yours etc . . .

She sat back and blew out a long breath of frustration.

'Granny,' she said, 'you got me excited for a moment. Ah well. C'est la vie.' She picked up her Pimm's and took a long, cool, self-commiserating mouthful.

Her phone buzzed. It was Henry.

'Hi, Henry, is everything okay?'

'Have you looked at your emails?'

'No, I've been going through the post. So much crap . . .'

'Check them now,' he said urgently.

'Okay, hang on.' She put her phone on speaker and looked at the screen. There was an email waiting to be opened. 'I've got it. It's from Granny's solicitor.'

'Open it.'

She did so and as she read it her heartbeat began to accelerate 'Oh. My. God,' she whispered. 'It can't be true.'

'It *is* true.' Henry's voice was gruff with anger.

Ella's hand was shaking as she gripped the phone. Swallowing hard to stop any tears she said, 'Our mother is alive?'

'Yes,' said Henry. 'And she wants to see us.' He was having

difficulty keeping the shock from his voice. As soon as he had read the message, relaxing with a pint on the Dolphin's oak bar and chatting to Kit, he'd excused himself and gone to the relative privacy of the pub car park to phone Ella.

He was scuffing the gravel with his shoes. 'I can't believe she's got the nerve.' He bit his lip, his face the definition of rage and pain. 'After all these years.' He pushed his free hand into his floppy fringe and pulled his hair. 'She's bloody alive. Well, I can tell you now, we are not seeing her.'

Ella sat down. 'But she's our mother.'

'Ha! She lost the right to call herself that years ago.'

'Henry, this is shock talking, we need time to think about it.'

'No, we don't. There's only one reason she'd come back. Because Granny's solicitor has told her that Granny is dead and that she is in for an inheritance. That's all there is to it.'

Ella loved her brother very much, but she didn't always agree with him. 'It must have been a shock for her to hear that. Her mother dead, her father too.'

Henry snorted and ran his hands through his floppy blond hair. 'Well, it was a bit of a shock for me too, you know, when I heard that my mum had run away. I was only two.'

'I know.' Ella looked at the garden she and Kit had started to plant. 'I can't imagine how she could leave you. She knew you. It was easier for me. I was just a baby. She didn't have time to know me. I don't have a clue what she was like . . . and that's why I'd like to see her.'

Henry sat on the wall of the pub's entrance, all the adrenalin leaving him. 'I don't know what to think. I was hoping they wouldn't find her. Or if they did, that she had died.'

'Don't say that!' Ella flopped into her squashy sofa. 'Is Kit still with you?'

'He's inside. I saw the email and came out to tell you first. He doesn't know.'

'Come home. The pair of you. Come home now.'

Ella had been hugging herself with joy just ten minutes ago. How quickly everything can change for the worse.

Ella took Henry's bag up to Kit's small studio and put it next to the single bed. It was getting on for late afternoon and through the open window a blackbird was singing in the magnolia tree. Instantly anger rose in her. How dare the bloody birds be so happy while her world was turned upside down? She shut the window with a bang, making the bird fly off. Good riddance, she thought to herself.

Downstairs she heard Kit's car pull up. She ran down and opened the front door.

Kit was looking serious, as if there had been a terrible accident and he now had the responsibility of the fallout. Which he had, she supposed.

Henry was pale and blowing out his cheeks in a childhood mannerism that always signalled upset.

'Hi,' she said softly.

Kit came to her immediately and put his arms around her. He felt the softness and sweetness of her incredible red curls then stood arm's length from her, his hands on her shoulders. 'You okay?'

She shook her head and at last felt hot tears springing to her eyes. 'Not really.'

Kit shepherded brother and sister into the kitchen and made them sit down. 'You both need a drink. Tea or alcohol?'

Ella settled for a cup of tea while Henry and Kit had large gin and tonics.

'Right,' said Kit, pulling out a chair from the table and sitting down. 'Tell me exactly what has happened.'

Ella looked at Henry. 'Do you want to tell him?' she asked.

Henry shrugged in reply and looked at his hands clenching the icy glass.

She looked at Kit. 'The solicitor has found our mother and she wants to see us.'

Kit was looking at her attentively. 'What do you think she wants after all this time?'

'Granny's money,' said Henry, flatly.

'Or,' said Kit trying to sound positive, 'she might be coming because she wants to see you two, after all she hasn't seen you for . . .'

'Almost twenty-five years.' Henry picked up his glass and drank.

Ella swallowed hard. 'The thing is, Henry has memories of her. Nice ones, I think.'

Henry grunted.

'They had had time to get to know each other. It was much more painful for him.' She looked at her brother. 'I should think.'

Henry said nothing but looked at the floor.

'Whereas I don't remember anything about her. I mean she left when I was only just over a year old,' said Ella, still watching Henry. 'That's why I want to see her.'

Henry glared at her. 'Really?'

Ella twiddled her fingers anxiously. 'I want to know what she looks like. Do we look alike? What she's been doing? Why did she leave us?' She wiped her nose as a tear ran down her cheek. 'Everything, really.'

Henry was angry. 'She's one selfish cow who doesn't deserve

to be listened to. I wouldn't be surprised if she's lied through her teeth anyway. She might not even *be* our mother. Just some strange woman who thinks she could get lucky. I wouldn't believe a word she said.'

'But, Henry, we must try. Then decide whether we want to be friends or not.'

'Friends? What are you talking about? She's a madwoman. We don't know anything about her. Correction, we know that she had two children by the time she was seventeen and she never told her own parents who the father – or fathers – were, and despite Granny and Grandad being kind and supportive to her, she ran away in the night and never looked back. What kind of person does that?'

'A sad person?' Ella said quietly. 'A person who finds themselves in a really hard place at the start of their adult life and can't cope. People run away all the time. Every day. She was not in her right mind.'

'Why didn't she come back?' demanded Henry.

'She was scared,' Ella said. 'Once you've done something like that, maybe there is no coming back.'

Henry gave a short laugh. 'Really? Not to have any curiosity about how your children turned out? Not even to see your own parents? Who, in case you had forgotten, never recovered from the worry of what might have happened to her?'

Ella drained her cup of tea, gripped by a sudden anger at his unkindness. She scraped her chair back and took her cup to the sink. She kept her back to her brother. 'Have you no empathy?' There was a tea bag in the sink. She fished it out and put it into the food bin. 'She was just a young girl, Henry. One who had got herself in a mess and she wanted to change that.'

'By walking out and leaving her shit to be cleared up by her parents?' sneered Henry. 'Brilliant.'

Kit, who had been listening to all this quietly, now intervened. 'You two getting angry with each other isn't going to help.'

'Oh, shut up. You know nothing about it,' said Henry, waving his hand dismissively.

'I know Ella,' Kit replied calmly, 'and I agree with her. You both need to meet this woman and find out who she really is. If you don't like her after that, then fine. It's over. You can all move on.'

Ella softened and, walking to Henry's chair, put her arms around his neck and hugged him. 'Kit's right.'

Henry clasped his sister's hands and pulled her closer to him. 'It hurts . . .' He spoke quietly.

'I know,' she said.

'Was it me?' His voice caught. 'Was it my fault?'

Ella took her arms from his neck and knelt by his side. 'How could it be your fault. You were only two. It might have been my fault. I was the final straw. A second mistake.'

Henry's tears began to fall. He angrily wiped them away. 'I hate her, Ellie. I don't want to see her and I don't want you to see her either.' He took her upturned face in his hands. 'Promise me you won't see her? I couldn't bear it.'

Ella saw the pain in her brother's eyes and made her decision. 'I promise I won't see her for as long as you don't want me too. But I can't promise that I'll never want to see her.'

He nodded and let his hands drop. 'Thank you,' he answered simply.

2

Agra, India, 2018

Sennen was nervous. More than nervous. What was going on in Cornwall? Her solicitor had promised to phone as soon as he had heard back from Ella and Henry and she'd been restless all morning. She walked to the shuttered windows of her hotel room and looked down on to the bustle of the street market. She could almost feel the heat and smell the dust through the glass. It was monsoon season, and although the clouds had now cleared, the last downpour had left deep puddles on the muddy street and in the awnings of the market stalls. She watched as a young woman in a rose-pink sari stepped out into the busy road and neatly sidestepped a couple of hungry dogs who took a sniff at her shopping, a plastic bag filled with colourful vegetables and herbs. A passing tuk-tuk beeped his horn and she waved at the driver in recognition, rows of golden bangles slipping up her arm and glinting in the hot sun.

Sennen watched as the woman continued her journey until

she was no longer in view. How jealous she was of that woman.

She began pacing her hotel room once again.

What had she done?. She twisted her wedding ring and stared at the phone by the bed, willing it to ring.

The letter that had started this turmoil was next to the phone.

A letter postmarked 'Cornwall'.

Cornwall. She'd walked away a long time ago. She thought of a quote from *The Go-Between*: 'The past is a foreign country; they do things differently there.' Who wrote that? If Kafir were here he would know. Kafir . . . one of the most erudite men she knew. Not that she knew many men. Her life hadn't all been roses, and right now it was just the thorns.

She sat on the bed, closed her eyes and began her private ritual of summoning Trevay in her mind's eye and walking its narrow streets and lanes. What were the little boats in the harbour doing now? Would any of the ones she remembered still be working or were they left in the silt, their hulks rotting down to skeletons? Or perhaps they'd been dragged up to The Sheds where all boats rested, used and unused.

She could smell the seaweed and the salt.

Hear the gulls laughing.

The splash of water as children launched their crab lines into the deep harbour.

Her mother painting at her easel on the beach. Her washed-out linen shirts and faded trousers glowing in the sun.

Poppa sitting at his pottery wheel. The shiny slip of water and clay covering his hands to his elbows.

She dared, for a moment, to think about Henry but, as always, the electric nerve pain of the thought stopped her. She couldn't even summon his face now. Or Ella's. She had been a wicked woman. And now, with the letter from Cornwall, they had found her and would make her pay.

It had come like a ghost summoning her to her grave.

There were several old addresses written on the envelope as it had chased her around the globe, before finding her here, in India.

When she had read it, locked in her bathroom, away from any inquisition, the sense of fear had almost compelled her to run again.

The letter told her that her father had died some years ago, her mother three years ago. They had died intestate, had made no will, so she was the sole heir to the estate. The house had been sold for a good price when the solicitor, acting as trustee, had rightly thought the market was at its highest. That money was now in a high interest account and it was hers. She or her solicitor should come to Cornwall. All that needed to be done was to prove her identity and sign some forms. She didn't even have to come to Cornwall, she could send a solicitor as her representative.

There was nothing about her children.

It took several days before she could formulate her reply. In it she expressed a desire to meet Henry and Ella and would only return to Cornwall if they wanted to see her.

The solicitor agreed to phone her when he had their answer.

She lay on the bed and allowed memories of her childhood to fill her thoughts.

She was on the beach at Shellsand Bay. Her father, nut-brown and strongly muscled, was swinging her round and round. He was smiling. His bright blue eyes twinkling in his tanned face and his deep laugh making her giggle. 'Daddeeeee.'

'Bill, darling, she might be sick,' said her mother.

'Are you going to be sick?' he asked Sennen.

'Noooooo,' she giggled.

'Would you like to come swimming with me and Mum?'

'Yeeessssss.'

He put her down on the warm sand. 'Get your rubber ring and we'll look for the mermaids, shall we?'

Sennen ran to her mother. 'Mummy, Daddy's taking us swimming.' She'd pulled at the slender, elegant hand of her mother. 'Come on.'

Her father stood ready in his dark-blue swimming shorts.

Her mother smiled, 'Of course. Let me just sort myself out.' Adela had been painting in the small sketchbook she always carried with her, capturing the likeness of fishermen mending their nets or lobster pots piled high on the harbour or the holidaymakers napping in the sun.

'I like that,' said Bill peering over her shoulder at her watercolour of the beach scene in front of them. 'Good colours.'

Adela stood up and put her hands on her husband's bare chest. She kissed him. 'Thank you.'

He kissed her back then held her slim body in his arms. She pressed her cheek against him and smelt the warmth of his skin.

'I do love you,' she said.

'And I love you.'

Sennen bashed her mother on the back of the knees with her sand spade. 'Come! On!'

Bill and Adela laughed and, taking Sennen in a hand each, they ran to the waves, swinging her between them. She had grown up surrounded by so much love and kindness. How could she have turned her back on them?

3

Cornwall, 1972

Adela was Cornish to the heart. Her parents had been wealthy landowners from Bodmin, her father the quintessential country squire and her mother a beauty of her day. Adela had wanted for nothing. The only awkward thing being that they were none of the things she actually wanted. Money, comfort, beauty, beaus – all were hers for the taking. But it wasn't what she longed for. She dreamt of being a great artist, living a rackety bohemian life in London, preferably Pimlico, which she had heard about and liked the sound of.

When she finally told them, it had caused much consternation for her parents, who had planned a husband, Anthony, handsome and untroubled by intellect with a rather lovely medieval manor house on the banks of the Tamar.

But it was not to be. At the age of eighteen she won a place at the Slade School of Art on Gower Street, Bloomsbury.

She refused her parents' offer of a nice little flat in Baker Street and, instead, put her name down for a flat-share with any of the new, female, students she would be joining up with. She would find out who when she arrived for her first term.

Her mother, a woman with a great capacity for organisation, decided her talents would be best spent taking her only child to Truro for the day and kitting her out with a new wardrobe of fashionable dresses and accessories and, as an afterthought, paints.

Come early September her father ordered his cherished Morris 6 to be serviced, polished and refuelled and drove her up to London in what he noted was record time. Nine and a half hours. It would have been even quicker if it hadn't been for the thick fog that had rolled over Dartmoor and a puncture on the A38.

Adela had waved him off to his club, where he would spend the night before the return journey the following day, and set about her new life with enthusiasm.

Her new flat, off Marylebone High Street, was small but clean and her flatmates were fun. There was Elsie, who was Irish and smoked, and Kina, who tied her hair with bright cotton scarves and wore boy's jeans. She was from Jamaica and was the most exotic person Adela had ever met.

Together they shared everything, including Kina's fashion sense. Within days Adela's pretty dresses and gloves, were taken off their hangers and bundled into Adela's suitcase under her single bed. Now Adela hunted the jumble sales and bric-a-brac stalls for overgrown jumpers and men's shirts which she knotted at the waist and loose canvas trousers. For a brief moment she tried smoking too but she really couldn't get on with it so took, instead, to drinking halves of bitter when she met fellow students in the pub.

The first year flew by and, returning to Cornwall the

following summer, she was surprised by how much she had missed it.

Her mother wanted to know all the London gossip. She had none. Had she been to Harrods? No. At which restaurants had she dined? Again, none.

Had she met any nice boys as she would be delighted to invite them to tea? No, but if I do I shall let them know.

Why did she wear such shabby clothes? I like them.

Wouldn't she like to get her hair styled? It's fine as it is.

It was towards the end of August that Adela took herself up to the golden fields of swaying corn in order to paint the local men who were getting her father's harvest in.

Her mother had hung string bags of bread, cheese and pasties on her handlebars and in her panniers she had placed bottles of cider to give the men a snack. When Adela had arrived, the men, stripped to their vests, had cheered and stopped work to enjoy their break. She knew most of them by sight, if not by name, as they had been getting the harvest in for as many years as she could remember.

Perching on whatever they could find, the bolder amongst them asked about her new life in London. She told them about the London pubs she visited and the life-drawing classes where the models were naked.

There was one boy, wide-shouldered and sunburnt with very blue eyes and very white teeth who lay on his shirt and listened but didn't look at her or join in.

She had never seen him before.

When the snack was done and both thirsts and appetites quenched, Old John, her father's stockman, called the men back to their labours.

The new boy thanked her for the food and drink and introduced himself as Bill. His hand was rough and strong in hers as she shook it. 'Will you be here tomorrow?' he had asked. 'I'm not sure,' she replied.

He smiled as he put his cap on and picked up his pitch fork. 'Nice to meet you,' he said and strode back up the field.

'Who's that new boy helping with the harvest?' she asked her father over dinner that night.

'Aha,' smiled her father. 'No need to ask you which one. All the girls are after him.'

Adela looked at the asparagus on her plate and stabbed it. 'I was just wondering.'

Her father gave a sly look to her mother and said innocently, 'He's a good chap, actually. I know his father. Nice man but awfully worried for the boy. He doesn't want to join the family firm. He's down in St Ives, working with some pottery chap. Pity.'

Adela couldn't help but bristle. 'Pity? Because he prefers art to business?'

Her mother leant over and touched Adela's hand. 'No dear, your father is mischief-making. The boy – William, I think his name is?' She looked at her husband who nodded. 'William, is a super chap, although a bit of a leftie.'

Adela couldn't help but laugh. 'We are all a bit "leftie" now, you know.'

'We are not!' Her father banged the table.

'Well, I am,' said Adela calmly.

Her mother gasped and clutched her throat. 'Oh darling, is that why you dress like a man?'

Adela shook her head smiling. 'No, Mother, I dress like this because it's comfortable and practical and all my friends do the same.'

Her father took a mouthful of pork pie and mumbled, 'I told you we shouldn't have let her go to London.'

Her mother ignored him. 'But, Adela, dear, if you want a husband you must at least try to look pretty.'

'I'm not sure I want a husband.'

'But, dear . . .' Her mother was putting two and two together and making six. 'Do you not like men?'

Adela put her knife and fork neatly on her plate and said nothing.

'I mean,' her mother continued, 'it could be just a phase you're going through. I remember at boarding school there were girls who got quite friendly but they got over it in the end.'

'Mother, stop, you are embarrassing Father, me and yourself.'

'Your father's a farmer, he knows all about these things.' She turned to her husband. 'Don't you, dear?'

Her father finished his wine and stood up. 'I'm going to let the dogs out.'

'Mother, you are terrible,' said Adela watching her father go. 'Now let's clear the table.'

The next day, Adela went back to the fields and was pleased when William waved at her and was one of the first to get a glass of lemonade and slice of cheese. 'Hello again,' he said. 'Are you painting today?'

Adela was putting out the bread and cheese and a few apples on to a linen cloth for the lads. 'It's so lovely up here, I thought I would.'

'May I see it when you're done?'

'It depends.' She smiled. 'I hear you're a potter?'

He took an apple and rubbed it on his trousers. 'My father has been talking to yours, I suppose?'

Adela smiled wryly.

'I'm an apprentice,' said Bill, 'down in St Ives?'

'Ah, Bernard Leach country.'

'I'm impressed.' He took a chunk out of his apple. 'Nobody here seems to have heard of him.'

'I'm studying art at the Slade.'

'Yes, I heard. Your father has been talking to mine.'

Adela laughed and Bill looked at her closely. 'That explains it.'

'Explains what?'

'The way you look.'

She looked down at her crumpled linen smock and rolled up trousers, and said defiantly, 'What's wrong with the way I look?'

'Nothing.' He grinned. 'I like it. You look like the type of girl who wouldn't mind getting caught in rainstorm, or pushing a car out of a ditch.

'Oh,' she said disconsolately.

'It's a compliment, believe me.'

'Didn't sound like one.'

She looked down at her scruffy sandals and brown, unshaved ankles. Self-consciously she tucked them under herself.

From the top of the field she heard Old John calling the lads back to work.

'Tell you what,' said Bill standing up and tossing his apple core into a hedge, 'what are you doing tonight?'

She looked at him suspiciously. 'Why?'

'I'm taking you out. I'll pick you up at seven.'

She had nothing to wear. The bed was littered with half a dozen garments which she'd had for years. Amongst which was an old dress she'd had since she was fourteen that was too short and much too tight; a pretty cotton skirt with a broken zip – and a horrible taffeta bridesmaid dress she'd had to wear for her cousin's wedding. Red faced from her bath and the putting on and taking off of so many things, she sat on the edge of the bed in despair. There was a soft knock at the door.

'It's Mother. Can I help?'

Adela sighed and flopped backwards on to the bed in despair. 'Come in.'

Her mother put her head around the door. 'I thought so. I found this. Any good?'

She was holding a Liberty-print cotton summer dress. 'I bought it ages ago. In a sale. It's too young for me. Too small, too. Try it.'

In the mirror, even Adela was pleased with her reflection. The dress was simple and hung a little loose on her but it was perfect. Her mother had brushed her hair into a neat ponytail and had attempted a little rouge and lipstick but Adela had been firm about saying no. Finally, her mother had stepped back. 'You'll do,' she said.

From downstairs they heard the bang of the old door-knocker and her father calling up the stairs, 'Prince Charming has arrived, Cinders.'

Bill had borrowed his father's car and drove Adela through the lanes and down to the pretty fishing village of Trevay. His shirtsleeved arm leaning on the open window, he chatted about this and that and gradually the knot in Adela's stomach began to loosen. As they came down the hill towards the harbour, Adela saw that the fishing boats were coming in on the tide, ready to land their catches on the quay. The sun was bouncing on the surface of the rippling sea making the light sparkle and flash.

'I love it here,' she said. 'I haven't been for ages. I could paint that sea every day.'

Bill parked the car outside the Golden Hind, picked up his jacket from the back seat and helped Adela inside.

'What will you drink?' he asked.

'Half a bitter, please.' She didn't see his amused smile as she looked around the dark and cosy bar. 'It's nice in here.'

Paying the barman, he carried his pint and her half towards the door. 'Let's take our drinks outside.'

The sun was beginning to set and the day was losing its warmth. She shivered a little as they sat on the harbour wall across form the pub and watched the fishing boats unload.

'Would you like my jacket?' he asked. 'Or I have a jumper in the car?'

'You'll need your jacket but the jumper would be lovely thank you.'

'Don't go away.' He set off for the car, Adela watching him. He was undeniably handsome, tall and muscular with an easy smile, the sort of man, she thought, one could fall in love with. She checked herself and looked back at the boat. She was only eighteen and she and Elsie and Kina had sworn to each other that they would play the field as men did, would never settle down with the first man they met. She looked over to him again. He was leaning into the car and reaching for something on the back seat. When he reappeared, he had the jumper in his hand and looked over at her with such a look that her heart jumped a little. She quickly returned her gaze to the boats, as if the unloading of their catches was of the utmost interest. She decided that, when he came back, she would be polite and cool. She would give no indication that she might find him attractive.

Adela waited a few seconds longer then glanced in his direction to see what was keeping him.

She saw at once.

Two girls were talking to him. Two *pretty* girls. One had her hand on his chest as she was talking to him, the other was pulling at his hand.

Adela's hand was shaking so much that she had to put her drink down. She looked over again. He was pointing at her and all three of them were laughing. At her? She felt her breath quicken and her cheeks redden. How could she escape?

Too late, he was coming towards her. 'Adela, meet a couple of old friends. Barbara . . .'

'Hello,' pouted Barbara, still holding Bill's hand.

'And Jill.'

'Hi,' said Jill, giving Adela a full top to toe scope.

'Bill . . .' Adela stood. 'I'm so sorry, I'm not feeling very well. I'll get the bus back.'

Bill frowned. 'Don't be silly, I'll drive you.'

'No, it's no trouble. I'll get the bus or ring my father. I don't want to spoil your evening.'

'Spoil my . . .' Bill was confused and exasperated. 'We've only just got here.'

Jill butted in. 'She'll be fine on the bus. Stay with us. We'll have a laugh.'

Adela stood fixed to the spot. Was she to be so easily shaken off?

Bill shook out his jumper and placed it around Adela's shoulders.

'Adela needs to go home and I shall take her.'

*

In the car, Adela said nothing. Her emotions were running high. She was elated that he had brushed those girls off but angry that he even knew them. Who were they? How well did he know them? Her father had said that all the girls were after him. Well, she wasn't. This would be the first and last time she would accept a date from him.

Her eyes slid over to look at him. His profile in the dark of the car was strong but his lips were tensed as he ran his hand through his hair. He felt her gaze and looked over at her. 'How are you feeling?'

'Okay.'

'Are you sure it wasn't something else?' She wondered if he was teasing her.

'Too much sun maybe,' she said.

'You don't get sun in London?' He was teasing her.

She turned to look out of her window and didn't give him the courtesy of an answer.

'I was looking forward to tonight,' he said. 'What did I do wrong?'

'Nothing.'

'Was it the girls?'

She shook her head, refusing to look at him.

'I grew up with them. They're fun.'

'Good for them.'

He slowed the car in the lane leading down to her family farm. The headlights picked out an owl on a gatepost as he brought the car to a halt and turned the engine and head-lights off, then they sat without speaking. Only the gentle ticking of the engine cooling broke the silence.

'Adela,' he said gently.

'Why have we stopped?' she asked.

'I wanted a chance to talk to you. Without interruption.

We've got at least two hours before your parents will be expecting you back.' He settled in his seat, his back to the driver's door. 'What's the matter?'

'Nothing.'

'Feeling better?'

'Yes.'

'Good. So talk to me.'

'About what?'

'Tell me about who you are and what you want out of life.'

'I'm Adela Trip. I'm eighteen. I'm an artist and I want to make a living from my work. Is that enough?'

'Uh huh. Do you have a boyfriend?'

She shook her head, then dared to look into his eyes. 'Do you have a girlfriend?'

'No. Not at the moment.'

'Oh.' She smiled. 'And so who are you and what do you want to do with your life?'

'Right now I'd like a pint and some fish and chips. That was how I had planned tonight.'

'Sorry I messed it up,' she said shyly.

'I forgive you.' He was teasing again. 'Shall we start afresh?'

She bit her lip but managed a smile. 'Yes please.'

'Good.' He turned the engine on and reversed the car. 'We'll go over to Pendruggan village. There's a great pub there called the Dolphin. Proper beer, good food and quiet. Fancy it?'

From then on the evening went smoothly. Bill was an easy person to be around and Adela made him laugh with her stories of her flatmates and her tutors, two of whom were Graham Sutherland and Lucien Freud. He told her about his work with the pottery and the great Bernard Leach who was teaching him. 'He's a genius, Adela. I'd like you to come down and meet him.'

'That would be lovely.'

'Good. By the way, can you play darts? The board has just come free.'

She surprised him with her skill at darts and took a game off him straight away.

'Have you been having lessons?'

'Beginner's luck,' she laughed. 'Or maybe I've spent the last year in London learning to play in our local?'

'Right, if that's the case,' he picked up his darts, 'no more Mr Nice Guy.'

The drive back to the house was very different to either of the previous drives that evening. Now they were comfortable together, the small silences between them serene and pleasant.

At the front door, she thanked him.

'Will you be up at the harvest tomorrow?' he asked.

'It's my job to bring you all your snack, isn't it?'

'Ah yes. That'll be the reason you come up.'

'Nothing else.' She chewed her lip, hoping and fearing that he might kiss her. She tipped her head up to his and in a low voice said, 'So. See you tomorrow?'

She half-closed her eyes and waited. He hesitated, then stepped off the front step and walked backwards towards his car.

'Yes. See you tomorrow.' He opened the driver's door and bent to get in. She watched the way he folded his long legs into the seat and sat down. Being so tall, his head touched the roof. As he started the engine and the car began to pull away he leant out of the window and said, 'Did I mention how lovely you look in that dress?'

She stood for a long time, watching his taillights grow smaller until they disappeared from sight.

4

Pendruggan, 2018

Once Ella had promised not to meet their mother, Henry, Ella and Kit had a reasonably happy weekend. After a gin-fuelled sleep on the first night, Henry had quite a hangover. He lay in bed, hoping the throbbing of his head would subside enough to allow him to get up and go to the bathroom. There was a knock at his door. It was Ella carrying a mug and a foil pack of pills. She pushed the door open with her foot. 'Are you feeling as bad as Kit?'

'Worse,' he groaned.

'Gin head. Big time.' Henry was aware of his sister approaching the bed and placing the mug and tablets on the table next to him. 'There's coffee and paracetamol.'

'Thank you,' he said, waiting for a wave of nausea to pass.

'Full Cornish breakfast will fix you. I'll call you when it's ready.'

After a few minutes he managed to raise himself from the pillow and attempt the coffee. It was good. Hot and very strong. He threw the tablets into his mouth and washed them down.

There was another knock at the door. It was Kit, bleary-eyed and wearing a scruffy, short, towelling dressing gown and stubble. 'Showed the gin who's boss, didn't we?' he said, sitting on the edge of Henry's bed, his head in his hands.

'How much did we have?' murmured Henry.

'I remember opening a new bottle and then throwing it away once it was empty.'

'Oh.'

'Yeah.'

'Boys,' Ella called up the stairs, 'breakfast is served.'

A young man's powers of recuperation are not to be under-estimated, and with the coffee and painkillers, plus Ella's enormous fry-up, by lunchtime they were almost functioning human beings once more.

They were sitting in the garden of Marguerite Cottage, warming themselves like cats in the drowsy sunshine. 'What shall we do this afternoon?' Ella drawled from her deckchair. 'Anyone fancy lunch out?'

'Love some,' said Kit reaching for her hand. 'Only you had better drive as I think Henry and I would never pass a breath test.'

'Pizza is what you need.' Ella gathered herself and got out of the deckchair as best she could. 'You need carbs, rehydration and some fresh air. We'll get all that in Trevay.'

'The old place looks very gentrified,' Henry remarked as he watched the little town of his childhood slide past his back-seat window.

'Would you like to see what they've done to Granny's house?' Ella asked over her shoulder.

'Sure.'

Ella pulled the car up on the corner of their old road and the three of them got out and walked up the short but steep lane to White Water. Henry stuck his head over the garden wall. 'They've kept Poppa's palm trees going,' he said.

'I know. I stayed here for a few weeks in the summer, remember? Our old courtyard for the sandpit and bikes has gone, though. They've put in a conservatory with a pond and a fountain.'

'Oh yes,' said Henry,' I can just about see. There are a couple of people having a coffee in there.'

'They'll be the B & B guests.'

'Double glazing and plantation shutters. Granny would think that *very* bourgeois,' Henry chuckled.

'Do you think so?' asked Ella, standing on tiptoes to get a view. 'I think she'd approve.'

Henry stepped back and rubbed the grit of the granite wall from his hands. 'Memories, eh?'

'Yep,' said Ella.

'I like the big window in the attic,' said Kit. 'Is that where your grandmother had her studio?'

Ella poked him in the ribs. 'You painters. All the same. Where's the best light? Can I get a tall canvas in there? Is there enough space for my paints?'

'So it *was* her studio?' asked Kit, fending off any more pokes by catching Ella's wrists.

'Yeah,' said Henry. 'Poppa had his space downstairs for his wheel and stuff, and the kiln was in the garden. That'll be long gone now.'

'Yeah, it is,' said Ella. 'Do you remember the excitement when we were allowed to open it up after a firing and find our pots?'

'Rubbish every one of them. But Poppa always told us they were great.' Henry smiled then rubbed his temples.

'I think your hangover needs feeding,' said Ella and she took Henry and Kit's hands in her own. 'Pizza time, boys.'

After a decent lunch, they went for a walk up to the headland and down to a small beach known only by locals and the odd inquisitive holidaymaker.

Henry picked up a slate pebble and sent it skimming across the smooth sea.

Ella counted the bounces. 'Six. My go now.'

They watched as Ella's stone bounced nine times before sinking beneath the water. Kit came up behind her and hugged her. 'Not fair. You've been getting practice in.'

'Poppa taught us. I think his record was twenty or something mad like that,' she said.

Henry sat on a damp rock and looked out to the horizon. 'We had some good summers here, didn't we, Ells?'

She sat next to him and put her head on his shoulder. 'Remember how good Granny was at French cricket?'

'When she wasn't painting,' said Henry. 'We've still got her painting books and sketchpads somewhere, haven't we?'

'Yeah, they're in Clapham. The loft, I think.' She tapped her brother's knee with her knuckles. 'How is Mandalay Road?'

'Nice and quiet without you.'

She gave him a pinch. 'I didn't expect to be staying here in Cornwall.' She looked over to Kit who was staring into rock pools. 'You do like him, don't you?'

'I've known him less than a day, but I've managed to spill all the family secrets and get blind drunk with him. What is there not to like?'

'He's a nice person,' she said thoughtfully. 'I really like him.'

Kit turned from the rock pools and looked up. 'My ears are burning.'

'They should be,' laughed Henry. 'Are your intentions towards my sister honourable?'

'Not altogether,' smiled Kit, walking towards them.

Henry turned to his sister. 'And is that all right with you?'

'Very,' she said, catching Kit's hand.

That evening the three of them lay sprawled around the lounge watching a movie on Netflix, full of Ella's cottage pie that she'd had ready in the fridge. Henry was on an armchair, Kit and Ella snuggled on the sofa, when they heard a key in the lock and the familiar sound of eight dog feet, tapping on the hall floor as they rushed to the door, then a voice calling, 'The bloody roads are full of idiots! Terrible road-works on the A38 and I'm absolutely starving.' A tall handsome man appeared at the door followed by two Afghan hounds that strolled in and flopped on the nearest rug. He surveyed the empty plates on the coffee table. 'Bugger. Have you already eaten?'

Kit and Ella jumped up. 'There's plenty left. I'll warm some up,' Ella said as Kit made the introductions. 'Adam, may I introduce you to Ella's brother Henry? Henry, this is my cousin, Adam. He's the landlord.'

Henry and Adam shook hands and Ella returned from the kitchen with a steaming bowl of cottage pie. 'Darling, sit down and eat while I give Celia and Terry their supper.'

'You're an angel.' He kissed Ella's hand as she passed him, taking the dogs with her.

'So,' said Adam, settling into his chair and blowing on a forkful of food, 'I've heard a lot about you, Henry. At last we are able to give you the once-over.'

'I rather thought I was here to give Kit the once-over, actually,' Henry laughed.

'And the verdict?' asked Adam, munching.

'Not bad at all.'

'We have bonded over gin and pizza,' smiled Kit. 'Anyone fancy a beer?'

Henry rubbed his chin. 'My liver is feeling a lot better, so yes please.'

'That's the spirit.' Kit went to the kitchen.

'What happened last night?' asked Adam, wiping a drop of gravy from his chin.

Henry sat back in his chair and wondered how to explain. 'I don't know if Ella has told you that we were brought up by our grandparents?'

Adam, concentrating on his food, nodded. 'Yep. Your disappearing mother has featured large over the last few months. The business of tracking her down for your grandmother's will?'

'Well, they've found her,' sighed Henry.

Adam swallowed his mouthful. 'Is that why you got hammered last night? Well, that's great.'

Henry stayed silent.

'Or is it?' asked Adam.

'Ella thinks it's great but I really want nothing to do with our mother, our grandmother's money or . . . anything.'

Kit came back with Ella, each carrying two cold bottles of beer. Celia and Terry loafed behind them.

Adam took his beer from Ella. 'Henry's just told me about your mum.'

Ella looked anxious. 'Her turning up? It's early days and quite difficult to get our heads round, isn't it, Henry.'

'Not yours.'

'Let's not start all that again,' said Kit.

Adam scooped up the last mouthful of cottage pie and put his plate down on the floor, pushing Terry's inquisitive nose out of it. 'So, Henry, you're staying here, are you?'

'If that's okay with you?'

'Oh, fine. I'm off again tomorrow, got a couple of weeks training in St Thomas's A & E. Serious trauma stuff in case of terror attacks. You can use my room.'

Ella saw Henry's puzzlement. 'Adam is a doctor, Henry. A very good one.'

'You can trust me,' laughed Adam.

Kit grabbed the television remote and unfroze the film they had been watching. 'Let's forget about all that tonight.' He picked up his beer and put his feet on Celia to tickle her tummy. 'Tonight we relax. Cheers.'

Henry left for London after breakfast the next morning. Ella had packed a pasty and a coffee flask in a cardboard and put it on the back seat of the taxi.

'That should keep you going.' She leant through the front window and kissed him. 'I love you, bro. Come back soon.'

'As soon as I can, but the office is really busy at the moment.'

'But the profit is good?' Ella raised her eyebrows, mocking him.

'Recession? What recession?' He tweaked her nose the way he knew annoyed her. 'The old Ruskies are still buying lumps of prime London real estate, lucky for me.'

Ella rubbed her nose crossly. 'Drive carefully.'

'I will, and Ella, thank you for saying you won't see that woman.'

'Mum.'

'Whatever. She can come, take the money and go. She doesn't deserve to see us.'

'It'll be okay.'

Kit came forward and leant on the car roof. 'Come and see us again soon.'

'And you look after my sister.' Henry said. 'She's had enough crap in her life. She doesn't need more.'

On the train from Bodmin, Henry's head was full of his mother. He couldn't forget the hurt that his grandparents had endured for all those years. He laid the responsibility of their unhappiness squarely at her door. What kind of mother would just piss off, dumping her children with parents who had only ever given her every helping hand they could? They had loved and supported her and she repaid them by running away without a backward glance. Not a note, not a phone call.

What a cow.

He had no desire to see her or listen to any pathetic excuses or apologies.

And who the bloody hell was his father? Was he the same man who fathered Ella?

Poor Ella. A girl needed her mum. Granny did her best, but even so . . .

On and on his thoughts went until he had exhausted his brain. Putting on his headphones he got out his laptop to watch a film he'd downloaded but he couldn't concentrate and eventually returned to looking at the world racing past his window while he brooded.

'So, do you like my brother?' Ella asked, nestling in to Kit as they walked on the beach that afternoon.

'He's got a bee in his bonnet about your mum, hasn't he?' he said, putting his arm around her.

'He remembers bits about her. Vague stuff, but I think it was nice things – and then suddenly she was gone. So, like a bereavement, he still grieves unconsciously.'

'And what about you? Do you want to see her?'

'I've promised Henry now.'

'That doesn't answer the question.'

'I'm curious.' They walked together in silence for a while before she said, 'Yes, I'd really like to see her. I'd like to know why. What happened. Who my dad is. I've always wanted to know, but Granny and Poppa had a sort of unspoken thing so that we didn't talk about her. Poppa was brokenhearted when she left and Granny bore the brunt of his grief whilst grieving herself.'

'Must have been hard for them.' Kit pulled her closer and kissed the top of her head. 'How old were you again?'

'Thirteen months. Henry was two. Not so bad for me – I have no memories, not even impressions. But Henry knew her. I mean really knew her. Had cuddles and bedtime stories and walking on the beach and playing. Somewhere in his head he must have those feelings. No wonder he's so angry.'

Henry arrived at Mandalay Road, Clapham at the same time Kit and Ella were talking. His taxi drew up, double parked, and he paid the cabbie before hauling his weekend bag over his shoulder. He stood motionless before suddenly throwing up Ella's pasty and coffee on the kerb outside his front door.

There were several letters on the mat as he pushed the door open. Bills and a catalogue. He picked them up and chucked them on the hall table, went into the kitchen to switch the kettle on before making himself a cup of tea. While the kettle was boiling he went up and dumped his bag on his bed and had a quick pee.

Downstairs, sitting on the sofa with his mug of tea, he looked around his home. Above the fireplace was one of his grandfather's paintings: a small girl with red hair sitting on the quay at Trevay with a crab line in her hand. It was unusual in that this was one of the very few canvases Poppa had painted. Poppa was the Potter – Granny was the painter.

In front of him was an Indian carved coffee table. His grandfather had brought it back from a trip to Rajasthan and Henry and Ella had always had their Friday night supper of fish and chips on it, rather than at the big kitchen table. It was their treat and marked the start of their weekends.

'Argh,' he said angrily to the empty room. 'I am *not* going to see that woman.' The sofa sagged as he leant back into it. His grandmother's again. She and Poppa had bought it when they first married and moved into Pencil House. A ridiculously tall, thin house that was one of the landmarks of Trevay. A place where visitors still stood and had photos taken of themselves. His own mother, born in that house, had grown up with this sofa, just as he and Ella had. He tried to imagine his mother as a child, sitting where he was sitting, having a bedtime story read to her. Being hugged by Granny or Poppa just as he and Ella had been. Well, she was not coming back to take this from him. Or the paintings. Or the table. Or the bloody wine glasses. They were his. His and Ella's, as was every stick of furniture or cutlery in this house.

5

Bill and Adela waited for two years before they married. Adela wanted to finish her degree and Bill wanted to make sure he had enough savings to begin married life in a home of their own.

Tucked up in the chill of Adela's Marylebone bedroom they talked of their future.

'Do you think we can afford to start a family straight away?' Adela had asked hopefully, her face pressed into the warmth of Bill's chest.

'How much do babies cost?' he had asked.

'Not much. I'll ask around the family for the essentials. I'm sure my old pram is stuck in the attic somewhere. We can use the kitchen sink as a bath and I'll feed the little mite myself so . . .'

She heard his laugh rumbling in his chest as he tightened his arm around her.

'What are you laughing at?'

'Your practicality and frugality. Most women would want brand-new everything.'

51

'Well, I don't. And I have a few books of Green Shield stamps that I'm sure would get us a cot.'

He kissed the top of her head. 'And where would we live? This garret of yours is fine for us but it would be a squeeze for three of us. And I don't fancy carrying the pram up and down three flights of stairs.'

'I always imagined us going back to Cornwall,' she said quietly. 'My parents have spotted a tiny place in Trevay, on the harbour.'

As she lifted her head to check his reaction to this piece of news, he saw the longing in her.

'I'm not having handouts from your parents.'

'No, no. Nor me. And I hadn't said anything to them about looking for something. Honestly.'

'Then how do they know about it?'

'My mother sent me something.' Adela shifted herself from her arms and slipped out of bed. She tiptoed across the icy lino and reached for a newspaper stuffed into her handbag and got back to the warmth of her bed as fast as she could. 'Here, look.' She turned to the properties page and handed it to him. 'There.' She pointed.

He scanned the small advert and blurry picture.

'What do you think?' she asked, tucking herself around him again.

'It's a derelict shop.'

'An old chandler's, actually.'

'But not a residential home.'

'That's why it's such a good price.'

'No indoor bathroom? No bedrooms? No kitchen and no heating? And it'll be freezing.'

'But, stuck between those two houses as it is, it will keep itself warm.'

He said nothing.

She pressed on. 'Bill, it's so pretty, and I don't mind living in a building site and I can do lots of labouring for you. Between us we could build the home we really want.'

He held her anxious gaze. 'You really like it?' he said.

She nodded, her fingers crossed under the eiderdown. 'Don't you?'

'Hmm,' he said, wanting to keep her in suspense. 'We could go down this weekend and take a look at it?'

She sat up clutching her hands to her chest. 'Could we?'

'Why not?'

To their delight, the second-class train compartment was empty. Bill put their small, shared suitcase up in the netted luggage rack while Adela opened up their packed lunch. 'It's only egg sandwiches and ginger nuts, I'm afraid,' she said, fussing over the greaseproof-wrapped packages and passing him one. 'Oh, and I've put the last of my chicken soup in the flask.'

Sitting together, watching as the smoky London scene beyond the glass began to morph into suburbia then farmland, they munched and chatted and did the *Guardian* crossword until, leaning their heads together, they fell asleep to the rhythm of the train.

Newton Abbot, Exeter and Plymouth sped by in a drowsy haze until the guard, in a comforting West Country voice called along the corridors, 'Bodmin Parkway next stop. Next stop, Bodmin.'

As the bus rattled onto Trevay Harbour and came to a stop, Adela and Bill collected up their bits and jumped off.

'There it is,' Adela said with renewed energy, pointing at a very tall, thin building, 'I can see the estate agent waiting.'

They hurried across the road, past the Golden Hind pub and turned left into the narrow lane where the building stood, squeezed in between its neighbours.

It was at least a hundred and fifty years old. Dressed in clapboard, its white paint peeling, it carried two floors above the front door. The estate agent greeted them.

'Mr and Mrs Tallon, I presume? Tim Baynon.'

They all shook hands.

'Welcome to the Old Chandlery . . .' Mr Baynon began his spiel. 'There's been a lot of interest in the property, I can tell you.'

'Really?' asked Bill incredulous.

Adela glared at him and addressed the agent: 'I'm sure. It's absolutely gorgeous.'

Bill shot her a murderous look. And as Mr Baynon took a set of keys from his pocket and put them in the rusted lock of the warped front door, Bill pulled his wife aside and whispered, 'Don't act too keen. He'll bump the price up.'

Adela tutted, and whispered back, 'I want him to know we are serious buyers.'

She pushed past him and followed the agent, who had given the door a couple of kicks to open it, leaving a lump of damp and rotting wood on the mat, into what had been the shop.

'As you see,' Mr Baynon was all pomposity, 'all the original fixtures and fittings are still intact.'

Bill looked at the empty shelves lining the walls and the shop counter covered in dust. 'Seen better days,' he said.

'So much character,' countered Adela.

Mr Baynon continued his tour into the room behind the shop which housed an old Raeburn range and a large butler's sink. 'And beyond is the garden.' Grandly he lifted the latch of the old back door and showed them a patch of wasteland no bigger than a couple of wheelbarrows. 'Sun all day.'

Adela could see that Bill was losing interest. 'Can we see upstairs?'

A steep and narrow staircase took them up to the first floor which housed two small rooms back and front. The second floor was the same.

Adela felt certain that Bill would never agree to live here. As he and Mr Baynon chatted on the tiny landing, she walked towards the window of the uppermost front room, her heels knocking on the bare floorboards. She rubbed the dust and grime from one of the small square panes and looked out. Trevay and its harbour were laid out before her like a drawing from a child's picture book. She tried the rusty latch and after a couple of thumps with the heel of her hand it opened. Sunlight, sea air and the call of gulls flooded the room. She almost laughed at the simple joyousness of it all.

She heard footsteps behind her, followed by Bill's hand on her waist as he stood next to her.

She laid her head against his shoulder. 'Someone will make this into a lovely home,' she sighed.

'Yes, we will,' he answered.

She looked up at him, all alert. 'What?'

'I've put an offer in. My Baynon is going to let us know in a couple of days.'

She hugged him, then pulled away and pummelled him. 'You bugger! I thought you hated it.'

'Just my poker face.'

'Oh, darling.' She kissed him, then a horrible thought crossed her mind. 'You didn't offer him a stupidly low price, did you? We'll definitely lose it if you have.'

'I've offered what it's worth to us. Which is more than it's worth to anyone else.'

'I love it.' She hopped from one foot to another.

'I love it too. It's mad. It's too much work. It's totally impractical. Who buys a building that's as tall and thin as a pencil?'

Adela laughed and leant on the filthy window sill to look out at the amazing view.

'That's what we'll call it. Pencil House.'

They got the keys and moved in within three weeks. The Raeburn only needed a good service and soon warmed the house through. Bill, always good with his hands, made the old shop counter into a kitchen unit, and built a sturdy kitchen table top out of the shop's shelves. Adela started upstairs. She swept, she washed and she painted everywhere and everything. Slowly, Pencil House was becoming a home.

At weekends they would take themselves off on bus rides, discovering seaside towns and hidden coves and simply immersing themselves in each other and life they were building.

It was about four months into their arrival that Adela began to feel sick in the mornings. The doctor confirmed her pregnancy and the following spring their daughter arrived.

Bill and Adela were as besotted with her as they were with themselves.

'What shall we call her?' asked Bill holding her for the first time by Adela's hospital bed.

Adela smiled. 'I would like to call her Sennen,' she said.

'Sennen?' asked Bill, puzzled. 'Why?'

She grinned. 'Remember that evening on Sennen Cove last summer?'

'Oh.' Bill remembered. 'When I . . . when we . . .'

She nodded. 'Yes, darling. Your daughter was conceived on Sennen Cove.'

A few days later Bill went to collect Adela and Sennen from the hospital. He'd bought himself an ancient red Ford Anglia for the occasion. 'Oh, Bill, it's wonderful,' exclaimed Adela when she saw it. 'Can we afford it?'

'For my wife and daughter, nothing is too much.' He opened the door for her and got her settled with Adela wrapped in her arms.'

When they got to Pencil House he told her to stay in the car while he opened up and took the bags in, then, when he was ready, he scooped Adela, who was still cradling Sennen, into his arms and carried them both over the threshold with Adela laughing and protesting until he placed her on the sofa.

'Welcome home.' He bent and kissed her. 'I am so proud of you.'

'What on earth for?'

'For making Sennen for us.'

'Well, it took both of us.'

'But you did the hard work.' He knelt by Adela's knee and lifted the shawl his mother had knitted from Sennen's face. 'Hello, my darling. We are three – and nothing and nobody will ever tear us apart.'

6

Pendruggan, 2018

At Marguerite Cottage, the day that Henry had left Pendruggan, making Ella promise not to meet their mother when or if she came back, Adam and Kit were cooking supper. Although they were cousins they were more like brothers. Adam, the elder, making suggestions as to how to dice an onion correctly and Kit arguing that the kitchen was a shared domain and if he was cooking, he'd do it his way.

Adam shrugged and started to lay the table. 'More wine, Ella? Supper will be a while.'

He poured a good slug of rosé into her glass and she excused herself. 'I'll take this into the lounge, if you don't mind?'

The boys barely looked up as they had started a ridiculous debate about whether to put chives on the new potatoes or mint.

Ella sat on the rug next to Celia and Terry and rubbed their ears. 'Don't tell Henry,' she whispered, 'but I would really like to meet my mum. I wonder what she's like? Do you think she'd like me?' Terry rolled over so that she could tickle his tummy. 'You don't have a care in the world, do you, Terry.' She turned to Celia who was in ear-tickle ecstasy, her eyes half-shut in bliss. 'Celia, you're a girl. What do you think my mum is like? Is she all bad? Selfish? Feeling guilty at what she did? Or is she funny and beautiful and clever and desperate for us to forgive her? Hmm? Do you think we could be friends? I'd like that. I really, really want to know. I want to see her. Is that too bad of me?'

In Clapham, Henry had ditched his tea and started on the wine. The anger inside him was building. If that woman was thinking of coming back and playing happy families, she had another think coming. But if she did come back, at least he would have the satisfaction of her seeing that, despite the pain and the chaos she had created, he and Ella had survived and done very well without her. Who needed her? She needed to be told some home truths. She needed to face up to the carnage, the wrecked lives of her parents, God bless them. Let her come and take the money and piss off back to wherever she'd come from. *He* didn't need her. *Ella* didn't need her. And he'd like to say that to her face. She deserved to see what she left behind and know what it's like to be rejected. He took another mouthful of wine and swilled it down as he picked up his phone and, in an impulse of fury, dialled Ella's number.

Ella stopped tickling the dogs and reached around for her phone. She checked the caller ID. 'Hi, Henry.'

'We *are* going to see her.' Henry emptied the bottle into his glass.

Ella felt her heart jump. 'Really?'

'Yes.'

'I'm so glad . . .'

'And I am going to tell her exactly what she's done. I am going to look her in the face and really tell her what I think of her.'

7

Trevay, 1995

Adela and Bill had taken the children to the beach. Adela loved her grandchildren dearly but she was exhausted looking after two little ones. They were growing up so quickly, she wished with all her heart that Sennen could see them. As the sun beat down on Shellsand Bay, Adela rested her eyes, just for a moment, listening to Henry's squeals of laughter above the crashing of the waves.

'Mama!' shouted Henry stamping his little feet in the shallow ripples of the sea. 'Mama!'

Sennen crouched as well as she could with her burgeoning pregnancy, and said, 'Smile, Henry. Smile for Mummy.' She pressed the shutter on her Kodak disposable camera just as her one-year-old son scrunched his eyes and gave her the broadest of grins. 'That'll be a good one,' she said, winding the film on.

Adela and Bill were sitting a little way up the beach, using the cliff face as a windbreak. Bill was asleep, Adela was watching her daughter and grandson.

'Darling?' She shook Bill gently. 'Darling?'

Bill woke up. 'Was I dozing?' He stretched, then put a hand to his eyes to check on Sennen and Henry. 'Are they okay?'

'I think so,' said Adela. 'She's being rather good with him today.'

'I think you're being very good with both of them.' He looked at her affectionately over the top of his Ray-Bans.

'I do worry. She's only just coping with Henry and now another baby on the way.'

'It's not quite what we were thinking of, is it?'

'No.' Adela steepled her fingers under her chin. 'Every child brings joy, we know that, but . . .' She shook her head. 'I do worry.'

'What are you worried about, Granny?'

Adela knew she'd been dreaming, but it was so real, so tangible, as she opened her eyes to see a smiling Henry standing in front of her with a crab net.

'Did I fall asleep?' She smiled at him.

'Grandad wants to take me and Ella swimming but you have to come too, to help Ella because she's not big like me.'

She reached out and stroked her grandson's soft cheeks. 'No, she's not as big as you, yet. Your swimming is coming on nicely. But you will teach Ella when she's big.'

Henry grabbed her arm and pulled her out of the nest of towels she'd created for herself against the cliffs where she and Bill always made camp.

'Quick, Granny, or Ella and Poppa will be finished before we get there.'

Henry pulled Adela down the damp and rippled sand to the water's edge where Bill was bouncing Ella's toes in and out of the shallow ripples.

'Hello, old thing.' He smiled at her. 'The water's not too bad.'

'Granny was asleep.' Henry told Bill.

'Was she snoring?' asked Bill conspiratorially.

'She was more sort of blowing air through her lips. Like Bert when he purrs.'

'Ah yes,' said Bill nodding his head as if Henry had given him the most important piece of information. 'She does that.'

Adela wasn't embarrassed. 'Well, Poppa farts when he's asleep.'

Henry burst into laughter. 'Poppa Farts! Poppa Farts!'

Ella, catching the fun and laughter, stuck her bottom out and began blowing raspberries through her teeth.

'That's quite enough, thank you,' said Bill, lifting Ella on to his shoulders. 'Who wants to find the seahorses?'

'Meeee!' shrilled Ella holding tight to her Poppa's ears.

'And meeeee!' shouted Henry running through the waves.

'And meeeee,' sang Adela as she skipped after them all, putting aside her post-dream sadness.

That night, after Adela had bathed Henry and Ella and dressed them in sweet-smelling pyjamas, Bill came upstairs to read the nightly story. Adela kissed the children and sat on the floor between their beds as Bill settled down with Enid Blyton's *The Magic Faraway Tree*. He read one chapter and then, after much pleading, read another.

'One more?' asked Henry sleepily.

'Ella is asleep. She'll be cross if we read on without her,' whispered Bill.

Adela stood up and gently tucked Ella and her teddy a little more cosily. Then she dropped a kiss on Ella's sleeping forehead. 'Night-night darling.'

Bill was settling Henry down. 'Did you read Mummy that story?' Henry asked, his bright blue eyes sharp with a need to know.

'Yes,' said Bill. 'I did.'

'Did she like Moon-Face best?' Henry settled himself more deeply into his duvet.

'Of course.'

'Good.'

'Sleep tight now. See you in the morning.' Bill ran his hands through Henry's soft hair.

'I will.'

'Night-night, Hen,' said Adela kissing his head. 'Love you.'

'Love you too.' Henry managed, before accepting sleep's kidnap.

Downstairs Adela watched as Bill mixed two gin and tonics. 'I dreamt about Sennen today. On the beach. She was being so good with Henry . . . so good.'

Bill clinked two cubes of ice into each glass and handed her one. 'But she couldn't keep it up.'

'She tried so hard, we expected too much of her.'

Bill sat in his favourite armchair and sipped his drink. 'Are you hungry?'

Adela swallowed the threatening tears no. 'No.'

'Oh, for God's sake,' he said impatiently.

A tear slipped down Adela's cheek. She raised her hand to wipe it away.

Bill shifted in his chair and after a while said, 'Cheese and biscuits? I've got some nice Yarg.'

'Okay.'

'I'll bring it in on a tray.'

'Thank you.'

He left for the kitchen.

Adela looked out onto the small courtyard beyond. On the washing line hung their swimsuits and trunks and beach towels. They'd be dry by morning if it didn't rain tonight, and another day would take her further away from her daughter.

Where was Sennen?

What was she doing?

Was she well?

Was she thinking of them?

Did she miss her children?

Adela put her hand in one of the deep pockets of her cotton, sun-bleached trousers and pulled out a handkerchief. She rubbed away the drying, salty track of her tear and wiped her nose.

It was more than five years since Sennen had gone, leaving Henry and Ella in her and Bill's care. Her heart had begun to grow a thicker tissue around the damage that had been caused, but now and again the pain caught her unawares.

Bill suffered too, although he couldn't admit it. Or perhaps, she wondered, he didn't have the words. There were no words big enough.

Friends had tried to empathise, well-meaning and kind.

Some of them had said harsh things about Sennen. Selfish. Cruel. Better off gone.

But the gravitational pull of the hole that was left drew Adela and Bill deeper until their fingers were clinging by the tips.

Bill arrived with two plates.

'Here you are.' He handed her one. Cheese, two digestive biscuits, a few slices of apple and celery. 'Enough?'

She nodded.

'So,' he said, easing himself back into his chair, 'what's the plan for tomorrow?'

'I thought I'd paint the courtyard walls with Ella. She wants a mermaid. She wants to glue some shells to it.'

'Good.' Bill carefully cut into his cheese and balanced it on his biscuit. 'Henry and I are going to work in the studio. He's getting very good on the wheel. We might try a jug tomorrow. Good practice.'

At bedtime that night, as Adela waited for the milk to boil for their Horlicks, she saw a spattering of rain on the window. She called out to Bill who was at the top of the stairs. 'I'm just going to bring Sennen's bathing costume in. It's started to rain. I'll bring the Horlicks up in a minute.'

Bill hesitated a moment on the stairs. Should he correct her? Remind her that the costume was Ella's not Sennen's? He closed his eyes and shook his head. No. He would say nothing. Remembering one of his mother's old sayings, he murmured to himself, 'Least said soonest mended, Bill. Least said.' And walked slowly to the bathroom.

8

1993: The Night Sennen Ran Away

Down the narrow lane she ran. Down to the bus shelter. It was empty. Her pulse was thumping at the base of her throat. She looked at her watch – eleven forty-five – and checked all around her again.

'Hiya,' said a voice in the shadows.

Sennen jumped. 'You scared me.'

'My dad took ages going to bed!'

Sennen shrugged. 'Are you nervous?'

'A bit.' Rosemary was Sennen's oldest school friend. She was shivering. 'A bit cold, too.'

Sennen checked to see if anyone had spotted them. The coast was clear.

'Let's do it,' she said. 'Come on.'

They walked up the hill and out of the village, leaving Trevay and its sleeping inhabitants behind.

At the top of the hill the two girls stopped and looked around. The moon was streaked across the low tide and the black silhouettes of the roofs and church spire were geometric and inky against the horizon.

Sennen blew out a long stream of breath.

'You sure you're cool about this?' asked Rosemary.

'Yeah.'

'Henry and Ella will be all right?'

'Yeah.'

The main road out of Cornwall was ahead of them. 'Listen,' said Sennen. 'Car.'

A set of headlights came into view and Sennen stuck her thumb out. 'It's now or never.'

The car slowed and stopped. 'Where are you going?' asked the lone, middle-aged woman driver.

'Plymouth, please,' said Sennen.

'Both of you?' asked the woman, clocking their appearance and their rucksacks. 'Running away?'

'No,' said Sennen, 'it's my parents. They're in France, on holiday. Our dad's been taken ill so we're catching the overnight ferry to see him. Mum said to hitch. We haven't got much money, you see.'

'Roscoff?' asked the woman.

Rosemary couldn't speak but Sennen said, 'Yeah.'

'You're lucky it was me who stopped, then,' said the woman, reaching round to unlock the door to the back seat. 'There are a lot of funny people about. Hop in.'

Sennen got into the front seat, leaving Rosemary to get in the back.

'Thank you very much,' said Sennen. 'My sister and I are ever so grateful, aren't we, Sally?'

Sennen looked around at 'Sally' with a cheeky grin. 'Aren't we?'

'Yes. V-very,' stammered Rosemary. 'Thank you.'

'Hello, Sally and . . .?' said the woman looking in her wing mirror and pulling away.

'Oh, I'm Carrie,' said Sennen with conviction. 'What are you doing out so late tonight?'

'I'm a midwife. Just delivered twins. Two little boys. Identical. I'm on my way home now.'

'That's nice,' said Sennen. 'Sally and I are twins too. Not identical though.'

The journey was remarkable only for the number of stories Sennen could weave about her bond with her twin, their father's weak heart and their mother's enormous worry about them all. Finally, the illuminated gates of the ferry terminal were in front of them.

'We'll jump out here, please,' said Sennen, feeling a fresh thrust of nerves and adrenalin.

'Sure? I can take you to the ticket office if you like?'

Sennen and Rosemary were already climbing out of the car. 'No, this is fine. We've got our tickets. Bye.' They shut the doors and waved at the woman who was doubtful about leaving them but she was tired and ready for bed and the girls seemed nice and sensible so she waved to them and headed for home.

The girls shouldered their rucksacks and headed off to the ticket office. 'Two tickets for Spain, please,' said Sennen as she delved into her bag for her wallet and passport.

'Santander return?' asked the tired man behind the glass.

'We're not sure when we're coming back,' said Rosemary, finding her courage.

'Two singles, then.' The man didn't look up as he printed out the tickets and took the cash. 'Follow the signs to the ferry. Sails in twenty-five minutes.'

The two girls spotted the signs and ran to the boat. They

clattered onto the gangway, laughing and breathless. Stepping on to the deck, Sennen dropped her rucksack and hugged Rosemary. 'We've only bloody done it! We're on our way to Spain.'

In Trevay, Ella woke and began screaming from her cot. Adela woke too. She listened. Would Sennen get up and see to her? After a couple of minutes, with Ella's crying becoming more agitated, the answer was clearly, no.

Adela didn't want Bill to be disturbed. He would stop her from helping, so she got out of bed as quietly as she could and padded onto the landing. Sennen's door was closed. Sighing with frustration and irritation at her daughter's lack of commitment to her children, she crept into the children's room.

Ella had managed to pull herself up by the cot rails, her tear-streaked face scarlet with the effort of crying.

The crying stopped when she saw her grandmother, to be replaced with shuddering gulps.

'Come on, you,' said Adela, lifting Ella into her arms. She put her hand under Ella's bottom and felt the damp creeping through her baby-gro. 'Got a wet bum, have you? Let's get you comfortable.'

Adela changed Ella's nappy and Baby-gro then walked around the small room with her granddaughter on her shoulder, cooing soft words until the precious baby rubbed her eyes and grew limp. Back in her cot with teddy close by, Adela left Ella sleeping. On her way back to her own bed she glanced at her daughter's closed door and forgave her her selfishness. What seventeen-year-old, with A levels looming, wouldn't be asleep?

*

At six fifty the next morning, Henry shook Bill awake. 'Poppa?'

'Yes?' rumbled Bill, emerging from deep sleep.

'Where's Mummy?'

Bill stretched his arms above his head. 'If she's not in her bed she's maybe downstairs.'

He turned over and put an arm around the sleeping form of Adela.

Henry shook him again. 'She's not, and Ella done poo.'

Bill lay still for a moment reluctantly allowing the realisation that he had to get up seep into his muscles. He turned round to face Henry.

'All right, old chap. Tell you what, you wake Granny and I'll make tea.'

Bill stood on the landing and glowered at Sennen's closed door. She really hadn't been pulling her weight recently. Yes, she had exams, but he and Adela were bending over backwards to help her through school while doing all they could to support her and Ella and Henry. He tucked his cotton sarong a little more tightly around his waist and headed downstairs. He would have words with Sennen later. She had to stop leaning on her mother so much.

Adela, woken by Henry, changed Ella's nappy. 'Shall we wake Mummy up now? She might give you a nice cuddle in bed.'

Henry said crossly, 'Mummy not in room.'

'Well, let's go and look for her,' said Adela smiling at both children.

'Where the bloody hell is she?' demanded Bill, having searched the house and garden.

'Shh. You'll frighten the children,' said Adela, full of fear herself. She closed the door to the lounge where Henry and Ella were watching *Bananas in Pyjamas*.

'Maybe she's gone over to Rosemary's for breakfast. Or to do revision,' she said, trying to keep the wobble from her voice.

They called Rosemary's family who told them that Sennen was not with them and that Rosemary was still asleep.

Five minutes later they called back.

Bill rang the police.

The church bells were ringing five in the afternoon when Sennen and Rosemary disembarked in Spain.

The sun still warmed the day and the girls were hungry.

They found a small pavement café and ordered coffee and eggs. Cheerfully, they raised their cups to freedom.

Adela and Bill ushered the uniformed officers into the kitchen, and offered coffee and biscuits as a way of making things appear normal. The disembodied crackle of speech from their radios was unsettling and the gleam of the badges on their hats, which now lay on the table, were alien and officious.

The officers sat on one side of the table, Bill and Adela on the other. One was broad-chested and ruddy-faced. The other reminded Adela of a vole, long-nosed with prominent teeth and sandy hair.

Adela told them all she knew since she'd last seen Sennen the night before.

Officer Vole was hovering his sharp pencil above his notebook.

'So, the last time you saw or spoke to her was when she went up to bed?

Adela squeezed the tissue in her hand. 'Yes.'

'Did she seem upset at all? Last night or in the past few days?'

'No.'

The sharp pencil scratched a note.

'Did she take any money with her?'

'Oh,' Adela looked at Bill puzzled, 'I don't know. She didn't have much.'

Bill was glad to be able to do something. 'I'll go and look.' He stood up, scraping the kitchen chair on the floor.

'I'll come too,' said the other policeman, cramming the rest of a digestive biscuit into his mouth and followed Bill out of the kitchen.

Adela swallowed the rising lump in her throat. Left alone with Vole she said, 'She's never done anything like this before.'

'A lot of youngsters do this sort of thing. They usually come home when the money runs out.'

He looked up as Bill and his colleague returned.

'Darling,' asked Bill, putting his hand on Adela's shoulder, 'do you still keep the housekeeping in your dressing-table drawer?'

'Yes?' answered Adela with fresh anxiety.

'How much?' Bill asked gently.

'Almost three hundred pounds.'

Bill sat down heavily. 'It's gone.'

Adela let her tears flow.

The broad-chested constable coughed uncomfortably. 'How was she coping with the children?' he asked, reaching for another biscuit. 'To have two kids before you're seventeen is pretty tough.'

Bill raised his voice. 'My daughter is a very good mother and, as a family, we have pulled together. My wife and I have given her every support. She loves Ella and Henry. There's no way she would abandon them.'

The police officers gave each other a sceptical glance.

The vole said, 'But she has.'

Bill felt his anger rising. 'No.'

'Can you give us the name and address of the children's father?' asked his colleague.

'No,' Bill spat.

Adela put a cool hand on his arm and said, 'We never knew who the father was. Sennen wouldn't tell us.'

'I see,' said Vole, jotting this down in his notebook. 'So it's possible there could be two different fathers?'

'Look,' said Bill, 'my daughter—' Adela looked at him sharply and he corrected himself, '*Our* daughter . . .' He took Adela's hand. 'Is missing. We want you to find her.'

The policemen left, promising to keep them in touch with any developments but repeated that most runaways turned up pretty quickly.

The next three days passed in a turmoil of worry, grief, anger and disbelief. Rosemary's parents came round and the four of them tried to think if there had been any clues to their daughters' disappearances.

Henry and Ella were fractious and naughty. More than once either Adela or Bill would raise their voices at them which only brought more tears and tantrums.

At the end of the week, the police began to take the idea that the girls may have come to harm, seriously.

Photos of Sennen and Rosemary were given to the newspapers and the local television station.

Witnesses came forward.

A psychic said she had spoken to them in the spirit world

and their bodies would be found in a disused tin mine.

A taxi driver said he'd given them a lift to a party out in Newquay until the genuine passengers came forward.

A midwife turned up at Plymouth police station to say she had given two girls answering the description, but not the names, a lift to the Plymouth Ferry Terminal. They were going to Roscoff, France to see their sick father.

A man who had been working in the ticket office that night thought he might have seen them and that they had bought two tickets to Santander, Spain.

Slowly the police put the runaways journey together and got in touch with the Spanish police.

'They'll be back before you know it,' Tracey, the family liaison officer, told Bill and Adela. 'With their tails between their legs.'

Sennen woke up cold and stiff and with a hangover. Next to her Rosemary twitched in her sleep and murmured something unintelligible. 'Hey,' said Sennen shaking her. 'What's the time?'

Rosemary turned away irritably. 'Dunno.'

Sennen gave up and crawled out of the makeshift bed in the basement apartment. She rubbed her face and gave herself a scratch. Last night the room had looked okay, but this morning she saw it for what it was. A shaft of sunshine from a narrow window illuminated the mattress on the floor and the worn blankets on top of it. She needed a pee. Stepping over her abandoned shoes she opened the bedroom door onto a corridor. She smelt coffee coming from a room at the end. '*Ola!*' a cheery female voice with a Mancunian accent called from what Sennen assumed was the kitchen.

'Hi. Which door is the loo?' asked Sennen.

'The one with Che Guevara on it,' the voice replied.

The mouldy smelling bathroom housed a shower, a loo with a wobbly seat, and a small basin with a dripping tap.

She had her pee then swilled her mouth with cold water and splashed her face. A speckled mirror told her she had a spot on her chin. 'Shit.' She gave it a squeeze, rinsed her face again, retreated and followed the smell of coffee.

'Surprised to see you up so early.' The girl was in her early twenties. She wore short dungarees, with a bright cotton scarf tied round her head. She handed Sennen a cup. 'Get this down you.'

'Thank you,' said Sennen.

'I remember my first night here,' the girl said. 'I'd got the train from Manchester to Portsmouth, then hitched a ride with a long-distance lorry driver all the way through France and Spain. Decent bloke. Had a daughter my age. Want a bread roll?' She picked up a brown paper bag and pulled out a small baguette. 'Got no marmalade or owt, though.'

Sennen took it gratefully, breaking it into small pieces, hoping she could keep them down. Her hangover was pretty fierce.

There was the sound of the bedroom door opening. Rosemary wandered out wearing a Snoopy T-shirt and tiny knickers. She sat down on a vinyl-covered stool. 'I feel shit,' she said bleakly. 'Morning.'

'Morning. Bread roll?' said her hostess brightly.

Rosemary reached for one and started eating.

'So,' said the girl putting her tanned legs on the table and sipping her coffee, 'what's the real reason you're here? Tell your Auntie Rachel.'

Rosemary looked at Sennen who was thoughtfully chewing her bread.

'Our parents chucked us out,' Sennen said.

Rachel's eyes narrowed. 'Really?'

Sennen pulled her lips down at the corners and nodded. 'Yeah. Apparently, I am a bad influence on Rosemary.'

'Well, I know you two can drink.' Rachel got up and opened a kitchen drawer. She rooted around then grabbed a brown pill bottle. 'This should help your hangovers.'

Rosemary, round-eyed, shot a frightened look at Sennen. Rachel laughed. 'I'm not a dealer. It's aspirin.'

Twisting the lid off, Sennen downed two tablets. 'Thanks, Rachel. For last night. I don't know what we'd have done.'

'Yeah well,' Rachel shrugged, 'I know those people who were buying you drinks and you looked as if you needed rescuing, so . . .'

Sennen's hazy memories of last night were of a group of three handsome young Spaniards who'd found them wandering from the docks into the town and offered them dinner.

'They seemed nice,' said Rosemary. 'I liked them.'

'Yeah, they're okay, but you need your wits about you. Mateo is a player.'

Sennen thought back. 'Mateo in the white jeans?'

'The one and only. Not the type to take home to your mother.' Rachel sighed. 'I know from personal experience.' She retied the scarf in her hair. 'Moving on, what's next for you two? You need a job. Somewhere to live.'

Rosemary, who was feeling rather homesick and would have done anything to catch the next ferry home, looked pleadingly at Sennnen – who ignored her.

'We were thinking of bar work or chambermaiding, perhaps,' Sennen shrugged. 'Anything.'

Rachel got to her feet and put her mug in the sink. 'You can stay here for a week or two. After that you're on your own. I've got to go to work in an hour, so get dressed and I'll take you into town with me. We'll ask around.'

Rachel's apartment was underneath an old and ugly residential building which had many windows broken. As the three girls climbed the dark and smelly concrete stairs to ground level, Rachel explained that the building was due to be demolished. 'I've been here for three months now. One of the better squats I've known.' She pushed a heavy door and they found themselves on the street.

Sennen and Rosemary squinted at the sudden sharp light. Rachel found some sunglasses and perched them on her nose, sniffing. 'Gonna be hot today.'

As they walked, they passed small parks with ladies walking dogs and men sitting in the shade watching the ladies walking the dogs.

Café tables and umbrellas spilt out on to the pavement, the smell of the lunchtime tapas reminding Sennen that she could do with some breakfast.

They walked for about fifteen minutes, turned a corner, and saw the sea sparkling ahead of them with a long stretch of beach running to their left and right.

Sennen caught her breath. 'Wow.' She put her arm around Rosemary's shoulder. 'Fancy a swim?'

Rachel pulled them along. 'You can have a swim once we've found you a job.'

They walked for another mile or so, the heat building all the time. Sennen was hot and uncomfortable, Rosemary was thirsty and tired. 'Where are we going?' she bleated.

'Right here,' said Rachel.

They had stopped outside a busy café bar sitting in the shade of several trees opposite the beach.

'Come and meet my boss.' She shouted to a small man with a big belly who was working at a coffee machine. 'Ola, Tomas!'

He looked over at her and lifted his chin in greeting. He glanced at Sennen and Rosemary.

'Not more of your street urchins, Rachel?.'

'Tomas, these are friends of mine, just arrived from England. I was at school with them.'

Tomas turned away from her and shot a jet of hot steam through a pipe. 'You think I was born yesterday. You have been at school with all the girls in the UK?'

'I am very popular.' Rachel laughed, then putting her head on one side and blinking coquettishly said, 'Please, Tomas? Sennen and Rosemary just need a little tiny job.'

He gave a guttural throaty snort. 'Experience?'

Rachel nudged Sennen.

'Oh yes,' Sennen answered convincingly, 'I've worked in lots of cafés and pubs at home. I love it. Meeting so many interesting people.'

'Don't overdo it,' Tomas replied, smiling, 'I can tell bullshit when I hear it.'

'And I'm *very* good at that too,' said Sennen.

Tomas laughed. A deep laugh that wobbled his belly. 'Okay. I give you girls aprons and Rachel will show you what to do. By tonight I will see if you are good.'

It was a long day. The café was popular with tourists and locals and whatever language barrier there may have been the girls got over with sign language and a smatter of O-level Spanish.

Tomas watched them all day, shouting disapproval and orders or nodding silently.

It was gone midnight before the last customer left.

'Clear the tables and I will tell you my decision,' he told them.

At last the place was tidy, bar and glasses cleaned, chairs upturned on all the tables except one, where Tomas sat reading a newspaper.

He gestured for them to join him.

Rosemary sat down yawning. 'Tired, eh?' Tomas asked.

'Yes.'

'You work hard today. You were good with the customers.' He looked at Sennen. 'You are cheeky. Too much chat, but I think they liked you.'

Rachel clapped her hands. 'Told you they were good.'

He slid a sideways look at her. 'I tell you before, I was not born yesterday. These two have no experience. All bullshit.'

He put his newspaper on the table. 'No more lies. I will give you the job but bring me no trouble. No boyfriends, no police. Understood?'

Rosemary nodded. 'Thank you.' She looked at Sennen who was looking at Tomas's newspaper. 'Sennen,' she said. 'What do you say?'

Sennen tore her eyes from the paper. 'What?'

'We've got a job. Tomas has given us the job.'

'Oh . . . right. That's great.' She turned to Tomas. 'May I have your paper?'

In bed that night, Sennen looked at the newspaper again, at the photo of a young man in a sequined black biker jacket, swirling a magician's wand and a wolfish smile. He was here. He had told her he would be. He had laughed when she said she would follow him. She couldn't wait to surprise him. She read the article. Amongst the Spanish words she managed to translate were 'Senor A'Mayze seria en el Teatro Arriaga hasta el 30 do Septiembre.' So now she knew he was at Arriaga Theatre until 30th September. She had six days in which to surprise him.

The work at Tomas's Café was hard but as the days passed her feet got less sore and the heat more bearable. They were earning good tips and Tomas was pleased with them. On the night of 29 September, Sennen asked Tomas if she could have the next night off.

'Por qué?' he asked suspiciously.

'I have to go to the dentist.'

He laughed. 'No, you don't. You are meeting someone? A boy, perhaps? Not the dentist, anyway.'

She decided to tell – almost – the truth. 'Tomas, I want to see the magic show at the theatre in town. I have always loved magic and one of my favourite magicians from England is in the show and . . . Don't tell Rachel or Rosemary. They will laugh at me.'

Tomas looked right into her eyes. 'I smell the bullshit,' he said. 'But, I will give you one night off . . . to see the dentist . . . and then you will be back. Si?'

She flung her arms around him. 'Si, si. Gracias, Tomas.'

He peeled her off him. 'But you still have to work tonight and tomorrow.'

'Of course.' She hesitated before asking, 'May I have my wages?'

He shook his head. 'Not until the day after tomorrow.'

With no money she couldn't buy a ticket, but it didn't matter. She left work early and went back to the squat to shower and change. Looking in the small, speckled mirror she saw a slightly thinner, now-freckled, face. Her sun-lightened hair gleamed as it hung over her tanned shoulders. She looked really pretty. What a surprise he was going to get.

She walked into town, soaking up the evening sun. People were promenading, hand in hand, or sitting on the pavements under coloured umbrellas sipping cold wine or beer. A tapas bar was playing a pop song. Sennen relaxed. The music put a bounce in her step and confidence in her heart. Tonight was going to be the best night of her life.

Outside the theatre, an excited crowd was milling around, laughing and calling to each other. Sennen looked closely at the photographs of the performers hanging in the glass cases of the outer walls of the building.

There were names and faces of famous magicians from all over the world but she couldn't find Ali's. At last the crowd thinned as they went inside to find their seats and she could get a closer look. In a group photo of the cast, she saw him. Fourth from the end, next to the cabaret dancers in rhinestoned leotards with feathers in their hair and fake eyelashes. He was looking straight out to the camera, his dazzling smile lighting his face, his eyes looking right at her. She put her hand to the glass and touched him. It suddenly all seemed worth it. 'Ali. I'm here to surprise you. Not long now. I have missed you.'

She had two hours to wait. She sat in a side-street café next to the stage door and ordered a coke, her eyes glued to the theatre's exit. She could hear the band through the back wall and the applause from the audience as the last curtain call was taken.

She finished the coke and, leaving the money by the empty glass, she walked to the stage door. She was the first person there. Soon the fans would have escaped the theatre and be here, jostling with their programmes for autographs. She stood her ground as they started to arrive.

The stage door opened and a gaggle of the girl dancers appeared in leggings and warm cardigans, still with their showgirl make-up on. Their boyfriends swiftly escorted them away. Next came some men carrying musical instruments, then two glamorous women, a double act, Sennen supposed, who signed a few autographs and then . . . there he was.

Her heart missed a beat. His dark hair was even longer, hanging sexily in his eyes and tumbling over his shoulders. He beamed at the autograph hunters as they pressed forward.

She held back, wanting to freeze this moment for as long as she could. He signed a woman's ticket and, giving her pen back, looked around for the next person who wanted his attention. And saw her. At least, she thought he did. He reached for another pen, signed another programme, posed for another photograph then reached his hand out to her. She took it. 'Hello,' she said smiling at him. 'Surprise.'

He smiled back in confused recognition, then froze. He dropped her hand.

'Ali. It's me,' she said, suddenly fearful.

Another woman's hand reached to grasp his. He smiled now, but not at Sennen. He was looking at someone behind her. 'Darling,' he said.

Sennen turned. A pretty blonde with long legs was pulling him from the crowd. 'Ali, come on. I promised the babysitter we'd be back.'

Sennen stood between them. 'Ali? It's me, Sennen.'

He knew who she was. His eyes told her that. For a second he stared back at her with what, fear? Panic? The woman pushed Sennen out of the way. 'Excuse me, love. He needs to get out of here.'

Sennen fell back as Ali swept past, looking anywhere but at her.

When Rosemary and Rachel got home later that evening, Sennen was already packed.

'What are you doing?' asked Rosemary, puzzled.

'You're going back,' she said, struggling with the straps of her rucksack.

'What?' asked Rosemary.

Sennen looked at her, as though she were a halfwit. 'It's what you want isn't it?'

'Well, yes, but . . . not right now. I'm sort of enjoying it now.'

Rachel, leaning against the bedroom door, held her hands up. 'I know Spanish dentists can be bad, but this is ridiculous.'

Sennen turned on her. 'It's nothing to do with a dentist, I just . . . I just want to go. Okay?'

Rachel shrugged. 'No skin off my nose. I'm going to make a cuppa if anyone's interested.'

Alone in their room, Rosemary sat on the bed and watched as Sennen gathered up her passport and make-up.

'What's happened?' she asked gently. 'Is it Henry and Ella? Are they okay? Are you missing them?'

Sennen sat down and burst into tears. 'I don't know. I just . . . It's me.'

'What's you?'

'I just want to leave here, okay?'

'Henry and Ella will be pleased to see you.'

'Stop talking about them!' Sennen rubbed her tears away ferociously.

'But you're their mum.'

'Shut up! I don't want Rachel to hear. Forget about them. I have.'

'Have you?'

Sennen dissolved into tears again. 'No,' she sobbed. 'But I want freedom. I don't want to be judged any more. I don't want my *sainted* parents looking at me in their disappointed way any more. I don't want to be woken up at all hours of the night. I want to sleep, and lie in – and be *me* again.'

'I'd love to have a baby,' said Rosemary quietly.

Sennen pulled herself together and wiped her nose. 'That's what I thought, too.'

'But I'll have their dad to help me,' said Rosemary.

'Ha,' Sennen scoffed, stuffing a pair of socks from the floor into her rucksack, 'assuming he'll want to hang around.'

'I'm sorry.' Rosemary passed Sennen a clean tissue. 'I shouldn't have said that.' She watched as Sennen rubbed the smeared mascara from her face. 'Any chance that their dad would help you?'

Sennen laughed bitterly. 'Oh no. Absolutely not.'

Through the long night Sennen and Rosemary talked. Eventually Rosemary persuaded Sennen to return to Cornwall with her in the morning. 'We'll get the earliest ferry. We'll go to your parents first and explain. I'll be with you. By tomorrow night you will be in your own bed and Ella and Henry will be so happy to have their mummy home.'

They got up and left the squat before Rachel woke up. Sennen left a note saying thank you and to tell Tomas that they were sorry, and Rosemary left half of her tip money next to it.

The sun was coming up as they walked towards the docks. The first boat from England had just come in and the cars with their shiny GB stickers were disembarking. The girls had to cross the road to the ferry terminal to buy their tickets and waited as the cars went by. A man driving an estate car full to the gunnels with luggage, two children in the back and his wife in the front, slowed to wave them over.

Rosemary lifted her hand in a wave of thanks. The wife stared at them. She nudged her husband, then lifted a newspaper from her lap. Sennen saw the photos of herself and Rosemary on the front page.

'Run!' she said sharply to Rosemary. 'Hide your face and run.'

In the terminal they dashed into the ladies loo, out of breath and panicking. 'They saw us,' gulped Sennen. 'Shit. We're in the papers.'

Rosemary went white. 'We must be in so much trouble!'

Sennen searched for her purse. 'Here.' She shoved what money she had into Rosemary's hand. 'Take it and go. I'm not coming with you.'

'But you must! You said you would,' Rosemary pleaded. 'We'll go together. It'll be okay.'

'Go and buy a ticket and get on that boat,' ordered Sennen.

'I'm not going without you,' Rosemary sobbed.

Sennen rubbed her forehead with the back of her hand. A bad headache was setting in. 'Okay, okay.'

Sennen checked around her. The building was quiet. A handful of foot passengers were waiting to buy their tickets but the cars were already embarking. Sennen could hear the metallic thump and rattle as each vehicle drove over the gangplank into the bowels of the ship.

There were no police and nobody waving copies of British

newspapers about. 'You get your ticket. I'll just get a drink from the shop over there. Do you want anything?'

'No, I'll be fine.' Rosemary had calmed down and was looking much happier. 'See you at the ticket office.'

In the small shop Sennen went to a display of cuddly toys. She picked up a pink pony with a white fluffy tail and a green dragon with silvery wings. She stuffed them in her pockets while the lady shopkeeper had her back turned then marched to where Rosemary was waiting. She took the toys from her pocket and handed them over. 'Give these to the kids, will you? Tell them they're from me.'

Rosemary giggled. 'No, you give them to them.'

Sennen said nothing but looked at her feet.

Rosemary's face fell. 'You're not coming, are you.'

'I can't.' Sennen began walking backwards, increasing the distance between herself and her friend. 'Go. Be happy. I'm fine. Thank you.' Sennen turned and began running.

Rosemary shouted, 'Sennnen! Sennnnnneeeeeen.'

But Sennen didn't stop.

It was cold when the ferry docked in Plymouth. Rosemary stood on deck, watching the coast grow closer until she could see the red and white stripes of Smeaton's Tower sitting on the Hoe. She was shivering.

As soon as she disembarked she went to the first phone box she could see. She rang the operator and asked to reverse the charges to a number in Trevay. She heard her mother's worried voice accept the call and cried with sheer relief. She promised to stay right where she was until the police arrived to take her home.

They were kind and gentle to her, offering tea and a bacon roll in a Happy Eater, en route.

She said no, but would they please take her to Sennen's parents first, as she had a special present and a message to give them.

Adela opened the door and gave a shocked shriek. Her hand flew to her mouth, eyes wide.

'I'm so sorry, Mrs Tallon. I'm so sorry,' said Rosemary stepping forward.

'Where's Sennen?' Adela came out of the front door and looked around to see if Sennen was hiding. Ready to jump out.

'She's not here. She's not coming back.'

Henry and Ella came to the door, Bill behind them. 'Rosemary? Where's Sennen?'

Rosemary pulled the toys from her pocket. 'She gave me these to give to the children.'

'But she couldn't bring them herself?' said Bill, stiffly.

'She wants you to know she's okay,' Rosemary told him.

'Thank you,' said Bill to the police officers standing behind Rosemary. 'Please take Rosemary home.'

Rosemary held the toys out to Ella and Henry. 'These are from your mummy.'

The children came forward shyly and took them.

'What do you say?' whispered Adela automatically.

Henry said, 'Thank you. Where Mummy?'

Before Rosemary could answer, Bill took her elbow and turned her towards the gate.

'I think you'd better get home to your family. They've been worried. I'm glad you are home.'

'I'm so sorry, Mrs Tallon, I really am,' Rosemary tried to say, but she was crying with fear now. 'I tried to get her to come back.'

One of the two police officers took Rosemary's arm and led her to the car. His colleague hung back and said, 'I'm sorry we are not bringing your daughter to you this time. We will be questioning Rosemary and will tell you all we know as soon as we can.'

'Understood,' said Bill formally. 'Thank you.'

And he closed the door on them.

9

Bill was struggling to keep the anger and grief that burned in him from destroying the careful balance of the fragile reality that he and Adela had fought to create for Henry and Ella.

Adela was fussing with the children. Henry was questioning her.

'Where Mummy? She come home?'

'Not yet, darling, but she sent you these lovely toys.' She heard the front door close and watched as Bill's familiar shape walked away from the house.

'Not like dragons.' Henry bent down to Ella who was swinging her pink horse by the tail. 'You like your horsey, Ella? It from Mummy.'

Adela's tears flowed and she hurriedly looked away so that the children didn't witness them. 'Well, I think I'll get us all a nice drink. Who wants a biscuit?'

Rosemary's parents came over the next day, but their happiness at having their daughter home and their guilt that Bill and Adela didn't made the meeting uncomfortable to the point of being unbearable.

The police passed on the little information Rosemary had given them and the Santander police could only confirm that Sennen had left the area, leaving her job and her accommodation.

Adela kept a watchful eye on the effect all this was having on Henry and Ella. Ella seemed fine but Henry's sadness at his mother not being there had become an anger in him. The easy-going toddler was replaced with a child who shouted when crossed and slammed doors with fury.

Adela buried herself in caring for her grandchildren, while Bill spent more time walking by himself or immersing himself in his work.

A month or so later, Adela came home from a walk with the children and caught him searching in the cupboard under the stairs.

Stepping over the vacuum cleaner, a box of old jigsaws and all the general detritus of many households, she asked him, 'Darling, what are you up to? Can I help?'

He backed out of the awkward space, his back bent and a cobweb in his hair.

'Where are the photo albums?'

Henry charged past them and disappeared into the back of the cupboard. Ella toddled in after him and a row started immediately.

'Out, Ella. This my camp.'

Adela was glad of the interruption. She knew exactly where the photo albums were and they were not in the cupboard. She had been so agitated about Sennen running away that she'd hidden them in the loft. Some instinct told her that they would be too distressing for Bill to look through while his grief was so raw.

'Henry, can't Ella join you in there? There's plenty of room.'

'No!' Henry shouted from the darkness. Ella began a high-pitched wailing.

'Oh, for God's sake!' Bill went back into the cupboard and pulled Ella out, kicking.

'Don't kick Poppa, please.' Adela held her arms out to Ella and Bill passed her to him.

'Just like her mother. Always wanting her own way.' He was getting angrier.

Adela decided to do the right thing. 'The albums are in the attic. Behind the suitcases.'

'Well, who the bloody hell put them up there?' Adela didn't need to answer. He had already stomped off to get the step-ladder.

Left with Ella crying in her arms and Henry making monster noises from the back of the cupboard, she felt like screaming herself.

But she didn't.

She took a deep breath, coaxed Henry from his camp, and gave both children some milk in their sippy cups and fairy cakes.

Later, with the children ensconced in front of *Top Cat* on the television, she found Bill sitting on an old suitcase in the attic, going through all the photo albums. She sat with him and looked as he turned each page.

Sennen as a baby in her cot bought with Green Shield stamps.

Sennen learning to swim, rubber ring around her, Bill holding her up.

Sennen on her first day at school standing grimly next to her satchel.

Sennen looking so young and yet so tired holding a newborn Henry.

Sennen pushing the old pram. 'Is that Henry or Ella in there?' Adela asked over Bill's shoulder.

'Henry,' said Bill softly. 'Look at that mop of hair.' He turned another page.

Sennen pregnant, with Henry on her hip.

Sennen with a tiny Ella on her lap and Henry leaning in to say hello to his baby sister.

'Why are we looking at these now?' asked Adela, sensing Bill's rising anger and his deep, deep sadness.

'I wanted one more look before I burned them,' he said.

'What? No!'

'Yes. If Ella and Henry are to have a good life, a full life without this gaping hole where their mother should be, I am going to have to fill it in.'

'Bill, don't. They should know what she looked like. You already took down all the photos we had of her. Please . . . Let's just keep these in the attic. Forget about them that way.'

'She's broken my heart.' He bent his head to his chest. 'I miss her too much. I can't bear having her here, but not here, any longer.'

Adela put her arm around him and pulled his head onto her shoulder. He started to cry. More tears than she had ever seen him cry before.

'She'll be back one day, I'm sure of it,' she said softly.

But Bill built a fire in his kiln and put each album on to it and watched as they burned to ashes.

Sennen was gone.

10

Pendruggan, 2018

Ella jumped off the sofa with excitement and threw her arms around Kit. 'That was Henry on the phone. He wants to meet our mum after all.'

'Careful!' Kit balanced the two mugs of coffee in his hands. 'What changed his mind?'

Ella took the cup he offered her and got herself comfy on the sofa, her feet under her. 'I'm not sure, but he said he wanted to meet her to show her exactly what she'd missed all these years.'

Kit sipped his coffee. 'Good. I thought he'd be harsher than that.'

'Well, and to tell her to her face what he thinks of her.'
'Oh.'

Ella wasn't bothered. 'I don't care! We are going to see our mum and I won't feel like an orphan any longer.'

'Is that how you've felt?'

'Yes, now I come to think about it. All those times at school:

97

concerts, plays, art shows. No mum or dad like my mates.' She picked at the buttons on her cardigan. 'Granny and Poppa were amazing, but they were Granny and Poppa. Not Mum and Dad.' She stopped fiddling with the buttons and looked at Kit. 'Do you think she'll tell us who our dad is?'

'Do you want to know?'

'Yes.'

'Well, ask her.'

'I'll wait and see. Test the water. I can't just spring it on her.' She laughed. 'One parent at a time is best, don't you think?'

Henry, with a rather thick head, rang the solicitor's office the next morning. He asked to speak to the senior partner, Mr Penhaligon, an elderly man who had been his grandparents lawyer for decades.

'I'm sorry, but Mr Penhaligon is not in the office today. He hasn't been well and has handed all his clients to Miss Palmer. Would you like to speak to her?'

Henry waited while she connected him. A young, efficient female voice came on the line.

'Mr Tallon?'

'Yes, good morning. I don't know how much you know about my family history but . . .'

'Mr Penhaligon has passed me your files and I am as up to speed as I can be. I am aware your mother wishes to meet you and you are reluctant to do so?'

'Well, I was, but having thought about it, I would like to meet her. Yes.'

'Excellent. I shall let her know. Where would you like to meet? Here? In our Trevay office? Or do you have somewhere else in mind?'

'Your office would be a good neutral place I think.'

'Exactly so.'

'And my sister only lives in Pendruggan, so it'll be easy for her to get there too.'

'Good. Well, I shall phone your mother today and ask her to make her travel arrangements.'

'As soon as possible, please.' Henry chewed his lip. 'Has she far to travel?'

'I am not at liberty to tell you where she is located.'

'Oh. Is she in the UK?'

'No, she is not.'

Sennen felt sick with anxiety. Who was she doing this for? Her parents? Her children? Or was the reason more selfish? For herself?

Why would Henry and Ella want to meet her after all this time? She had proved herself to be unreliable, feckless and worthless. She paced around her simple hotel room, the whirring breeze of the ceiling fan neither doing anything to cut through the heat, nor helping her thoughts speed around more quickly. Why did she want to see them so much? To ingratiate herself? To show them that she was a decent person? The sort of person who wouldn't walk out on her two children unless she had very good reason?

And what had been her reason? Really, there was none. She couldn't cope. That was the bottom line. She couldn't cope and didn't want to cope. The truth was as basic as that.

Her mobile phone rang. She scrambled in her handbag.

'Kafir?' Her husband.

He was brief. 'Have you heard anything?'

'Not yet.' She hugged the phone to her ear, imagining the feel of his beard on her face. Softly she asked, 'How are you?'

'How do you think?' he said tersely.

She shrank into herself, hungry for his forgiveness. 'I'm sorry. I know I should have told you.'

He paused, then murmured, 'Yes, you should.'

'Please, Kafir. Please don't.' She lay flat on her hotel bed wretchedly pressing the phone ever harder to her ear, the pain of it stopping her tears. 'I know I have hurt you, but please, please don't push me away.' Her voice faltered.

Kafir was silent. She imagined him pulling at his beard the way he did when he was angry. Eventually he said, 'Go and find your English family. You have much work to do.'

'Yes.' The enormity of her mistake crushed her.

'But . . .' said Kafir.

'Yes?'

'Let me know how it goes.'

'Thank you, Kafir. That means so much . . . Kafir?'

But he was gone.

She rolled her face into the pillow and gave way to helpless tears. She had to atone for her past, face who she had been when she walked away from her parents and two helpless babies. Had the girl she had been gone? What scared her most was, that in trying to finally to face her past, she could end up destroying another family. Was she now turning her back on *them*?

The phone by her bed rang. Wiping her eyes, she picked up and croaked, 'Hello?'

'Mrs Tallon-Singh? It's Deborah Palmer. Your solicitor in Trevay?'

Sennen sat up, alert. 'Yes?'

'I have good news. I have just heard from your son and daughter – and they have both agreed to meet you here in Cornwall. When shall I say you will arrive?

11

Ella was literally singing with happiness. She couldn't sit still and bounced up the stairs to find Kit. He was in his small painting studio, working on a canvas of a grumpy cat for its besotted owner. The skylights above poured bright sunshine onto the cat's ginger pelt and whiskers.

'Very handsome,' Ella said.

He looked up, brush between his teeth, turps rag in his hands.

'Hiya,' he said, speaking like a ventriloquist. 'What do you think?'

'Lovely.' She ruffled his hair and kissed his cheek. 'Today, everything is lovely.'

Kit took the brush from his mouth. 'Is this anything to do with your mother?' he smiled.

'I'm so excited.' She squeezed him. 'Can you imagine what this is like for me? For all these years I've wondered about her. Where was she? Did she think about me? Was she dead? Was she happy? Was she in a nunnery? And now I know she'll be here. Soon. And I shall be able to see her face. Hear her voice.' She sat down on the little stool next to Kit. 'Do you think she'll like me?'

Kit pulled a face. 'Seriously? Darling, she's going to love you.'

'God, I hope so. And I hope Henry isn't too hard on her. He's so angry.'

'He'll come around.'

Ella frowned. 'He'd better. I don't want him messing this up.' She jumped up and skipped around the room. 'I am so bloody happy! And a bit scared and . . . Oh, I don't know. A bit of everything.'

'Do we know when she's coming?'

'Not yet. The solicitor is sorting it.' She stood behind Kit with her arms around his waist and began to nibble his ear.

'Are you trying to distract me?' he said.

'Yes.'

'It's working.' He closed his eyes enjoying her light kisses. 'We do have the house to ourselves,' he breathed softly.

'What are you suggesting?' she murmured, her warm breath tickling his neck.

'I was thinking . . .'

'Hmm?'

'We could take the dogs for a walk?' He twisted in his seat and took her face in both hands and kissed her. 'Or, they can wait a bit . . .'

When they finally came downstairs, Celia and Terry were waiting for them. Terry's long feathery tail wagged as excitedly as an aloof Afghan hound allows itself to get, and Celia got to her feet languidly and strolled to the back door.

Out on the cliffs the dogs pulled at their leads, eager to investigate any fresh new smells and unleash the energy in their legs. 'Off you go, then,' said Kit to them, 'and don't forget to come back.'

They took off like rockets, leaping over the gorse bushes and tamarisk, full of the sheer joy of being alive.

Ella laughed into the wind as it hit her face and blew her hair into her eyes. 'They are as happy as I feel.' She held her arms out and twirled and jumped across the soft grass path.

Kit was happy for her: she so deserved to be happy. She knew nothing about her parents or what they looked like, she might never know who her father was, but now she was on the brink of finding out who *she* really was.

A stab of anxiety made his stomach knot. There was every chance that this longed-for meeting may turn out painfully.

He caught her hand and pulled her to him. 'I'll always be there for you. You know that, don't you?'

She stopped dancing and looked at him. 'Will you really?'

He nodded.

She kissed him, and they walked along watching the waving flags of the dogs' tails as they explored every bush.

'I've been thinking,' said Kit. 'Maybe the solicitor's office would be too formal a place to meet your mother, and Marguerite Cottage a bit too emotional.'

Ella scooped her hair out of her eyes. 'In case it goes badly?'

Kit scratched his cheek and looked at his feet. 'I'm not saying it will go wrong, but maybe neutral ground?'

Ella saw the truth of what he was saying. 'But where?'

'Let's have a think. Something will come to mind.'

'We'll talk to Henry,' said Ella, 'We need to agree together.'

They began to walk on again. Ella rather solemn and thoughtful.

'I'd like to be there too,' said Kit. 'If you would like me to?'

Ella stopped again. 'Would you?'

'Of course.'

'I'd like that.'

'Good. Then I'll be there.' He pulled her close to him and she warmed her hands under his fleece. 'I want to look after you, Ella.' He kissed her nose. 'Always.' He was nervous. This wasn't exactly planned and yet it seemed the perfect moment.

'I do mean always. Ella, I know we haven't known each other long. Just a few months, really, but I love you and I wonder if we could get engaged? It would be some good news to tell your mother.'

Ella stared at him, her mouth slightly open. 'You want to marry me?'

'Yes.' He hesitated. 'If you want to marry me?'

She took a deep breath. 'Oh blimey!' She felt her heart beginning to speed up. 'This has to be the best day of my life. Yes, I'll marry you, you lovely boy. But you've got to get down on one knee.'

Kit laughed and looked around to see if they were alone on the cliff. In the distance he could see a couple coming towards them. If he was quick they wouldn't catch him. He fell to his knees and took Ella's hand. 'Ella Tallon, will you do me the honour of being my wife?'

'Let me think about it. It's all so sudden.' She grinned from ear to ear. 'Oh, all right then. YES!'

'Can I get up now?'

'Yes. I love you, I love you, I love you!' She pulled him to his feet as the two walkers got closer.

Kit hurriedly brushed the grass from his knees as the walkers arrived.

'Congratulations,' they both said. 'Couldn't help but see it all. Did she say yes?'

As Ella and Kit walked back home, Celia and Terry loping beside them, worn out after their exercise, Ella took Kit's hand. 'Can we get married in church?'

'Oh, definitely. You're not going to do me out of seeing you walk down the aisle, all eyes on you.'

'You're so soppy.'

'Soppy is my middle name.'

'Shall we keep this to ourselves for a bit?' She asked, 'Until we get used to the idea? I think, with all that's going on, this happiness might get lost.'

'Whatever you want . . . Mrs Beauchamp.'

12

Truro, 1989

Sennen had been a happy child, until she was eleven, when she was sent away to school.

'It's only Truro, and you'll be home every weekend. You'll love it,' said her mother, packing a case with starchy new shirts and scratchy skirts, every sock and vest with her name sewn inside.

Almost overnight, she hated her unusual name, hated her parents, hated all the friendly, hippy student artists who lived in her house and got to spend every day under the tuition of her mother and father while she was sent away, but most of all she hated the other girls in the new school.

They were the sort of girls who had cool, Liberal/Tory parents. The mothers wore designer outfits and make-up. Their fathers drove flash cars. Holidays were spent skiing in Klosters or sailing in Nassau. They were called Sara, Claire, Emma, Lisa.

No one was called Sennen.

'What's your name again?' asked a particularly appalling girl called Samantha, as Sennen was unpacking her case in their small dormitory.

'Sennen.'

'Why?'

'It's after the cove. Sennen cove.'

Samantha smirked. 'I think nanny took us paddling there when we were small. My little brother had diarrhoea. He shat all over the beach.'

Two other girls, the remaining roommates, were listening as they also unpacked.

Samantha turned to them. 'What are your names?'

'Katie,' one said. 'Hi.'

'Em,' said the other.

Samantha swung back to Sennen. 'This is Sennen. Sounds a bit like senna, doesn't it. I'm going to call you Senna Pod from now on.'

Sennen hid her flaming cheeks by stuffing her empty case under her bed as she'd been told. 'Why?'

'Because,' Samantha paused waiting for Katie and Em to join in with her joke, 'they give you the shits.'

There are many ways to deal with bullies. You can either stand up to them, or tell someone, or hide your pain and go off the rails.

Sennen chose the latter. If there was a wall to be climbed, a rule to be broken, or a boundary to cross, she did it. She grew a small gang of acolytes around her and by the age of fourteen was a dab hand at smuggling booze and cigarettes into her shared study. Her detentions were many but her academic marks held up. Teachers either loved her free spirit and creativity or loathed her for her insubordination and sharp wit.

Adela and Bill would always apologise when a major misdemeanour meant they were called to a meeting with the headmistress, but to them, Sennen was merely a creative soul who meant no harm. They were secretly rather proud of their bold daughter and when she came home she was a ray of sunshine.

It was the Christmas before her fifteenth birthday that Sennen got a holiday job backstage at the Pavilions Theatre in Trevay. She was to be one of two assistant floor managers for the pantomime season.

It was *Cinderella* and Buttons was to be played by the latest winner of the TV talent show, *New Talent*. He was a brilliant young magician, offsetting the corniness of his profession with a rock and roll image.

His real name was Alan Chisolm.

His stage name was Ali A'Mayze, and from the first time Sennen clapped eyes on him, she was in love . . .

During rehearsals she was given the job of being his runner. Anything he wanted she got, willingly.

On the final tech run rehearsal, there was a crisis. Alan had developed a sore throat. His singing voice was in danger. A doctor was called and, after examination diagnosed mild laryngitis. Sennen sprinted to the chemist with the given prescription and brought it back, beaming. 'Shall I take this to Mr A'Mayze's dressing room?' she asked the company manager who should have delivered it himself but was distracted by a problem on stage.

'Okay, but knock first and don't stay too long. He's got to rest his voice.'

She had never been allowed into the star dressing room before. She knocked tentatively. A whispery voice answered, 'Come in.'

He was lying on the cushioned sofa which acted as a day bed. The room was warm and he was wearing a tight T-shirt over boxer shorts. 'Is that my prescription?' he mouthed inaudibly.

'Yes.'

He beckoned her to him and took the small bag from her. 'Water?' he managed.

Sennen quickly filled a tumbler from the sink in the corner of the room and returned. 'Here you are.'

He smiled and popped one of the tablets between his wickedly sensuous lips. 'Thanks.'

She stood for a moment in case he needed anything else.

'It's okay,' he croaked. 'I'll be fine. What's your name again?'

'Sennen.'

He nodded again and held his hand out to her. She took it and he pulled her down to him, his strength sending her off balance so that she half fell onto his chest whilst banging her knee on the wood of the sofa.

'You're nice.' He smiled, then pulled her mouth down to his lips and kissed her in a way that the boys in Truro never had. Not knowing quite what the protocol here was, she kissed him back until he let her go.

'Good girl. That's the best medicine.'

She stood up and rubbed her bruised knee. Was she dismissed? He smiled and, closing his eyes, waved her out.

She left the room and closed the door gently behind her. Shit. He fancied her. Wow. She might be his girlfriend.

The rest of the day she was in a state of suspended bliss but she had no further meaningful contact with him for the next couple of days as they ran through the dress rehearsals. She jealously watched as he chatted to the dancers and cosied up to the actress playing Cinderella. Once or twice she took him a coffee as requested, but that was it. She understood that he had to concentrate on the work so she bided her time.

First night was a huge success. To a full house, the curtain rang umpteen calls. As he finally came off stage she was waiting for him in the wings. He saw her and hugged her, then picked her up off her feet and spun her round. 'I was good, wasn't I?' he panted. She could feel the sweat through his shirt.

'Yes. You were wonderful.'

He put her down. 'Didn't they love the levitation scene with the Ugly Sisters at the ball? I do it so well, even I'm amazed!' He was chuckling with the buzz of his own success.

Sennen was excited for him. 'They did,' she agreed. 'It's brilliant and you are so funny when you do it.'

'Yeah.' He grinned not so modestly and winked. 'Between you and me, I am bloody good.'

One of the Ugly Sisters, a man called Graham, walked past and pinched Ali's bum. 'You can run your magic wand over me anytime, young man.'

'I'm spoken for,' Ali grinned.

'Lucky fella,' sighed Graham, taking Ali's arm. 'Come on, love, get changed, I want the first dance at the party.'

The two men sauntered off to their dressing rooms.

The stage manager walked past her, 'Stop mooning over the boy wonder and reset for tomorrow. Two shows a day from now till mid-January, no time for slacking.'

The first-night party was in full swing by the time Sennen

arrived. She hadn't had time to change out of her working black trousers and T-shirt and was rather dusty and grimy, but she'd managed a spritz of Calvin Klein's Eternity – well, a rip-off market stall version, pinched from the wardrobe mistress – and she was good to go. Hell, this was Show Business and she was part of it.

The venue for the party was the stalls bar. She grabbed a glass of coke and wandered through the sea of people in search of Ali.

She didn't get far. Adela and Bill found her first. 'Darling, that was so much fun,' Adela said kissing her daughter's cheek. 'Did you hear Dad laughing?'

Sennen shook her head, eyes searching over Adela's shoulder. 'Can't hear much backstage.'

Her father grabbed her in a bear hug. 'So proud of you. My daughter in the theatre.'

She hugged him briefly still scanning the crowd. 'I'm only the assistant stage manager. ASM's are lowest of the low.'

'It's the oily rag that keeps the engine turning,' insisted Bill.

An elderly couple approached Bill and Adela, greeting them warmly. Sennen took advantage of the distraction and melted away.

Ali was in a dark corner at the back of the bar. He was sitting on a claret velvet banquette, on his own, with several empty glasses in front of him. 'Hi,' said Sennen shyly. 'What are you doing on your own?'

'I'm bloody annoyed.' He looked at his empty glass. 'Get me a drink, will you?'

'They won't serve me. I'm not old enough.' She sat next to him. 'Why are you annoyed?'

He stood up. 'I'll get them. What do you want?'

'Oh. Coke, please. Thank you.'

She noticed how he steadied himself against the wall as he got up and wondered how much he'd had already. 'Don't go away,' he instructed her.

'I won't.' She hugged herself. He really did like her. And she had him all to herself.

After a short queue at the bar he returned with a large gin and tonic for himself and a coke for her. He sat down heavily before raising his glass to her. 'Cheers, Sally.'

'Sennen,' she giggled.

'I knew that. Just kidding. Drink up.'

She raised her glass and sipped. It wasn't just coke. 'What's in this?' she asked.

He winked at her and put his finger to his lips. 'A little bit of what you fancy.'

'Lovely.' She smiled at him and took a big swallow, feeling a mystery warmth meander down to her tummy. 'So why are you so annoyed?'

He leant back and reached across the velvet to hold her hand. 'That stupid cow playing Cinderella keeps making passes at me and I'm just not into her. She's pissed me off.'

Sennen thrilled to this. 'Stupid cow,' she agreed.

'I like you, though.' He squeezed her hand.

'Do you?'

Adela and Bill arrived. 'There you are,' said Bill, pink from too much wine. 'Mum and I are off now. So come on and we'll get you home.'

Before Sennen could think, Ali, who had let go of Sennen's hand as if it were hot metal, said, 'Your daughter is a gem. I don't know what any of the company would do without her. A little star, she is. Would you let her stay a bit longer? I'll look after her and bring her home. You have my word.'

Adela looked at Sennen and back at Ali. He seemed nice enough and was, anyway, at least ten years older than Sennen if not more, and Sennen was a sensible girl. 'What do you say, Bill?'

'Fine, but not too late,' shrugged Bill.

'Bye, Mum. Bye, Dad.' She waved at them. Ali waved too. As soon as they were out of sight he took her hand again and kissed it. 'Fancy getting out of here? Somewhere we can talk?'

His shabby hotel was in the shabbiest back street of Trevay. His room was up three flights of crooked stairs and had a sloping floor so that she felt she was walking up hill to the bed. The room was decorated with thoughtless design, the carpet brown with beige swirls, the curtains pink and unlined, hanging limply from the plastic rail, the sagging bed covered with a threadbare lilac-coloured candlewick spread. Sennen, feeling warm and relaxed from whatever had been in her coke, flopped down on to the bed and laughed. 'I thought my dormitory at school was bad.'

He was rustling about in his suitcase and produced a bottle of vodka with a flourish. 'Ta-da! And for my next trick I shall magic up a couple of plastic toothmugs from the bathroom.'

'I like vodka,' said Sennen, seriously. 'One of my mates smuggles it in to school. Her dad likes the good stuff, buys a case at a time. He never notices a bottle missing.'

Ali came back with the mugs and poured some vodka into each. He rolled a spliff and lit it, then bounced onto the bed next to her. 'Ever smoked a joint?'

'Yes,' she lied.

'Good girl.' Lying back on the bed he took a lungful then passed it to her.

She took a small puff. 'Nice.' She smiled at him and passed it back.

He put it to his lips and inhaled slowly. She watched as he held the breath deeply and then let the smoke curl slowly from his nose and lips. 'That and the Bacardi I put in your coke will relax you nicely,' he said.

She did feel pretty good, now he mentioned it. She took another sip of her vodka.

He propped himself up on one elbow and looked down on her. 'So . . . Sally, Susie, whoever you are.'

Sennen giggled. 'Sennen.'

'Sennen. Do you know how attractive you are?'

'Er, no,' she giggled again.

'Well, you are.' He leant over and kissed her. She responded warmly.

'Hang on,' he said, 'I just need to get something. You can never be too sure, can you?'

'I suppose you can't,' she said, not getting his meaning.

'Let me just nip to the bathroom. I need a slash anyway.'

Sennen put her drink on the bedside table and stretched her arms above her head. He obviously really fancied her and she liked the way he kissed. She ran the fingers of her right hand over her lips, then reached for her glass again and drank it all down.

She waited for him.

Five minutes later he still hadn't appeared.

'Ali?' she called quietly. 'You okay in there?'

Getting no answer, she got off the bed and knocked on the cheap plywood door. 'Ali?'

She heard something like a snore. 'Ali?'

She turned the handle and the door opened.

He was sitting on the loo, trousers round his ankles, head resting on the wall next to him. 'Ali! Wake up.'

She put her arm around him and got him to stand up. 'I must have had a little too much of my voddy friend,' he slurred.

'Come on. I need to get you on the bed.'

Sennen managed to shuffle him – difficult with his trousers round his ankles – to the bed and get him lying down, albeit at an uncomfortable angle. She took his trousers off, trying hard not to look at his nudity.

'Ali? I'm going to go home now. I'll have to walk. Don't worry, I'll be all right.' She picked up her small canvas bag and tied her trainers. 'Thank you for a lovely night.' She bent down and kissed him, but he was dead to the world. 'See you tomorrow then. Bye.'

Downstairs, behind the studded leatherette reception, sat the night porter. He stared at her. 'All right?'

She blushed and stammered, 'Yes, thank you.' She pushed the glass front door open and stepped outside. A wind was whipping up from the harbour and racing up the narrow street. She felt the rawness of it stinging her cheeks and nose and pulled her duffle coat closer.

As she walked the quiet, deserted road and turned the corner at the bottom heading for home, she saw the first snowflakes of winter falling from the inky sky. She stuck her tongue out and caught one. This must be the perfect end to the most romantic night of her life, she thought.

The next morning the snow was slush but she was up early, energised, ready for work and brimming with the excitement of seeing Ali again. The daily matinees were scheduled for

2.30 and the evening shows were at 7.00. She got all her jobs done swiftly: fresh water in the wings, props laid out, stage checked, costumes distributed to the dressing rooms, coffee and tea ready in the green room. Ali and all the cast were expected to be in the theatre by 1.55. At 1.45 she positioned herself artlessly in the stage doorkeeper's office, to make sure she was the first person he saw when he came in.

Everyone had arrived with a couple of minutes to spare, except Ali.

The company manager, doing his rounds, was not amused.

'Mr A'Mayze will be getting a warning unless he's here in five minutes,' he huffed, checking his watch. 'Let me know the moment he's here. In the meantime, I'd better get the understudy ready. And you'd better tell everyone that all the magic stuff will be cut this afternoon.'

Ali strolled in with ten minutes to go, black sunglasses on, the fringes on the sleeves of his black leather jacket swinging.

'Where have you been? You've got ten minutes,' whispered Sennen as she dragged him to his dressing room. 'You're in trouble.'

He stopped dead in the middle of the narrow corridor and pulled his arm from her grip. 'I'm the star of the show. It won't start without me.'

Sennen wrung her hands, her stomach churning. 'Please, please get ready or your understudy will be on.'

Ali pushed his shoulders back and his sunglasses into his hair like an Alice band. His eyes were bloodshot and had dark circles beneath. 'We'll see about that.' And he strode off to his dressing room.

Somehow, he did get ready, leaving the audience to wait fifteen minutes. When he finally bounded on to the stage, shouting, 'Hello, boys and girls, mums and dads, my name's

Buttons. What's yours?' he got a huge round of excitable applause, mostly from the mums.

Between shows Sennen fetched him a sandwich from the café next door and a large, strong black coffee. He barely acknowledged her. 'How's your throat?' she asked, leaving a KitKat on his dressing table.

'Sore.' He made great show of swallowing with painful effort.

'You don't look very well,' she ventured.

'I'm fine. Bit of a headache, that's all.'

She went to the door. 'See you later?'

'Maybe.'

'If you need me, just call.'

After the second show, as she was making her way to his dressing room, she saw him with an older woman in a fur coat heading for the stage door. If he saw her, he didn't acknowledge her.

'Who was that with Ali?' she asked the stage doorkeeper, trying to keep her voice light and disinterested.

'His agent, I think.' He looked astutely at Sennen. 'Don't you go falling for him. He's nothing but trouble. I caught him trying to corner our Cinderella last night. Poor girl, he was like an octopus. All over her.'

Sennen was outraged. 'Actually, it was she who was after him. He's not interested in her.'

'Really? Too old for him, I expect. He likes 'em young. So don't you go near him.'

Her walk home was cold in more ways than one. The stars were clear and bright and the cold wind nipped her fingers and nose but there was no snow and no Ali by her side. She went over what had happened the night before. He had told her he liked her, he'd invited her back to his room and been sweet. He was working so hard – no wonder he'd fallen asleep. She was glad she'd been there to get him safely into bed. She would have to be very supportive of Ali. He was carrying the success of the show and he wasn't feeling well. She wouldn't put him under any pressure. She would simply be there for him and help him in any way she could.

All theatres shut their doors on Christmas Day. Actors and crew either spend the day with their loved ones or sleep the clock round. Sennen was tired. She had worked hard looking after her own job, as well as Ali, and it hadn't gone unnoticed. The company manager, her boss, had praised her and suggested that if she wanted a career in stage management he would be happy to employ her. She dreamt of working with Ali always.

Her mother woke her on Christmas morning with a cup of tea. 'Happy Christmas, darling.'

Sennen turned over without opening her eyes. 'I'm tired.'

'It's ten o'clock.'

'So?'

'It's Christmas morning and Father Christmas has been.'

'Let me sleep.'

'Just another ten minutes. Don't let your tea go cold. We are all waiting downstairs to open the presents.'

'I'll be down later.'

'Your tea is right there.'

'Mum! Go. Away.'

Time ran like quicksilver. Christmas came and went; New Year was celebrated and Sennen became a slave to Ali. He mostly ignored her, but threw her the odd crumb of a compliment which she savoured and took home to replay in her endless fantasies. Finally, in the middle of January, the panto run was up.

Sennen always stood in the wings to watch Ali's audience participation scene before the finale. She absorbed every joke, every glance, every move.

Ali would pick three children from the audience and bring them up onto the stage. Kneeling down to their height he would ask them silly questions and make eggs appear from behind their ears and pound coins from under their tongues.

When they were finished, she was the person who handed over a marvellous and always huge teddy bear as a prize so that every child in the audience was instantly jealous.

When the children had been safely delivered back to their proud parents, Ali would shout, 'Ladies and gentlemen, boys and girls, Cinderella, my best friend, is marrying Prince Charming and we are all invited to the wedding! See you in a minute!'

Running off stage his dresser would wrench off his costume and speedily Velcro him into his sparkly wedding outfit.

Sennen always had a small towel ready for him to mop the sweat running from his scalp. Usually he took it from her without a word, but that night, the last night of the run, he said, 'In my dressing room there are some gifts. They're labelled. Bung them round to the right people, would you?' He winked as he said it and gave her hand a squeeze then ran back on stage for the wedding finale and curtain calls.

She dashed to his room and found a pile of seven identically shaped parcels. She read the labels. One each for the principal members of the cast and one for her. She held it in her hands and pressed it against her chest. He had thought of her. Now he was acknowledging their relationship. She

opened the parcel. A book. *Ali A'Mayze's Simple Magic Tricks.*
It sold in the foyer for £4.99.

She felt a little let down.

She flicked through the pages back to front and then saw
his handwriting on the first page. He had dedicated it to her.

> *Dear Sally,*
> *Thanks, Doll,*
> *Ali A'Mayze*

And he'd drawn a little heart with a magic wand waving
above it.

The dressing-room door opened and he walked in. 'Jesus,
that was something. God, they couldn't get enough of me.
Eight curtain calls. Love it. Get me a drink, would you?' He
sat down at his dressing table and looked at himself in the
mirror, checking his hair and teeth.

'What would you like?' she asked.

'There's some champagne in the fridge.' He pointed to the
small fridge by the daybed. 'Pour yourself one, doll.'

'Thank you.' She smiled. She knew he really *did* remember
her name. 'And thank you for my book.'

He was creaming the make-up from his face. 'They'll be
worth a lot of money when I'm in Vegas.'

She went to the fridge and found the champagne, already
open, and poured it into two tumblers. 'Why did you write
Sally inside it?'

'Did I?' He took the tumbler from her. 'Just a little joke.
You are my mystery girlfriend, aren't you?' He patted his
knees, inviting her to sit on them. She did and immediately
thought back to when her father used to do the same.

'This is nice,' he said, jiggling his knees up and down to

make her giggle. 'Drink your champagne up and we can have another.'

He was so gentle as he stared into her eyes. Whispering loving words as his hand crept up inside her T-shirt and gently stroked her breast. His kisses were lingering, soft but passionate. He carried her to the daybed and took off her jeans and knickers before caressing her stomach and inner thighs. He was still dressed in his costume. The lace and taffeta of his knickerbockers scratched against her thighs as he told her how much he loved her.

When he had finished, he rolled off her and patted her arm. 'Well, that was very nice.'

Sennen's head was swimming with a mix of happiness and alarm. She understood what had just happened and she was proud of it. She had lost her virginity. To a man. Not a boy. A man who had told her he loved her.

He got up and kicked off what remained of his costume. 'Right, I'm off to the party.' He saw the undelivered presents. 'Haven't you done those yet? Hurry up.'

She didn't make the party. Being part of the backstage crew she had to pack props and costumes into the huge wicker travelling skips and load them onto the pantechnicon that had reversed into the scene dock ready to take it all back into store for next year. By the time she had done everything and made a final check that every dressing room was empty and the stage clear, it was almost 3 a.m.

When she got to the stalls bar, it was dark. She saw the shadows of empty glasses and beer bottles and could smell the thickness of tobacco'd air, but there was not a soul to be seen.

She called out, 'Ali?' She ran to the silent auditorium. 'Ali?' she called again. She heard footsteps on the stage and turned quickly in relief. 'Ali! I'm here. I thought you had gone.'

He was holding a torch and she couldn't see him behind it.

'Come on, whoever you are,' a gruff voice said. 'You got no home to go to?'

It was the stage doorkeeper on his rounds. He shone the light on her face. 'Is that young Sennen? If you're looking for young fella-me-lad, he's long gone. Come on, let me see you off the premises.

13

It was three weeks short of her fifteenth birthday, when she had already missed two periods and was regularly sick after breakfast, that Adela, who had hovered on the landing listening at the loo door, asked her if she was bulimic.

'Darling, I know that there is a lot of peer pressure to be slim nowadays, but you are lovely just the way you are.'

Sennen scowled and pushed past her mother to get to the sanctuary of her room. As she went to shut the door behind her, Adela put her hand out stopped her. 'Sennen, I'm worried for you. Don't shut me out. Would you like to see the doctor?'

Sennen flounced to her bed and fell face first into the pillow. 'No,' she mumbled.

'Darling, talk to me.' Adela sat on the bed and stroked Sennen's hair. She was feeling out of her depth. She tried again. 'You can tell me anything.'

She waited patiently for an answer, then shook her daughter's shoulder. 'Tell me. Please. Is it school? I know you didn't like it at first, but it's okay now, isn't it?'

She felt Sennen breathe deeply, then expel the air loudly. 'I'm pregnant,' she mumbled.

'What?' asked Adela gently. 'I couldn't hear you.'

'I'm pregnant.'

If asked, Sennen wouldn't have been able to say what she thought would happen next, but what she hadn't expected was the calm acceptance of her parents and their incredible support.

The doctor confirmed the pregnancy and then offered her solutions. A termination, an adoption, or keep the child. When he said this, in the clinical serenity of his consulting room, Adela and Bill were sitting either side of her. They said nothing, allowing Sennen to make her decision. Eventually she murmured, 'I want the baby.'

Adela beamed and clasped Sennen's hand. 'Good,' she said.

The doctor watched her over the frames of his half-moon glasses and asked the question her parents hadn't felt able to ask. 'And the father? Will he have any part in the baby's life?'

Sennen shook her head.

'May I ask who the father is?'

Again, Sennen shook her head.

'I see. Does he know that he has a child on the way?'

Bill gripped Sennen's hand tightly.

'No,' she said.

The doctor looked down at her notes on his desk and thought for a moment. 'You are very young. Your life will never be the same again.'

'She has us,' said Adela firmly.

The doctor frowned. 'That is true, but Sennen is a minor and the boy who did this to her was breaking the law.' He looked at Sennen and in a serious voice asked, 'Tell me, were you forced into having sex? Or did you know what you were doing? And did you do it willingly?'

Sennen closed her eyes and thought of that night and how Ali had made her feel. She nodded.

'You weren't forced into doing something you didn't want to do?'

She shook her head.

'Are you still seeing the boy?'

She shook her head again.

'Because if you are, I shall prescribe you some contraception. You do know what that is, don't you.'

'Of course she does,' Bill said. 'She won't be needing it.'

'Well, then.' The doctor sat straight and clasped his hands. 'I will write to your school and explain your circumstances. There is no need for you to give up your studies – indeed, your child will need a mother who is well-educated. Look after yourself: no smoking or drinking, be kind to your parents and I'll see you in four weeks.'

Henry Alan William Tallon was born at the end of September, 1991, with both his grandparents in attendance.

It was decided that Sennen would stay at her school in Truro to finish her exams and come home at weekends to be with Henry. In the meantime, Adela and Bill would care for him.

Back at school she was ostracised. Girls whispered about her as she walked the corridors or queued for lunch. Even her small coterie of daredevil friends shrank from her. No one asked her, and she told no one about Ali.

Thinking back, she realised that this was the time when she had begun to feel something that made her more than different. Of course she was different; which other of her friends had a baby? But a new and dangerous pit of teenage melancholy opened up in front of her. Who was she? She was neither child or parent. Her own parents had taken control with ease and efficiency. Henry was more theirs than hers. All her waking thoughts and sleeping dreams were filled with the desperate anxiety of trying to find Ali. If only she could contact him, he would come and sort all this mess out. He loved her. He had told her so, hadn't he? She longed to confide in Adela. To tell her about Ali. To have her help her find him. But she didn't know where to begin. And she had an uncomfortable suspicion that they would turn against him. They would accuse him of . . . well, she wasn't quite sure. He had not taken advantage of her. That was a fact. She had wanted him. But why hadn't he tried to contact her?

As soon as she knew about the baby she had asked for the address of his London agent from the Pavilions Theatre and written to him, asking if he could phone her as she had some news. After a few weeks she received a letter from his agent's secretary, thanking her for 'her interest' and enclosing an unsigned cheesy postcard photo of him.

When Henry was born, she wrote again, and this time received a leaflet with the dates of the *Ali A'Mayze On The Road* tour. She scoured the schedule and her heart sang when she saw that, for one Sunday night in November only, he was coming to the Pavilions.

She planned how she would tell him about Henry. He would be so happy. He would hold her and promise to take care of her. He would be so sorry that he hadn't been there for her, but now, everything would be all right.

She took fresh interest in Henry and whispered her secret

to him when she bathed him or took him for walks on the harbour.

Adela and Bill noticed how much happier she was. 'She's doing so well, isn't she?' said Adela, watching from the kitchen window as Sennen showed Henry the late butterflies on the buddleia.

Bill slipped his arm around Adela's shoulder. 'She is. And so are you.'

Sennen counted the days to seeing Ali again. She'd asked at the theatre if they needed any backstage help for the show. They didn't, but she could work front of house as an usherette.

At last the day arrived. The dress code was black trousers or skirt with a white blouse. She had a stretchy mini skirt that was a little too tight over her baby tum and borrowed a white shirt from her mother. She bought some sheer black tights and wore her old knee-high black leather boots. By the time she'd wound her hair into a bun and put on a little eye make-up and lip gloss, she looked very presentable.

'My word, you do look smart,' said Bill when she came into the sitting room. 'I'm very proud of you. Not many girls with a baby and exams would want to go out and earn a little money. Very proud indeed.'

'Thanks, Dad. Would you give me a lift down?'

'Yep. Let me just find my keys.' He wandered off into the hall.

Her mother came in from the kitchen with Henry on her hip. 'Let's have look at you.'

Henry blinked and burped.

Adela patted his padded bottom. 'Very high praise for your mummy indeed, Henry. Now say goodnight to her and say "See you later, Mummy".'

Sennen kissed them both, told them she loved them, and with a happy, hammering heart, left the house.

Standing at the back of the stalls as the house lights dimmed, leaving just a single spotlight on the crimson velvet curtains, Sennen's breathing was shallow and ragged with anticipation.

Prerecorded rock music blasted through the auditorium and a deep, slow voice announced 'Ladies and Gentlemen, you are about to witness incredible things. Things that will shock you, and fill you with awe. Tonight is a night you will speak of in hushed tones as your children, grandchildren and great-grandchildren beg you to tell them the story. The story of the night you witnessed real magic.' The audience gasped and giggled as the single spotlight snapped out and they were left in a silent blackness . 'Ladies and gentlemen, for one night only I give you: Mr Ali A'Mayze.' The voice dragged out the last syllables as a deafening peal of church bells rang through the audience. From the roof above them a spotlight revealed a coffin, lowering itself towards the stage.

Sennen had her heart in her mouth. Any moment now she'd see him.

The coffin stopped about a metre from the stage floor and floated free of any wires that she could see. A female under-taker walked slowly from the wings to the spotlit box. She drew a glinting silver sword from a scabbard beneath her cloak and proceeded to wave it all over the box to prove it was merely hanging there in space. A curdled scream came from the back of the stalls and made Sennen jump out of her skin. She and the entire audience turned to see what it was and, in that split second, the coffin crashed to the ground and from it leapt a powerful scarlet motorbike with Ali sitting astride it, revving the engine.

Sennen couldn't breathe. The audience began to cheer and applaud. Ali spun the back wheel until smoke poured from it. The crowd were in the palm of his hand. His eyes, outlined in black, stared at them until they felt he was looking into their souls. Sennen shivered with anticipation. He smiled, baring his teeth and in a white flash both he and the machine were gone.

Another gasp.

A man in an overcoat and cloth cap got out of his seat and ran down to the stage shouting, 'Where is he? Where is he?'

The audience didn't know who he was.

The man ran to the spot where the bike had been. He stopped, bent down and examined it. His back to the audience. Then slowly he took off his cap and then his coat and spun round with his arms wide open. 'You didn't think I'd leave you without a show, did you?'

It was him. Ali.

Sennen clutched her hands to her chest and yelled his name and was drowned out by eight hundred people doing the same.

She stood in a dream as she watched the show. This was the father of her baby. Her future. She couldn't wait to see him and tell him about Henry.

The show finished. She stood at the back of the stalls until the place had emptied, then made her way backstage and headed for the star dressing room. Her hands were shaking as she knocked on the door.

'Who is it?' asked a male voice. Not Ali's.

'Sennen.'

The door opened a crack and a small round man looked her up and down. 'Mr A'Mayze is not having visitors.'

'Who is it, Keith?' Ali's disembodied voice asked.

Keith curled his lip and said to Sennen, 'What's your name?'

'Sennen. I worked with Ali in the pantomime. Last Christmas.'

Keith relayed the message. Ali answered.

'Yeah? Okay, let her in.'

Keith opened the door wide and there he was. Naked but for his jeans, his long curls damp with sweat, his eyes looking her up and down. 'Yes?'

'Hi. You were great tonight. Truly. I can't believe you are actually here.'

He narrowed his eyes and looked at her more closely. 'I know you . . .'

'Yes,' she smiled.

'Sally? Susie?'

She laughed at his old joke. 'Sennen.'

'Of course.' He stood up. 'I'm fine now, Keith. I'll meet you back at the hotel.'

Keith was put out and his bottom lip jutted sullenly. 'I haven't sorted your laundry yet.'

'Out. Now. Sennen's an old friend of mine.' Ali looked at Sennen and gave her the kind of smile that made her whole body flush.

Keith was not happy and took his time, gathering up his coat and felt beret. 'Don't be late,' he said as he left the room.

'Want a drink, gorgeous?' Ali asked as soon as he'd left. 'I've got some wine in the fridge. Sit down.'

She sat on the same daybed where he had made love to her almost a year ago. He watched as her mini skirt slid up her thighs. 'I like your boots.'

'Thanks. How are you?'

'Right now I couldn't be better.' He poured the wine and,

handing her a glass, sat down next to her. 'How are you? Busy year?'

She giggled. 'You could say that.'

He was looking at the buttons of her shirt. 'You really do have lovely breasts.'

She melted. 'I have missed you so much, Ali.'

He put his wine down and kissed her, pushing her down on the bed.

'I love you, Ali,' she said.

'I love you, babe.' His face was hot as he opened her shirt and squeezed her breasts from her bra. 'And I really love these.'

It was a bit more comfortable than the first time and he took a little longer than before. He lay next to her panting. 'Pass my glass, would you?'

As she sat up her tummy rounded in her skirt which was pushed up to her hips. He took the glass. 'You've put a bit of weight on, haven't you? I remember you being a bit skinnier. Mind you, I don't mind a bit of curvy flesh.'

'Don't you?' She took a sip of her wine and lay back, looking into his eyes.

'Not on a young girl. It's like puppy fat. Don't want it on an old bird, though.'

She was so happy. 'Did you get my letters?'

'Where did you write?'

'Your agent.'

'No. They answer them.'

'I thought so. Otherwise I'd have heard from you, wouldn't I?'

'Maybe. I've been touring all year. It's hard for things to find me.'

She put her hand to his cheek. 'I understand.'

'I love a girl who understands.' He smiled down at her.

'I love you, Ali,' she whispered as he began kissing her again.

'I love you, baby.'

Keith, listening at the door, knew exactly the right moment to knock and get Ali out of there.

'Sorry to disturb, but there's an important call for you at the hotel, Ali. You must come now.'

'Oh, right.' Ali stood up and zipped his jeans. 'Babe, I've got to split. It'll be to arrange a meeting about my European tour – going to happen over the next two years. Scandinavia, Holland, Belgium, Italy, Portugal, then the final gig in Spain, lovely Spain in September '93. You must come when I'm there.'

Sennen was bewildered at this sudden departure. 'Which hotel are you in tonight? I could come over in the morning. I've got someone I want you to meet.'

'Great. It's the, erm . . .'

'Starfish,' said Keith handing Ali his T-shirt and coat.

'See you, babe. Bye.' He went over and kissed her. 'Thanks for everything.'

14

The next morning, she bundled Henry into his pushchair, escaping her mother's questions on the pretext of a need to get nappies, and set out for the Starfish Hotel.

She couldn't wait to see Ali's face when she told him that Henry was his son.

His family.

Her family.

In her shoulder-bag she had her little camera ready for the photo she had been longing for.

The well-groomed receptionist looked up from her desk and smiled warily.

'Can I help you?'

'Yes. I've come to see Mr Ali A'mayze. He's expecting me.'

The receptionist gave a patronising smile. 'I'm afraid he's already left.'

'Oh.' A distant alarm bell began to ring in Sennen's heart. 'Did he say where he's gone? Is he at the theatre?'

The receptionist revealed a set of perfect teeth behind her lacquered lips. 'No. He checked out before breakfast. He had

135

to catch a train.' She remembered her flirty conversation with him very clearly.

Panic flooded, Sennen. 'Are you sure?' she asked. 'Maybe he's booked under his real name? Alan Chisolm?'

'Yes, I'm sure. Mr A'Mayze has definitely left.'

Sennen felt her heart actually crack with pain. Henry began to cry. 'Did he leave a message for me? Sennen Tallon?'

'I'll check, but I'm sure he didn't leave any messages.' The receptionist made a show of checking the cubbyholes behind her. 'No, I'm sorry.' She gave Sennen a professional beam and turned her attention to a couple who were next in line.

They were staring at Sennen and tutting as Henry's cries grew louder.

'Okay. Thanks,' she said, and pulling Henry's little jacket around him she hurried away in confusion and shame.

A few weeks later, she told Adela and Bill that she was pregnant . . .

When she came, Ella was a beautiful baby with a mass of red curls and a happy nature. Bill and Adela idolised her from the start. Henry was not so keen – like many a firstborn he didn't like sharing his mother with an interloper.

Sennen was cornered. Her loving, generous, caring parents watched her every move, were there for Henry and Ella's every cry. They were stifling her. Why didn't they confront her? Demand to know who this boy was who had fathered their grandchildren?

Sennen overheard them one morning in the kitchen as she was coming down the stairs for breakfast. She paused and quietly listened.

Bill was talking. 'If I ever find out who that lout is, I'll knock him from here to the middle of next week.'

'And what good would that do? What's done is done and it is our duty to protect Sennen and give her all the security and time she needs. She will tell us one day, I'm certain.'

'We aren't protecting her, though. She's not seventeen and she's just had her second child. We somehow let that happen.' Sennen heard Bill stirring his coffee loudly. 'I'm going to ask her outright.'

'You are not.' Adela sounded adamant. 'She is a woman and a mother. This is her body and her life and I want to make this transition for her as easy as possible. Family show-downs are not going to help. I want her to look back on all this with happy memories, not rows.'

Sennen wanted to run into the kitchen then, tell them all about Ali and ask for their help in finding him, but instinct told her that once that lid was off there would be only hell to pay. No, she told herself, one day, when Ali came back, they could explain together, when the time was right. For now, they asked no questions, gave her no pressure, wrapped her and their two grandchildren in unending love – and she hated them for it.

She dropped her friends, the ones that were left, before they dropped her. Only Rosemary, a girl who Sennen had never known well, came over because she loved playing with children.

Adela and Bill encouraged the friendship. 'Rosemary's a nice girl. We like her and she's good for you, Sennen. Why not go to the pictures at the weekend? We'll babysit.'

Sennen wanted nothing less, but Rosemary could be a means to an end. Instead of going to the cinema, Sennen took Rosemary to the pub and introduced her to Bacardi and Cokes and, over time, planted the idea of holiday in Spain.

They were walking on the harbour wall, eating chips. 'Don't

you ever feel like running away?' Sennen asked, chucking her chip paper into a bin, and missing, then passing Rosemary a Consulate menthol cigarette.

'No,' said Rosemary.

'I've got a friend in Spain. Fancy coming with me?'

Rosemary shook her head. 'Who is it?'

'A guy.'

'I don't think my parents would let me.'

'They don't need to know.' Sennen smiled slyly. 'We could just hitch to Plymouth, catch the ferry and be gone. Back before they knew it.'

'Really?'

'Have you got a passport?'

'Yes. I had for when we went to Oberammergau, in the Alps, on a school trip.'

'Money?'

'Some in the post office.'

'Okay. Leave it with me and I'll make a plan. Don't tell anyone.'

'What about Henry and Ella?'

'In a kind of a way, I'm doing this for them.'

'Oh, I see,' said Rosemary, clearly not seeing at all.

And now here she was, seventeen, on a ferry to Spain, abandoning her children to look for their father.

15

Trevay without Sennen

The black void left by Sennen was impossible to avoid, yet too painful to explore.

'How could she leave Ella and Henry?' Bill, staring out of their bedroom window, looking out over the roofs of Trevay and down to the sea.

He was like a wounded bear. He could neither sit down nor stand up without doing the opposite in moments.

'Please, Bill . . .' Adela tried to soothe him. 'We need to stay calm, for Henry and Ella. They are missing her terribly. Henry woke up at two this morning, sobbing his little heart out.'

'How could she do it, Adela? We have never judged her. Always loved her.' He wiped his broken eyes. 'Is she even still alive?'

Adela came towards him and put her arm around his shoulder. 'She's a young woman breaking free from her life. She needs to find herself.' He dropped his head onto her shoulder and sobbed. She stroked his head in the same way she had stroked Henry's just a few hours before. 'She'll come back.'

He broke away from her, angry. 'We were too soft on her. Should have been tougher. When she first told us about Henry, I should have shaken sense into her. How can a teenager deal with a baby? We should have demanded to know who the father is. Some little toerag out there is running around Trevay laughing at us, at her, at Henry.' His voice was rising, the words almost choking him.

'Darling, please – don't let the children hear you.' Adela put a hand on his arm but he shrugged her off.

'Just scraped her O Levels. Will miss her A levels. She's cruel and stupid.' He sat on the bed, his head in his hands. 'Where did we go wrong? I honestly thought I knew her, but I don't. She was laughing at us. Using us all along. She's ruined her life and the lives of Henry and Ella.' He stood up and walked to the window, banging his hands down on the sill. 'I never want to see her again. I will never let her back into this house. Never. It's Henry and Ella we must focus on now.'

Adela clutched him. 'Stop it, Bill. Stop it. You're hurting. You don't mean those things. She's Sennen. Our daughter. You love her. We all love her. She'll come back to us.'

Bill looked at her with sneering pity, 'Not while I'm alive.'

'Bill!' Adela was frightened. 'That's a terrible thing to say and untrue. She will come back and you will be alive and we will be a family again.'

He crumpled then. Adela watched the man she loved break down in front of her. She put her arms out to him and he came to her like a child. He clung to her, his whole body shuddering with every sob.

*

When Rosemary returned from Spain, without Sennen, and came knocking at their door with the presents for the children, Adela was even more worried for Bill. He took the toys and put them in the dustbin. He sat for hours in Sennen's room crying and finally burnt all the photos they had of her.

The doctor arranged for grief counselling, which Bill refused to attend, and it fell to Adela to care for him. She quietly carried the burden of the children, her husband, the house and her own desolation, never allowing the internal scream that deafened her to escape her lips.

At Christmas Sennen sent a postcard from Madrid. The message read,

> *Dear Mum, Poppa, Henry and Ella,*
>   *Happy Christmas. I'm okay. Don't worry.*
>   *Lots of love*
>   *Sennen*

Adela, always the first up in the house, picked it off the mat and read it. She never told Bill. It would upset him too much. She didn't have the strength to face that. Greedily, she kept it for herself.

Sennen never forgot their birthdays. Each year, from somewhere in Europe, cards would arrive. All with the briefest of messages and always ending with 'I'm okay. Don't worry.'

Adela kept them all for herself, and the years passed. Henry and Ella got through primary school well enough and were happy popular children. Ella had a real talent for art, which

Bill delighted in. She was the apple of his eye and wherever he was Adela would usually find her with him, chatting and laughing.

Henry was a good boy, but quieter, with a quick temper. He was good at maths and accumulating money. At school he ran an illicit tuck shop, selling penny sweets he'd bought from the newsagents for twice as much in the playground. The head teacher, whilst acknowledging his entrepreneurship, had to ban him, but it didn't stop Henry: he simply sold the sweets outside the school gate, and therefore outside the school's jurisdiction, instead.

Adela had always run a small ad hoc painting school for young artists, providing bed and board as well as classes. Sennen had hated having to share her parents with them and after she left, Adela stopped doing it.

It was Henry who suggested she should start it up again. 'How much would you pay me to help?' he asked.

'It depends,' she said, thinking about what needed to be done. 'I shall have to give the spare bedrooms a lick of paint and maybe make some new curtains.'

'I will paint. You and Ella can do the curtains,' said Henry. 'I'll do it for twenty pounds a room.'

'Ten pounds and you have a deal,' laughed Adela.

'Ten pounds for the small rooms. Fifteen for the big ones. Including Mum's.' He held his hand out to seal the deal.

'No. No, not Sennen's,' Adela replied.

'Granny, Mum's room has been a shrine for too long.'

'It is not a shrine.' Adela was firm.

'It is a shrine, Granny. If Mum ever came back, she'd think she'd never been away. And anyway, Ella would like that bedroom.'

'Would she?'

Henry nodded. 'Yep. She's almost thirteen and her room is tiny. She needs the space to grow up in.'

Adela sighed. 'Do you want a cup of tea? I'm going to put the kettle on for Poppa.'

'Don't change the subject,' Henry said gently. 'I was allowed a bigger room when I was twelve. Don't baby her.'

'I'll ask your grandfather.'

Bill was accepting of the idea. 'She's been gone over a decade. It's time to move on, Adela.'

'It's the last bit of her we have. It feels so final,' Adela said sadly.

'No, Adela. We have Henry and Ella to think of.'

Ella was delighted. 'Can I choose the curtains, Granny?'

'We'll go into Wadebridge and have a look.'

'Can I have Cath Kidston roses and matching wallpaper?'

'We'll see.'

It didn't take long to erase Sennen. Her posters, books, old make-up and dusty shoes were sorted into rubbish or charity piles and Bill filled his car and drove them away for good.

Adela felt winded, dizzy and teary but she kept a cheery face and only twice had to go to the end of the small garden to cry silent tears.

A week later and the room was transformed. Ella had kept her mother's old patchwork bed quilt, stitched by Adela's mother when Sennen was a toddler, and her old teddy, Buster, but apart from those two things, no trace of Sennen remained.

Bill and Adela took in four art students and set up a new daily routine. Adela began to enjoy cooking the 8 a.m. break-fasts for seven and Bill started to shake off the malaise which had dogged him since Sennen's disappearance. He began to lead stimulating conversations about art, politics and religion around their old kitchen table.

On wet days the students would have lessons in painting and drawing with Adela, or working clay by hand or on the wheel with Bill.

Once or twice a week there would be outings to Bodmin Moor, the cliffs around Trevay, or the beach of Shellsand Bay.

Laughter was again spontaneous in the house.

Henry did well in his GCSEs and was opting for Economics, Maths and Business Studies for his A Levels. In contrast, Ella excelled in English and her short stories were achieving some acclaim in the school magazine, but it was her painting that was her strength. From canvases of wild seas whipped by fierce winds, to small and delicate watercolours of field mice and wild flowers.

Lying in bed one night, Adela with Bill's arm around her and her head on his chest, said, 'I hope we've been good parents to Ella and Henry.'

Bill stroked her hair. 'Better than with Sennen, you mean?'

'I hope so.'

'Perhaps we were too good to Sennen.'

'I think of her every day.'

'I know.'

'I hope she's happy.'

'That's all we can hope for.'

'I've never stopped loving her.'

'There was a time I thought I hated her, but now I can remember her with love.'

'Do you think we'll ever see her again?'

Bill inhaled deeply and Adela felt her head move against his ribs. 'I really don't know. But we have each other, Adela.

And Henry and Ella. You've been so selfless with them. I was no help, was I.'

She pulled herself up and looked into his loving, familiar eyes. 'Do you regret burning her photos?'

He nodded. 'I was not in my right mind.'

'I know. But we pulled together.'

'Little did I know that the girl I fell in love with at harvest time would be so strong. It's been hard for you.'

Adela kissed him softly. 'Love at first sight for me.'

'Foolish girl.' He smiled at her.

'That's me.'

'Don't ever leave me, will you?'

'No.'

He hugged her. 'I love you Adela.'

'I love you, Bill.'

Adela woke early. Bill was still sleeping so quietly she left him to make herself a cup of tea. She loved mornings like this. It was late September and the house was slumbering around her. She opened the back door and went out into the small courtyard to sit and drink her tea. The air was warm and fresh. She filled her lungs with it and leant back in her seat to feel the early sunshine on her face.

She thought about Bill. He had been so badly hurt when Sennen had left, and suffered so deeply. But now the Bill of old was coming back. She could see a future for them both now. Not the one they had imagined, but there was a future. They were still young, only in their fifties. Henry and Ella would be leaving home in a few years and then the world was their oyster. She'd always been keen on taking a cruise. Bill laughed at her. 'How very middle class of you, darling.'

But she knew that if she asked him to join her, he'd come like a shot.

Bill wanted to keep chickens. She had always said no, but, why not? Life was for grabbing with both hands. Sennen had done it. Why not them?

She finished her tea and went back into the kitchen to get breakfast started. The smell of coffee and sausages was always enough to get everyone out of bed and around her table. Bill was the only one absent.

'Ella, darling,' said Adela, 'go and get Poppa, would you?'

'I'll go,' said Henry, 'I've forgotten my phone anyway.'

When he returned a few minutes later, ashen and alone, Adela knew.

She put the milk jug she was carrying down and flew past Henry and up the stairs.

Bill was lying on his side as he always did. He was pale, but still warm to her touch. She stroked his forehead and kissed his lips before lovingly closing his sightless eyes.

PART TWO

Sennen Comes Home

16

Pendruggan, 2018

Ella was a cat on hot bricks. She needed to spend the day cleaning Marguerite Cottage so she shooed the dogs out into the garden and sent Adam and Kit out to collect Henry from Bodmin Parkway station.

'Don't come back too early. Go for a pint or something. Supper will be ready at eight.'

Kit pulled her to him. 'Darling, the house looks great. *You* look great. Your mother will love all of it – and if she doesn't, she's not worth a jot.'

Ella swatted him away. 'Go.'

When they had gone, Ella started on the bathroom. She had no idea whether her mother would want to stay the night, but she would probably need the loo in any event, and she'd better have the spare bed made up in case. In the end they had decided that Marguerite Cottage would be the best place for the meeting.

When upstairs was as she wanted it, she went downstairs.

The lounge was dusted and vacuumed, the small cloakroom scrubbed, and the kitchen floor, sink and cupboards wiped and polished.

The last job was to empty the bin. She gave it a quick spritz of air freshener before putting a new liner inside it.

Done.

'Right, Ella,' she said pulling off her apron, 'you can have a coffee.' She opened the cupboard above the kettle and pulled out a jar of instant. It was empty. She swore under her breath and took a quick inventory of anything else she might need to buy. Loo paper, tissues (there were bound to be tears) butter, milk, tea bags and bread (in case her mum stayed for breakfast).

She had made a quiche and a chilli con carne that were awaiting in the fridge, and she had plenty of beer and wine.

'Right, if I've forgotten anything, it's tough,' she said to Terry and Celia who had been allowed back into the house and were lolling in their beds, and set off for the village shop.

Queenie was behind the counter as always, reading the words on a packet of nicotine gum with an unlit cigarette in her mouth. She looked up as Ella came through the door, ringing the little bell above it.

'Ella, duck.' She coughed. 'Do you think this is any good? It says chewing it will help me cope with the withdrawal of not having me cigarettes.'

'Do you want to stop smoking?'

'No. I love me fags.' Queenie waved her cigarette as proof.

'So why are you looking at the gum?'

'I dunno. Maybe I should think about me health in the long term.'

'How old are you, Queenie?'

'Oh, you cheeky mare.' Queenie pushed her smeary, pebble-thick glasses up her nose. 'I'm as old as me tongue and a little bit older than my teeth.'

Ella smiled. 'How long have you been smoking?'

'About a hundred years.' Queenie's wheezy laugh brought on a coughing fit.

'Well,' said Ella, 'it's up to you, but after a hundred years it's not going to make any difference now.'

Queenie took her hanky from her sleeve and wiped her eyes. 'That's what I thought. Now, how can I help you, duck?'

Ella passed her scribbled list to Queenie who squinted at it and began collecting the bits together. ''ave a look at them magazines while I do this. That celeb, the one with the big bum, 'as got a lovely new 'airdo. It would suit you with all them lovely red curls you got.'

'I haven't got time at the moment. My mum is coming to see Henry and me tomorrow.'

Queenie, searching the grocery shelf, snapped her head round, on the alert for gossip. 'Oh yes?' she said. 'Your mum that left you and Henry when you was nippers? The local papers had her picture on the front pages for weeks.'

'Yes,' Ella replied, feeling uncomfortable.

'Oh my gawd, you'll be feeling a bit mixed, I expect?'

'Yes.' Ella scratched her cheek and tried to swallow down the sudden lump in her throat. 'Mixed is the right word.'

The bell on the shop door rang again. It was Simon, the vicar.

'Hello, Ella, Queenie,' he said jovially. 'Lovely day today.'

'Hmm,' said Queenie putting her head to her shoulder and nudging it towards Ella in a secret signal to Simon. 'Ella's got quite a lot on her mind, though.'

'Oh really?' asked Simon, not being able to fathom Queenie's coded signals. 'Why's that?'

'My long-lost mum is coming to see Henry and me tomorrow for the first time in more than twenty-five years.'

Simon looked at her thoughtfully. 'Is there anything I can do?'

Ella shook her head slowly and tried to smile, but the waiting tears beat her to it. Simon took a clean cotton handkerchief from his pocket and, as he passed it to her, pulled up one of the old armchairs that Queenie had scattered around for just this sort of emergency. 'Sit down,' he said.

Ella sat and apologised. 'I'm so sorry. I'm fine. I'm just being silly.'

'I'll make you a cuppa. You stay there,' ordered Queenie.

Simon dragged another chair over and sat down next to Ella. 'I remember how Penny was when her mother – well, her stepmother – died. It was something she couldn't possibly prepare for.'

'I'm so nervous.'

'Of course you are.'

'Will she like me?'

'She jolly well should do. You are a daughter to be proud of.'

'But Henry is so angry with her and I'm worried he's going say something awful that will make her go away again.'

'Where are you meeting her?'

'At Marguerite Cottage.'

Simon thought for a moment. 'Why not use the vicarage? Penny and I can be there, not to interfere, but to be on hand if things get a bit . . . emotional?'

Ella wiped her eyes. 'Oh, Simon, you are so kind.' Fresh tears rolled down her cheeks. 'But I couldn't do that to you.'

'But wouldn't you like to? It would mean a neutral space.'

She nodded. 'Yes. It would be lovely.'

He patted her hand. 'Consider it done. What time is she arriving?'

'We don't know yet. Her solicitor is ringing in the morning.'

'Well, the vicarage will be ready for you at any time. It is yours for the day and Penny and I will be right there for you.'

Sennen's flight from India had arrived at Heathrow at the same time as Ella left Queenie's shop, feeling a lot better than she had and excited to tell Henry that the meeting would be at the vicarage.

Sennen unbuckled her belt and looked out into grey drizzle. Nervousness gripped her. Why was she doing this? She should be back home in India with Kafir, her husband. But he'd been so angry with her when she had had to tell him about Henry and Ella.

'How could you deny the existence of your own children? To me? You are someone I don't know any more. What else do you have in your box of lies?'

He had told her to leave their home. To go back to Cornwall. To apologise and make peace with her children. Only then would he consider the future of their marriage.

He had frightened her with his appraisal of her. He was a good man. A moral man. What sort of woman was she? For years she had managed to bury the past. She had never forgotten a birthday or Christmas, always sending a card, but she had given neither her parents or Ella and Henry an address with which to find her. And now her parents were dead and her children had agreed to see her. But they must hate her.

In the terminal she handed her passport to the Border Control guard. 'Welcome home at long last, Mrs Tallon-Singh,' he said, smiling.

Guiltily, she held her hand out for the passport. 'Thank you.

Yes. It's been a long time.' And scurried through to baggage reclaim and customs before exiting the building and taking her first breaths of British air for so many years. After a moment or two she steadied herself and found the car hire office.

The M4 was wide and clean and well-organised, nothing like the madness of India's roads. The rental car smelt new and was easy to drive. She had never driven on the left before, but after a few miles her confidence grew. At Bristol she stopped for a coffee and the loo, then pressed on to Cornwall and arrived in Trevay in the late afternoon and drove to her solicitors, Penhaligon and Palmer. Deborah Palmer, young and new to the family firm, welcomed her into the office with a handshake. 'We meet at last,' she said, smiling.

'Yes. At last.'

Sennen estimated Deborah to be in her late twenties, petite in her smart suit and with an air of complete professionalism.

Sennen looked around her. The offices were old and crooked, smelling of dry rot. Built at the top of Trevay, the building was surrounded by new-build homes and a large supermarket with a petrol station. Sennen remembered when it had all been open fields where ponies had been kept. She would often walk up to feed them hay and Polos during the school holidays.

Deborah was opening a file on her desk. 'How long is it since you've been back?'

'A very long time,' Sennen said wistfully. 'A lifetime. It's changed a bit.'

Deborah looked up and smiled. 'I'm sure it has, but I think the old town is recognisable. I've booked you into the Starfish hotel, near the harbour. Do you know it?'

Sennen's mind went straight to the horrible morning that

she had walked into that hotel with Henry in her arms, ready to be with Ali for the rest of her life. The look of dismissal on the receptionist's face, the humiliation. She squeezed her eyes tight, the shame burning her.

'Yes. I know it.'

'The best on this coast.' Deborah flicked through the file. 'I've just had a phone call from your daughter, Ella.'

'Yes?' Sennen was anxious. Had Ella decided not to see her after all?

'They have chosen the vicarage in Pendruggan as your meeting place.'

'Why?'

'I think that she and Henry – and I rather agree with them – believe that neutral ground, No-man's land, if you like, would be sensible.'

'Are they very religious?'

Deborah smiled. 'The vicar, Simon Canter, and his wife Penny are friends of theirs. In fact, Ella was nanny to their daughter, Jenna. I think she does still do the occasional day for them.'

'That's nice.' Sennen's mind was racing. There was so much she didn't know. 'And Henry?'

'He works in London, something to do with property. A commercial surveyor as I recall.'

'Golly. That sounds grand. He must work very hard.'

'He has come down on the train today. Ella suggests that tomorrow's meeting is at eleven o'clock. How does that suit? You may be tired after your journey and want to start later?'

'No, that will be very good. Thank you.'

'Right, I shall pick you up from the Starfish at about ten thirty.' Deborah closed the folder and stood up. 'Here's some reading for you.' She handed the folder over. 'Just to get you up to speed. Nothing too difficult. Just some background and legal stuff that I shall be asking you to sign.'

Sennen took it. 'Thank you.' She collected her coat from the back of her chair and then said, 'I'd rather not stay at the Starfish if that's okay?'

'Of course. Would you like me to book somewhere else?'

'I'll find a B and B. I'd like to find my feet a bit. I'll phone you to let you know where I am.'

She followed her nose to the main road into Trevay. It was all so familiar and yet so dreamlike. Had she really lived here? Left here?

She turned onto the hill that would take her down to the pretty little fishing town and almost gasped as the beauty of the harbour and the houses that lay spread out beneath her. Her memories had faded the sheer beauty of the place. How could she have forgotten?

Her hands shook as she changed gear, slowing down to take it all in. Instinct took over and she guided the car to White Water, her parents' home. Which was just the same although much smarter. It had a conservatory, now, and pretty shutters at the windows. She inched past slowly. The front door was a different colour but there was the downstairs loo window she'd climbed out of and the gate she'd walked through as she made her escape. There was a sign on the wall. *White Water Bed and Breakfast. Vacancies.*

It took a split second for her to make her mind up. She was coming home.

The landlady came to the door, wiping her mouth of crumbs. 'Do excuse me. I'm just making a batch of scones for tea

tomorrow and I can never resist one while they're warm! Can
I help you?'

'Hello,' said Sennen shakily, 'I see you have a vacancy.'

'For tonight?'

'Yes.'

The landlady, a slender woman in her forties, wearing a
simple dress and with her hair piled on the top of her head
with tendrils escaping attractively, opened the door wide.
'Come in.'

Sennen stepped over the threshold and looked around. In
her parents' day the house had been full of Bill's pots, large
and small, some gathering dust, others filled with dried
grasses or teasels.

The walls had been filled with Adela's large canvases of
nudes or swimmers or both, which burst with exuberant
colour and movement.

In their place now were subtle grey painted walls and stark
window sills. It was lovely. But it wasn't her home.

'I'm Amy and my husband, John, is usually here, but he's
out on the boat. Come into the lounge and I'll get you settled.
Would you like a drink? Glass of wine?'

'That would be lovely,' said Sennen, following her into the
room where her parents had sat in their old armchairs
discussing art, or politics or listening to the radio. Adela had
painted the walls sunset orange and on the old table there
had always been bowls of fat chrysanthemum, daffodils or
sweet peas depending on the season.

The room was now a shrine to grey in all its hues. The
floor tiles were graphite, the walls a light slate, the ceiling a
shade of mist and the linen curtains . . . well, Sennen could
only describe them as Drizzle.

Amy invited her to sit on the taupe sofa.

'Isn't this room lovely?' Amy sighed. 'So peaceful. An artist and his wife used to live here and it was sold to a couple who started it up as a B and B a few years ago, and then John and I took it over at the beginning of the season. We've made some changes in the décor. It was very dated.'

'It was a potter who owned this,' said Sennen. It seemed important to correct the woman. 'His wife was the artist.'

'Did you know them?' smiled Amy, interested. 'I'd love to know more about the place.'

Before Sennen could think of a suitable answer, a ping came from the kitchen.

'That's the next batch of scones. I'll get you your wine and then take you up to your room. Sea view with en suite? Or garden view, which is quieter but no en suite?'

Sennen smiled, thinking how chichi Adela would have thought the phrase en suite.

'Garden view, please,' she replied.

Sitting in her parents' house for the first time in all these years, she closed her eyes and allowed memories to flood her mind.

In this room, she had told her mum and Poppa that she was pregnant.

In this room, the Christmas tree had always stood in front of the big window and she and Adela had covered it in a handmade myriad of shells and driftwood. And on the top, they had always put a mermaid with wings rather than an angel.

Where were those bits now? Had Henry and Ella kept them in the old cardboard box? Or were they rotting under some municipal rubbish tip.

So long ago, and so far away.

'Mrs Tallon.' Amy jolted her back to the present. 'You're tired after your trip, aren't you? John often has a doze in that chair. Most comfortable in the house, he thinks. Here,' she passed Sennen a glass of wine, 'take this and I'll show you to your room.'

As they climbed the stairs Sennen felt an odd sensation. Not regret. Not fear. She turned it over in her mind before she got it.

It felt like the first steps to coming home.

17

Ella hadn't slept well.

The night before, in the pub, Henry had had too much to drink and had been moody and tetchy.

Ella had tried hard to soothe him. 'It's a good idea to meet Mum at the vicarage, don't you think.'

Henry had barked a bitter laugh. 'I suppose so. At least we'll have an expert on hand if she needs to be exorcised.'

Ella had tightened her lips and glared at Kit, blaming him for the fact that Henry was drunk.

Henry put his pint down. 'I need a leak.'

When he'd gone, Ella had a go at Kit. 'How many pints has he had?'

'I think this is his fourth.'

'Four? Four? For God's sake, Kit.' She glared at him. Ella was furious and turned to leave the bar but walked smack into a returning Henry.

'Whoops, Sis. You need to look where you are going.' He was laughing, 'Or learn to handle your drink better.'

Ella, incandescent, turned on both of them. '*I* am not drunk. I'm going home.'

Kit watched her walk away and, draining his pint, set out after her with Henry following. In the car park he went to her. 'I'm sorry. Sorry. It's just this thing with your mum coming. We are all jumpy. Come here.' He held his arms out to her and she went to him.

'That was our first row,' she said.

He held her a little tighter. 'At least we've got it over with.'

Sennen woke up in what had been her parent's bedroom. The window was where it had always been, but everything else had changed. The sleek Scandinavian bed, dressed with a linen throw and cushions, was a far cry from the heavily carved one she had leapt into each birthday and Christmas morning.

But she had slept very well in this one. Better than she had hoped.

Considering the day ahead.

The day she had longed for and dreaded in equal measure.

There was no going back now . . .

There was a gentle knock at the door.

She sat up, giving her hair a quick comb with her fingers before calling, 'Come in.'

Amy appeared with a tray of coffee and a newspaper. 'Good morning, Mrs Tallon-Singh. It's a lovely day out there.'

'Thank you so much.'

Amy placed the tray on the bedside table. 'How did you sleep?'

'Very well, thank you.'

'Good.' She pushed the plunger on the cafetière. 'Busy day planned?'

'I hope so.'

'Well, enjoy your coffee, and we'll see you for breakfast at eight thirty. Okay?'

'Lovely.'

When Amy had gone, Sennen got out of bed and went to the window. Opening the plantation blinds she looked down on her old garden. She flattened her nose against the cold glass and tried to see around the corner of the house, down to the harbour. The tide was out and she imagined she could smell the salty dankness of the weed in its bed; seagulls strutting to peck at amputated crab claws, the sand sucking at their feet.

A wave of sorrow slapped her in the stomach. Why had she waited so long? She drew back from the window and sat on the bed, sipping her coffee. She closed her eyes and tried to picture the faces of her parents. It was difficult after such a long time. She concentrated hard, but each time she thought she had found their likeness the images slipped from her brain. Silently she said, 'Mum? Poppa? Can you see me? Do you know I am here?' When there was no answer she opened her eyes and said to no one, 'I have come back.'

In Pendruggan, Ella was making two huge plates of sandwiches: cucumber with the crusts off and cheese with a good dollop of pickle.

Henry, bleary-eyed, slopped into the kitchen wearing baggy shorts. 'Who are they for?' He took a crust, put it in his mouth, and began to fill the kettle.

'For the meeting. A distraction.'

'Oh.' He rubbed his head. 'Got any aspirin?'

She pointed with her bread knife.

'Left-hand drawer next to the sink.'

He opened the drawer and pushed things around until he found the packet and threw two tablets into his mouth, swallowing without water.

He leant back against the counter, waiting for the kettle to boil. He scratched his chest and yawned.

Ella pushed past him. 'You stink.'

'You're welcome.'

'You need to be ready by ten thirty.'

'What time is the old bitch getting to the vicar's?'

'If you mean our mother, I've told you, eleven.'

'If she bothers to show up.'

Ella turned on him. 'Stop it! It's going to be a hard enough day as it is without you being so horrible. Today means a lot to me – and if you can't or won't see that, then I'll see Mum by myself and you can get the hell back to London and your money-mad chums.'

He held his hands up in mock surrender. 'Okay, okay. I was only saying: just don't expect it to be all kisses and white doves.'

'Shut up.'

The skittering of dog claws in the hall announced Kit's arrival.

'Morning. I do hope I am not hearing the snarling of siblings. What's going on?'

'Nothing,' said Ella through gritted teeth.

'Good. Let's keep it that way.' He kissed Ella. 'Fancy a walk on the beach?'

'Bless you, yes,' said Ella thankfully.

'My pleasure – and Henry,' Kit added, 'you had better get shaved and showered. Don't let yourself or your sister down.'

*

Bang on ten thirty the little party from Marguerite, clean and smart, pale and nervy, left for the vicarage, carrying two plates of sandwiches, a Victoria sponge, an extra litre of milk and some tea bags.

Penny opened the door. 'What's all this?'

'I couldn't expect you to feed us as well as give us your home,' said Ella, putting the cake box into Penny's outstretched hands. 'You've done so much for us.'

'Come into the kitchen and let's get our strategy right before your mum and the solicitor arrive.'

Simon was putting his car keys into the dish by the back door. 'Hello, Ella. How are you doing?' He came forward and hugged her.

'Okay. A bit nervous. Is Jenna at playgroup?'

'Yes, just dropped her.'

'Is she enjoying it?'

'Taken to it like a duck to water. Miss Davis said she was the most confident child she had this year.'

'That's my girl,' laughed Penny.

Ella hugged the Aga. 'We went for a walk on the beach this morning. There's a cold wind getting up.'

'Oh, for God's sake,' Henry grumbled, 'can we stop talking about the weather? Our mother is about to arrive and I don't even know if I'll recognise her.'

Simon passed Henry a cup of coffee and sat next to him. 'During difficult times like this, the power of small talk is often underestimated.'

Ella gave Simon a grateful smile across the table.

'Mum must be pretty nervous too,' she said.

Henry shifted in his chair. 'She bloody well ought to be.'

Simon took a gentle steer on the conversation. 'What do you hope for from this meeting, Ella?'

'Erm, I think . . . I think I want us to all get on with each other and trust that maybe we have a future. As a family.'

Henry was exasperated. 'Really? You think this might be one big happy ending? I believe she's come for one thing and one thing only, and it's not her darling children. It's Granny and Poppa's money. End of.'

'That's a very strong point of view, Henry,' said Simon softly. 'She may have come to atone for the past.'

Henry crossed his arms defensively.

Penny spoke. 'Tell me what the pros and cons of meeting your mother are for you, Henry.'

'The only pro is hers. She takes the money, tells us she's very sorry she dumped us, and buggers off back to the hole she crawled out of.'

'Put like that, I wonder why you are here at all.'

'To hear how she tries to justify herself.' And he added quietly. 'For my sister. For Ella.'

'I see.' Penny turned to Ella. 'How about you?'

'I want to know why she left us. To try to understand. To find out who she really is. If we share likes and dislikes. To see who we look like. All that stuff, really.'

Henry folded his arms and grunted.

Kit looked up at the kitchen clock. 'Five to eleven. Anyone needing a pee, go now.'

As they left the kitchen, Penny took Ella's hand. 'You'll be okay,' she whispered. 'She's your mum and anyone who could have such a lovely girl like you can't be all bad.'

Ella's butterflies were churning. 'You will stay in the house, won't you? In case?' she pleaded.

'I'll be in the kitchen all the time.'

Penny led Ella into the vicarage drawing room. She had lit

the fire and put a huge jug of roses on the piano. Ella's throat tightened with emotion. 'It looks lovely. Thank you, Penny.'

'It's the least I could do.'

Ella's eyes were shining with unshed tears. 'I'm scared.'

'Only natural.' Penny patted her hand and let her go. 'Simon and I will bring the tea and sandwiches in at about half eleven. You might need a bit of light relief by then.'

The heavy knocker sounded on the front door. Ella jumped. 'This is it.'

She went into the hall where Kit and Henry stood uneasily. Simon took over. 'You three go into the drawing room, I'll let them in. Close the door behind you.'

They did as they were told and listened as Simon went to the front door.

'Hello. Good morning. I'm Simon. How do you do.'

A woman's voice replied. 'Simon. Good to meet you. I'm Deborah Palmer, Mrs Tallon-Singh's solicitor. We spoke on the phone?'

'Indeed we did,' said Simon.

'And this is Mrs Tallon-Singh.'

'You are very welcome,' Simon's voice said. 'Come along in. Henry and Ella are in the drawing room.'

In the drawing room, Henry and Ella looked at each other, then at the door.

'Go on in,' they heard Simon say.

The door opened; Ella stretched her mouth into a welcoming grin while her eyes were round with apprehension.

Henry looked at his feet and then at a photo in a silver frame of Penny and Simon's wedding day, anywhere but at the door.

A woman's voice, strong and smoky, said, 'Hello, Henry. Ella.'

Both children looked up.

She was tall. Ella judged her to be almost six feet, wide-shouldered, slender and rangy. Her long hair, once fiery red, was now hennaed with silver strands glinting at the roots.

Ella recognised it as her own Titian curls.

Henry's chest had constricted to the point where he couldn't take a breath deep enough without panting. God, how he hoped this woman couldn't hear it. This woman who had his face, his nose, eyes, mouth, brow . . . She was staring at him. What did she want? If she thought he was going to rush into her arms and call her Mummy she had another think coming. He walked to an armchair and sat down, his arms folded.

'Well, then,' said Simon hovering by the door, 'I'll leave you to get to know each other. Penny and I will bring refreshments shortly.' He walked out into the hall, closing the door behind him. Why the hell did he say that? Get to know each other? Refreshments? He pulled his handkerchief from his pocket and rubbed the sheen of perspiration from his head.

Sennen smiled and sat on the sofa.

She was wearing a calf-length, billowing dress in jewel colours with a soft, midnight-blue scarf, mirrored and beaded, around her neck. On each wrist she wore rows of golden bangles. Her eyes were heavily lined with kohl and her skin was very tanned.

Henry was thinking, 'Of course. A bloody hippy.'

Ella thought, 'This is my mother.'

Kit thought, 'Oh, shit.'

Simon tiptoed to the kitchen where Penny's eyes were out on stalks.

'And?' she asked desperately.

'Tall. Very tall for a woman.'

'But does she look like a nice person?'

'I couldn't tell.'

'Oh, you are *hopeless*.' Penny looked at the clock. 'Roll on tea and sandwiches.'

In the drawing room Ella stood in a quandary. Where should she sit? Next to her mother on the sofa and risk looking needy? Or take an empty armchair and risk looking judgemental.

The solicitor solved the dilemma by taking the sofa. Kit loyally sat on the arm of Ella's chair.

The solicitor began. 'So I'm Deborah. Debbie. And you know I have just joined the practice because your grandparents original lawyer and senior partner of the firm has finally retired due to ill-health. But I am well acquainted with your family's history and I am honoured to be here on this important day.'

Henry made a noise in the back of his throat, somewhere between a growl and a groan. Ella flicked her head towards him and gave him daggers.

Sennen said nothing. She felt sick. The open fire was making the room overly hot and she could feel the sweat prickle her top lip.

Henry hated her. He was making that quite clear. She raised her kohl-rimmed eyes to look at him, to drink him in. Her little boy was now a man, a man who looked so like Poppa, well-muscled and tall, with a mouth, which while scowling now, had clear laughter lines around it.

She dropped her gaze. Of course he hated her. Once he had loved her. Hung onto her legs, climbed on her lap, kissed her with his sticky lips. And she had left.

She turned her head and looked at Ella. So like Ali. Neat,

clever hands. Perfectly straight nose. Indigo eyes. But she had Sennen's wild red curls.

She couldn't blame either of them for their silence. Saying their names aloud as she had entered the room had been involuntary. A reaction, more like a prayer than anything else.

It had set the room on edge.

She decided to remain still and silent and wait for what might come.

18

Deborah took a file from her bag and began sifting through it. 'I have here copies of the valuation of Mr and Mrs Tallon's estate.' She passed one to Sennen, then stretched her arm out to Henry and handed him the remaining sheets. He took one and passed it on to Kit who gave it to Ella. Debbie continued, 'When Mr Tallon died nine years ago, he left everything to Mrs Tallon. When Mrs Tallon died, she left no will. However, in our role as executors we took advice from you, Henry and Ella, and due to the fact that you were both now living in London, you agreed that we should sell White Water, your family home. The monies from the sale of the property were invested by us. They remained so as we searched for your mother as she would be the sole beneficiary, if alive, or if proven to be deceased, her descendants, you, would become the beneficiaries.'

She turned to Sennen and smiled. 'Thankfully, we tracked you down.'

Sennen wasn't listening. She was reading the page in her hand.

Henry, white-faced, was reading his copy.

Ella's hands were shaking as she scanned hers. 'Golly. It's a lot of money,' she said.

Henry screwed his sheet into a ball stood up and walked to the fireplace. He tossed it into the flames. 'Well, that's all our darling mother's now.' He turned to look at her. 'You've got what you came for, now off you trot.'

Sennen stood up. 'Henry – I know you are angry . . .'

Henry laughed cruelly. 'Angry doesn't cover it.' He looked at his sister. 'Come on, Ella. She's got what she wants. You and I have coped this far without her. We don't need her or her money.'

Sennen reached for his arm but he swerved from her touch. She pulled back, stung. 'Henry, please.'

Fury suffused him. 'Do you know how old Poppa was when he died? Hm?'

Sennen gripped her hands, twisting her fingers.

'Well?' he shouted. 'No? You haven't a clue have you. Have you?' He stared at his mother and raked his hand through his hair. 'Selfish bitch. He was fifty-nine, that's all. He should be here now. He should be here to walk Ella down the aisle, if and when she gets married. He should be enjoying a comfortable retirement. But he's dead.' The last words were filled with pain and venom.

Sennen hung her head and Henry took a step closer. 'And do you know what killed him?'

Sennen shook her head and whispered, 'Don't. Please stop.'

He continued. 'You. You broke his heart.'

Ella put her hands to her face in horror. 'Henry, stop. Don't say such things.'

'Why not? It's true.' He glowered at the room. 'And because he died, Granny died too. The two people she had loved most in the world had gone. Her beloved husband and her feckless tart of a daughter who wasn't worth her love.' Henry saw the pain in his mother's face but couldn't help sticking the knife in deeper. 'Do you know that they removed every bit of you from our home? You hurt them so much that every trace of you was taken from the house. No belongings, no letters, no photos. You were deleted. It was as if you didn't exist.'

The room hung in stillness, the bitterness of Henry's outburst ricocheting through the air.

There was a knock at the door and Penny came in with a tea tray followed by Simon with sandwiches and cake.

'Thought you could all do with a cup of tea,' Penny smiled.

Deborah, remaining seated, managed, 'Lovely.'

Kit came from Ella's side towards Penny. 'Let me help you.'

Henry had thrown himself back into his chair and was biting his nails, staring into the fire.

Ella held back tears, her anger directed at Henry.

Sennen smoothed her multi-coloured dress and rearranged her scarf. 'That's very kind of you, but I have to leave.'

'So soon?' asked Simon anxiously.

'Yes,' Sennen replied and looked at Debbie. 'Would you take me back to Trevay, please?'

Deborah took the cue seamlessly and collected her bits together. 'Of course. Thank you so much for hosting this initial meeting, Simon. Penny.' She looked at Henry and Ella and held out her hand. 'Call me when you are ready.'

Ella got up and shook her hand. 'Thank you. We need time to . . . You understand?'

'Of course.' She looked over at Henry who was still chewing his fingers. 'Goodbye, Henry.'

The room emptied, leaving Ella and Henry with Kit, holding the teapot, in shocked silence.

'Well,' said Henry dryly, 'that went well.'

Ella let rip. 'You stupid idiot. You couldn't have made it worse, could you? That was our mother. You may not want to know her but I bloody well do. Granny and Poppa would be ashamed of you. They loved her. They loved us. They would want this to be a happy ending, but oh no, not you, you want to play life's victim and smash anything good that might come to us.'

'Who's playing the victim now?' Sneered Henry. 'I'm protecting you, Ella. Can't you see that? The minute you got close to her she'd kick you in the teeth and leave again. She'll break your heart and I'm not going to let that happen. Leopards do not change their spots.'

Ella began to cry with frustration and shock. 'She came out of love. Love for us.'

'Nope. It's love of money. That's why she's here.'

'You don't know that. People change. You haven't given her a chance. I want to know why she left and where she's been. Then I can make up my own mind and not have you doing it for me.'

Henry looked at his watch. 'Kit, would you be kind enough to take me to the station. I need to be back in London.'

He looked at Ella, sitting tear streaked and shaky in her chair. 'I'm sorry, Ells, but it's better you face reality.'

19

Sennen hadn't looked back as Deborah drove her out of Pendruggan village and down to Trevay. Neither woman spoke until Deborah drew up outside White Water's gate.

'I'll call you tomorrow?' she asked.

'Maybe the day after,' said Sennen. 'I need time to process what's just happened.'

'Understood. Get some rest.'

Sennen got out of the car.

'And Mrs Tallon-Singh,' said Deborah, 'these things are never easy at the start, but don't lose hope.'

Sennen let herself in through the newly familiar front door and climbed the stairs. The house appeared to be empty. She was glad; she could do without Amy coming out of the shadows bringing tea and questions.

On the landing she hesitated. A memory of bringing Henry home from the hospital suddenly assaulted her, his tiny hands and sweet lips, the fear that she wouldn't cope without Ali, the overbearing kindness of her parents choking her to the point where she didn't know who she was any more.

The hours she spent fantasising about finding Ali and becoming a family . . .

Across the landing was the door of her old bedroom. She held her breath, listening for any sound in the house indicating that she wasn't the only person in it. She had done this before, on the night she had left.

Black spots were forming in front of her and she felt weak and desolate. Her brain was foggy. A primitive reflex forced her to breathe again and she steadied herself on the smooth banister.

She looked at her hand on the wood. So like her mother's. Freckle-skinned and slender, long fingers. 'An artist's hand,' Poppa had always told her.

She closed her eyes and crumpled to the carpet.

'I am so sorry,' she whispered. 'I didn't mean to hurt anyone. I meant to come back. I didn't know you had died. I should have been here. For you and Henry and Ella. I've been so selfish and unkind. I would do anything to turn the clock back. Forgive me . . . Forgive me. Please.'

A ping of an incoming text sounded from her bag. Kafir. It must be Kafir. He hadn't contacted her since she had left India, although she had sent him several texts telling him she had arrived and asking after the children.

She scrabbled for the phone and checked the screen. It was from Deborah, checking that she was okay. She let the phone drop back.

Lying on the simple Swedish bed in her parent's old room, she closed her eyes.

Too tired to cry.

She felt leaden, almost relaxed.

The tumult of the meeting had drained her.

What had she expected?

After all these years.

She had left Santander on a train heading to Madrid.

For a few months she picked up casual bar work. She kept herself free of friendships and men, her only goal to eat, sleep and work. She ruthlessly scythed thoughts of home from her memory.

That first Christmas her postcard home was a picture of a female flamenco dancer. Her skirt was made of real fabric and lace and was sewn onto the card. She imagined Henry and Ella's little fingers stroking it. She had written something like 'Happy Christmas, don't worry.' She thought now how she'd feel if she received something similar from her children.

She had yearned to go home, but the shame of what she had done and fear of how she would be met, the trouble she'd be in, the punishment she'd face, kept her away.

She grew up fast.

From Madrid she travelled to Barcelona, learning the language, and how to survive. Bar work, shop work – anything that would pay for a little rent and food – she took.

But she never forgot the birthdays of Henry and Ella and would send cards, minus any hint as to her whereabouts, to the children and her parents on their special days.

Ali, she refused to think about.

One weekend a workmate suggested a trip to Sitges, a seaside town not far from Barcelona and renowned for its party atmosphere. She turned it down. 'Not my kind of thing,' she had said. But the girl wouldn't take no for an answer. 'You need some fun. A dance. A snog. A boyfriend.'

Sennen finally gave in. What else would she be doing on her day off? Her washing?

When they got there, the girl dumped her almost immediately for a handsome lifeguard and she was left to fend for herself.

It was almost lunchtime and she didn't want to sit on the beach feeling exposed and alone, so she found a café, with shaded awnings and scarlet geraniums and ordered a coke and a menu from the handsome waiter who began to chat her up.

'We have good tapas. Let me choose the best for you and maybe a glass of wine?'

She handed the menu back to him. 'Okay, but not the expensive stuff.'

He smiled. 'What are you doing on your own?'

'Having lunch.'

'Of course, I know that, but no friends meeting you?'

'Nope.'

'I can be your friend.'

'I'm fine.'

'Okay, I'll get your lunch.' He walked lightly through the tables and customers but was soon back with her food. He put it down with reverence and started chatting her up again.

'You're English?'

She nodded and began to eat to put him off.

'Your Spanish is very good.'

'Thank you.'

'My name is Emmanuel.'

She stopped eating. 'Please . . . I like to be on my own. Thank you.'

He put his hands up in surrender. 'Okay, okay, but I don't like to see sad girls eating in my bar. It is bad for business.'

He turned his attention to a group of four young men who had arrived noisily at a table behind Sennen's.

'You call me if you want anything,' he said to her as he went to welcome them warmly. Emmanuel clearly knew them well.

Sennen watched the four new arrivals as she ate. They spoke French and were very camp, flirting with Emmanuel outrageously.

Emmanuel played up to it, throwing his eyes to the heavens and saying, 'Ooh la la,' every time they said something a bit saucy.

Sennen caught his eye and ordered another glass of wine.

'My friends are very funny, no? You are not so sad now.' Emmanuel smiled as he poured the wine. 'Would you like to meet them?'

She shook her head.

'Please. They won't bite. Not you, anyway.' He smiled and held out his hand to her. Reluctantly she took it and he pulled her from her chair and introduced her to the boys.

'May I introduce Miss English?' He pulled out a chair for her. 'She won't tell me her real name and she is sad and has no friends.'

The boys sighed and pulled tragic faces, putting their right hands against their hearts as one. She tried not to laugh. 'My name is Sennen.'

The four men stood up and introduced themselves, one by one 'Serge.' 'Antoine.' 'Noa.' 'Clement.'

'The four musketeers?'

'Of course,' said the one called Serge. He was very tall and thin, with a large nose. 'Only we are much more fun.' He winked.

'They are here working in the Pigalle club,' explained Emmanuel.

'As what?' asked Sennen.

Serge pointed to the smallest of the troupe. 'Noa. Please.'

Noa instantly washed a hand over his twinkling face and revealed a frightened one behind it. He leapt onto his chair and began to search four invisible walls for a way out.

Sennen watched, enchanted.

He bent over from straight hips and began to feel for a trapdoor. As he bent over he pretended to fart and popped up straight again to mime an apology. He bent over again; the same thing happened and he wafted a hand under his nose. He did it a third time and fainted.

'You're mime artists!' said Sennen, clapping.

'Oui, mademoiselle,' said Serge. 'You win the star prize – which is to have another glass of wine and join us.'

The warm afternoon sun slowly dropped and the stars and lights of the café's canopy soon twinkled over the balmy evening.

Sennen had had enough wine to feel safe with these kind and funny strangers. When Serge put his arm around her she put her head on his shoulder without fear – the first time since Ali.

'You are very sad, Mademoiselle Sennen. Who has done this to you?'

'Too long a story.'

'I am all ears.'

She told him her miserable tale, leaving nothing out.

'C'est tristesse,' he said. 'You need to find another boy to erase the memory.'

'That's the last thing I want.' She picked up her wine glass and drank. 'I'm happy just as I am.'

'How old are you?'

'Almost twenty.'

'Oh well, you are very old.' He patted her hand and smiled.

'Tell me about you,' she asked.

'Of course. Well, I met Noa in Paris and we fell in love. He made me laugh and here we are. We were a little duo, writing and performing on the streets. One day we see Clement and Antoine busking outside Notre Dame. They are very good robots,' he said with great pride. 'So we convinced them to join us.'

'Was that hard?'

'Not really. They were hungry, we fed them pizza – et voila!' He laughed at the memory. 'You will see our show. We are very good. We have been in Spain all summer in the night clubs, doing our show, and now we are ready to go back to France.'

'Paris?' she asked.

'Paris, of course.' He gave a Gallic shrug. 'Want to come with us?'

'I can't.'

'Why not? You have told me you have no boyfriend, no family. We will look after you. Come and work for us.'

'I'm not an actor or anything.'

'Can you use a washing machine?'

'Yes.'

'That's it. Tous nos félicitations! You are the new Head of Wardrobe for Pour Le Silence.'

'Pour Le Silence?'

'Oui. That is what we are called.' He raised his eyebrows and asked in mock surprise, 'Do you know them?'

She played along. 'I've heard of them.'

'Parfait. They will love you. Okay, we go to Paris on Thursday.'

She spent almost seven years with the troupe. They travelled across Europe entertaining crowds of sometimes more than a thousand, sometimes only twenty.

Sennen graduated from laundering and mending their costumes to designing costumes for them. The more elaborate and outrageous, the more the group loved them.

One afternoon, as she was stitching feathers to a codpiece, Serge came looking for her. 'I have exciting news.'

'Tell me then.' She broke a bit of thread off with her teeth.

'We are going to England,' he announced.

Her heart lurched. 'Oh?' She avoided his eye.

'Yes. How long is it since you have been home?'

'What do you mean?' She stayed fixed on her stitching. Her hands were trembling.

He clicked his tongue. 'Home. To England.'

'It's no longer my home.'

'But we will need you to show us around.'

'Whereabouts in England?'

'Edinburgh, for the carnival.'

She was relieved. Just about as far from Cornwall as you could get. 'It's the festival, not carnival, and it's Scotland, not England.'

'Scotland? Will it be cold?'

'Not in August.'

'Good.' He pretended to shiver and warm his hands on her face. 'I don't like snow.'

'You'll need to wear some tartan,' she said already drawing sequined kilts and sporrans in her mind's eye.

'Like Jean-Paul Gaultier?' he said with excitement.

'Yessiree.'

He got up and did a little jig. 'The boys will be soooo happy.'

The boys were a huge success in Edinburgh and appeared on as many British talk shows and entertainment programmes as they could until they were found smoking hash in a BBC dressing room, so the work dried up and they returned to Paris.

Bickering broke out amongst them and eventually Noa walked out on Serge and ran towards an Italian waiter. Serge, heartbroken, left for his parents' home in Provence.

Pour Le Silence were no more.

Sennen was heartbroken, but she needed to find another job.

Through the grapevine she heard that a respected German ballet company were looking for a costume design assistant for an all-male production of *The Jungle Book*.

She got the job and within two weeks was in Berlin.

The production toured the world for five long years and she went with it. Europe. Scandinavia. South America. West Coast America. Australia. New Zealand. The Far East and finally, India.

20

Henry got off the tube at Clapham Common and headed towards 47 Mandalay Road, just as the London commuters were arriving home and the nightlife lovers were coming out.

The pavements smelt of a recent shower, and the restaurants and cafés were enticing people in with promises of smiling waiters, warm lights and fun.

He felt anything but fun. He knew he'd hurt his mother and Ella, that he'd said some terrible things – but what did they expect?

On the long train journey up from Bodmin, he'd turned the whole scene over and over in his mind. The woman he'd met today was not the mother he thought he remembered. He had thought he would know her. But the vague memories of sitting on his mother's lap, pointing at the pictures in a children's book were no more. All he now had in his mind's eye was redheaded bohemian who *couldn't* be his mother.

The phone in his pocket vibrated. He pulled it out and looked at it. 'Bugger off, Ella.' He terminated the call.

It was the sixth call he'd had from her since he'd left Cornwall. She must have phoned every half an hour and, in between, left texts ranging from kind and pleading, to tears and anger. Meeting his mother had turned his world upside down. The way she had said so little and been so unmoved by the whole experience . . . She hadn't explained or apologised for the past. She hadn't asked him, or Ella, anything about themselves.

Selfish. Cold. Cruel. Disinterested.

And what was this *Mrs* Tallon-Singh about? So she'd married and given herself a fancy double-barrelled name. Well hoo-bloody-rah for her.

A thought struck him.

She was young enough to have had a second family.

Now it all came clear to him. Yes, that was it. She had a new family and could do with some money. The old family, him and Ella, could go to hell. She done it before so it would be so easy for her to do it again.

His gut was seething. He could murder a pint. At the top of Mandalay road was his local, the Kings Head. The doors opened and a young woman in a leather biker jacket stepped out with her arms around a young man. They brought with them the waft of beer on the breeze, a waft he allowed to surf him to the bar.

'He's not answering his phone,' said Ella, banging hers down on the table. 'What a pig-headed, rude man he can be. Can you believe how awful he was today?'

Kit, rather more on Henry's side than Ella's, was noncommittal. 'I think he was just being honest. It was how he feels and he told her.'

Ella was horrified. 'Our *mother* was there, in front of us

after all these years, and instead of making her feel welcome, he was horrible. No wonder she felt she had to leave. I'm impressed she didn't give him a piece of her mind.'

They were in the lounge of Marguerite Cottage, sitting on opposing chairs rather than their usual position on the sofa together.

'I'm just saying that I could see his point of view.' He watched as Ella's face grew darker and quickly added, 'Just as I see yours.'

'Do you?' she asked angrily.

'Darling, of course I do. You know I do. But I'm a bloke; maybe I'm not so good at expressing it.'

She pulled one corner of her mouth up sullenly while defensively reaching for a cushion and holding it against her chest. 'Huh.'

'What does *huh* mean?'

'Just huh.'

He changed tack. 'Hungry?'

'No.'

'G and T?'

'No.'

'Okay.' He thought of something to say that wouldn't be too contentious. '*Coronation Street* is on in a minute. That always cheers you up.'

Ella burst into tears and left the room.

Henry was on the outside of two pints and feeling just a little bit better, when a hand caressed his shoulder. 'Hi, Henry.' Soft, heavily lipsticked lips kissed his cheek. He looked over his shoulder to see who it was and his spirits rose.

'Oh, hi, Ashley.' Glossy brunette hair, thick eyelashes, and great fun. When he had first come to London, he had rented a room in a flat she shared with two other girls. For Henry, Ashley was the one that had got away. Maybe tonight was his lucky night.

'Long time no see,' she said and smiled.

'Yeah. Sorry. Work. Stuff. You know how it is.' His eyes scanned her braless breasts, suspended inside a tiny, strappy crop top. 'Want a drink?'

'Sure. A Cosmo, please.'

Henry caught the eye of the barman and shouted Ashley's order plus another pint for himself. 'So,' he said, adopting his best pulling voice, 'what's new?'

She flicked her hair. 'I'm modelling, now.'

He tried to make himself more comfortable on his bar-stool 'Yeah? Given up the old temping lark, eh?'

The barman delivered their drinks. 'Cheers.'

'Cheers.' They raised their glasses and drank.

'What sort of modelling?' asked Henry, casually.

'You wouldn't be interested?'

'Wouldn't I?'

'It's rather . . . adult.'

He felt his pulse quicken. 'I think I could handle that.'

Her very white teeth bit her bottom lip charmingly. 'Well, it's for . . .'

'Tell me.'

'Underwear.'

'Oh yes?'

She laughed, then sexily revealed. 'Thermal underwear.'

He blinked twice as what she said sank in. She was laughing. 'Long johns and vests.'

He started to giggle and the more she laughed, the more he laughed, until he was wiping tears away. 'Ashley,' he managed, 'You have no idea how much I needed to laugh tonight. Another Cosmo?'

Ella, in bed, lay on her side as far from Kit as she could manage. She felt more lonely than she had felt since Granny had died.

Her mother was back, the woman who had deserted her before she could even remember, had come back. Ella couldn't believe it was just for the money. No, she had come out of love – or, if not love, at least curiosity, just as Ella was curious about her. And Henry, her stupid brother, had behaved like an absolute child.

Anger infused her grief and brewed a painful stew of emotions. Why were men such idiots? How could Kit sympathise with Henry? How was her mum feeling right now after Henry's appalling outburst?

Ella imagined how disappointed Sennen must have been in them both today. No affection. No kindness. No attempt at reconciliation. God, how awful Sennen must be feeling now. Well, she, Ella, was going to meet her mother and make amends. In the morning she'd phone the solicitors and fix another meeting. Just her and her mum. Sod Henry.

Henry was very, very drunk by chucking out time.

Ashley was surprisingly sober and realised she was responsible for getting him home. 'Come on, time for us to get out of here,' she said grabbing an arm and put it across her shoulder. 'Good job I do kettle bells in the gym. Knew it would come in handy.'

'I love you, Ashley,' Henry slobbered. 'How come you and I have never got it on, eh?'

'You know why. Our house rule, remember? Never sleep with a flatmate.'

'But I'm not your flatmate now, am I?'

'That's true, but,' she sighed, 'my fiancé really wouldn't like it.'

'What's he got that I haven't?'

She laughed. 'You always were a trier. Come on, let's get you home.'

She managed to get him to his front door and find his keys in his trouser pocket. 'Here you are. Home sweet home.' She got him over the threshold and propped him against a radiator while she closed the door. He slid to the floor. She stepped over him and went to find the kitchen and coffee.

Henry crawled on all fours along the narrow hallway towards the lounge.

'Are you all right in there?' Ashley called, spooning sugar into a mug. 'Caffeine, mega dose, on its way.'

She found him on the sofa trying to turn the television on. 'This bloody clicker doesn't work. Bloody batteries I 'spect.'

Ashley took it and had a good look. 'Batteries are fine. It's just that this is a calculator. Now settle back and drink this.'

'Are you mothering me?' he slurred plaintively.

'No.'

'I need mothering, though. You see, my mum left me when I was little. I saw her today and I was very mean to her. My sister is cross with me.'

Ashley forced a mouthful of coffee between his lips. 'Drink.'

He took a mouthful then pushed the mug away. 'I'd like a whisky.'

'You're not having one.' She gave him the mug. 'Hold this and drink.'

'Okay.' He used his free hand to brush his fringe out of his eyes. 'I think I have to apologise.'

'No, you don't. We all get a bit pissed sometimes.'

'Not to you, no, to my mum. I was a horrid . . .' He began to sniff. 'I think that's why she left me. Maybe it was my fault. Something I did? And now I've been awful again and she'll go away again and my sister will never speak to me.' He broke down into wretched sobs. 'I missed her so much. Granny and Poppa tried their best but I felt their sadness. Why did she leave us all so miserable?'

Ashley sighed and put her arms around him. 'Come on, then. Let it all out. I'm here.'

When he'd cried himself to sleep on the sofa, Ashley removed herself gently so as not to disturb him and went in search of a blanket. Once she was sure he was settled and safe, she wrote him a note telling him not to waste any more precious time and to apologise to his sister and mother and go back to see them as soon as possible.

Then she let herself out of the house and disappeared into the night.

21

Sennen was lying in her room at White Water, channel hopping. So many channels. So much rubbish. Eventually she settled on a biopic of Audrey Hepburn but her mind refused to concentrate and she turned it off. What was she even doing here? Why come back and disrupt the lives of the two people she had abandoned? She had denied their existence, had never been there for them, when they scraped a knee or needed her. She'd been running. Scared. She knew her parents had turned their back on her as she had turned her back on them. She was an outcast who had had to reinvent herself, her heart under lock and key, lying deep in an impenetrable carapace of loss and self-hatred.

But then, Kafir had found her. Loved her and believed all she had told him, the made-up stories of her childhood and loving parents. At the beginning of their relationship she couldn't tell him about Henry and Ella. And later, when she knew he loved her and she lived within their safe and secure marriage, and she had wanted to tell him the truth, it was too late. She tricked herself into believing the past was in the past. Dead, buried and unable to rise up and bite her. Kafir would never find out.

And that was the second terrible mistake of her life.

She rubbed her hands over her eyes and tried to remember why she had thought running away, leaving Henry and Ella to her parents, had been in any way a good idea. Who had she been all those years ago? What had she imagined her future would be? She groaned into the empty air of her parents' old room. This time she had nowhere to run to.

She picked her phone up for the umpteenth time to see if Kafir had messaged her. He hadn't.

She argued with herself. If she sent him another text, would she seem desperate? If she didn't, would she seem uncaring? Should she send a message telling him how selfish he was and that he couldn't stop her from seeing the children? She would take him to court. They would divorce. He could visit for two weeks in the summer holidays.

Would he fight her? Yes, he would. He was a proud man with high morals and innate kindness and he hated injustice.

Had she lost another family? She was sure that Henry would never want to see her again. Ella might, but she couldn't be certain of that, either. She bashed the pillows behind her head into submission and picked up the phone again. She'd throw herself on Kafir's mercy. She had already gambled one family for another and possibly lost both. She had nothing left but her dignity.

The text she sent was an honest account of her day and how awful it had been. She asked after Aali and Sabu and told Kafir she loved him. She finished with her wish for him to speak with her – and added that she needed him more than even she had known.

*

Kafir. Even his name made her happy.

When she had arrived in India, all those years ago, she was no longer the girl who had left Cornwall. The ballet had toured Kerala, Goa and Delhi before its final end in Agra, Rajasthan. She wasn't sorry. Five years of touring was enough for anybody and she wanted to unpack her suitcase and call somewhere home. On the last night, cast and crew made their quiet farewells and took flights back to wherever they called home. They would never be together in the same group, sharing the same adventures, dancing the same dances again.

Sennen was envious that they had somewhere to return to. Partners, parents, families. She had no one. She wasn't welcome back in Cornwall any more. She told herself that this was what she wanted, that she was lucky to have her freedom, to be liberated from the bother of other people. So she stayed in Agra and looked for lodgings.

This was the city of the Taj Mahal. The mausoleum built of ivory white marble; the world's greatest monument a man has ever built to his dead wife.

Sennen had to see it. She went in the early morning – the best time to visit, according to the friendly concierge at her cheap hotel. And he was right. The day was still cool and the queues of air-conditioned coaches, spilling out tourists from around the globe, had not yet arrived.

Outside the famous walled grounds, trinket vendors and small children called out to her, holding Taj Mahal snow-domes, pens, postcards, mugs and all manner of delightful tourist tat. She couldn't resist a snowdome and paid too much for it but the small girl with a pink frilly dress and crutches pulled her heart strings.

Putting the treasure into her cotton shoulder bag, she walked to the great archway for her first glimpse of the shrine.

Shimmering in the early light, a bright blue sky behind it and a grassed garden with many still water channels in front of it, stood the Taj Mahal.

This was what the love of one man could do for one woman. She walked forward into the garden and saw a group of Canadian tourists gathered round a white marble bench, one of many set symmetrically around the garden. She stopped and eavesdropped, listening to what the Indian guide was saying.

'The late Princess of Wales sat right here on this very bench. You remember the photo?' he asked them. They nodded, wryly.

'Diana, the girl who married a future king but one who did not love her as Shah Jahan, the Moghul Emperor, loved his favourite wife, whom he called Mumtaz Mahal, which means Jewel of the Palace. Taj is the Indian word for Crown and that is why this building is called Taj Mahal. You understand?' His audience nodded. 'And now you would like pictures taken on Diana's bench, yes?'

Sennen moved away, not wanting to witness the scramble for mawkish photos. She was glad that she was single, with no chance of having her heart broken again.

The teenage girl she had been was gone. Replaced by this quiet woman who asked little of anybody.

There had been no boyfriend after Ali. She withdrew from relationships and told herself she was entirely happy being self-contained and free of complication. It wasn't that she didn't attract male attention: she was a very striking young woman. Her mane of glorious Titian curls fell around her shoulders, framing her pale-skinned, lightly freckled, face; her eyes were wide and lively, her long legs carried her tall, willowy frame with elegance. To herself, however, she was almost invisible. An invisible woman with too much height, too much hair.

Agra was a busy city, colourful and noisy. She enjoyed finding herself a room in a large house full of 'waifs and strays' as she thought of them, herself included.

She joined early morning yoga class and became friendly with the women there. They took her to the markets and introduced her to the exotic produce on sale and taught her how to cook with them.

Sometimes she held small dinner parties, trying out her new skills, and was gratified when her dahl was approved of. She lived simply and inexpensively, expecting nothing. If this was to be her life until the end, she was content. She lived like that, taking in mending and alterations, while residents came and went, some more pleasant than others, growing truly close to none of them. Then Tanvi arrived one afternoon, a childless widow who took the room across the hall from Sennen's, on the second floor of the house. Sennen liked her and their friendship grew. Soon they took it in turns to invite each other over to their rooms to take chai each Wednesday at four o'clock.

On one particular Wednesday it was Sennen's turn to invite Tanvi for tea, and when Tanvi knocked, Sennen was finishing off a pair of curtains that she had made from a bolt of glorious saffron-coloured cotton from the market.

'Come in,' called Sennen, snipping the last thread from the final drape. Tanvi appeared with her usual offering of sweetmeats. Today it was gulab jamum, an Indian version of sticky doughnuts.

She put them down on the small tea table and admired the curtains. 'So colourful.' She clapped and went to feel the fabric between her fingers. 'And good quality. Who are they for?'

'Me. I need something to cheer the room up,' smiled Sennen. 'I just need to press them and then I'll put them up.'

Tanvi looked at the high curtain rail surrounding the French windows leading onto Sennen's balcony. The existing curtains drooped exhaustedly.

'You have a ladder?' asked Tanvi.

'I'm tall, I'm sure I can reach standing on a chair.'

'And risk hurting yourself? No, no, you need a man to do this.'

Sennen smiled ruefully. 'And where would I find one?'

'My nephew. He is tall, and,' she gave Sennen a sly look, 'handsome and single.'

Sennen shook her head. 'Not him again! If I didn't know you better I'd think you were matchmaking.'

'I am,' laughed Tanvi.

'I'm sure your nephew is marvellous, but I am happy as I am. You know that. I'll make the chai.'

She walked to a corner of her room where a small kitchen, basic but perfectly practical, was set up. She lit the gas and put the kettle on the hob.

Tanvi was still sizing up the height of the curtain rail over windows. 'I cannot allow you to hang your glorious curtains without assistance.'

Sennen took the boiling kettle and poured it into her dented, chased-silver teapot. 'You make the rules for me, do you?'

Tanvi tutted. 'I care for you. I was joking about you liking my nephew, but I could come and get him to hang them – you give him chai and that's that. Nothing more.'

Sennen brought the tea tray to the table. 'Well,' she admitted reluctantly, 'it would be helpful. I tried to get the old ones down last night but I couldn't reach far enough. Does your nephew have a ladder?'

'If he doesn't, he can borrow one.'

Sennen weighed up the inconvenience of having a stranger in her room, versus the difficulty of doing the job. 'Okay. You can ask him. But I'll pay him for his trouble.'

'He'll come tomorrow afternoon.'

'You haven't asked him yet.'

'He will come. What time? I'll make sure he won't be late.'

It was arranged for five thirty the following evening and Sennen spent the following morning tidying her bedsitting room. No man had been here since she had arrived and her bed looked too intimate. She disguised it with a scarlet piece of beaded cotton, found in the general store across the road, and put two large, green, silk bolsters at either end. She hoped it looked more like a sofa.

She baked a few samosas in case the nephew might expect some food and then she waited.

At five thirty came Tanvi's recognisable knock. 'Come in,' called Sennen from the kitchen. Tanvi came in with a twinkle in her eye and a tall, very handsome, man in a pink turban behind her.

'Hello.' Sennen walked towards him, her hand outstretched. 'Thank you so much for coming to help me. It was your auntie's idea.'

He had the smoothest skin she had ever seen on a man. The whites of his eyes were like mother of pearl, his pupils like liquid chocolate.

He smiled broadly, showing perfect teeth. He put down the small stepladder he was carrying, took her hand and shook it. 'I am Kafir. What my aunt orders, I do.'

Tanvi touched his arm and looked at Sennen. 'Didn't I tell you she was very pretty? And almost as tall as you.'

He had the grace to look embarrassed.

'What have I said?' asked Tanvi. 'I only say what I see.'

Sennen waved a hand towards her kitchen, 'Would you like something to drink?' she asked.

'That would be kind,' he said, 'After I have put up the curtains, maybe?'

He set up his stepladder and Sennen held them still at the bottom, acutely aware of his long, strong legs so close to her face. She found herself noticing how nicely his jeans fitted.

'Here . . .' He handed down to her an end of the first curtain. His hands were beautiful. 'Now if I can just . . .' He reached over and unhooked the other end. 'Can you take this? It is a bit dusty.'

'Goodness knows how long they have been there,' said Sennen.

'I will go and get a duster,' said Tanvi, 'I have one in my room.'

Alone together, Kafir, still on the ladder, looked out at the view. 'You have a better view than Auntie and a bigger balcony.'

'Tanvi says that her view is better. She likes the garden, but I like the noise coming up from the street. I sit and watch life go by.'

'So you are nosey?' he said, looking down at her, smiling. He really did have lovely teeth.

'A bit,' she laughed.

'Here we are, here we are.' Tanvi came back waving a long-handled feather duster. She passed it up to Kafir.

'Better stand back down there,' he told the two women, 'I may disturb a few spiders.'

Within ten minutes, the three of them were standing back

200

and admiring their work. 'Very nice,' said Tanvi. 'Your sewing skills are excellent.' She looked at Kafir. 'The curtains in your house need updating. Sennen could do them for you.'

Kafir politely shook his head, 'My curtains will do as they are, and why would Sennen wish to make me new ones.'

'It would be something to keep her busy.'

Sennen was loading a tray with samosas and lemonade and heard what Tanvi had said. 'It's true. I could do with small jobs to keep me occupied.' She picked the tray up. 'Shall we have this on the balcony?'

There was a short flurry for the moving of the tea table outside and shaking the yellow bougainvillea blossoms from her outdoor chairs.

Sennen handed around the plate of samosas and poured glasses of fresh lemonade.

'May I ask what do you do?' asked Kafir, munching a samosa.

Tanvi interrupted and told Kafir all that she knew about Sennen's work.

He listened attentively. 'So that is how you have come to be in Agra?'

'Yes. More lemonade?'

'Thank you.' Kafir lifted his glass towards her and she poured some more. 'These samosas are very good,' he said taking another.

'She is a very good cook too,' Tanvi said. 'And she's still young.'

Kafir quietly rebuked her. 'Auntie, you must know you are embarrassing Sennen and me. Please.' He drew his finger over his lip. 'Stop talking.' He turned once more to Sennen. 'What did you study at university?'

Sennen laughed ruefully. 'I left school at sixteen and started to travel. I am qualified for nothing.'

'But you are a seamstress?'

'Well, yes, by default.'

'Do not talk yourself down. You have a creative skill that we are losing in schools. Too many parents want their children to be doctors or solicitors.'

Sennen put her glass down. 'So may I ask what you do?'

'I teach.'

She smiled. 'Medicine or law?'

'Neither. Economics.'

'He got his degree at the London School of Economics in London,' Tanvi pitched in proudly.

He scratched his ear self-effacingly. 'Auntie, I'm sure Sennen knows many people who went to the LSE.'

'I don't,' said Sennen. 'In fact, I've never been to London.'

She told him about her early years in Cornwall, painting a rather exaggerated picture of herself that was less than true and entirely missing out the existence of Henry and Ella.

'How wonderful that your parents let you go,' he said.

'Yes, well, they are artists and rather bohemian. They encouraged me to experience the artist colonies of Europe,' she lied.

'When did they last see you?' asked Tanvi.

And before she really knew what she was saying, Sennen said, 'Oh, I'm sorry to say they are no longer with us. I don't really like to talk to about it but they were very loving, kind parents.'

Tanvi leant forward and gently took Sennen's hand. 'Well, now you have me and our weekly chai afternoons.'

'Oh yes. My mother would have loved your recipe for the gulab jamum. Now tell me all about you, Kafir.' And, as simply as that, Sennen had rewritten her past and made her parents ghosts.

'Well,' said Kafir standing up some time later and collecting his stepladder, 'I have taken too much of your time.'

Sennen stood too. 'You have been very kind. Let me give you something for your time.' She went to her purse on the disguised bed.

'To see you happy with my work is enough.' He smiled and went to the door. 'Come along, Auntie. Let us leave Miss Sennen.'

As she closed the door on her visitors, thanking them both again profusely, she looked at her room and its new curtains. The colour was just right.

The evening had been just right.

Something inside her had shifted a little.

As if someone had poured a little oil on to a rusted bolt.

22

It was the cramp in Henry's calf that woke him. His face was squashed up against the arm of Granny's old sofa and he was dribbling on one of Ella's hand-embroidered cushions. His unsquashed eye felt sore and he rubbed a hand over it. It was gritty with the dried salt of last night's tears.

It all came back to him. His awful behaviour at the vicarage. Drowning his sorrows. He had cried. He was an idiot.

He tried to stand on his cramped leg and limped painfully to the kitchen. He needed some paracetamol.

He poured a glass of water, necked the painkillers and went back to the sofa.

How was he going to make amends to Ella after he said all those terrible things yesterday?

Ella woke up very chirpy. She had slept well, having made the decision to meet her mother without Henry. What was stopping her? She rolled over and spooned Kit, stroking his tummy to wake him up.

'Morning, Kit,' she whispered into his ear.

'Morning,' he said guardedly. He wasn't certain where this was leading.

'Sorry about last night.' She nibbled his neck.

'Okay . . .' he replied slowly.

'I'm going to forget about Henry and see Mum by myself.'

'Riiight.'

'Would you come with me?'

'I don't know. Do you want me to?'

'Of course. She's going to be your mother-in-law.' Ella shifted her weight and sat on top of him.

'Oof,' he said, 'you're heavy.'

'Tell me you'll come to see Mum or I won't get off you.'

'Get me a cup of tea and we'll talk about it.'

She kissed him and jumped off the bed. 'Thank you.'

'I haven't said I will yet.'

'You will.'

Snuggled back in bed and drinking tea, Ella talked about her childhood. 'It was good, really. Better than if Mum had been around, probably. She was so young. I can't imagine what it was like for her. Seventeen and with two children. I sort of don't blame her for running away.'

Kit, wisely, said nothing. He drank his tea and listened.

'When Henry and I got chickenpox, he started crying for Mum. I think that's when I realised I didn't have one. Granny and Poppa were so good to us, though. They took in all these funny art students and taught them everything they knew about art and pottery. Those students really loved Granny and Poppa. Henry and I would get a bit jealous sometimes.' She twisted her red curls round her fingers as she talked. Kit watched her.

'You got your mum's hair.'

'I know. That was a shock. Having never seen even a photo of her, I had no idea. Do you think she's attractive?'

'Yeah. She's all right.'

'I wonder if I will look like her at her age,' she mused.

'How old is she?'

'I'm not sure. About . . .' She did some mental arithmetic. 'I'd say about forty-one or two.' She stopped. 'I don't even know when her birthday is. Or what sign she is.'

'Weird.'

'Yeah. She's missed all my growing up. Henry's growing up too. She won't know how well he did at business school or how well he's doing now. Or about the time he fell off his skateboard and broke my arm.'

'Really?' asked Kit.

'Yeah. I just happened to be in the way. Poppa was so good. Whizzed me off to the cottage hospital in Bodmin and got me fixed. I milked it like anything. Henry had his pocket money stopped for a month.'

'Poor Henry.'

'Poor me, actually. It bloody hurt.'

'Come here,' said Kit, lifting his arm so that she could nestle against his shoulder. 'It must have been very hard for your grandparents, but they did a fantastic job. I really like Henry.'

Ella looked up into his eyes. 'What about me?'

'You're not so bad.'

Ella's phone rang. 'Hello?'

'Hi, Ells, it's me.'

Ella rolled her eyes and mouthed to Kit, Henry, then said aloud, 'Hi.'

'I'm really sorry about yesterday.'

'You should be.'

'I'd like to come back to Trevay?'

'Why?' Ella didn't want to make this easy for him.

'Because . . .' She heard him sigh with frustration. 'Because I want to apologise to Mum in person. And get to know her. Like a civilised man should do.'

'Hmm,' said Ella.

'Don't make this difficult. Ells, please.'

'When are you thinking of coming?'

'Tomorrow? Can I stay with you?'

'I'll have to ask Kit.'

'Well, could you let me know? Then I'll arrange it with work. I'm due a bit of extenuating circumstances.'

'I was thinking I might see Mum on my own first,' Ella said airily.

'Oh. I see. Of course. I understand.'

'I'm going to phone Deborah today and sort a meeting out.'

'Will you let me know what's decided? I really do want to make amends.'

'Yeah, well. I'll bell you later.'

Sennen still hadn't heard from Kafir. She'd woken, very early, after a dream that he was on the next flight to Cornwall, bringing Aali and Sabu with him.

She checked the time on her phone – 5.45. The start of her day, but Kafir would be well into his. He would have given the children breakfast, taken Aali to school and Sabu to the nursery he loved. She imagined Kafir planning what he would cook them for dinner. Aali liked everything, but Sabu was picky. He liked rice and flatbreads and chicken, but most vegetables he shunned. Sennen smiled to herself, thinking how Kafir would get so cross after making a special cauliflower curry or vegetable bhaji. Sennen always had a supply of tarka dal in the freezer for Sabu. She hoped now that there was still some left. She had better put lentils on the list. She checked herself. What was she thinking? She was not there, in India, not able to feed her own children. The thought inevitably took her onto the hamster wheel of anxiety that turned towards Henry and Ella. She hadn't been there to feed them, either. She had no idea of their likes and dislikes. The wheel turned another circle and took her to a place of self-flagellation. How could she have done what she'd done to all four of her children? Who was she? *What* was she? The emotional pain in her gut speared through her, made her restless.

Getting out of bed, she got up, got dressed and let herself out of the sleeping house as quietly as she could.

The harbour was as still as a millpond, the reflections of the fishing boats and pleasure boats shining in its glassiness.

A couple of gulls cackled above her and flew out over the water.

She stood against the harbour wall and listened. She heard another seagull, high among the slate roofs and chimney pots, skittering on the tiles, the gentle lapping of the sea against the hulls of the boats, the whistle of man walking his dog.

She closed her eyes and breathed in. Immediately, she was twelve. Poppa was looking over her shoulder and guiding her hand as she drew the line of a fishing boat in pencil, on her sketchpad.

'Remember what you know about perspective. That boat is face on to you. Think how big it is in comparison to the back . . . That's it.' He stood back and watched her childish work, her tongue between her teeth as she concentrated. 'You'll be giving your mum a run for her money,' he had said.

She screwed her closed eyes up tightly and shook herself. It was too late for regrets.

She walked around the harbour and down the narrow lane that connected with a network of smaller lanes crouching behind the sea. The old butchers, that had had the greengrocers next door, now knocked into one big 'holiday clothes' shop. The windows displayed jolly blue and white striped T-shirts, shorts, summer dresses and warm jumpers. She saw her reflection in the glass and realised how odd and foreign she must look in her long Indian skirt and scarf. Perhaps she should treat herself to a little shopping? Become a person of Trevay again. Yes, after breakfast when the shops were open, that's what she would do.

She crept back into the house and checked her phone. Nothing.

She switched on the radio, ran a bath and thought about what her new wardrobe of clothes should look like.

Breakfast was quick, just a coffee and cereal. Amy wanted to engage her in a discussion about sausages versus chipolatas for breakfast but Sennen made an excuse and escaped to the shops.

She needed some jeans. She went into the first shop that had clothes in the window and spoke to the young male assistant. 'How do people wear jeans nowadays? I mean, of my age. I want to look as if I understand fashion without looking laughable.'

He was a nice-looking boy with a cheeky face and wispy beard. His hair was shaven around the sides with a long top bit caught in a ponytail. 'What do you mean laughable? You look great. I love the Indian vibe you've got going on.'

'I have lived in India for a long time. But I'd like to look a little more local. Less foreign.'

'Cool. Whereabouts in India?'

'Agra. Do you know it?'

'Nah. I've been to Goa, though. Really cool place.'

'Yes. I have been there too. Very hot.'

'Yeah. It was. So what size are you?'

'A medium I'd say.'

He gave her a funny, mocking look. 'I mean jean size.'

'I have no idea.'

He ran his eyes over her. 'You look like a 28-29 waist and you've good long legs so . . .' He riffled through a pile of jeans and pulled a pair out. 'These are straight legs, but I'll see if I've got some boyfriends or skinnies. Do you like high or low rise?'

'I have no idea what you're saying,' she laughed.

'Go in the changing room and try these first.' He chucked her the jeans and obediently she took them to the changing room. She pulled up the zip, straightened the legs and gave herself a good hard stare. She was so used to seeing herself in the loose Indian trousers and tops that she loved, she was amazed to see that her stomach was, if not exactly taut, flatter than she had thought. She turned to the side and observed her profile. Her bottom looked smaller, her hips too.

She heard the assistant outside the curtain. 'How are they?' he asked.

Nervously, she drew the curtain back; her dress, that she hadn't bothered to take off, was hoiked up around her waist.

'What do you think?'

'Too big. I'll get the size down. Length's good and I like the low rise on you.' He handed her another two pairs. 'Try these. One's boyfriend, the other's skinny.'

'Okay.' She pulled the curtain back, stared at herself again. She felt a change. Maybe there was a glimmer of the person she had been or could be?

The young man came back and slipped the new, smaller jeans through the curtain.

She tried the boyfriends first.

He didn't like them. 'No. Hand them back. With your figure, I think the skinnies are best for you.'

Obediently, and thrilled by his compliment, she wriggled into the skinnies.

'Proper rock chick,' he said when she revealed herself. 'All you need is some flats or a pair of ankle boots – preferably with spiky heels – and you're good to go. Now just try the smaller straight ones.'

In the end she had the skinny's, the straights, a pair of Superga trainers, a couple of lovely soft cotton tops that fell, very fetchingly, off one shoulder, and a cream, cable-knitted sloppy joe pullover.

At the till, clutching her bag of goodies, she said, 'Thank you so much. You have been very kind.'

He handed her the receipt. 'Enjoy. You know where I am if you want anything else.'

She left the shop feeling ten feet tall. Her mind was on getting herself a pair of ankle boots when she heard her name being called. She looked in the direction of the voice and saw a woman, her own age, waving at her across the road. 'Sennen? It's Rosemary!' the woman shouted.

Sennen stared, open-mouthed, 'Rosemary!'

Rosemary crossed the road and hugged her. 'My God, what are you doing back here? I was only thinking about you the other day. Have you time for a coffee?'

Sennen, completely taken aback by this sudden encounter, said, 'Erm, well . . . I was . . .'

Rosemary cut her off. 'Just half an hour. I'm buying.'

*

The coffee shop was busy and the two women took a little while to reach an empty table, in a far corner near the loos, stepping across pushchairs and toddlers.

'You get settled and I'll go and order. Latte? Cappu?'

'Just a tea, please. Black, no sugar,' said Sennen. She was still reeling from the second collision of her past hitting her present in two days.

'So,' said Rosemary, 'what are you doing here? Visiting the children? I thought they had gone to London after your mum died?'

Sennen felt an anxiety headache creeping into the back of her eyes. 'It's all rather complicated, actually. Yes, I have come to see the children but the meeting didn't go very well.'

Rosemary eye's shone with compassion. 'Do you want to talk about it?'

Sennen surprised herself with how much she wanted to tell Rosemary everything that had happened since putting her on the boat at Santander, and it all came out.

The telling of the story in the cramped Cornish coffee shop, transported her back to the moment, standing in her bright, Indian kitchen, pans and herbs hanging from the ceiling, when she had told Kafir her secret.

At first his face, his glorious beautiful face, was clouded with confusion, followed by heartbreak and then pure, white hot anger, that the woman she had told him she was had never existed. He was married to a liar and a cheat. Sennen relived the moment as she told Rosemary.

'I had to tell you, Kafir,' she had wept. 'They have found me and I must go back.'

'You wouldn't have told me otherwise? You would have kept up the pretence forever?' he had shouted.

'It's not like that. I have been shamed by my lies. You have no idea how much I have wanted to tell you.'

'Then why didn't you? Did you think so little of me that you couldn't be honest with me?'

'No, no.' Her words came in sobs. 'I thought you wouldn't want me, that I was used goods, that you couldn't marry me because I have two illegitimate children.'

'You really think that I am that unsophisticated? You don't know me at all, do you?' He looked at her coldly. 'And I surely don't know you. What other lies have you told me?'

'Nothing. Nothing else.'

'Other than you told me that your kind and loving parents died long before they actually did die? You conveniently killed them off?'

'Well, yes. And I am so ashamed. But, it seemed easier and . . .'

'Sennen, I am sorry for you, but I am even sorrier that our marriage was based on your lies.'

She crumpled then, her shoulders hunched, her face in her hands.

Kafir watched her. 'So what are you going to do?'

'I must go home. I must sort it out,' she snivelled.

'And if I told you that I won't allow you to go?'

She stared at him in surprise. 'You wouldn't do that, would you?'

'Why not? You are my wife and it is your duty to stay with me and the children.'

'Yes, but . . .' She was confused; he had never been such a person. 'I *have* to go. You understand why, don't you?'

He folded his arms and looked at his feet.

'Kafir? Come with me. We can take the children.'

Still he said nothing.

'Please, come with me? I need you.'

'No. I shall stay here. Someone has to look after Sabu and Aali. If they haven't got their mother they will need their father. But I will get you a ticket to go home and you will face your first children and you will beg their forgiveness.'

'What will you tell Sabu and Aali?'

'The truth. It is better they know while they are young.'

'And us? Our marriage?'

'I can't promise anything. You have turned my world and the world of our children upside down. We will need to pray and think. Now, I shall pick the children up from school and you must pack. Do not be here when I get back.' He turned his back and walked out of the house.

Rosemary listened, occasionally offering a paper napkin in lieu of a tissue, and reaching over to rub Sennen's hand.

'You've been to hell and back,' she told Sennen simply.

Sennen wiped her nose and sighed. 'My own making.'

'Surely Kafir will come around.'

'I don't know. He can't understand how I could have lied to him. I am not the person he thought he'd married. I've hurt him.'

'Yes, but your two little ones . . .' Rosemary struggled to remember their names.

'Aali and Sabu,' said Sennen.

'You're are not turning your back on them, are you?'

Sennen pressed the heels of her hands into her eyes and rubbed at them. 'No. But I feel, oh, just . . . shit right now. I've let everyone down. My parents, my four children and my husband. And all because I made a huge mistake when I was so very young.'

Rosemary leaned in. 'I've always wondered, who is Henry's father? Did he hurt you? I mean were you . . . ?'

'It doesn't matter who he was. He was even more selfish and stupid than I was, and no, he didn't make me do anything I didn't want.'

'And Ella's father?'

'The same person.'

'I see. Do they know who he is?'

'No. I am the only person.'

'Even he doesn't know?'

Sennen shook her head, her mouth drawing a tight line.

Rosemary looked at her old friend with kindness. 'I think we need another tea and coffee.'

When Rosemary came back, she brought biscuits and a round of cheese and pickle sandwiches. Sennen forced herself to cheer up. 'So, I've bored myself and bored you too, so come on. Your turn. What has happened to you over the last twenty-five years?'

'Well, I'm a quarter of a century older,' laughed Rosemary.

'What happened when you got back from Spain. Were your parents furious? Did they hate me?' asked Sennen.

'No. They were happy that I was okay. I felt guilty because they were so nice about it.' Rosemary paused. 'And I felt so sorry for your parents.'

Sennen's throat tightened. 'You saw them? Took the toys for Henry and Ella?'

'Yes. I asked the police to take me to your house before they took me home. I gave them the toys but your father was very angry. He shut the door on me and I was too scared to see them again.'

'Angry?' Sennen felt tears pricking her eyes.

'Yes. But polite. You know what I mean? I think he was angry because I was on his doorstep and not you.'

Sennen dropped her head to hide her tears. 'And now my children are angry because I am on their doorstep, and not their granny or poppa.'

'Two wrongs don't make a right.' Rosemary said quietly. 'You can understand how they feel. You just have to show them, tell them what you feel about them and how much you've missed them.'

'Maybe.'

Sennen's phone rang. She snatched it up. 'Hello?'

'Mrs Tallon-Singh, Deborah Palmer here. I have news. Your daughter wants to see you. Just the two of you.'

Sennen sat up and looked at Rosemary. 'No Henry?'

'No Henry.'

'When?'

'Tomorrow. Afternoon. I've suggested tea at the Starfish hotel. Three thirty.'

'Oh, yes, yes. Thank you.'

'Perfect. See you tomorrow.'

Sennen put the phone down. 'Rosemary, you've brought me luck. Ella wants to see me tomorrow. For tea at the Starfish.'

'I could come with you, moral support and all that, if you'd like?

'Oh, Rosemary, would you?'

'What are old friends for?'

The two women parted with a plan to meet in the Starfish reception the following afternoon and Sennen began shopping again. She needed to get ankle boots for tomorrow's tea with Ella. What a difference a cup of tea and an hour with an old friend made. She determined to take Rosemary out for dinner in the next couple of days and find out how the last twenty-five years had treated her. Rosemary had shown her such kindness today, more kindness than Sennen had shown her when they were young.

Her spirits lifted. Maybe she wasn't such a bad person after all. She had made mistakes, huge ones, but now fate was offering her a chance to atone.

With a fresh bounce in her step, she put her shoulders back and forged on. On the corner, where the pet shop used to be, was a hairdresser's. She hadn't had her hair cut for years. If it got too much she would simply lop at it herself. In the window there were model shots of young women wearing the latest styles. She compared them, unfavourably, to herself. She put her hand to the glass and screwed her eyes up to ascertain how busy the salon was.

She could make out six chairs with six mirrors, a short row of backwash sinks and a reception desk. Only two of the chairs were occupied by clients. One, an older man, was being given a trim by a young woman, the other was occupied by a woman with red curly hair like her own. A man in his thirties was combing it through and bending to hear what she had to say.

Sennen gasped and pulled herself around the corner and out of sight. Ella. Had she seen her? Would she think she was stalking her? Sennen held her hands to her burning cheeks and told herself to calm down. The worst thing to do would be to run away, up the street, in case Ella was even now leaving her chair to catch her. She held her position and painted an unnatural smile on her face while pretending to find the parking permit sign fascinating. After a few moments she knew Ella would not appear. Phew. Sennen headed for the lane that would take her back to White Water, where she sat on the edge of her bed and thought about Ella. Bless her, she was obviously getting her hair done to look her best for meeting her mum tomorrow.

Sennen quickly dismissed the idea. 'Don't make it all about you,' she told herself.

She lay on the bed and tried to sleep but the welcoming arms of oblivion were not playing her game. She got up, did some yoga poses to relax herself, then hopelessly tried to meditate. Finally, she gave up. Her mother had always suggested a good walk to get tired. 'Ozone in the lungs. Always done the trick for me.'

Sennen smiled at the memory. She picked up her scarf and phone and tucked a twenty-pound note in her pocket in case of emergency and went for a walk.

She intended to walk down to the harbour, turn left past the Golden Hind and follow the path up over the cliffs towards Sundown Beach, which would take her to Tide Cove and on to Shellsand Bay. But intention and action are very different things. Once out of the front door she didn't turn right to the harbour. She turned left up towards the back of Trevay and its church, St Peter's.

The doors were locked. She rattled them in annoyance. She was hot and could have done with having a quiet moment of reflection in the cool of the building.

She reprimanded herself again. 'You're a very selfish woman today. Stop it.'

She found some shade and a bench under an ancient yew and sat down gratefully.

'What the hell am I doing here?' she asked herself. 'I want the beach and the wild ocean, not this mournful garden.' She looked around at the ancient, lichened gravestones. But still she did not move.

She knew why she had come.

She began searching for her parents' graves. She was methodical, walking up and down the lines, wonky though they were, searching for the Tallon name. She didn't even know if they had been buried. It would be like Poppa to want to be cremated and scattered in the ground to feed the crops and trees. And Mum would have done whatever Poppa thought was right. And if they were buried, would they even be in this churchyard?

She stopped and caught her breath. An emotion, she couldn't identify, possibly shame, certainly fear, was sending a tremor through her. She felt them. They could see her, she was certain.

Looking around to make certain she was on her own, she said quietly, 'Mum? Poppa? Where are you?'

A blackbird fluttered from a nearby bush and startled her. He flew to the top of a gravestone some twenty paces from her and cocked his head. She challenged his beady eye. 'You're tricking me Mr Blackbird. And I'm not falling for it.'

He flew to another stone and another. Reluctantly, she followed him, glancing at the names on the memorials he had landed on. All strangers.

Ignoring the bird, she began her methodical search again. Some headstones were so interesting she stopped and read them, enjoying the history and mystery of each.

Eventually she reached the furthest corner and the boundary of the garden. The drystone wall had a seat set into it and she sat, feeling the warmth of the slate seeping through her skirt. It was peaceful up here and, beyond the roofs of the town and its harbour, she could just make out the sea.

Would she be buried here? Would she be welcomed as a

child of Trevay? Or had she lost the right to be thought of as a local? Closing her eyes and tilting her face to the sun she pictured the mourners who would have sat here over the centuries, wiping their eyes, glad to rest their grieving limbs, imagined the gravediggers sharing a Thermos of tea as they took a break from their sweaty work.

Something light landed on her shoulder, making her start. It was the blackbird.

'You again?'

He hopped off her shoulder and on to the wall, then flew to two gravestones a row ahead of where she was sitting.

Curiosity hooked her. 'This is your last chance, Cheeky.' She got up and read the inscription.

William 'Bill' Tallon
Husband to Adela,
Father to Sennen
Poppa to Henry and Ella
So loved and so missed

Then she read the one next to it.

Adela Tallon
Wife to Bill
Mother to Sennen
Henry and Ella's Beloved Granny
No words will tell how much we miss you

The blackbird had gone.

She was alone.

She fell to her knees between the graves and spread her arms over both of them, weeping.

23

Eventually her tears ended and she sat, legs crossed like a schoolgirl, looking at both headstones.

The plots were edged with granite and covered in small, pinkish, marble-like stones. She picked one up and tossed it from hand to hand.

'Did you ever think you'd see me again. Mum? After the last time? I never thought I'd be back, that's for sure. The prodigal daughter?' She laughed. 'No fatted calf for me, though, is there, Mum? You made that very clear.'

A butterfly, possibly a cabbage white, she thought, rose from a patch of white clover and flew around her hand before settling on her father's headstone. Opening and closing its wings, it basked in the warmth of the day.

'Poppa, did Mum ever tell you about me coming back?'

Sennen shut her eyes against the daylight that was suddenly too sharp, too bright.

In her darkness, she saw her mother again, opening the front door to her. Adela had stiffened the moment she had seen Sennen. Her smile had dropped, her knuckles clenching the door as she stepped out onto the front step, pulling the door closed behind her.

'What do you want?' Her eyes searched Sennen's face. 'What have you come back for?'

Sennen felt awkward and small. This was not what she had pictured, but then again, what *had* she pictured? Her parents enfolding her with love and forgiveness? Her children hugging her, burying their faces in her skirt?

'I don't want them to see you,' Adela had hissed.

Sennen knew who she meant.

'I just wanted to see if you were okay? You and Poppa and Henry and Ella.'

'We are fine.' Adela was terse. 'Now.'

'Please, Mum, please, I've come back to explain. I've missed you all so much. Things have been so difficult.'

'Difficult?' Adela almost spat. 'I'll tell you what difficult is. Having a daughter disappear, that's difficult. Difficult is nursing your father through a breakdown.' Her face was twisting in strain at the memory. 'Losing you almost killed him. Both of us. And Henry and Ella.'

Sennen had taken a step forward to her mother, her hands reaching out to her. 'But I'm here now and I want so much to explain.'

Adela stepped back. 'There is nothing to explain and nothing of you left here.'

'But Mum . . .'

Sennen forced herself to come back to the present. 'That was not good, Mum. If you hoped to hurt me back, you succeeded. I'm so sorry for everything.' She turned her face to her father's headstone. 'I bet she didn't tell you about that, did she, Poppa? I was longing to see you. I needed your love and forgiveness. I honestly didn't realise I had hurt you so much.'

She lifted a strand of hair from her cheek and tucked it behind her ear. On the horizon, she could make out the blurred shape of a tanker heading east. For a moment she pictured herself on its bridge, twirling the ship's wheel and heading out to wherever the wind blew her. Then, with a rueful shake of her head, she addressed her father's headstone.

'I ran away. I ran and ran until I couldn't come back. God, I was frightened. But I so wanted, needed, to see you and Henry and Ella. In my heart I thought that maybe you'd welcome me back. That we could get over the terrible thing I had done and I could be Henry and Ella's mum again.' Sennen threw the stone she was playing with high in the air. She watched as it turned and sparkled then fell into the grass beside her. 'It was pretty horrible.' She turned to the grave of her mother. 'Mum made sure she told me how you had burnt my school reports, Christmas cards, photographs. She told me you had wiped me out of your lives. She called me selfish, hot-headed, too independent for my own good. She said that Ella and Henry had no memory of me and that you, Poppa, had told them I had disappeared and would never come back to them.' Sennen bowed her head in shame. 'Mum said I was dirty.' Her tears flowed again but there was no sobbing. 'I know I did wrong. But when I went to Spain it felt right. I was trying to make it right. Give the children their father. Be married. Live happily as you both had.' She sniffed and shook her hair back from her face. 'But . . . Mum told me that I was no good. That the shock of seeing me would kill you, Poppa. That the sight of me would give the children nightmares again, that you'd only just got them on an even keel . . . But all I wanted was . . . I was only twenty!' Her tears were bitter now. 'I screwed it all up. I lost him. I lost you. I lost the children . . . it's not too dramatic to say

I lost myself. Until a few years ago when I met Kafir.' She wiped her eyes on her sleeve. 'You would both love him. Kind, gentle, knows right from wrong, and he's a Sikh. Imagine. I married a glorious, handsome Sikh and we live in India. In Agra. Yes, the Taj Mahal is there and yes, it's beautiful. Kafir has given me two wonderful children. A girl first and then a boy. Aali, my daughter, is so wilful. She takes after me, you'd say. Strong. Defiant. Funny. She's coming up for six now. And then there's Sabu. He's three. So loving. He likes stories and colouring and cuddles.' Her legs were getting stiff in their crossed position so she stretched them out in front of her and lay down between her parents and looked at the sky. 'The sky's very blue. I think you'd call it heliotrope, Mum.' She shifted her head. 'And the clouds are blooming in the west. Big, smoky puffs. But I don't think it'll rain. I've seen Henry and Ella, you know. I've been summoned by your solicitor as sole beneficiary of your will. Typical of you, Mum, not to have made a will. Henry is very angry about it all and Ella is trying to compensate for him. I'm meeting her tomorrow. I saw her today but she didn't see me. She was getting her hair done. What a girl you've brought up. She's very beautiful, I think. Henry is handsome, but he was so cross with me he hid it well.' She smiled at the thought. 'So here we all are. You two, me, Henry and Ella. Back in Trevay. I'm not sure what will happen next, to be honest.' She rolled onto her stomach and plucked a long, seeded grass head. 'I threw the pebble in the pond all those years ago and the ripples are still hitting the shore. I may have lost Kafir and Aali and Sabu too.' She suddenly remembered meeting Rosemary. 'Oh, I forgot to tell you. You remember Rosemary? The girl I made run away with me? The one you liked? I bumped into her today. She was very kind. I told her everything . . . almost. She's coming to my meeting with Ella tomorrow. I'm going to explain to her what happened and ask her forgiveness. Would you wish me well? Please? No matter how old a child gets, we still want our parents' approval. I know I lost yours a long time ago, but . . .' Her voice broke and the tears came again like a sudden cloudburst in summer. 'Please. I love you both so much. Forgive me. Help me.'

24

Ella woke up to a showery day. The billowing clouds Sennen had seen the day before had poured their heaviest rain in the night and were almost spent.

Kit slumbered quietly next to her, giving her time to think about the day ahead. At least her hair was done.

She ran through her wardrobe rail in her mind. Not trousers, maybe a skirt – but what would she wear on top? Perhaps a dress would be better? Not too formal or too casual, something that was just her. In that case, it was a choice between the pale cream shift dress with lily-of-the-valley print or the black linen.

Black? Too funereal. She went for the sprigged shift. Demure but strangely sexy and very daughter-like – whatever that was. With her denim jacket over the top and heeled boots she should look just right.

She slipped out of bed and went to the kitchen to make a tray of tea.

*

'Kit?' She put the tray down on the blanket box at the end of the bed. 'Tea?'

'What time is it?'

'Six thirty.'

He groaned. 'Why so early?'

'I couldn't sleep and I've been thinking about meeting my mum today.'

'Oh,' he said without opening his eyes.

She went to the wardrobe and pulled out the chosen dress. 'How about this? With my denim jacket? I thought the black suede ankle boots would be good or do you prefer the nude strappy sandals?'

'I like them both.' Eyes still closed.

'But with this dress?'

'Boots.'

'I was thinking the sandals might be better.'

'Maybe you're right.'

'Kit, this is important to me.'

He surfaced from the duvet and opened his eyes. 'Babe, you look great in both.'

'Hopeless,' sighed Ella, 'but thank you for trying. Ready for tea yet?'

They had both drifted off back to sleep, wrapped around each other, when the doorbell rang.

'Who the bloody hell is that?' Kit groaned.

Ella got up and went to the window. 'There's a taxi driving away, without a passenger.'

The doorbell rang again. 'Okay, I'm coming.' Ella reached for her silky dressing gown and went downstairs.

'Hi,' said Henry from the doorstep.

'What are you doing here?' asked Ella suspiciously.

'Can I come in?'

'It's half past seven in the morning.' She stood back to let him in.

'I got the sleeper from Paddington.'

She smiled. 'Granny's favourite.' She closed the door. 'Want some tea?'

'I'll make it.' Henry put his bag down and looked up the stairs. 'Kit here?'

'Yeah, but Adam's at some conference. It's just us.'

Terry and Celia came from the kitchen, stretching their legs and yawning. 'Hello,' said Henry bending down to give them a friendly pat. Terry stuck his nose straight into Henry's crotch and Celia went round the back and did the same to his bum. 'Charming. Thank you.' He extricated himself as Ella went to put the kettle on.

'So why are you here?' she asked him again, reaching for the tea bags.

'I told you I wanted to come.'

'I also said that I would call you.'

'But you didn't.'

Ella stopped finding mugs and faced him. 'I want to see Mum on my own.'

'But why? We should be a united front.'

'But we are not united, are we? You don't want to hear what she has to say and I do.'

Henry rubbed his stubbled chin to think of an answer, but there was no answer. 'True.'

'So, I'm going to see her by myself. With Kit.'

'Well, that's not by yourself, is it?'

'No, but at least he's not emotionally involved.'

She poured hot water onto the tea bag and squidged it around in his mug. She hooked the bag out with the spoon and poured some milk in.

'Here you are.'

'Thank you.' He took a sip. 'That's bloody hot.'

'It's just come out of the kettle, hasn't it?'

'Don't be sarcastic.' She raised an eyebrow then went to the larder and took out a box of cereal. 'Want some?'

He shook his head. 'So where are you meeting her?'

'If you mean our mother . . . at the Starfish. For afternoon tea.'

He blew on his mug. 'Nice.'

'Yes.'

'What time?'

'Teatime.'

'You really don't want me there, do you?'

'After the other day when you were so rude? No.'

'I promise I'll be nicer.'

'No.'

'Please?'

'No. Let me build some bridges, then maybe.'

They heard Kit's tread on the stair. 'Hey, Henry, what you doing here so early?' he walked in to the kitchen and hugged his future brother-in-law. 'Hey, buddy. Come to give your sister support today?'

Henry looked at Ella pleadingly. 'I'd like to.'

She turned away and began to unload the dishwasher.

'Well, that's great,' smiled Kit, sensing the atmosphere.

'He's not coming,' responded Ella, her back to them. 'And that's that.'

Henry sensibly backed off the subject and the morning was spent walking the dogs on the beach. There were a handful of surfers out catching the waves, their sleek wet suits gleaming in the water.

'I haven't surfed for years,' said Henry wistfully.

'Are you any good?' asked Kit.

'Used to be, but,' he patted his slight belly, 'not as fit as I was.'

Ella scoffed, 'Soft Londoner.'

'Oh yeah, and when were you last in the water?' Henry bridled.

'Ah. Good point. I honestly can't remember.' She pushed her red curls out of her eyes. 'Tell you what, I've got a deal for you. You can see Mum with me today if – and it's a big if – you stay calm and are nice. If you can do that, we'll swim at the weekend. If not, no swim.'

'I'm not six.' Henry gave her a disgusted look. 'I can swim when I bloody well want.'

'Okay,' Ella said airily, 'in that case you can't see Mum today.'

He glared at her for a moment, weighing the situation up. 'Okay. It's a deal. I'll button my lip.'

Sennen was trying on her new jeans. She was going for the straight-legged pair, with a white cotton shirt she'd got in a market in India years before. In front of the mirror she turned from her right side to her left. For years, the climate – and the modesty required of being Kafir's wife – had meant she had always shrouded herself in loose clothing. She picked up the hand mirror on the dressing table and looked at her rear view, and was more than pleased with the power of Lycra. Her hips were slim, her bottom lifted and her long legs looked longer than ever. She slipped on the new white sneakers. She'd do.

She walked from White Water to the old hotel that stood

tall just above the harbour. In her youth, she had gone there for the occasional Sunday lunch with her parents and remembered how high the ceilings were and the great sea view from the dining room windows. Then it had been past its Victorian heyday, when holidaymakers would make the tiring train journey from London to Cornwall and spill out on to the platform of the long-gone Trevay station.

Now, with the harbour behind her, she looked up at it. The beige pebble dash she remembered had been given a sparkling coat of white paint. Every one of the myriad of windows was gleaming and the steps, once chipped and dirty, were now smooth granite. Twenty-five years ago she had stood here with Henry in her arms to find Ali. And now she was here with her heart in her mouth to get her children back.

St Peter's clock struck the half hour. It was time.

The young woman at the reception desk looked up from her computer terminal. 'Good afternoon. Welcome to the Starfish. Can I help you?'

'Yes, I'm having tea, a family tea.'

'That will be in the bar. Can I have the name?'

'Oh, I think it'll be booked under . . .' She didn't know. Would it be Tallon? Or Deborah's name. She was saved by a hand on her shoulder.

'Sennen, have I kept you waiting?' It was Deborah.

Relief flooded Sennen. 'I've only just got here.'

Deborah spoke to the receptionist. 'I've booked tea for three of us. The name is Palmer. Have the other guests arrived yet?'

'Not yet. Perhaps you'd like to wait here?'

Sennen was embarrassed. 'I've invited an old friend, a bit of moral support, so there will be four of us. Is that okay?'

'No problem,' said the girl behind the desk.

Sennen checked with Deborah. 'Do you think it's okay to have my friend with me? Do you think Ella will mind?'

Deborah took Sennen's arm, which she noticed was trembling, and led her to one of the enormous white sofas in the reception hall. 'We could check with her first?'

'Okay, yes.' Sennen bit her lip nervously. 'Or Rosemary could always wait for me here.'

'Indeed,' smiled Deborah taking a seat. 'You look very nice,' she remarked.

'Thank you,' Sennen said, looking down and reminding herself of what she was wearing. 'I haven't worn jeans for over twenty years. Are you sure they look okay?'

'Absolutely.'

Sennen smiled gratefully and began to absorb her surroundings. The squashy sofas, colourful rugs, tall candles in huge bell jars, the assortment of beach shoes, buckets and spades for anyone who wanted to use them by the front door. 'Gosh, this has changed.'

'I believe it's been a very recent thing. It was becoming almost derelict, but a businesswoman from up country saved it. Apparently, she used to come here with her family in the sixties.'

'She's done a good job.' Sennen had her own final memory of the hotel. She looked at her hands, damp with perspiration.

Deborah spoke. 'How are you feeling?'

'Nervous.'

'It won't be as bad as the other day. Ella on her own will be a different Ella to the one with Henry.'

'I hope so.'

There was activity at the door. Sennen looked up as Ella came in. Kit was by her side and Sennen automatically got to her feet. 'Ella.'

Ella spotted her and smiled warmly. 'Mum, hello. I've brought a surprise with me.' She stood aside and Henry came in, looking anxious and, Sennen was astounded to see, a little sheepish. 'Hi,' he said.

Sennen was thrilled. 'Henry, I am so glad.'

There was a moment's unease as to what should happen next before Ella stepped forward and kissed Sennen with a hug.

Henry, after a short hesitation, followed suit.

Kit thought he'd better do the same.

Sennen felt dizzy. The closeness of her children, the smell and feel of them, was overwhelming.

'Are you all right?' asked Ella taking her mother's hand. 'You look a bit shaky.'

'I'm fine. So lovely to see you.'

Rosemary arrived. 'Sorry, am I late?'

'Rosemary, perfect timing.' Sennen introduced her: 'This is my oldest friend, Rosemary. Would you mind if she joined us for tea?'

Ella and Henry exchanged glances. 'This is *family* business,' Henry said.

'Of course it is.' Rosemary's easy smile was charming. 'I shall wait out here. I can make myself cosy with a glass of wine and people-watching.'

Sennen shot her a thankful look. Rosemary responded with a supportive wink.

The bar was quiet; only two other tables were taken which meant the waiters were able to be very attentive. Deborah had booked the best table overlooking the sun terrace and the harbour.

The business and flurry of getting everyone seated and

the ordering of the tea was a welcome respite from the over-powering sense of occasion.

As usual, Deborah set the ball rolling. 'After our initial meeting a few days ago, may I thank you for taking the time to proceed with the matter at hand?' She reached for her bag on the floor and began to pull out an A4 wallet of paperwork. Sennen stopped her.

'Maybe we should start with just talking to each other?' She directed her attention to the children. 'I'm sure you have lots of questions to ask me?'

Ella and Henry exchanged glances, then Ella plunged in, 'Well, the one thing we really want to know is, who is our father?'

'If he's the same person,' Henry muttered under his breath.

Deborah sat back and started to click the top of her pen. Kit gripped Ella's trembling hand.

Sennen took a deep breath. 'Yes, Henry, you have the same father.'

'I knew it,' said Ella with satisfaction. 'Who is he?'

'I have never told anyone until now. I think I always knew you had to be the first I told.'

The table held its collective breath, all eyes on Sennen.

A waiter sashayed past, holding his pen and pad to his chest. 'Is everything okay?'

'Bugger off,' growled Henry. He did.

Sennen gathered herself. 'He was much older than me, in his late twenties. He worked at the Pavilions Theatre where I had a holiday job. I fell in love with him, but when the holidays ended he had to leave. I was very upset.'

'Where did he go?' asked Ella.

'He had to go back to London. We lost touch.'

Henry had his arms folded tightly across his chest. 'But he'd got you up the duff by then?'

'Yes.'

'Did he know you were fourteen?'

'No.'

'I don't suppose you wanted to keep me?'

Henry's words were like a slap in the face. 'Of course I wanted you.'

'Until you didn't and walked out on us.'

Ella glared at him. 'Henry!'

'It's okay.' Sennen gave Ella a gentle smile. 'Really. It's okay.'

'What did Granny and Poppa say?' Ella asked.

'After the initial shock they couldn't have been kinder. Granny was with me when you were born, Henry. Poppa was out in the waiting room and she called him in to see you.' Sennen's memories flooded back: 'He – he held you and t-told you that you were very welcome.' She gave a small laugh. 'He wanted to call you Mabwyn.'

Henry glowered at her.

'It's Cornish,' Sennen went on. 'It means child of a child, I think.' She looked at Deborah for back-up.

'I'm afraid I don't know,' Deborah said, 'but I can check Google.' She turned to her phone.

'So why Henry?' asked Henry, feigning boredom.

'It's a king's name,' she told him.

Henry rolled his eyes, 'Oh please. I was hardly your little longed-for prince, was I? What was the bloke's name?'

'Your father's name was . . .' She coughed, her throat suddenly dry. '*Is*, I suppose, Alan.'

Henry leant back and looked at the ceiling. 'Thank God for small mercies. I've never liked that name. Did you tell him about me?'

'I tried to. I came here, to this hotel, with you in my arms. He was staying here. But he'd already gone on to another job.'

'What work did he do?'

'He was a young magician,' she told them.

'Wow. Was he handsome?' asked Ella.

'I thought so.'

'Describe him to me. Or do you have a picture of him?'

Sennen could see the dreams in Ella's eyes. 'No, I don't have a picture, but he had long curly hair and always wore a leather jacket and jeans. He rode a motorbike.'

'Sounds very romantic,' said Ella.

'Oh, puh-leeze,' scoffed Henry. 'Sounds a complete tosser.'

Ella turned on him. 'Maybe that's where you get it from.'

'Stop it,' Sennen said loudly, exerting some maternal authority. 'This isn't easy for any of us.'

Deborah put down her teacup. 'I think it's time for a break. Sennen, would you like to get some fresh air?'

Sennen fidgeted with her hands then picked up her bag, 'Yes. That's a good idea.'

When they'd gone, Ella began to chew her hair and Henry anxiously jiggled his legs.

Kit was thinking. 'Is she telling the truth, do you think?'

'Of course she is,' Ella said swiftly.

Henry stretched across the table and crammed a small cucumber sandwich into his mouth. 'It's all very Mills and Boon. Long hair, leather jacket, motorbike. What a knob. I'm not sure I believe her.'

Kit frowned. 'Actually, I believe I do.'

Ella clutched his hand and kissed him. 'Thank you! Oh, thank you, Kit.'

*

Sennen and Rosemary were sitting outside the hotel on a comfortable swing chair. Deborah had made for the loo and Rosemary had brought a glass of wine and a cigarette out with her. She shook the packet towards Sennen. 'They're not the menthol we used to smoke, but would you like one?'

Sennen almost laughed. 'Yes, but I haven't smoked in decades and I'm worried I'll be sick.'

'How is it going?' asked Rosemary inhaling deeply.

'Henry hates me,' said Sennen.

'He's a little boy lost, that's all. He has memories, however deep, of you and him together.'

'I don't know.' Sennen picked at the chair cushion. 'He doesn't want me here.'

'Oh, he does. If you were to pick him up in your arms now and hold him tight, he'd burst into tears for missing you.'

'If I thought that was true, I'd do it.'

'Don't fight him. Stay calm. Be honest. You are the parent here. And don't you forget it.'

'I think it's too late for that.'

Deborah came back with freshly powdered nose and lipstick. Shall we go back?'

Sennen nodded. 'Yep.'

As Sennen stood, Rosemary said cheerfully, 'I'll have a large margarita for you as soon as it's over. Tequila is a cure-all.'

'I'll need it.'

Rosemary patted her arm. 'Once more into the fray, old friend. Once more.'

Back at the table, Sennen saw how depleted the sandwiches and scones had become. 'I'm glad you've had something to eat.'

'I saved you a scone.' Ella pushed a plate towards Sennen.

'Thank you.' Sennen was touched. 'I will in a minute, after I've told you more about your father.' She sighed, a deep slow sigh and began again. 'After you were born, Henry, I had no idea where . . .' She stumbled over the name. 'Where Alan was. I went back to school to do my exams and Granny and Poppa looked after you. The doctor had said that I needed to be able to get a good job after school so that I could look after you properly and they agreed with him. But,' her throat was again tight with tears, 'then, Alan came back to Trevay. To the theatre. It was only for one night. I was working as an usherette and saw him afterwards.'

'And you couldn't keep your knickers on?' sneered Henry.

Sennen ignored him. 'And I was so pleased to see him. We met after the show and yes, he and I made love. He asked me to come to the Starfish the next morning and that's when I brought you to meet him, Henry, but he had already—'

'Pissed off,' Henry said with less antagonism than before. 'What a charmer.'

'Yes,' Sennen rubbed her forehead, 'and I decided, very naively I admit, that I would go and find him and tell him about you, but I didn't know that you, Ella, were already on the way. When I did, I waited until you were born and safe with Mum and Poppa and then, knowing that he was in Spain . . . I went to find him.'

Ella burst into tears.

25

Deborah discreetly left the table and went to fetch Rosemary. 'I think you may be needed.'

Rosemary did the only sensible thing anyone could do in the circumstances and ordered two margaritas, one for herself and one for Sennen, and a bottle of wine with four glasses for the others. 'Send them to the party in the bar, would you?' she told the waiter and went to see for herself what was happening.

Sennen was comforting Ella. 'I was so happy to know you were coming. I was.' She rocked her daughter gently in her arms. 'It was a wonderful feeling, and when you were born, Poppa and I had the idea to give you Granny's name. But two Adela's would be confusing so we called you simply Ella instead.'

'He always told me that,' sniffed Ella.

'Here,' Sennen gave her her own crumpled tissue, 'wipe your nose.'

'So that's why you went? To find Alan and tell him about us?'

'Yes. And I regret it. Leaving you was the most terrible thing I have ever done.'

'Did you find him?' Henry asked.

Sennen shook her head. 'No.'

'Oh, Mum. How awful for you.' Ella was holding Sennen. 'Did you ever find out where he was?'

'No, darling,' Sennen said gently, 'I never spoke to him again.'

Rosemary and the drinks arrived. 'Somewhere in the world the sun is over the yardarm and you all look as if you need a drink.'

Henry looked at her darkly. 'Who actually are you?'

'I am the girl who ran away with your mother to look for your father. Here, have a glass of wine.'

Henry took the glass she offered him, dumbstruck.

'It takes a lot of guts to do what Sennen did,' said Rosemary 'And a lot of guts to come back and tell you both about it. She has thought about you every day of her life. Can you say the same?'

'What do you know about it?' Henry jeered. 'You've appeared from nowhere and now you're telling us you know all about it.' Henry took another large mouthful of wine and reached again for the bottle.

'We went to Spain, got jobs, found a place to live, a revolting little squat but it was safe enough. Your mum was determined to find your father and bring him home to you. All she wanted was to make you into one happy family.'

'Where did you look?' Ella asked Sennen.

'The theatres. I knew he was touring in Spain. I thought I had found him but . . .' The image of Ali's cold face refusing to acknowledge her at the stage door, the woman calling him, telling him to hurry up and get back for the babysitter, flashed jaggedly in her brain. She swallowed hard, wanting to tell the truth but still protect her children. 'I thought I had found him but it was not him. The man I found was married with his own children.'

'Why didn't you come home then?' asked Henry.

Sennen had no answer. 'I don't know. I wasn't thinking straight.'

'But Rosemary came home,' said Ella. 'Why didn't you come home with her?'

'I was too afraid . . .' offered Sennen.

'No,' said Rosemary, 'you were brave. Braver than me. I was homesick, desperate to come home.' Rosemary looked at Henry and Ella. 'Sennen took me to the ferry. I thought she was coming home with me, but she decided not to and I left her. I never should have come back without her, but I did, and it's something I have regretted always.'

She turned to Sennen. 'I am so sorry I left you.'

'This is all very touching,' Henry refilled his wine glass, and pointed it at Rosemary, 'but after you'd dumped your best mate and come back why didn't you tell anyone where she was? The police could have picked her up.'

'I did tell them, Henry,' Rosemary said. 'And I brought back the news that she was okay, presents for you two and a message about how much she loved you.'

Ella, hands in her lap, was leaning forward on her knees, hungry for more. 'Did you bring the presents back?'

'Oh yes. As soon as I got off the boat in Plymouth, I rang the police to tell them where I was and they took me straight to your house so that I could tell your grandparents that Sennen was safe and deliver the presents. You were very little, only just walking. I don't suppose you'd remember.'

'I do,' said Henry his eyebrows wrinkling in his effort to

recall. 'Ella got something pink and fluffy, and I got a dragon, with silvery wings.'

'Yes,' said Sennen, remembering. 'Did you like them?'

Henry's face was a mixture of confused emotions, then his face crumpled. 'I did – but Poppa put them in the bin.'

A fresh pain of parental abandonment skewered Sennen.

Rosemary passed her a glass. 'Drink your margarita,' she advised.

Sennen took a sip and said, 'Ella, Henry – did you get my postcards? Birthday and Christmas cards?'

They looked at her blankly. 'No.'

Deborah cleared her throat. 'I may be able to help. During Mrs Tallon's last illness, she asked her previous solicitor, old Mr Penhaligon, to collect several items from the house and take them to the office for safe-keeping. They remain in my care. One is a shoebox which holds many items of correspondence.'

Sennen put her hand to her chest, tears springing into her eyes. 'So she kept them?'

'It would appear so.'

'But she couldn't show them to the children or to Poppa because he couldn't bear anything about me to be in the house?'

Deborah nodded. 'It sounds harsh, but is a likely scenario, yes.'

'Can I see them?' Sennen's voice was shaky.

'Yes. They are among her personal affects which are now, legally yours.'

Sennen was now weeping soundlessly. Fat, glistening tears slid over her bottom lashes and made their way over her cheeks and into the creases around her mouth, then down to her chin where they hung like crystals before falling to her lap. 'I'm so sorry I wasn't here when they died.' Her voice was small and pleading. 'I wish I had known. I could have told them how much I loved them, thanked them for looking after all the mess I left them in.'

Henry crossed his arms tight over his chest and looked at the floor. Ella didn't know what to do. Her instinct was to go to her mother and hold her, but Sennen looked so vulnerable and withdrawn that she daren't touch her.

Eventually Sennen looked up and asked Deborah, 'Did your office try to find me?'

Deborah nodded. 'Of course.'

'I see.' Sennen wiped her nose on the back of her hand. 'I see.'

'We wouldn't have wanted you there anyway,' Henry said.

'No,' Sennen replied quietly.

Ella shifted. 'I would have loved you to come but you had managed to hide yourself so well.'

'Yes.'

'I could take you to their graves if you'd like?' Ella offered softly.

Sennen reached for her bag and, taking out a tissue, blew her nose. 'That's kind of you, but I have been to see them. I went yesterday. They are in a beautiful part of the churchyard.'

'Poppa chose the plots long before he was ill,' said Ella. 'He said it would be quiet up there.'

'It is,' smiled Sennen sadly, 'and the inscriptions on their stones are lovely. I was surprised to see that I was included. Whoever did that was very kind.'

Ella glanced at Henry, who had stuffed his head deep into the neck of his sweater. 'That was Henry's idea.'

Henry shifted in his chair. 'And now we come to the reason you are finally here. To collect your money and go.'

'No,' Sennen said clearly, 'No. I came to find you and Ella.'

Henry snorted. 'Not too hard a job. We were here all the

time. Unlike you. Ever since Granny died solicitors' letters have been chasing you around the world. What did you do? Every time one found you did you run again? Why turn up now if it's not because you need the money?'

Ella reached out to her mother with longing. 'Tell us about your life. Where you live. What you do.'

Sennen inhaled deeply and closed her eyes. This was the moment that she had dreaded. She opened her eyes and spoke. 'Well, I am married. To a lovely man. He's Indian. A Sikh, actually. We've been married for six years. His name is Kafir.'

'How wonderful,' Ella said with kindness.

Sennen looked at her gratefully. 'Yes. I am lucky. We live in a small house in Agra, just the four of us.'

Henry leapt at this. 'Four of you?'

Sennen's stomach twisted. 'Yes. We have a daughter, Aali, and a son, Sabu. Your half-sister and -brother.'

Henry sat back in his chair, his glass of wine on his chest. 'I knew there was something,' he said slowly. 'So Granny's windfall is for them, is it?'

Sennen again shook her head. 'No. I am here to heal the damage I did.'

'Ha!' Henry had a cruel smile on his face. 'Too late for that, Mother.'

Ella was still taking in the news that she had a brother and a sister. 'How old are they? The children?'

'Aali is five and Sabu three.'

'Are they here? Did they all come with you?' asked Ella.

'No.' But before Sennen could say more, Henry jumped in.

'So that's why you're here.' Henry sat forward in his chair, his hands gripping the sides. 'He's not here because he doesn't know about us.'

Sennen licked her lips nervously now. 'Not until a couple of weeks ago.'

Henry narrowed his eyes like a mongoose spying a snake. 'How did he take the news?'

'He, erm, he was angry that I hadn't told him before.'

'I'll bet he was,' drawled Henry. His eyes gleamed. 'He'd married a liar, hadn't he? A woman with a very chequered past.' He drained his wine glass. 'Poor sucker. I bet he chucked you out – and with nowhere else to go you came back to us.'

'It's not like that.'

Deborah put her hand up. 'Maybe we should stop there.'

Ella was shaken. She clutched Kit's arm. 'You all right?' he asked.

'Yes.' She looked at Sennen. 'Are you okay, Mum?'

Sennen was getting a tissue from her bag. 'Sure. Yes. I'm fine. I'm just so sorry to have hurt you and Henry. So sorry.'

Henry got to his feet and hissed, 'God, this is such a joke. This woman,' he pointed at Sennen, 'left me when I was a toddler and now, what a surprise, she's walked out on her next two as well. History repeating itself.' He picked up his jacket. 'Come on, Ells, we're going. Leave her to her own mess.'

'No,' said Ella.

Henry shrugged. 'Fine by me but don't expect me to offer sympathy when she hurts you again, and she will. I promise.' He threw two twenty-pound notes on the table. 'That's for the wine.'

Without looking back, he walked out of the hotel to find the nearest bar.

Sennen remained in her chair, drained and exhausted and shut her eyes. Pandora's box was open.

Rosemary called the waiter over and ordered two large margaritas.

Ella looked at Kit, not knowing what to do.

Deborah packed her bag and addressed them all. 'In my experience, family matters can and do improve. But it takes time.' She stopped and looked at Sennen. 'Mrs Tallon-Singh, don't take this as a final outcome. With gentle support we will get there. There will be a satisfactory, if imperfect, conclusion, I am certain. Try to get some sleep. Goodbye.'

She went to the ladies' loo and looked at herself in the mirror. She was glad that her professional face remained intact. She liked Sennen, for all her mistakes, and Ella was demonstrably kind and loving. Henry, however, was less than congenial. Behind his handsome face lay a spoiled child. But she vowed that she would do everything in her professional power to make things bearable for them all.

Outside the hotel she set off for the small house she had rented while she looked for one to buy. On the way, she passed the small and lively wine bar where she was becoming a regular. She had refused any of the drink offered at the meeting, but now seriously felt she deserved a drink. At the bar she was welcomed. 'Hello, Debs. Bit early for you, ain't it?' said the chirpy barmaid.

'Never have I needed a glass of Pinot more, Lily.' She climbed onto a bar-stool.

Lily opened the glass-fronted wine fridge and reached for a bottle. 'Small or large?'

'A pint glass wouldn't be too big.'

'You earned your money today, then?'

'I hope so.' The large wine glass, frosted with condensation, was begging her to take a sip of its contents. It was cold and fruity, with just the right amount of acid. She licked her lips.

'God, that's good. I'll have a bag of crisps too, please, Lil. Haven't had a chance to eat today.' She looked around the bar. 'Anyone interesting in?'

'A bit early yet,' said Lily passing her the crisps. 'But there is one good-looking bloke here. Never seen him before.' Lily looked around her. 'I think he must be in the gents. I hope so. He hasn't paid yet.'

Henry finished his pee, washed his hands and looked at himself in the mirror. 'Come on, buddy. You're a big boy now. Who needs this shit? Get on with your life. *She* has.'

He dried his hands and walked unsteadily back to his bar-stool.

A petite woman in a business suit had her back to him, talking to the barmaid. He clocked her slim legs in their sensible court shoes and thought he might have a crack at her. He walked towards her as the barmaid nodded in his direction, saying something to the woman, who turned. Deborah, the legal tart. He almost doubled back to the gents but she had seen him. 'Henry.' She patted the bar-stool next to her. 'Join me for a drink?'

'I've already got one, thanks.'

'Okay. Shall we drink together? Or alone like a couple of saddos?'

He looked at his pint sitting all by itself on the bar just a few feet away. 'Okay. We'll drink together, on the promise that we don't mention my mother.'

'Done deal.' She smiled.

He got his pint and hauled himself up onto the stool beside hers. 'So, where shall we start?'

'Tricky opener,' she teased. 'How about you first. Tell me about your work in London.'

He eyed her up. Without her legal face on, she was really quite pretty, in a girl-next-doorsy kind of way. 'I am in an office with a lot of other guys – and some women, you'll be pleased to know . . .'

'Why pleased?'

'Well, you're probably a feminist so I don't want you to think I live in an altogether male world.'

'I'm not *probably* a feminist. I *am* a feminist. So as long as I treat you as an equal, you may treat me as an equal.'

'Oh, right, that's me told.'

'Carry on. Large office. Mixed sex and . . . ?'

'Yeah, I'm a corporate surveyor for an expanding company and I check out plots of valuable land for people who want to make squillions.'

'Are you good at it?'

'Yes. I got a good bonus at the end of last year.'

'So you're doing all right?'

'Aha, now, you're trying to get me to say I don't need Granny's money. Leading the witness?'

'Would I do that?' She curled her lips up into one of the prettiest smiles Henry could remember. 'But you have a house in London?'

'Clapham, and before you ask, yes, old Mr Penhaligon, Granny's solicitor, gave me a little money for the deposit, on the understanding that if my mother was ever found, then I would pay it back.'

'Could you?'

'No. After the mortgage and the bills there's not much left at the end of the month.'

'But your bonus?'

'I helped Ella a bit and . . .' He stopped, realising he'd told her too much. 'Bugger.' He said and drank his beer.

Deborah laughed. 'Sorry. It's force of habit. Getting people to confess.'

He was mildly impressed. 'So, you do criminal stuff as well as probate, do you?'

'Yes, but when Old Mr Penhaligon retired the offer to come down here was too good to miss. I decided I loved the sea and Cornwall more than the workings of the criminal mind.'

'I'll drink to that.' He emptied his glass. 'Another?'

'I think I need to eat more than crisps first.'

'I'll get the menu.'

He ordered the drinks and two plates of whitebait with chips. Lily took his money and winked at Deborah. 'Why don't you two find a table and I'll bring it to you? There's one round the corner in the snug. It's a bit dark but it's private.'

She wasn't kidding. Two wall lights with red lampshades cast a boudoir effect over the small space filled by a table and two armchairs. They made themselves comfortable.

'Your turn,' Henry said. 'Tell me about you. Ever been married?'

'Close. I broke off an engagement when I came down here.'

'Why?'

'He had a daughter from a previous relationship and didn't want to live three hundred miles away from her.'

'Fair enough. Although,' he smiled, 'she's going to miss out on some cracking holidays.'

'Yes, and I'm missing out on marrying a nice man.'

Henry didn't know how to reply to that.

'What about you?' Deborah asked. 'Anyone special in your life?'

'Lots of girls, obviously, but I have no plan to settle down anytime soon.'

'Love 'em and leave 'em eh?'

'I've told you too much again! How do you do this, Deborah?'

'Debs, please.'

The whitebait and chips arrived and they tucked in.

Debs had a good look at him from under her eyelashes. A slick City Boy hair cut; a body that suggested regular trips to the gym and clean hands with well-shaped nails. His face was slightly irregular, but attractively so, with a tiny scar below his bottom lip and a crooked nose. 'Were you ever a rugby player?' she asked, picking up a whitebait and scooping it into a pile of tartare sauce. A glob of it dropped on the lapel of her jacket which she failed to notice and Henry was much too gentlemanly too mention.

'Yeah. Why?'

'I saw the scar.'

He rubbed at it. 'Teeth went through. Broke my bloody nose at the same time.'

'Do you still play?'

'No. I like to run. Do a few weights still. Swim.' He thought about Ella. 'I was supposed to be swimming with Ella and Kit this weekend but I think I've blown it now.'

He told her about the deal they had made.

'You can come swimming with me instead.' Debs surprised herself for saying it. The wine was having too much of an effect on her.

'Sure. Love to,' he said, touchingly pleased.

She looked at her watch. 'Well, that was lovely.' She pushed her empty plate away and finished her wine.

'You're not going, are you?'

'I must. I have an early office meeting tomorrow.'

'Do you have far to go tonight?'

'No, I'm just around the corner.'

'Let me walk you back.'

She was on her feet now, looking for her purse in order to pay the bill. 'Not at all. It's been a nice evening after a difficult day and I promise that all we have spoken about tonight will remain confidential.'

He stood up too. 'I insist on walking you.'

She relented. 'Okay, but I'm paying this bill. My treat.'

He held his hands up in submission. 'My treat next time.'

Lily said goodnight to them both as they left the bar and smiled to herself.

Debs and Henry began walking towards the lights of the harbour.

'Hasn't changed much since I was a child,' mused Henry. 'We used to crab off the wall here. Poppa had a little boat that he'd take out mackerel fishing. I didn't like it much. Hated the poor things gasping before he knocked them on the noggin.'

Debs laughed. 'Noggin?'

Henry put her arm through his. 'Don't laugh at me.'

'It's such a great word.'

'Lots of good words Poppa had. He was a lovely man, even after his breakdown. Granny was so strong. God knows what would have happened to Ella and me without them.'

They walked on, past the lane leading to Debs' house, and down to the water. The small town was quiet. Their footsteps echoing off the ancient cobbles. He led her to a wooden bench at the end of the harbour wall where they could hear the sea quietly lapping in the darkness.

There was a cold breeze and Debs pulled the lapels of her jacket up to stop the draught running down her neck.

'Cold? Here.' He put his arm around her and hugged her to his side. 'Better.'

'Thank you.'

She closed her eyes and noticed the warmth of his body and then the scent of his cologne, musky and masculine. 'What aftershave are you wearing?'

'Creed.'

'It's lovely.'

'Sitting here, with you, is lovely.'

She lifted her head and gave him a puzzled look. 'Really?'

He had to kiss her, so he did.

'That was unexpected,' she whispered as they broke apart.

'It was.' He smiled. 'Shall we do it again just to make sure it wasn't a fluke?'

This new and surprising closeness flowed over them with ease. Finally, Debs broke away. 'I know this is boring, but I really do have to get up early.'

'I know. And I must get home to Ella and apologise.'

'You can't drive. You've had too much. I can give you a coffee at home. Sober you up?'

He kissed the tip of her nose lightly. 'Thank you.'

They walked back up to her little house that sat in the middle of a terrace of old fishing houses. It began to drizzle as she put the key in the lock.

The door opened into her unlit tiny lounge.

She closed the door behind them, took Henry's hand and led him upstairs.

26

Ella and Kit left the Starfish shortly after Deborah. Ella had given her mother a warm hug. 'I'm sorry about Henry. I'll talk to him.'

'I'm sorry I have caused such friction,' Sennen said ruefully. 'I honestly hadn't meant to. But I don't regret coming home and seeing you both.'

'Would you like my mobile number?' asked Ella.

Mother and daughter swapped numbers and said their farewells, promising to be in touch soon.

Now, only Sennen and Rosemary were left.

'Another margarita?' asked Rosemary.

'Oh God, yes.' Sennen slumped in her chair and exhaled loudly. 'What a day.'

The margaritas arrived and the two women sipped on them peacefully and thankfully.

'Ella's a good girl, and so like you,' said Rosemary.

'I like the look of Kit,' smiled Sennen, relaxing further into her chair. 'They seem comfortable together.'

Rosemary stretched her legs out and kicked her shoes off. 'Henry's hard work though.'

'Yes.'

'Anything from Kafir?'

'No.' Sennen felt suddenly wretched. 'What have I done?'

'The right thing.'

'But have I? Why do I keep making a mess? Ella and Henry don't need or want me and I've thrown away my marriage. I'm going to lose Aali and Sabu, my parents rubbed me out of their life . . .'

Rosemary shook her head. 'Oh, hello. Nora Negative has arrived!'

'Shut up.'

'If Posy Positive were here she'd be congratulating herself. She's come home, her kids are at least willing to meet her, she has a family in India who love her very much—'

'They don't,' Sennen groaned. 'They'd be here now if they did.'

'The reason Kafir is not here is because he's hurting, and he wouldn't be hurting if he didn't love you to bits. After all, it's not as if you've been unfaithful to him, is it?' Rosemary had a terrible thought. 'Is it?'

Sennen gave a short laugh. 'Absolutely not. Alan was my first and Kafir the last, with no one in between.'

'Really?' asked Rosemary, more interested than she should be.

'Really.'

'Even I managed more than that.'

Sennen looked at her friend. 'Tell me. Tell me about all that has happened to you since I put you on the ferry.'

27

Henry woke up in Deborah's bedroom – and immediately regretted it. What the hell had he been thinking? Without moving any part of his body, other than his eyes, he took in his surroundings. Everything was very white. Ceiling, walls, duvet cover, wafting curtains against the open window where daylight was creeping. He swivelled his eyeballs with some discomfort to the right. There was Debs, lying on her back and gently snoring.

He needed to leave.

Feeling like James Bond avoiding the hidden laser alarms, he inched himself out of bed and quietly picked up his clothes which were scattered on the floor, tangled with Debs'. She coughed. He ducked. She was quiet and then the snoring started up again.

He felt a heel but he really had to get out of here. Ella would be furious. He mustn't tell her. Under no circumstances. But would Debs spill the beans? He wondered whether he should wake her up and tell her this had to be a secret between them, but, coward that he was, he crept downstairs and left a note by her kettle. *Morning. Had to go. X*

He let himself out of the front door and ran as quickly as his hangover would allow him.

In the glove box of his car he found a roll of extra-strong mints and put four in his mouth to kill any telltale aromas of alcohol. Ella had the nose of a bloodhound.

As he drove out of Trevay, his mouth open to cool his burning tongue, he tried to come up with a feasible story as to why he hadn't come home last night but as Henry coasted towards Marguerite Cottage, the engine switched off, he noted, with joy, that all the curtains were still closed.

He put his head on the steering wheel in relief and to ease the pain.

Once inside the cottage, he tiptoed up the stairs, across the landing and towards his bedroom door. He congratulated himself as he placed his hand on the handle.

'I've been so worried.' Ella had appeared from the bathroom and was tying up her dressing-gown belt. 'Where have you been?'

Henry leapt with fear and screamed, 'Fuuck!' whilst clutching his chest.

'Shh,' said Ella crossly. 'No need to wake Kit up.' She stepped towards him and sniffed. 'That old trick.' She put her hands on her hips. 'Extra-strong mints will never cover the amount of booze you've sunk. Come downstairs. I want to talk to you.'

Meekly, he followed her.

Debs woke up and stretched from top to toe. She smiled, remembering last night. She rolled over to see Henry's adorable little face but he wasn't there. He must be downstairs making a coffee. She would help him. She got out of bed and walked naked down the stairs, hoping to seduce him again. 'Henry?' she called seductively. He was not in her tiny front room. She padded into the galley kitchen. Not there either. Then she realised, he must be in the bathroom which was just beyond the kitchen. 'Henry?' she called. 'I'm making coffee. Hot, strong and sweet. Want some?' She arranged herself in what she hoped was an attractive nude stance outside the bathroom door but she couldn't hear any movement. She put her ear to the door and then tapped. 'Henry? I'm putting the kettle on now. Coffee, tea or me?'

She chuckled as she went to the kettle and then she saw his note.

She ran to the empty bathroom and was sick.

She heard her phone ping as she walked gingerly from the loo, feeling better but weak.

She looked at the message and swore. Sennen wanted to know if she'd be free for another family meeting, this time in Deborah's office. *I need to make my position clear to Ella and Henry about my parents' legacy. Would you be free at 10? And arrange for them to be there?*

Debs rubbed her temples, poured herself a coffee and then replied. *What a marvellous idea. I am free at* . . . She stopped and looked at the clock on her radio – 09.00. She swore. Hastily she typed, *Yep 10 is perfect. Will text them.*

Ella poured boiling water into the two mugs and stirred in milk and sugar. She passed one to Henry. 'Get this down you.'

'Thanks,' he said obediently, trying to remember his fictitious backstory.

'So,' Ella pulled out a chair and sat at the table, 'where were you last night?'

'I found a pub and had a few drinks. To be honest, I wasn't thinking straight. The shock of discovering an Indian family and all that was too much.'

'Uh huh,' Ella said patiently, crossing her legs and waggling a slippered foot. 'And then where did you go?'

'Nowhere.'

'Where did you sleep?'

'In the car.'

She looked at him. 'I will ask you again: where did you sleep?'

'I told you, in the car.'

'I don't believe you.'

'It's true.' He flopped back in his chair like a teenager denying he cheated at his exams.

'So why, when I asked Kit to go and look for you, did he find your car empty?'

Henry's brain was not functioning as fast as he'd like, 'When was that?'

'Just before midnight.'

'I went for a walk to sober up and woke up on that bench down by the harbour wall. Poppa's crabbing bench?' He was rather pleased to have added a touch of truth, but was clutching at straws and he knew it. However, it was bang on target. Ella's natural empathy kicked in.

'Oh no,' she wailed, 'it was so cold last night. You must have been freezing.'

He nodded pathetically.

She stood up and kissed the top of his head. 'I'll run you a nice hot bath.' As she got to the stairs her mobile phone, sitting next to Henry on the kitchen table, trilled a text. She called over her shoulder, 'Would you check that for me?

'Sure.' His hangover was pounding but he valiantly focused

his eyes on the name of the text. He blenched and swallowed hard. It was from Deborah.

'Read it to me, then,' said Ella, hanging on to the bannister.

'It's from, er, Debs.' He cleared his throat. 'Deborah.'

'Oh? What does she want?'

'She says, Mrs Tallon-Singh would like to meet you and your brother at 10 this morning in my office. Would you mind passing this message to Henry and letting me know if you will both be attending?'

'Great. Tell her we'll both be there.' Ella took a couple of stairs two at a time.

Henry wavered. 'Wait, let's think about it. Isn't it too soon after last night? I mean, yesterday afternoon.'

'Not at all. Strike while the iron's hot.'

'But the last two meetings have ended up in rows.'

Ella returned from the stairs and entered the kitchen. 'Which is why we need to move on. The money Granny left is hers. End of. When that's sorted we can begin to build bridges. I was saying to Kit last night how lovely it would be to go to India and meet our little brother and sister.'

Henry rubbed the back of his neck. 'Do we have to do this today?'

'Yes.' She took his hand. 'Now come and be a good boy and have a bath.'

Sennen read Deborah's text and smiled. Here was another chance to prove to her children that she was not thinking of herself where her parent's money was concerned. She contemplated getting up and having a shower.

Rosemary popped her head around the bedroom door.

'Morning. Sleep well?'

'Wonderfully well. The margaritas did their job.'

'Good. I bring caffeine in case you need a lift.'

Sennen stretched out in the pretty little bed in Rosemary's spare room.

'Thank you for last night.' She sat up and took her coffee cup from Rosemary. 'You've been such a friend. I can't believe how much you've helped me . . . when really, you should have steered well clear. I was awful to you when we were young and I am truly sorry.'

'Forgiven. We all learn from other's mistakes.' Rosemary sat on the end of the bed, tucking her feet under her.

'But anything could have happened to us in Spain. I bet your parents hated me. '

'Well, let's just say you weren't exactly top of their pops,' said Rosemary with a wry smile. 'After the initial anger and interrogations – have you taken drugs, had sex? – they calmed down but kept me on a pretty short lead. When I met Ray, the man I married, they were relieved. Dad knew his father from the Rotary club, so he already had the stamp of approval. I wanted to make up for my teenage misdemeanour and make my parents happy, so Ray and I married very quickly.'

Sennen sat up and pulled her pillows behind her to get more comfortable. This was going to be a long conversation. 'I'm assuming you aren't with him now?'

Rosemary looked in to her coffee. 'No.'

'Tell me about him.'

'Oh, he looked great, on paper. Tall, dark, handsome, attentive, generous. Everyone told me I had made a terrific catch and I managed to convince myself that I was in love.' At this she plastered on a huge smile, a brave smile. She didn't fool Sennen.

'But?' asked Sennen.

'He was . . . a bit jealous.'

'Difficult?'

'Understatement, my dear,' Rosemary said bluntly. 'I had a little job in the chemist on the harbour. Remember Miss Tangye, the pharmacist?'

'Oh yes.' Sennen smiled at a memory. 'She sold me my first box of tampons. So discreet and kind. She took me to one side and explained how they worked.'

'Bless her. Yes, she was lovely and I loved working there. I was right in the hub of village life – which is what Ray didn't like.'

'Why?'

'He would come home with a couple of beers inside him and accuse me of fancying the men who came in for ordinary things like razors or shaving foam, but he said they came in because I was flirting with them. I wasn't.'

'What happened?'

'My dad got ill and Miss Tangye gave me as long as I needed off to give me time to help Mum nurse him.'

'Oh dear, that must have been very hard. How old were you?'

'Mid-twenties, I suppose. Anyway, when he died, Mum still needed me and Ray encouraged me to stay at home. There were certainly less rows then, but, when Mum started to feel herself again and I was ready to go back to work, Miss Tangye told me that Ray had already told her I wasn't coming back and she had employed someone else.'

'He what?'

'Yeah. But anyway, I was so tired after Dad died, with the worry of looking after Mum and everything, I accepted it and was actually glad to have time to myself for a bit. But the more time I had, the more time he had to control me.

He hated me seeing friends, phoned me all the time to find out where I was. I had to give him details of my plan for each day and he would check up on me.' Rosemary's eternally upbeat persona began to slip. 'Then the drinking began. And he began to hit me.'

'Whaat?' Putting her coffee cup down, Sennen leant forward and threw her arms around her friend.

'Yeah. Shameful eh?'

'For him yes,' said Sennen stoutly.

'No. You'd think so, but I was the one who was shamed. When I finally told the family I was leaving him, they turned on me. Apparently, it was my duty to stand by him. He was going through a rough patch. He was family. Huh. Some family. Even when it came out that he'd been having an affair with a woman I had been close to, they blamed me for being a boring wife. God, it was awful.' She wiped her eyes on her pyjama sleeve. 'Anyway, I divorced him – or rather, he divorced me, for unreasonable behaviour.'

'No! How come?'

'I don't know, really. Anyway, I simply couldn't fight any longer, I was just so tired with it all.'

'Typical small town mentality,' said Sennen angrily. 'And all the time I was running away, I envied you. I imagined you in a cosy home with a couple of children and Sunday lunches in the pub.

'I envied *you*,' said Rosemary quietly. 'You got away and I could have gone with you.'

Sennen moved up the bed and hugged her old friend. 'In lots of ways I wish I had got on that bloody ferry in Spain and come back with you. What a pair we are.'

'What a pair we *were*! But here we are, older, not much wiser but together again.'

Rosemary sat back. 'And you have so much to look forward to. Having Henry and Ella back in your life and starting afresh, no lies, with Kafir and your little ones.'

Sennen rubbed her hands over her face and through her hair. 'God, I hope so. And what about you? Do you have anyone special?'

'Yes.' Rosemary's eyes lit up. 'Someone very special.'

'And?' Sennen's romance radar pinged into life.

'And I am sure you will meet very soon.' Rosemary looked at her watch. 'If you're going to get to Deborah's for the meeting you'd better get in the shower.'

28

Deborah downed her coffee, sped upstairs, then sped down them, remembering she had to clean her teeth. She gave herself a cursory cat lick then added deodorant and perfume. She told herself she could come back after the meeting for a full shower.

Back upstairs she found clean underwear but no tights. It was much too cold and her legs were too white to go bare-legged so she unhooked her tights from last night's knickers and yanked them on.

She opened her wardrobe door and immediately cursed herself. She'd forgotten to collect her second-best business suit from the cleaners. She stared at yesterday's suit. It was in a sorry heap on the floor. Bugger! She scooped it up and ran down to the kitchen and threw it into the tumble dryer with a shot of Febreze.

Back upstairs, she sat at her dressing table and looked in the mirror. A bit of touché éclat, blusher and lipstick should sort her out. In her make-up drawer she came across a couple of Nurofen and tossed those down as insurance, then fixed her face. Her shaking hand made a bit of a mess of her flicky eyeliner but an extra coat of mascara camouflaged that.

She ran downstairs, pulled the refreshed suit from the tumble drier, ran back upstairs for a neat white T-shirt and shoes, and made it to the door by 9.27. Taking a deep breath, and raking a hand through her unwashed but passable hair, she stepped out of the house and walked to the office.

Miss France had been the secretary for Penhaligon and Palmer Solicitors for as long as anyone could remember, but when Old Mr Penhaligon retired, so did she. Her replacement was a young law graduate called Grace who was far too qualified for the job but was happy to take on any conveyancing work as well as general office work.

'Morning, Debs.' Grace scanned her boss from head to toe. 'Want me to go out for a coffee?'

'Thank you, how kind.'

'Rough meeting yesterday, was it?'

'You could say that.'

'Looks like you haven't slept a wink. Up all night, were you?'

'Why do you ask?'

'Your suit has a stain on the jacket and there's a hole in your tights.'

Deborah looked down in despair at the dried blob of tartare sauce and said the first thing that came into her head. 'It was a dog – it jumped up at me on the walk in.'

'Tall dog.' Grace raised her eyebrows in disbelief. 'I'll pick up a pack of wet wipes and some new tights while I'm out. Latte? Large?'

'Anything other than American tan.' Deborah was already heading for her office.

Grace shook her head and laughed. 'I mean the coffee, not the colour of your tights.'

As soon as Grace left, Deborah went to her office and began setting it up. First, she opened the only one of the large casement windows that actually did open, the other being long stuck with paint, to let the underlying pong of dry rot out, then she tidied away a pile of case files sitting on the floor next to her desk, and finally assembled a selection of chairs for her three clients.

On the wall above her desk was a foreboding portrait of Mr Penhaligon, the founder of these chambers. She surveyed him.

'Well, Mr P, it's Debs here. Goodness knows how it has happened, but I'll try to look after your old practice as best I can. I went to Oxford, you know. Got a 2:1. Sorry it wasn't better.' She hitched her skirt up. 'Sorry about this; I had a bit of a situation this morning. Don't look.' She pulled off her torn tights and threw them in the bin. 'You probably know that I broke the cardinal rule last night and slept with a client's son. Not very smart, I admit. And I have a hangover. So, I'd like all the help you can give me, please.'

The outer door slammed and Grace walked in. 'Large latte, extra shot and nearly nude.'

'Thanks.' Deborah grabbed at the packet of tights. 'How much do I owe you?'

'Nothing. You'd do the same for me.'

Deborah thanked her, then looked at the clock. 'Mrs Tallon-Singh is due in seven minutes. Would you hold her until I'm ready?'

'You're the boss.'

*

Deborah pulled on her new tights, settled into the chair behind her desk and took a mouthful of the lifesaving coffee.

Sitting back in her chair she closed her eyes, lowered her shoulders and took a few deep breaths.

Her headache was almost bearable.

Opening her eyes, she opened the file in front of her.

The legacy due to Sennen was quite substantial. Certainly enough to help Henry with his mortgage. She banged her hand on the desk. She must not think about Henry Tallon.

She sipped some more coffee and concentrated.

Yes, the money could help both Sennen's older children and there would still be enough to help her second family too.

If she were asked, that is what she would advise.

Then maybe Henry would come down to live in Trevay and they would fall in love and . . . She banged the desk again. Stop it.

Her door opened. It was Grace. 'Mrs Tallon-Singh is here.'

Deborah laid her head on the desk for just a moment then sat up, as bright-eyed as she could. 'Please show her in.'

She got up and met Sennen at the door.

Today Sennen smelt of patchouli and was wearing her new jeans with an Indian kaftan.

Deborah was always surprised by Sennen's height and had to resist standing on tiptoe as Sennen bent down to shake her hand.

Sennen looked at the chairs and asked hopefully, 'Three chairs? Ella and Henry are coming?'

'They're certainly invited.'

'Oh, that's good. I have made some decisions and it would be better if they were both here when I say them.'

'It's always useful,' smiled Deborah. 'Has Grace offered you a coffee?'

'Yes. She is taking the orders as we all arrive.'

There was the sound of someone else arriving. Grace knocked at the door and announced Ella, who was holding tightly to Kit's hand, and Henry. Deborah was pleased to notice he looked worse than she felt. He kept his eyes firmly on the carpet.

Ella bent to kiss her mother on both cheeks. 'Hello, Mum, you look nice.'

Sennen could have wept for this kindness. 'Thank you, Ella. So do you.'

Suddenly the room felt a little cramped and over warm. Deborah started to feel flustered and faint. The room slid under her feet. She sat down.

Grace noticed. 'Do you need more chairs, Miss Palmer?' she asked with professional calm. 'And before I get the coffees, perhaps I'll open another window?'

'Chairs, yes thank you but the window is a bit . . .' She swallowed rising nausea. 'A bit erm . . .' Deborah gripped her desk.

Henry leapt up and, Deborah could tell, he almost immediately regretted it. He steadied himself on the back of his chair. 'Let me help you.' He crossed to the window and, after a few goes, managed to thump it open. 'There.' He took the opportunity of a gulp of fresh air. 'Now chairs, where are they?'

Grace pointed out a heavy chair in the outer office. 'Maybe that one?'

'Of course.' He made an effort to produce his winning Tallon smile. 'Could you direct me to the gents first?'

'On the landing. First left.' She looked at the beads of sweat on his forehead and shaking hands. 'Are you all right?'

'This family stuff is very emotional.' He wiped a hand across his brow. 'Do you have any aspirin?'

Grace knew a hangover when she saw one. 'I'll get some when I go on the coffee run. It might be a bug.' Grace narrowed her eyes. 'Miss Palmer isn't looking too good today either.'

'Really? I must just . . . on the left?' She watched as Henry scurried to the loo.

'Will that be everything, Miss Palmer?' asked Grace, fifteen minutes later, coffee and aspirin distributed and everyone seated.

Deborah gave her a thankful smile. 'Yes, thank you.'

Grace closed the door silently behind her.

Deborah sipped some coffee, quelled her mild nausea and began. 'You all now know the extent of Mrs Adela Tallon's estate. As her nearest living relative, everything now passes to Mrs Sennen Tallon-Singh. That is the law.' She looked at Sennen, who held her hands to her mouth as if in prayer. Deborah continued, 'All that needs to be done is to sign the relevant documentation and the money will be placed into Mrs Tallon-Singh's bank account.'

'Thank you,' breathed Sennen, 'it's almost too much to take in.'

Deborah stood up and offered her hand to Sennen. 'Congratulations.'

'You don't know what this means to me.' Sennen held out her trembling hand. 'It's a miracle.'

Henry shifted loudly in his seat. 'So that's it, is it?'

Deborah chanced a quick glance at him. 'Yes.'

'What about Ella and me?'

Ella put her hand on his arm. 'Henry, the money is not ours.'

'It shouldn't be hers.' He looked at the faces around him. 'Just saying. I'm allowed to say what I think, am I not?'

Deborah opened her mouth to speak but Sennen beat her

to it. 'I have something to say. To you all. I have been thinking about what to do for the best with this windfall. What my parents would want me to do with it. So here it is.'

Ella looked at both Kit and Henry and smiled. 'You see?' she said. 'I knew Mum would be fair.'

Henry frowned and gave Deborah a filthy glare as if it were her fault.

Sennen went on, 'I hope you will all approve.'

Henry put his elbows on his knees and his head in his hands and groaned. 'Please don't let it be the local cats' home.'

Sennen ignored him and turned her attention to Ellla and Kit. 'I'm thinking of starting a painting school, here in Trevay, in memory of Mum and Poppa. The Tallon School of Art.'

Ella's eyes lit up and her mouth opened in joy. 'Brilliant. That's a wonderful idea.' Sennen held her hand up in front of her to stop her. 'And, I should like it if you ran the school. You and Henry between you.'

Ella sat still, pink-faced with happiness, clutching at Kit's hand. 'Oh, my goodness. Oh. Oh. It's perfect. Mum, thank you. Granny and Poppa would be thrilled.' She turned to Henry. 'Isn't it wonderful, Henry?'

Henry scratched his elbow and pursed his lips. 'I have a job in London. A good one. Why the hell would I want to run an art school?'

Kit had promised himself that he would say nothing in this meeting, he was only there to support Ella, but he couldn't allow Henry to pour cold water on her happiness. 'You could be a sleeping partner.'

'Oh, fuck off,' said Henry, appallingly, 'this is nothing to do with you. You're just my sister's boyfriend.' He stood up, almost knocking his chair over. 'I've had enough of this fairy la la land crap.'

Ella was horrified. 'Henry! Please. Sit down. Just listen. Please.'

Henry looked over at Sennen who was sitting with her eyes firmly on him. He stared back. 'And how long will you be around to help with this school?' he asked. 'Because Ella hasn't the faintest idea of how to run a business.'

Ella bridled. 'I can learn.'

Henry ignored her and directed his anger towards Sennen. 'As soon as things go wrong, when bills aren't paid and the bailiffs come knocking, you'll run away again, won't you?'

Sennen kept calm. 'I never meant to leave you forever.'

He splayed his hands out in front of him and looked bewildered. 'And yet you did.'

'I'm back now,' she answered patiently.

'For how long?' asked Ella, gently.

'I'm not sure.' She twisted her wedding ring.

Henry said quietly, 'And how much will you be taking home to your other family?'

Sennen shrugged. 'Nothing.'

'I don't believe you,' Henry said coldly.

'Please, Henry, I am just trying to do a good thing, the right thing.'

'Why start now?'

'Stop it,' pleaded Ella. 'If it's going to make you so beastly, let Mum have all the money. We have everything we have ever needed: Granny and Poppa's love, their memories and keepsakes, their art. We don't need anything else, least of all their money.'

Henry shouted, 'What about my mortgage? What about you?'

'Stuff it,' said Ella peacefully. 'Mum can do what she wants with it all. She never had what we had.'

Sennen blinked back a torrent of grief. 'And that is the sorrow I carry with me forever. I lost them. I lost you.'

'Oh, this again!' Henry waved her words away.

Ella spoke. 'It's a kind and generous thought, but if it's going to cause this much trouble, no thank you.'

Henry began to laugh. A rumbling laugh that swelled in his diaphragm and soared from his lips. He wiped his eyes. 'This is ridiculous.'

Sennen's mind was whirling. 'But I want to help you.'

Henry scowled at her. 'We'd rather go without, thank you.'

Deflated and confused, Sennen shook her head. 'This is not how I hoped it would turn out. I'm sorry. I've come in all guns blazing and not thought things through at all. Maybe . . . maybe we could let this lie for a bit. Sit on it. Have a think. But I want you to know that this is something I would really like to do for you.'

'Thank you,' said Ella, 'but perhaps it's all just a bit too sudden.'

'Yes. Sorry.' Sennen picked up her bag and took Deborah's hand. 'Thank you. For everything.'

'My pleasure. The money will be in your account by this afternoon.'

Sennen looked at her children. 'May I take you out to lunch?'

'You must be joking,' mumbled Henry, looking at the floor.

Ella glared at him then turned to her mother. 'Yes, please. I would love to have lunch.'

Sennen was grateful. 'And you too of course, Kit?'

Deborah saw them all out as Henry fumed silently.

Deborah walked quietly back to her desk and sat down. 'That was the worst meeting I have ever had.' She kicked her shoes off and drained her coffee. 'Well done.'

'What is she thinking?' Henry was biting his thumb. 'She may as well give it all to the cats' home.'

'Instead of you?'

Henry gave a shamefaced grimace. 'I'm sorry I left you this morning. Without saying goodbye.'

'I didn't notice,' she said coldly.

'Ah. So last night didn't happen?'

'No, it didn't.'

He looked at her lapel. 'Although you do have a tartare sauce stain on your jacket, evidence that it did.'

Deborah placed her hand defensively on the stain.

He looked at the rubbish bin by her desk. 'And a pair of torn tights in your bin.'

'I don't have time for you, Henry. Last night was a mistake.'

'Oh dear. I rather enjoyed it.'

She shot a look at his smugly handsome face and put her head on her desk in shame. 'I have a terrible hangover,' she mumbled.

'Me too.' He stretched his arms above his head. 'If you're not too busy, how about we take the afternoon off and blow away the cobwebs?'

Sennen walked Ella and Kit down to a small fish restaurant on the corner of the harbour. Rosemary had suggested it and she was waiting outside. She greeted Sennen with a kiss. 'How did it go? No Henry with you?'

'No,' said Sennen,

'But you're okay?'

Ella put her arm around Sennen's shoulders and replied, 'Yes. We are okay but ready for a glass of something cold and white.'

The cheery waitress put them at a window table. The day

was warming up and she had opened the sliding windows onto the view of passers-by and the harbour. Sennen took in a lungful of the salty air curling around them.

'I shall miss this when I go back home.'

Ella was dismayed. 'You're not going soon, are you?'

'I have to go back eventually.'

The waitress arrived, causing a distraction as she handed them menus. 'Fish of the day is on the marble counter.' She pointed to a counter in the centre of the room, heaped with ice and an abundance of seafood including lobster and crab.

'Anything to drink?'

Rosemary chose a bottle of Sancerre for the table, then took Sennen to choose her fish.

The restaurant was filling up with more lunch customers. Voices bounced off the white ceramic tiled walls and their chair legs scraped the ceramic floor.

While they were alone, Kit took Ella's hand, 'Ella, why don't we announce our engagement to Sennen today? It'll be some good news for her.'

Ella bit her lip. 'I don't know. I don't want her to think I'm trying to keep her from going back to India . . . although . . .'

Rosemary and Sennen returned. 'We've chosen the monk-fish,' Rosemary told them, 'How about you two?'

'Dover sole, I think,' said Ella, closing the menu.

'Me too,' smiled Kit. He squeezed Ella's hand conspiratorially and readied himself to break their news but the waitress arrived to take their order.

When she had gone, Rosemary wanted to know how the meeting had gone. 'An art school? That's marvellous and would do so much for Trevay,' she exclaimed.

'It feels right,' agreed Sennen, 'only Henry thinks it's a waste of money.'

'I'm sure he'll come round,' said Ella loyally. 'He doesn't like things changing too quickly. It took him a long time to settle in London after leaving here and he had a lot of grief counselling when Granny died.'

'Did he?' asked Sennen. 'Oh, poor boy.' She put her head in her hands. 'I hadn't thought of how Mum's death would affect him. Affect both of you.'

'It was very hard.' Ella thought back. 'Losing Poppa was awful, but we stuck together and Henry helped Granny get through. They were very, very close. When you left, Granny became everything to him. He remembered you, you see. It was easier for me because I didn't.'

A weight of guilt and regret lowered itself onto Sennen's shoulders, pressing down on her neck, pushing her into her chair so that she physically slumped. 'Of course, yes.'

The waitress arrived with the monkfish. 'Roasted monkfish for two with crushed potato and watercress sauce.'

Kit prepared again to announce the news of their engagement, but, with ineffable timing, the waitress reappeared.

'Two Dover soles with buttered leeks and shrimps.'

She placed them in front of Kit and Ella and standing back, clasped her hands. 'Is there anything more I can get you? Some bread? More water?' She looked at them. 'No? Well, call me if you need anything.'

Sennen had lost interest in her food. 'Ella, I can never explain how sorry I am to have made such a mess and taken so many wrong turnings. If I could turn back time I would never have left you. Sorry is just not a big enough word. All I can say is that I am here for both of you now, for as long as either of you need me or want me.'

Ella's eyes began to brim with tears. 'Don't, Mum. What's done is done and I want to get to know you now. Properly. Henry will come around.'

'But I have missed so much. Birthdays, Christmases. Mum and Poppa.'

Kit took his moment. 'Sennen, you haven't missed it all. Ella and I are engaged to be married . . . if you don't mind?'

29

Agra, 2010

Every time Sennen admired her curtains she couldn't help but remember Kafir. He was very handsome and his courteous nature and charm were very attractive. If she wanted a man, he was certainly the type she would go for but a man was the last thing she wanted. She was happy as she was.

This morning she was going down to the market to buy some trims and tape for a set of curtains she was making for a new client. She picked up her cotton shoulder-bag, threw a shawl over her shoulder and let herself out of her room.

She wondered if she should knock to see if Tanvi needed anything brought in, then decided against it. It was early and Tanvi liked a lie-in.

Sennen stepped out into the heat of the morning sun. The market was already set up and looked fresh and inviting in the shimmering haze. She stepped off the uneven kerb and walked into the heart of the stalls. A couple of blond dogs with curly tails trotted behind her. They walked as if doing dressage; slightly sideways, crossing their back paws with each step. She addressed them. 'Good morning, girls, and how are your puppies today?' The smaller dog with long nipples looked at her with expressive eyes. 'Hungry? Shall I get you something? Come on, then.'

The dogs followed Sennen, as they did most mornings, to a busy stall selling pouches of pet food.

'Namaste,' the young man behind the wooden crates greeted her. 'More food for the dogs? Every day you feed them. You are their mother.' He smiled his toothy grin.

'Namaste.' She put her hands together and nodded her head in respect. 'I can't let them go hungry. Not with their puppies.' She reached for her purse as he handed her the usual four pouches of food.

'Chicken chunks in gravy. Very delicious.' He laughed and licked his lips.

'Their favourite. Thank you.' The dogs scampered off behind the stall into the shade and she followed. There was a sheet of tattered canvas hanging from a wall by two nails. The two dogs immediately wriggled inside their shabby home where Sennen could hear the puppies whining. She knelt down and lifted the canvas.

'Here you are, then.' She opened the pouches and the dogs waited patiently as she emptied the food into two plastic bowls that she had put down weeks ago. 'There now. Dinner is served.' She ruffled their ears as they tucked in, and counted the bundle of puppies mewling in the dark recess of their home. All six were still there. 'See you tomorrow, girls.'

She replaced the canvas flap and stood up. First job of the day accomplished.

She walked back into the market and on through the teeming tide of shoppers who were pushing each other along or swerving to avoid those who had stopped to inspect a display of green beans, ripe tomatoes, mangoes or herbs.

Women in jewel-coloured saris, men in white shirts, ill-fitting trousers and dusty sandals, children laughing and twisting amongst familiar legs. This was her place.

Turning left, leaving the human river behind, she entered a more shaded, cooler part of the market. It was less busy and all the nicer for it. Here there were proper shops with solid walls and shuttered fronts. It was the haberdashery quarter of Agra.

Several of the shopkeepers greeted her by name. She stopped to swap pleasantries but headed on, knowing exactly where she wanted to be. And there it was.

'Namaste, Mr Kuranam.'

The proprietor, rotund and serious, looked up, smiled and clasped his hands to his belly. 'Namaste. You have come. I am keeping some very special fabric for you.'

'Did it arrive?' she asked excitedly.

He wobbled his head. 'From Jaipur. It is the very best. Let me show you.'

He walked into the murky depths of the shop, past the shelves bulging with bolts of exotic fabrics. She followed him.

He pulled out a large roll and thumped it down on his cutting table. The noise was muted, absorbed by the density of material around them. He unrolled it with pride. 'Look.' He rubbed the end between his fingers. 'Pure cotton and linen.'

She did the same, but knew not to look too impressed. 'How much?'

'I give you very good price.' He wobbled his head and smiled. 'Very good.'

'Mr Kuranam, you know I am a poor woman.'

He laughed. 'But the lady you are making these curtains for is a rich woman.'

'But if I charge her too much, she won't use me any more and I will be poorer still.' She grinned. 'And I won't be able to be your best customer.'

'Oh, Miss Sennen, you are naughty lady. Let me think.' He took a pencil from the pocket of his immaculately ironed shirt. 'How many metres?'

An enjoyable amount of bartering ensued, during which he tried to persuade her to buy several metres of Black Watch tartan – 'Queen Victoria's favourite' – but Sennen stuck with her original purchase and got him to throw in thread, lining and tape.

Mr Kuranam made a huge show of flapping open a large carrier bag and putting everything inside. 'You will never make me rich, Miss Sennen.'

'I don't believe you,' she laughed, momentarily losing concentration as she backed out of the shop. 'See you soon.' She fell, catching her foot awkwardly and falling hard on her left hip and elbow.

Mr Kuranam moved to comfort her. 'Come. Sit in my shop. A glass of water? Are you hurt?'

Sennen took his helping arm and checked herself over. 'I'm fine. A bit bruised, probably, but I'm fine. Thank you.'

'Would you like a chai? There is the café on the corner.'

She recollected seeing it. 'Yes, I think that would be a good idea.'

He insisted on helping her cross the road and finding her a seat in the shade. In rapid Indian he ordered and paid for a chai.

'You will be okay now. Just the ticket?'

Sennen gave a small laugh. She loved the way many Indians still used British idioms. 'Yes. Just the ticket. Thank you, Mr Kuranam.'

When he was satisfied that she was absolutely fine, and distracted because there were two potential customers hovering by his shop, he left her to her chai.

Her hip was rather sore but undamaged, she was certain. She lifted her sleeve and checked her elbow. The skin was scuffed and a small bruise was blooming, but otherwise there was nothing to write home about. She pulled her sleeve down and picked up her drink.

'Good morning,' said a vaguely familiar voice.

She looked up. Standing with the sun against his back, forming a golden halo around his head, was Kafir.

'Hello,' she said.

'Are you okay? I saw you looking at your elbow.'

'Oh, it's nothing – I fell out of a shop. Literally. But I'm fine.'

'Would you like to have it checked with the doctor?'

'Absolutely not. Chai is the best medicine.' She held her cup up to show him.

'May I join you?' he asked. 'I was wondering if I would see you today – I am on my way to visit Auntie.'

'What a coincidence.' She smiled, moving her large carrier bag from the empty chair beside her. He shouted an order for lemonade and sat down.

'You are up early,' he said.

'It's a habit now. I can't sleep in. It gives me a headache.'

'Me too. But it means I go to bed too early. I am not much of a night owl.'

'Me neither.'

Kafir's lemonade arrived and, as he took a sip, she took a

sly glance at him. Today he was wearing a pale blue turban, navy polo shirt and chinos. His dark beard framed his lips and accentuated their fullness. He was lovely. 'So, what have you been buying?' he asked, putting his glass back into its china saucer with a clatter.

'Buying more curtain fabric, but for a client this time.'

'May I see?'

Sennen opened the bag and he peered in. 'Not my cup of tea,' he said.

'Nor mine. A bit too overpowering.'

'You know that Auntie says I need new curtains?'

'But you don't think so?'

'I didn't, until I saw how nice yours looked the other evening.'

'Well, if ever you need some, I'd be happy to do them for you. Mates rates.'

'Mates rates? Lovely jubbly. That's funny. Do you like that comedy programme?'

'*Only Fools and Horses*? Gosh, I haven't seen it for years but my father adored it.'

'Do you remember the one where the man falls through the bar? It is very funny.'

She laughed 'Oh yes! David Jason. He's a Sir now.'

'The Queen knighted him? She must like the programme too.'

'I can imagine her and the corgis sitting down to watch it, can't you, gin and tonic in one hand.'

'Crown in the other.' Kafir laughed louder.

'Are you a royalist?' Sennen asked.

'Not really, but there is something very charming and old-fashioned about them, don't you think?'

'They aren't my thing.' Sennen stirred her chai.

'Auntie loves them.'

Sennen exhaled loudly. 'Don't I know it. I've seen her commemorative plates.'

'You are honoured.'

'So you are on your way to see her now?'

He looked surprised, as if he had forgotten, 'Ah yes! I shall walk you there, if you would like the company.'

She had never walked through the market with a man before. Handsome or otherwise. Maybe it was her imagination, but it seemed as if, walking together, they drew respectful glances from the passers-by. Women certainly noticed him and she wondered if, when they slid their eyes to her, it was in admiration, envy or surprise that she could walk with such a man.

As he talked by her side, she felt different. Taller. Prettier. She listened to his stories of growing up on this street and the history behind some of the older buildings. She hung on to all that he said and tucked them carefully away in a new box in her brain, to bring out and lovingly examine later.

Finally, they got to her building and they walked up the stairs to her landing. 'Let me put your bag in your room, and then I shall take up no more of your time.'

She fumbled for her key in her bag and he gently took it from her and unlocked her door. 'Where would you like your shopping?'

'Just there. On the floor. Thanks.'

He gave her her key and they said goodbye.

She watched him cross the wooden floor to Tanvi's room opposite.

His long, lean, elegant body bewitched her.

'Bye,' she said.

He turned and smiled at her. 'Bye.' Then he knocked at Tanvi's door and Sennen closed hers.

She couldn't wait for chai at Tanvi's the following Wednesday, but Tanvi didn't mention him and Sennen's natural reticence made it impossible to ask.

She found herself not leaving the house too often or for too long, in case he came calling. At least, it meant that she finished making the new curtains quickly, much to her client's happiness.

She thought about Kafir most of the time and was irritated that she knew so little about him. He was an economics graduate and a teacher, but where did he live? And, the stomach-churning question, did he have a girlfriend?

A month passed. She continued her weekly routine of chai with Tanvi, cooked a small dinner party for a few of the house residents and fed the stray dogs and growing puppies who were almost weaned. Of Kafir, though, there was nothing.

It was Tanvi who eventually brought him up. 'Kafir has been asking after you.'

Sennen's grip on the kettle almost slipped. 'Oh yes?' she said carefully.

'I have been telling him for weeks to ask you about his curtains but he is too shy.'

'Oh.' Sennen couldn't hide her disappointment.

Tanvi looked very put out. 'Don't you want the work?'

'I do.'

'Are you too busy?'

'No.'

'Then I shall tell him we are coming over to measure up.'

Sennen was nervous. 'When?'

'This afternoon. It's perfect. Wednesday's are his afternoon off.'

Sennen was again alert, 'Oh. I didn't know teachers have half-days.'

'Not normally. He's a part-time teacher.' Tanvi shook her head. 'He also works with children who have suffered emotional trauma.'

'Oh.' Sennen was surprised. 'Like a therapist?'

'A very good one,' Tanvi said with pride.

'Yes, I would think so,' said Sennen, her brain reordering and shifting all the mental files she had on him. She pictured him surrounded by smiling children, so grateful for his ministry. She smoothed her hair and smiled to herself.

Tanvi's hawk eyes caught her. 'Does that make him attractive to you?'

Sennen's cheeks burned and she answered primly, 'No. Not that he's not handsome, I mean, but it's an attractive quality in a man . . . to like children.'

'Ah yes.' Tanvi gave Sennen a knowing look. 'He would make an excellent husband and father.'

Sennen tutted. 'Don't start that again.'

'Start what?' Tanvi was all innocence.

'You know.'

They took a tuk-tuk to Kafir's home, which was a little out of the city on the road to Mangaleshwar Temple. Sennen didn't take tuk-tuks very often due to the cost and also because she enjoyed walking, but this trip with Tanvi was a treat. Sitting on the narrow back seat, pressed against her friend, with the breeze whipping her hair, she delighted in the exhilaration. The driver, she hoped highly skilled, sped through narrow gaps in the traffic that made her hold her breath and squeeze her eyes shut. He stopped for nothing, his thumb firmly pressed on the horn.

Hanging from his rear-view mirror and across the sun visor he had secured bright pink tinsel and golden tassels. Sennen remembered the fairs in the green fields of Trevay, the spinning lights and gaily painted carousel horses. All she needed to complete the picture was to have the driver shout, 'Hold on tight, here we go!'

'I'm loving this,' she shouted to Tanvi. 'So much fun.'

Tanvi patted Sennen's knee. 'You are too easily pleased.'

At last they pulled up in a quiet street dotted with small bungalows.

'This is Kafir's. Ignore his décor. You can work on that later,' said Tanvi climbing the two shallow steps to the verandah.

Sennen had butterflies waking in her stomach. What was she doing? Would he think her a stalker?

Tanvi knocked loudly, her tiny fist belying its power.

Sennen was ready to turn and flee when Kafir opened the door.

'Auntie.' He opened his arms, his face wreathed in smiles and hugged her. 'What a surprise.' He looked over Tanvi's shoulder and saw Sennen. She thought she saw his smile drop just for a split second, then he said, 'And Sennen. Welcome to my humble home.'

But it was humble only in so much as it was uncluttered. He led them through a small hall and into a simple sitting room with shuttered windows, two inviting rattan chairs, a table and a door opening onto a courtyard which was filled with pots of exotic fruit trees, flowering plants and herbs. In the sunshine there was a wicker lounger, with an open book lying beside it, and an empty glass.

'We've interrupted you,' said Sennen apologetically.

'Not at all. Let me make you a drink. I have Coca Cola which Auntie does not approve of but I love. Would you like one?'

'I would love one.' She smiled.

'And you, Auntie?' he said.

'Do you have 7 Up?'

'I do.'

'Then I shall have that.'

'It is as bad as Coca-Cola. Tut tut,' he said, as a parent might to a toddler. 'Are you sure?'

'It is less trouble for you than to find teacups.'

'That is very thoughtful.' He looked at Sennen, bringing her in on the joke. 'Make yourselves comfortable and I will bring the drinks and then you can tell me why you are here.'

He was an easy host, making his guests feel comfortable and important. He asked after Sennen's sore hip and elbow and Tanvi berated them both for not telling her about the fall and their meeting. He talked a little about his work and how few resources or desires there were to help children with their mental health. 'The point is,' he concluded, 'none of us is perfect. We are all a little mad. And we all need a little help at times.' He looked at Tanvi. 'Except my auntie. She is perfect and is right about everything, isn't that so, Auntie?'

'I'm glad you see that.' She nodded. 'Which is why I have brought Sennen to your home. She will make you new curtains.'

'I have shutters,' he said.

'They don't keep the heat in when it's cold.'

'Hello, this is India,' he said.

'You need curtains.' She folded her arms and stared at him.

He looked at Sennen. 'Apparently, I need curtains. What would you suggest?'

'I like your shutters.'

'He needs curtains,' said Tanvi obstinately.

'Well . . .' Sennen thought, then, 'A light muslin perhaps? To diffuse the light?'

'Perfect,' agreed Tanvi. 'And what about chair covers?'

'I don't do upholstery.'

'Cushions, then?' Tanvi insisted.

'Erm . . .' Sennen glanced at Kafir for help. 'Do you want cushions?'

'No, but I would like a rug.'

'I'm not an interior designer.' Sennen was embarrassed. 'I just make curtains.'

'But your flat is so lovely,' Tanvi interjected. 'Isn't it, Kafir.'

'I remember it being very charming and welcoming.' He thought back. 'The curtains were good and your balcony very pretty.'

'Thank you,' said Sennen.

'So, Saturday morning early you will go shopping for curtains and a rug,' Tanvi declared. 'I'm glad that is settled.'

'Is it?' laughed Kafir. 'Sennen may have plans of her own.'

Tanvi sniffed. 'Believe me, she has nothing else to do.'

'Excuse me,' said Sennen, 'I do have a life.'

'So tell me?' Tanvi challenged her. 'What are you doing on Saturday?'

'As it happens,' Sennen said, 'I am free this Saturday.'

Tanvi looked at Kafir in triumph. 'You see? Auntie is always right.'

At dawn the next day, Sennen watched as the sun crept over the wall of her balcony. She had lain in bed for hours, thinking about Kafir and how happy she was to be spending the morning with him. Of course, she told herself, he wouldn't be thinking the same. He was doing what his auntie expected of him and he was too kind to refuse her. He was not interested in her romantically. Why would he be? A thirty-four-year-old spinster who could sew curtains was hardly a great catch. But he had smiled at her while he'd been teasing Tanvi and been so attentive when he had walked her home through the market that time.

She threw back her sheet angrily. 'I am just the person who is making him curtains he doesn't want, and helping him choose a rug I know nothing about.' She swung her legs onto the floor. 'Now get up and shut up.'

She went to the bathroom on the landing that she shared with Tanvi. She showered and washed her hair, pinching some of Tanvi's excellent conditioning hair oil.

Back in her room she sat on her balcony, with tea, bread and jam, brushing her hair dry until it gleamed. It was past her shoulder blades now with flecks of grey at the temples, just as her mother's had been when she was a child. She stopped brushing and caught her breath. What were her parents doing right now? She looked over at her clock. They were about four and a half hours behind so it would be the middle of the night for them. They'd be in bed, slumbering peacefully next to each other. Then she thought of her children.

Henry would be almost nineteen, now. Probably at university. Maybe studying art. As a toddler he had always loved painting with her and Adela. She wondered if she would recognise the loving little boy who was now a man.

And Ella? She was seventeen, the age when Sennen had already run away. What had her parents told them about her?

Had they heard all the little stories of her as young girl? Did they think of her fondly? She closed her eyes and sent fervent waves of love to them all. 'Stay safe. Please stay safe.'

She heard a dog bark below. There were her two little canine friends promenading with their puppies, teaching them where best to scavenge for food. She called to them and they looked up. She dropped several pieces of her breakfast bread down and watched as they tussled for them before sauntering off, tails up and curly.

30

Kafir arrived on time, with Tanvi standing across the landing, checking that the plan was going as she wished.

'You both look very nice,' she said approvingly.

'Auntie, we are going to buy a rug, not go to a wedding,' he told her firmly.

Tanvi raised her eyebrows. 'That is a funny analogy to use. Don't you think, Sennen?'

'I think you need to stop being naughty,' Sennen said.

Kafir laughed his deep laugh and held his arm out for her. 'Take my arm and let us leave the naughty Auntie to meddle with someone else's life.'

Sennen tucked her arm through his and Tanvi watched them go and called after them, 'Be sure to show me the rug when you get back!'

The market on Saturday, even this early, was already packed. Sennen allowed herself to be guided by Kafir as he kept her arm close to his chest. It took longer than usual to get to the haberdashery quarter but when they did, the cool shade revived them.

Mr Kuranam welcomed her warmly. 'And who is this gentleman?' he asked, studying Kafir from top to toe.

'Namaste, Mr Kuranam,' Kafir replied, very formal. 'I am Miss Sennen's client, Kafir Singh.'

Mr Kuranam held a hand up in apology. 'A client! I am so sorry to embarrass. Miss Sennen is a good friend. Please, come in and tell me what you are looking for.'

Kafir chose quickly with Sennen's guidance. A linen voile that would drape well. 'Perfect choice, Mr Singh,' smiled Mr Kuranam, clearly not convinced that the relationship was solely a business one. 'I am certain Miss Sennen will make a good home for you.'

Kafir hesitated slightly but thanked him.

Sennen hurried them out of the shop. 'I'm so sorry, Kafir.'

'What for?'

'Mr Kuranam's presumptions.'

Kafir shrugged, 'It seems that a lot of people are making presumptions for us.'

Sennen giggled nervously, kept her head down, and, taking his arm, allowed him again to guide her to the rug shop.

They were invited in by a young man who offered them a seat before asking exactly what they were looking for. Kafir was stumped. 'I don't exactly know.'

The young man turned to Sennen for help.

'Well, let's start with colour,' she said. 'What is your favourite colour, Kafir?'

'Blue.'

'Dark? Light? Aqua?'

He thought. 'Dark?'

The young assistant sprang into action. 'I have good dark-blue rugs. Let me show you.'

Within minutes at least six beautiful rugs were unrolled in front of them.

Kafir was lost. 'Maybe they are too dark?'

'Let me get lighter ones.' The boy scampered off and returned with more rugs, this time in light blue. He unfurled them with pride before Kafir.

Kafir inclined his head in a suggestion that he liked them. 'What do you think, Sennen?' he asked.

'I think I prefer these, but with new drapes and your rattan furniture, maybe a cream or gold design would be nice?'

He stroked his beard. 'Maybe.'

'I get them,' said the eager young man.

Eventually Kafir chose a dusty pink pattern with a rich cream-coloured background.

'Very good choice,' said the boy. 'Taj Design. Agra knotted. Very nice rug.'

He and Kafir haggled over the price and, when both were happy, the deal was struck. The rug would be delivered that afternoon.

Kafir checked his watch. 'Time for a coffee?'

They walked to a small park where a café was set up in the shade of a grove of Banyan trees. Kafir ordered two coffees from the slender teenaged girl who was serving the tables.

'I have enjoyed this morning. Thank you,' Kafir said, stretching his legs out in the dust.

'Me too,' said Sennen, draping her shawl over her hair. 'The rug is very beautiful.'

They drank their coffee in comfortable silence, neither

feeling the need to talk. Sennen watched the sparrows hopping under the tables, pecking for crumbs.

'In Cornwall, where I grew up, we have lots of sparrows. My mother has a bird table outside the kitchen window. My father calls them Spadgers, I don't know why.'

'Do you know we have robins in India?'

'Really? I didn't think robins migrated.'

'Not your robins. Ours are called Indian Robins but they don't have red breasts. They are dark all over but quite tame.'

'Poppa, my father, had a tame robin in our garden. He would come to my father and take crumbs of cheese from his hand.'

'That's nice. We had a tame tiger who would take steak from my father's hand.'

'Really?'

'No. I am joking.'

She laughed. 'For a moment there . . .'

'Tell me about your home,' he asked.

She described Trevay and its harbour, the fishing boats and the hard life of the fishermen. She told him about her days of sun and rain on the beach, and the childhood of paddling, then swimming and eventually graduating to surfing. She made him laugh, telling him about the terrible things she did at school and the punishments that she received. And, finally, she described her house, her parents and their work with the art students.

'I would like to see Cornwall.' Kafir said. 'When I was in London, studying, there were students who talked about it, had holidays there, but we Sikhs get a little hydrophobic around the sea, or even the rain.'

'Why?'

He pointed at his head. 'The turban is not waterproof.'

She laughed. 'Do you never swim?'

'Yes, but maybe with something on that doesn't mind getting wet.'

'I never thought about that. But you take it off to sleep? And shower?'

'Of course.'

'I like your turban. It suits you.'

He inclined his head self-deprecatingly. 'Well, thank you. And may I say I have noticed you have very shiny hair?'

She reached up and felt it. 'I have something to confess. I sometimes pinch a little of Tanvi's conditioning oil from the bathroom.'

'I shall have to call the police immediately . . . or I can take you to the shop that sells all sorts of hair products. You can buy some for yourself and some for Auntie too.'

When they got to the shop, Sennen was enchanted by the toiletries. She bought two new bars of sandalwood soap, some body moisturiser and the hair conditioner for herself and Tanvi. At the till the assistant carefully wrapped and tied each purchase and asked Sennen if she'd like to buy some cologne for her husband.

Sennen flushed and was relieved that Kafir was on the other side of the shop. She whispered, 'We are not married. He is my friend.'

But the assistant was not to be put off. 'Can you not buy a friend a small gift? I have very special gentlemen's cologne on offer. See?' She squirted a tester onto Sennen's hand. 'Smell.'

Sennen put her nose to her hand and inhaled. It was lovely. The freshness of lime with a base of sandalwood and musk. She bought it.

*

The walk home was quite long but Sennen's senses were alive to everything she saw and heard. The birds in the trees, the warmth of the sun, the sound and feel of Kafir walking next to her.

Back at her house, Tanvi's door flew open as they reached the top of the stairs. 'Successful shopping?'

'Very,' smiled Kafir. 'Have you been waiting to catch us?'

Tanvi was all innocence. 'Not at all, but I was thinking you might be hungry?'

'Not at all,' said Sennen as Kafir said, simultaneously, 'Starving.'

That was all the encouragement Tanvi needed to produce plates of tasty food with fresh fruit juice.

Eventually, Kafir said he had to leave or he would miss the delivery of the rug. Taking their leave of Tanvi, he walked Sennen across the landing to her door. 'Thank you.'

'I haven't done anything.'

'But you will make my beautiful curtains and you have given me a happy day.'

'You have given me a happy day too.' She rummaged in her bag. 'I have a small, very small, gift for you.' She handed him the wrapped bottle of cologne. 'I hope you like it.'

'May I open it now?'

'Yes.'

His slender brown fingers with their well-shaped nails undid the string and unfolded the paper. He took the bottle out and read the label. 'But this is too nice.'

'Smell it. If you don't like it I won't be upset.'

He twisted the top open and put his nose to the glass. 'It's very nice.'

'Really? It was the woman in the shop; it was on offer and it might be like loo cleaner . . .'

He put his hand to her cheek. 'Stop talking. It is beautiful and it is kind of you.'

He looked into her eyes and she felt his gaze deep inside her. She closed her eyes and turned her cheek further into his hand.

'Now I must go.' He dropped his hand.

'Of course. The rug.'

'Well, goodbye – and thank you.' He made a small bow then turned and walked down the stairs.

She stood rooted to the floor. The skin of her cheek that he had so gently held felt cool. She ran her fingers over it with happiness and hope.

The following morning Tanvi knocked on her door. 'I have had a phone call from Kafir. He wants us both to go to see his new rug and he will be cooking us lunch. I have said yes, so hurry. We will get a tuk-tuk in half an hour.'

Sennen was filled with energy and excitement and was pacing the landing impatiently before Tanvi was ready.

'You look very pretty,' Tanvi said. 'What have you done to yourself?'

'Nothing.'

'Hm. Something has happened. You are changed.' She screwed up her eyes and peered at Sennen. 'Yes, there is a change in you.'

Kafir opened his door looking a little frazzled. 'I have moved the rug this way and that and I still don't know if it is right. Come and see.'

Under her bare feet, Sennen felt the softness of the wool. 'It's gorgeous – and perfectly placed. Tanvi, what do you think of the colour?'

Tanvi was pushing her toes, with sensual delight, into the deep pile of the rug. 'I was sure he would go for blue. He always liked blue since he was a little boy. But this I like.'

Kafir blew his cheeks out in relief. 'That is good. Now all you have to do is like my lunch. Are you ready?'

He had made a beautiful vegetable curry with fluffy rice and chapatti.

'My auntie's recipe,' he admitted, smiling at Tanvi. 'I have never cooked it before.'

'He has never cooked for a girl before,' said Tanvi.

'Yes, I have,' he protested.

'When?'

'In London.'

'Ha!' said Tanvi. 'When you were a student. That doesn't count.'

'Well, it's delicious,' Sennen said dipping her chapatti in the sauce. 'And thank you for having me.'

'You should invite him round for supper in return,' nudged Tanvi. 'She cooks well, Kafir.'

'I would like that very much,' said Kafir looking at Sennen. 'If you would invite me?'

And that was the true start of their courtship. He would finish work and come to her at least three times a week, always leaving by ten o'clock. It was two months before he kissed her and a year before they gently made love. Sennen had never known the true tenderness that a man could show a woman.

On her birthday he promised her a mystery tuk-tuk tour. She had to meet him, just before dawn, outside her house where he would be waiting.

It was cold as she stepped outside, wrapped in a large shawl, and the birds were starting to wake up. He was there, as promised, and helped her into the tuk-tuk.

As the little motorbike engine started, he put her hand in his, his warmth spreading into her. 'Happy birthday.'

She guessed where they were going when the driver turned in to the road leading up to the Taj Mahal.

Kafir paid the driver then helped Sennen out. Leading her under the gated arch and into the perfect peace of the gardens, he pointed to the horizon and the glow of the promised sunrise. Turning her to face him he said, 'This sun brings with it the day when it is in your power to make me the happiest of men.'

She could hardly believe what he was saying. She put both hands to her mouth.

He knelt down. 'You know I am in love with you, and you have told me that you love me in return. I would be most honoured if you would say yes to allowing me to be your husband.'

Sennen could not speak. This man, this wonderful, gentle, loving man wanted to marry her? She swallowed hard and looked deep into his upturned, honest eyes. 'Yes. Yes, please.'

He stood up and took her in his arms. 'Thank you. Thank you.'

'No,' she laughed, 'thank you.'

Tanvi came with them to Jaipur to ease the meeting between Sennen and Kafir's parents. There was some disappointment that he was marrying a non-Sikh, but when they saw how happy he was, and how charming Sennen was, they took her to their hearts.

Her new in-laws could not have been happier with their beloved son's choice. Kafir, at thirty-seven, had had few serious girlfriends and Sennen, now thirty-six, was unusual in that she had not been married before and, according to Tanvi, led a modest and boyfriend-free life.

The wedding was to be a quiet one, a civil ceremony to be followed by a more traditional wedding in the Gurdwara or place of worship.

A few days before the ceremony, Sennen was invited to meet with the Granthi, a woman who would officiate at the wedding. She was a handsome, devout woman with kohl-rimmed eyes and a darkly glossy plait.

'Do I have to become a Sikh?' Sennen asked anxiously.

'Only God can decide if we are true Sikhs, so no. Do you believe in God?' The Granthis asked.

'I think so. My family were not very churchy, though. I suppose I believe that God is within us all.'

The Granthi smiled. 'Sikhs do not show other religions in a bad light. We believe that there is one God and we see no racial or gender bias. We stay humble and honest. As Guru Nanak himself said, "I am not good, but nobody is bad."' She held her hands together as if in prayer and blessed Sennen. 'May you and your husband walk the rest of your lives together on one path. May there be openness and truthfulness, with no secrets to come between you.'

When the Granthi had finished, Sennen bowed her head in deference and the woman showed her out.

Kafir, waiting outside for her, waved. She waved back trying not to think what the Granthis had said about no secrets coming between them. Gradually, a dark stone of dread, so long and deeply hidden, began to glow white hot within her.

The memory, even now, scorched her as she watched Ella and Kit's glowing faces in the Cornish café.

'Engaged? That's wonderful,' she said.

Rosemary was calling for a bottle of celebratory champagne.

Sennen felt the wet tears on her cheeks. She was crying for herself.

'Oh, Mum,' said Ella pushing her chin up and her lips down, 'you sentimental old thing. Here.' Ella brushed Sennen's tears away with her fingers. 'You are happy for us, aren't you? I know this is all going very fast for you but Kit and I have been together for over six months now and I love him so much.'

'It's wonderful, darling.' She gulped. 'I wish you every happiness. Both of you.'

Somewhere a phone began to ring. It was coming from Sennen's bag down by her feet. 'Just a moment.' She retrieved the phone and checked who was calling. Kafir. Had she willed him to ring her. 'Hello? Kafir?'

'Yes. How are you?' he asked, the line so clear he might have been in the room next door.

'Where are you?' she asked, surging with the hope that he may actually be next door.

'At home. Just giving Aali and Sabu their dinner.'

Ella gave her mother a questioning look, mouthing at her, 'You okay?' Sennen nodded and pointed towards the front door before, getting up and leaving the noisy room. 'Are the children okay?' she asked, hoping that one of them hadn't been taken ill.

'Fine. They are fine.'

'That's good.' She stepped out on to the narrow pavement and leant against the old bowed wall. 'Have they asked about me?'

'A little. But no trouble. What is happening with you?'

'I've met Ella and Henry.'

'And?'

'Ella has just told me she's getting married. To a very nice boy called Kit.'

'I wish them well. What about Henry?'

Sennen burst into tears. 'I've mucked everything up. I should never have opened that bloody letter. I should never have told you. Never have come here. Henry hates me. And *you* hate me.' She was crying loudly.

'I don't hate you,' Kafir said softly. 'I think maybe you hate yourself.'

'Yes, I do. I've made a mess of my whole life even when I've tried to do the right thing. And I miss you and I miss the children.' She wiped her running nose on the back of her hand.

'When is the wedding?' he asked.

'I don't know. I think they've only just decided to get married.'

'Would you like me to come?'

Sennen was aware of two women on the opposite pavement watching her, wondering whether they ought to see if she was okay. She gave them a small thumbs up and a watery smile before turning her face to the wall, 'I . . . I don't know. It may be too soon. Ella would be fine, I think, but it might be too much for Henry.'

'I see.'

'It's not that I don't want you here . . .' She heard the bleat in her voice. 'I miss you. I love you so much.'

'And we miss you.'

'And I would love you all to be here, Kafir. I need you. I need to see you. All three of you. Please, please, you are my husband, I don't want this to break us.'

'I think you should work out the situation you are in with Henry and Ella first, before we begin thinking of our marriage.' She heard a child's voice calling him. 'I must go, Sabu is calling me. I will send him and Aali your love. Now I must go. Goodbye, Sennen.'

'Kafir?' she said weakly, but he had already ended the call.

31

Pendruggan, 2018

'Way-hay,' shouted Rosemary as the bottle of house champagne went off with a loud pop. 'You're just in time!'

Sennen, arriving back at the table having tried to repair her face, put her shoulders back and decided to be the happiest of mums, for Ella's' sake.

'Get me a glass,' she ordered.

The other diners, couples old and young, families the same, watched and couldn't help but be cheered by the obvious happiness emerging in front of them. Sennen took her filled glass and raised it to the room. 'Please celebrate the engagement of my elder daughter, Ella Tallon to the handsome Kit . . .' She realised she didn't know his surname.

'Beauchamp,' Kit said helpfully.

Sennen inclined her head towards him in thanks. 'Yes, Kit Beauchamp. He is to marry my daughter, and I couldn't be more pleased. Would you be kind enough to raise your glasses . . .' She acknowledged the beer and wine drinkers. 'Your beakers . . .' She smiled at the younger children. 'And your cups . . .' She winked at the older customers. 'And now – to Ella and Kit!'

The room responded with a cheering, 'Ella and Kit!'

'Thank you.' Sennen sat down. 'Well, that's got you two off to a good start I should say.'

Gradually the champagne bottle emptied and Sennen insisted on settling the bill. Finally, Kit and Ella said their grateful goodbyes, leaving Rosemary and Sennen among the debris of the table.

'Cocktail?' asked Rosemary after Sennen's credit card had been returned.

'Why not? I have had more to drink on my return to Trevay than I've had in sixteen years in India, and I like it.'

She couldn't have told you what time she got back to White Water that night, other than that it was very late.

She peeled off her clothes and dropped them on the floor, then in the bathroom, held the sink unsteadily with one hand as she cleaned her teeth with the other. Her make-up she ignored. In bed, she pulled the duvet up to her chin and fell asleep immediately.

She dreamt of the day she had told Kafir the truth about herself.

She had got home after collecting Aali and Sabu from school, to find the multi-addressed envelope in the hall. Her heart plummeted when she saw the postmark: Cornwall.

It could only be bad news, she knew. Mum or Poppa must be ill?

In the dream, she relived the moment she had taken the

letter into her bathroom and locked the door to read it. The torment of grief that overwhelmed her, reading of her parent's deaths, hit her again. She saw Kafir's beautiful face switch from love to betrayal as she told him the truth.

He had shaken his head, disbelieving her.

'How could you deny the existence of your own children? To me?'

He had stood tall over her as she knelt at his feet in supplication.

'I thought I knew you,' he said, barely believing. 'What else do you have in your box of lies?'

She grabbed his knees. 'Nothing. I promise. Please, Kafir.' But he had swiped her away as if she were nothing more than a fly. 'Go home. To Cornwall. Make your peace. Apologise to your children and hope that they forgive you. But know that to find your past you may have lost your future.' His words were like ice and he chilled her blood as he continued, 'I must protect Aali and Sabu. I will tell them you have returned to England and we don't know when you will return. Tonight you will leave this house. Stay in a hotel, if you must, but you must go.'

She had woken sweating and shouting, 'No Kafir. No.'

She sat up in bed, alarmed, and tried to steady her breathing. She took a gulp of the water from the glass on her nightstand.

She knew what she had to do, and by God she would do it.

She was up early and made sure she was looking her best. Downstairs, she had the briefest of breakfasts before dialling Ella's number.

'Hello,' answered Ella, sleepily.

'Hi, darling. It's Sennen – Mum.'

'Hi. You're up early.'

'Early bird catches the worm and all that, so I wondered, if you were doing nothing else today . . .' She took a deep breath to keep her resolve strong. 'If you might like to go wedding dress shopping. With me?'

'Oh.' Ella sounded unsure.

'If you're busy, I quite understand,' said Sennen, backing off.

'No, that would be great. I haven't even thought about it to be honest. We haven't even set a date.'

Sennen heard Kit's voice, drowsy and mumbling, 'Who is it?'

Then Ella, speaking off the microphone, 'It's Mum.'

'Is she okay?'

'Yes, she wants to take me wedding dress shopping.'

'Nice.'

Ella came back louder again. 'I'd love to, Mum.'

'Any shops you can recommend?'

'There's a shop in Truro that someone told me about.'

'Well then, let's go to Truro. I can pick you up from your house?'

'Okay.' Ella reeled off the address. 'Marguerite Cottage to the right of the church, down a little drive. Can you give me an hour to get ready?'

The next hour was sixty minutes of impatient agitation for Sennen. She walked to the newsagents, bought herself a paper, sat in a coffee shop, ordered a cappuccino and attempted the crossword. She checked her phone, strummed her fingers, paid the bill and was finally on her way to Pendruggan.

As she drove into the heart of the village she could see why Ella loved it. The village green was like something out of a children's picture book. There was the large farmhouse with its barns and milking parlour, the village stores next to the church and a row of attractive cottages, maybe two hundred years old, with slate roofs, well-tended gardens and pastel-coloured front doors.

She found Marguerite Cottage and, as she parked, Ella came bounding out of the front door, her red curls streaming behind her. She jumped into the passenger seat. 'This is so unexpected and all the more exciting for it,' she exclaimed. 'Thank you, Mum. I never thought this would happen. Me and you. Wedding dress shopping!'

Sennen began to reverse the car. She had butterflies in her stomach. This was something she had never allowed herself to imagine. She glanced at her beautiful, loving, kind and forgiving daughter as she shifted the car into first gear and set off.

'Thank you, Ella, for allowing me this,' she said softly.

Ella was putting her bag by her feet. 'Who else would I do it with?'

'If I hadn't have come back, you could have asked anyone.'

Ella turned to Sennen. 'But anyone wouldn't have been you.'

'You know what I mean. I am a stranger to you really. We hardly know each other, so, thank you.'

'Mum?'

Sennen slowed the car as she approached the junction to the main Truro Road. 'Yes?'

'We may not have spent my childhood together, but I do know you, even though I don't, if you know what I mean?'

Sennen stopped the car, waiting for a break in the fast traffic. She put her left hand out to Ella who held it tight. 'I do love you,' she said, her throat tightening with emotion, 'and this is so special.'

A car arriving behind her beeped loudly. She waved into the rear-view mirror and mouthed 'Sorry,' to the agitated driver, then, kissing Ella's hand, let it go and got on the road to Truro.

Parking in Truro took a little time, but once they'd got a space Ella quickly marched her to Truro Bridal Boutique. A petite young woman greeted them. 'Do you have an appointment?'

Ella's face dropped. 'Should I have made one?'

'It is recommended, but let me just check the book.'

Sennen held her crossed fingers in front of her face and Ella giggled. The assistant came back. 'Yes, we have a spare hour right now. What sort of style are you looking for?'

Ella gave a little jump of joy. 'It's just like *Say Yes to the Dress*.'

'What's that?' asked Sennen, catching her daughter's joy but not understanding.

Ella explained.

'Well, let's do it!'

The assistant, who was called Erin, took them through the initial questions.

'What sort of wedding are you having? Register's office or church?'

'Church,' said Ella definitely.

'And your budget for the dress?'

'Oh. Erm . . . about . . .' She hesitated, waiting for her mother to be shocked. 'Seven hundred pounds?'

'How much?' said Sennen on cue. 'I can make you one for a fraction of that.'

Ella went quiet. How could she tell her mother that she didn't want a homemade dress?

Erin said diplomatically, 'I think we can find something very beautiful for the bride within that budget.'

Sennen took the tacit rejection in her stride. She had lost the right, a long time ago, to give orders where Ella's needs were concerned.

Erin whisked Ella away into a fitting room while Sennen found a tasselled and buttoned velvet chair and sat on it gingerly, testing its sturdiness under her weight. Gradually her confidence in its strength grew and she tried to make herself comfortable. She glanced around, taking in the ruffles and drapes, the deep pile carpet and the scented candle on the payment desk. There was a huge mirror on one wall with a circular platform in front of it. Presumably for the bride to stand on and admire herself in full rig.

In the mirror, she saw herself. Her father used to describe her as 'rangy'. Tall, broad shoulders, narrow waist and hips, long legs. She stared into her own face and wondered where the young Sennen had gone. When had the smooth skin and unhooded eyes been lost among her sun-exposed skin? What would her mother have said to her right now? If things had been different Adela would have enjoyed this shopping trip. She would have loudly complained about expense and the over-commercialisation of two people getting married, but she would have been determined to share the fun. Sennen closed her eyes. Mum? Poppa? Look at me. I'm being Ella's mum. Helping her to choose her wedding dress. I can hardly believe it and I expect you can't either. So thank you. Thank you both for looking after her. She is perfect, and I know that that is down to you. Oh, I miss you. And I so wish you were here to see her . . .

The swish of the fitting room curtain interrupted her. She opened her eyes and gasped as Ella walked out in a confection of tulle, twinkles and hoops that swamped her perfect figure.

Sennen smiled nervously. 'Wow!' she managed.

'It's not me, is it?' said Ella.

'Um . . . I think you should try a few more before you decide.' It was as honest as Sennen was prepared to go.

Ella was whisked away again and modelled three more dresses, each more disastrous than the first.

Ella's spirits were sagging. 'Mum, maybe this isn't the shop.'

Erin, never known to lose a customer, sprang into action and tapped something into her iPad. 'Hang on, there may be just the thing, in the stockroom. We occasionally get sample dresses from the big designers for a very affordable sum. We should have some that have just arrived in stock. She swiped her screen several times then picked up the phone on the desk. 'I'll check the stockroom . . . Hi, Moira, it's me – has the Wang 2016 come in yet? Yes, I'll hold.' She covered the mouthpiece and said, 'She's just looking.' There was a long and silent wait until, 'Yes, I'm still here . . . a ten? Terrific!' She winked at Ella whose eyes were wide and desperate. 'Okay, thanks, Moira. Bring it up.' She put the phone down. 'Right, I've got a size ten Vera Wang 2016 – ticket price was two thousand pounds but we have it for seven hundred and fifty.'

Of course it fitted like a glove. A romantic, narrow fall of tulle which briefly hung on Ella's shoulders then slid over her waist, hips and ankles before puddling at her feet. She stood nervously in front of her mother for the final verdict.

Sennen viewed her as she might an Old Master in the Tate. Her eyes narrowed, her head first on one side then the other. Finally, she said, 'You look spectacular.' She stood and put her arms around her elder daughter and held her tight. 'So, so beautiful. And this is my treat.'

Ella flatly refused. 'No, Mum. The gift you have given me is you being here.'

'But I want to give you something special for your wedding day.'

Erin, starting to get tissue paper and dress bags from under the desk was listening and suggested, 'Will you be wanting a veil?'

Ella looked at Sennen. 'I would love a veil. But aren't they very expensive?'

Sennen laughed. 'Just like your Granny. But in this case I think she would tell you that it is never your extravagances you regret, it's your economies.' Then Sennen had an idea. 'I could make you one. A proper gift from me to you. What do you think?'

'Would you? Could you?'

'I've earned my living as a seamstress all these years – why not?'

'And so,' Ella finished off, 'I got the most gorgeous dress and then Mum bought the finest chiffon for my veil and that's all I'm going to tell you.' She put her hands around Kit's neck and kissed him. 'I am so, so, so lucky to have you, and Mum and Henry all here.'

Kit kissed her back. 'Talking of Henry, I haven't seen him since the meeting with Deborah.'

Ella smiled naughtily at him. 'Don't worry about him. He knows tons of people here who have a sofa to lend him. He'll come back when he's ready. But in the meantime, we do have the house to ourselves . . .'

Henry was spread across Deborah's sofa, wearing one of her T-shirts and little else. In front of him lay the remains of a cheese and pickle sandwich and two empty cans of lager. He was watching the cricket on Sky. He didn't take his eyes from the television as his phone rang. 'Yes?'

'Nice telephone manner,' Ella said. 'You're alive, then?'

'Yeah . . . Ooooh . . . Howzat!'

She sighed. 'You're watching the cricket.'

Sarcasm took over. 'Oh, hello, Ella, and how can I help you?'

'You can stop sulking for one thing.'

'I am not sulking, I'm getting on with my life.'

'Where? Are you back in London?'

'Not at the moment.'

Ella was getting irritated. 'I am not going to play twenty questions with you, just tell me: where the hell are you.'

'In Trevay, with a friend.'

'A lady friend?'

'Not right at this moment, but she will be back later.'

'I don't need to know the details. When are you going to come back and face all this stuff with Mum? You have got to let all these feelings of entitlement go. We have Granny and Poppa's furniture and art, and all our memories of them. She will *never* have those.'

Henry turned the sound down. He knew that Ella was right, but every time he thought of how his heartbroken grandparents were let down by his mother he was overwhelmed by a sense of injustice.

'It's just . . . oh, I don't know. It's just seeing her, here in Trevay. Trying to take over and make everything all right. Well, it isn't all right. It never will be all right. She doesn't know them better than us and Granny and Poppa would be spinning in their graves if they knew we were making it easy for her.'

'No, they wouldn't,' Ella said patiently. 'They loved her and would be glad that we have got her back.'

'I don't want her here. She can hop off back to her new lot, never to be seen again as far as I'm concerned.'

'Actually, she's staying on for a bit.'

'Why?'

'Kit and I are getting married.'

Henry couldn't help but be happy. 'Really? That's great, Ells. Does the poor bloke know what he's letting himself in for?'

'Oh, ha ha ha. But Mum is staying for the wedding. She's making my veil for me and she helped me to choose the dress.'

'Mommie dearest doing her bit to get you on side?'

Ella sighed. 'Please, Henry. She's our mother, and the idea of the art school and everything is a good one and I hate it when you distance yourself from me. Please, could you just try to be a bit more accepting? See things from her point of view?'

'You mean forgive her?'

'Eventually.'

'I'm not as nice as you.'

'But could you just try? For me? Just until she goes back to India?'

Henry ran a hand over his stubbled chin. 'For you, Ells Bells, I'll try.'

32

Sennen was having trouble sleeping. Her dreams were vivid and full of panic. She would find herself running from an unrevealed horror, but her legs wouldn't work, dragging behind her as if stuck in treacle or cement. Sometimes she'd be drowning in Trevay Harbour, other times she was lost in an Indian town she didn't know. The sun was beating down bringing the warm scent of the spices to her nose and she was walking in the busy market with her children, Kafir by her side. Then, abruptly, they were gone and she was lost and scared. She knew her family were in danger but her voice didn't work, and even though she screamed for help, no sound came and no one heard her. She would wake distressed and crying.

That morning, she woke breathlessly trying to quell the panic in her body.

Outside it was still dark and she could hear the patter of soft rain falling on the eaves.

She lay still for a while and tried to will sleep back to her but it was a fruitless effort. She checked the time. Six fifteen.

A walk, that's what she needed, to feel the earth under her feet and the elements on her face.

In the silent streets of Trevay she felt like the only person in the world. Down the cobbled lane, right onto Fore Street and then left onto the harbour. Here, there was a sign of human life. She could see the baker and her assistant working away in the kitchen behind the Old Bakery shop. The smell of fresh bread and pasties took her senses straight back to Saturday mornings with Adela, buying long French sticks and doughnuts for the students. On the way back from her walk she promised herself a treat.

On she went, down to the boats drifting on a high tide, the light drizzle cool on her face. She went past the Golden Hind pub, past the lane that led to Pencil House, until she found the start of the footpath that would take her over the cliffs towards the lighthouse and Tide Beach.

The cliff path was steeper than she remembered, but the view, when she finally reached the top, was as spectacular as it had always been. 'Million-dollar view for nothing,' her father had always said. Until now, she had never appreciated his words, but standing looking out over a horizon that stretched more than 180 degrees around her, she felt tiny yet huge. Alone but not lonely. Neither happy nor sad. She simply accepted her existence. The rising sun lit a golden path on the ocean below her and behind her a skylark began to sing.

She continued walking, thinking about how she had got to this junction in her life. She wasn't a bad person, but she had done bad things. Or . . . were they bad or just wrong? It hadn't been wrong to have Henry and Ella, but her decision to run away and look for Alan had been. She had hurt her parents, who hadn't deserved to be hurt, and now she was hurting Kafir, Aali and Sabu.

Henry was rightly angry with her. She had had no idea
that her parents were leaving her so much: she had not come
for the money, she had come to apologise, reclaim her children
and explain why she had left them. Was that selfish too?

But it was the money that was causing so much trouble.
Ella didn't want it. Sennen didn't want it. Perhaps she should
just give it all to Henry? But that didn't feel right either.

She kept walking and thinking. She passed the lighthouse,
crossed Tide Beach and found herself on Shellsand Bay.

The sand dunes glowed gold and the rain had stopped
and she spotted a small lobster boat cutting bravely through
the waves.

She sat on a barnacled rock and told herself she needed
to make a plan.

She must have sat there for over half an hour, cloaked in
regret and the desire to make amends.

She heard voices chatting breathlessly before she heard the
regular thud of runners' feet upon the sand.

She looked up. 'Rosemary!'

Rosemary, red-faced and wearing a neon yellow running
jacket and headband, puffed to a halt. 'Darling, what are you
doing up this early?'

'I might ask the same of you.' Sennen looked from
Rosemary to her companion.

'This is Jools. My partner,' Rosemary said. 'Jools, this is
Sennen.'

Jools shook Sennen's hand. 'I've heard a lot about you.' She
smiled. She was in her late forties, Sennen judged, with blond
hair tucked behind her ears and an open friendly face.

'What are you partners in?' asked Sennen.

Rosemary gave her a mischievous smile. 'Jools is my girlfriend. She was away on business when you spent the night.'

Sennen's eyes widened. 'Oh.' She tried hard to keep her voice level. 'Gosh. Fantastic.'

Jools laughed. 'I think so.'

'How did you meet?' Sennen was aware she was gabbling.

'Very romantically.' Rosemary took Jools' hand. 'She took me to hospital one night after Ray had had a drink too many.'

'I'm a police officer. Rosemary's husband had attempted to strangle her.'

'Oh my God.' Sennen was horrified. 'You didn't tell me about that.'

Jools put her arm around Rosemary. 'She's been through a lot, this one.'

Sennen nodded. 'Including the time I made her run away to Spain with me.'

'Oh, that was fun,' Rosemary insisted. 'Well, it wasn't then, but it's a good story now.'

'Come on,' said Jools, readying herself to run again, 'we've got another two miles and then it's coffee.'

'See you later, Sennen? Coffee in Trevay? Ten-ish?' shouted Rosemary as she set off.

'Great. See you then.' Sennen watched as they jogged off down the beach. 'Well,' she said to herself. 'Life is full of surprises. I never saw Rosemary as a runner.'

From the opposite end of the beach, Kit and Ella, with Terry and Celia chasing a ball, appeared.

'Is that Mum?' Ella put her hand up to shield her eyes from the brightness of the rising sun, 'Look, skimming stones?'

Ella cupped her hands to her mouth and called, 'Muuum! Mum!'

Somehow the words reached Sennen's ears on the ragged wind and seeing Ella and Kit she waved.

'Hi, Mum. You're up early.'

'Well, I've got lots to think about, haven't I?' Sennen hugged them both. 'Veils, weddings . . .' She bent down and tickled the dogs.

'That's Celia and this one is Terry,' said Kit. 'They are both drama queens but love chasing a ball. Watch.' He threw the tennis ball into the waves and both dogs sped after it.

'I have missed the sea,' said Sennen watching them. 'Really missed it. Agra is about as far from the sea as you can imagine. I've been trying my hand at skimming but I'm so out of practice. Watch.' She picked up a smooth sliver of slate and, with a flick of her wrist, loosed it at the sea. After two skips it sank. 'See. Rubbish. Poppa was good but Mum had the talent. Sometimes seventeen or eighteen bounces.'

'I remember that,' said Ella. 'I would usually have my birthday parties on the beach and she would always set up a skimming competition.'

'She did the same for me too, when I was little.' Sennen was surprised at how clear the memory was. 'Shall we have a go, now? Six stones each?'

Celia and Terry thoroughly enjoyed the game and, refusing to chase their tennis ball, began to swim out for the stones.

'Woohoo!' shouted Ella, her arms in the air as her last stone reached fourteen bounces. 'I win.'

'Oh, that was fun,' said Sennen breathlessly. 'I am going to miss you both so much when I go back.'

'No, you won't. As soon as we can we'll come out to see you and meet our new family,' said Ella stoutly. 'If you don't mind.'

'I want that more than anything. I'll show you both the Taj and we'll eat wonderful food and you'll love the market. I would love Henry to come too.'

'I'm sure he will,' smiled Ella. 'He can never bear to be left out of anything.'

Eventually, Sennen left them to return to Trevay, and Kit and Ella headed back towards home.

'I've been wondering,' Kit said, 'now that you've got your wedding dress, and before it goes out of fashion, or you get too fat for it . . .' He dodged a thump from Ella. 'That maybe, if you're free over the next couple of weeks, you would consider getting married to me?'

Ella jumped on the spot. 'You mean, book the church and cake and guests and . . . ?'

'That's the idea.'

'But don't we have to get a licence and read banns and get blood tests and stuff?'

'I don't think we need blood tests, but we can ask Simon about the rest.'

Ella hugged herself. 'Oh yes! We can just walk next door and into the church. How romantic is that? Hope it doesn't rain.'

'You look lovely in the rain.' He kissed her soft lips then buried his face in her perfumed hair. 'I have loved you from the first moment I saw you.'

She leant into him and closed her eyes. His arms felt so right as they held her. Six months ago she had no job, no boyfriend and no mother. Happiness had been sent to her by whatever transient passing fate had decided to drop on her shoulders. She held Kit tighter. 'I love you more than I can say, Kit. I promise to be a good wife. Faithful. Loyal. I will always be by your side, no matter what.'

'And I, Kit Beauchamp, promise that I will take care of you always. I will never let you down.'

*

Sennen walked back along the cliffs to Trevay alone. Her mind was splitting off in so many directions. How long could she feasibly stay? Until Ella was married? She didn't want to rush Ella and Henry but she also had two little ones.

Should she stay and help to build the art school?

But she wasn't sure if that was what Ella really wanted, not with Henry's negative response.

Should she run back to India and never come home again? But what was left in India? Did she have a marriage? Wouldn't Sabu and Aali be better off without her?

Or should she just run away to another life altogether. Leave both the mess here and in India and build a life somewhere else. She had done it before. She could do it again.

That was the simple solution. Simple for everyone. Clean. Done.

The cliff path was narrow now, the edge very close to the steep drop and the sea. She took a step closer and viewed the broiling waves below, crashing on to the mussel- and limpet-encrusted rocks; sharp and deadly.

She thought back to the stones she had been skimming just a short while ago. One stone could make many ripples. One person could create a storm that drowned others' lives.

She stepped back from the edge and sat on the grass tufted edge of the path. 'Where do I belong?' Her question was ripped away on the wind.

Closing her eyes, she lay back on the soft sward and allowed her senses to take in the thump of the thundering waves, the call of a gull, the chug of a boat's engine, the fingers of the wind brushing her cheeks and the tangy smell of salt and nature.

She couldn't tell when it started but she became aware of something, somebody, at her side. A presence.

She didn't dare open her eyes for fear of what she might

see. She knew who it was. She heard her. Not through her ears, but through her body. It was her mother. 'I am with you,' she was saying. 'All is well.' The words were repeated like a chant, a mantra, many times, until Sennen saw, in her mind's eye, her mother place a hand on her forehead. The touch filled her with peace just as the vision of Adela began to fade.

When the dream or mirage or apparition had left, Sennen lay still, allowing her conscious mind to absorb the knowledge she had been given. She opened her eyes and sat up. 'Thank you, Mum. Thank you for the answer.'

Simon Canter, vicar of Pendruggan, sat at the desk in his study and beamed at the happy couple in front of him.

'Congratulations. This is happy news,' he said. 'When were you thinking of having the wedding?'

Kit jumped in. 'As soon as possible because we don't know how long Ella's mum will be here for and we want her to be there, obviously.'

Simon looked at the large diary in front of him and turned the pages. 'There's a space two Saturdays from now but that would be too soon. We couldn't get the banns read in time, or . . .' He riffled through some more pages. 'There's an empty Saturday in six weeks.' He looked up and saw the disappointment in their faces. 'I mean, there are ways of doing this very quickly if you get a common licence. I can help you with that. It costs a bit but there will be no need for any banns to be read, so off we go.'

Ella sat forward to the edge of her seat. 'How soon could that be fixed?'

'As long as there are no hitches, I should think you'll be married in two weeks. Midday is a good time.' He blinked kindly behind his glasses.

Ella grinned at Kit. 'Shall we?'

'Why not?'

They left the vicarage, bouncing with happiness. 'I've got to tell Mum,' said Ella, beaming.

'Now?'

'Yes, before she does something stupid like book a flight back to India.'

'What about Henry?'

'I'll call him after I've spoken to Mum. He's going to have to give me away, after all.' Thinking of something she stopped. 'You'd better phone Adam – he will be your best man, won't he?'

'Yes. I suppose so.'

'And Jenna will be my flower girl.' Ella was zinging with happiness. 'She'll be perfect, carrying a little basket of petals to spread before me.'

Kit shook his head in bemusement. 'Really? Do we need all this?'

'I am only getting married once, Mr Beauchamp, so it had better be bloody perfect.'

Kit grabbed her and kissed her. 'Remind me, did I buy you an engagement ring?'

She squealed. 'NO! Well, not yet anyway.'

'We'll go shopping tomorrow.'

She hugged him, 'Thank you. This is all so exciting. When shall we send the invitations out?'

'Tomorrow?'

'Yes. Maybe Queenie has some in the shop.'

'They'll be from 1956 if she has.'

Laughing, they headed up to the Village Stores.

*

Queenie was sitting on one of her old but comfortable armchairs by the counter of the shop, her feet up on a plastic bottle crate, made more comfortable with a cushion on the top. As the bell tinkled on the door she struggled to her feet.

''Ello, me ducks. What brings you 'ere so cheerful?'

'Can you keep a secret?' breathed Ella.

Queenie's canny old eyes lit up behind her pebble-thick specs that were the size of re-entry shields. 'I'm known for me discretion, me.'

Ella put her arm through Kit's. 'Kit and I are getting married!'

'Never! Well, bless me. Ain't that lovely. When's this, then?'

'Two weeks tomorrow.'

'Oh, my good Gawd. Come and give me a kiss.'

She bestowed her whiskered kisses on both of them, then asked them what they had come in for.

'Wedding invitations.'

'Oh now, I've got some somewhere – 'ang about and I'll find them.'

Kit and Ella passed knowing smiles to each other as Queenie rummaged in the huge bottom drawer of an old haberdashery dresser. 'Ere, Kit. Give me a hand.'

Kit obediently went behind the counter and helped her lift a faded cardboard box onto the counter.

'Have a look in there, while I put me legs up again.' She went back to her chair and put her feet on the crate. 'They may be a bit out of date but that's cos they're vintage.'

Ella lifted the lid and put her hand over her mouth to stop herself from laughing. 'Queenie, these have got photos of Prince Charles and Lady Diana on them.'

'Dig a bit deeper, dear.'

'Oh, these are nice.' Ella held out a handful of cards that

had prettily painted forget-me-nots, primroses and larkspur on them. In silver writing they had either *The Happiest of Days is Here*, *Marriage Joy* or, rather more jocularly, *Aisle be Seeing You* written upon them.

'Let me look, dear.' Queenie held out her hand and looked closely at them. 'Oh yes, these are definitely vintage. Seventies, I should say. Do they have envelopes?'

Ella felt about in the box. 'No.'

'I'll find you some, but they might not fit. How many people you inviting? It's a pity your mum isn't here.'

'But she is!' Ella smiled excitedly. 'She came back!'

Queenie was dumbstruck. 'And no one told me?' she gasped.

'It's not a secret, but we've had a lot to talk about and we had to get to know each other without distractions.'

'I had the newspaper, here on me counter, with that poor girl's face looking out. I can still see it clearly. We thought she'd gone for good. Her poor parents were heartbroken.'

'Yes, it wasn't an easy time.' Ella wanted to change the subject, 'Anyway, I shall be needing about twenty invitations.' She counted in her head. 'No more than twenty.'

'Does that include me?' asked Queenie, pointedly brushing cigarette ash off her bosom.

'Of course it does.'

'Oh, good. I could do the catering if you like? Twenty of me famous pasties is easy for me to do.'

Kit said a little too quickly, 'We haven't talked about the reception yet.'

Queenie cackled naughtily. 'Got you there, boy. You have what you want, only I don't like prawns so don't have any of them, or vol au vents. Pastry gets stuck in my dentures.'

'Understood,' said Kit.

Queenie looked over at Ella. ''Ave you found enough cards, duck?'

'Yes, just about. I like that they are a bit mixed up and not the same.'

Kit paid for them and the extra envelopes and before he left with Ella he reminded Queenie, 'Please don't say anything to anyone just yet. About the wedding or Ella's mum. We don't want any more attention than necessary.'

Queenie held her hand up. 'Don't you worry about that. Me lips are sealed. Careless talk costs lives and all that.'

She waved them off from her armchair and watched as they walked back towards Marguerite Cottage. In her cardigan pocket, next to her smoking tackle, was her mobile phone. She pulled it out and punched a number into it.

''Ello? Beryl, is that you? I've got some news for you. But you mustn't tell anyone . . .'

PART THREE
Ella's Wedding Day

33

Pendruggan, 2018

'Mum, I've got some news,' Ella said down the phone. Sennen, in bed, sat up, the thrill of hearing her daughter call her Mum always filling her with joy. 'Is it good?'

'Definitely. *Very* exciting. What are you doing two weeks today?'

'Tell me.'

'Kit and I have set the date for our wedding.' The end of the sentence went up at least an octave and with added volume.

Sennen held her receiver from her ear until the shrieking finished, then said, 'Darling, that is so wonderful! Where?'

'You remember the church next to our cottage? Holy Trinity? There.'

'And this is in two weeks?'

'Yes. At midday. I'm going to ask Henry to walk me down the aisle and Kit's cousin, Adam, he's a doctor, is going to be the best man.'

Sennen bit her lip. 'How does Henry feel about me being there?'

'Mum, *you* will be there, Henry will be there – and it will be the happiest day of my life. Okay?'

Sennen loved Ella's optimism. 'I might need some help with an outfit. What do mothers of the bride wear? Do you want me to wear a hat?'

'Yes, hats, confetti, silly little kitten heels – and everything, please.'

'I can't promise kitten heels.'

'Mum, you will look gorgeous no matter what. I'm going to ring Henry now and let him know he's walking me down the aisle. Bye.'

Ella ticked Sennen's name off the top of her 'who to phone list' and dialled the next name down.

'Henry, it's me.'

'Hello, you.'

'What are you doing two weeks today?' And she poured out the good news before he'd taken a breath.

'And Mum is coming too.'

Henry said nothing.

'Henry? Are you still there?'

'Why do you want her there?'

'You know why.'

'I can't help how I feel, Ells.'

'She's your mum.'

'Well, we all have a cross to bear.'

'Henry, I'm not going to beg. Will you give me away and behave like a brother should? Or are you really prepared to break your sister's heart?'

'Resorting to emotional blackmail won't help.'

'How about wheedling?' She coughed and pitched her voice

girly high. 'Pleeeeeese, Henry. You're my brother and I love you. And you love me, don't you?'

'You know I do.'

'So you'll do it? It should be Poppa, I know, but it would make him so proud of you if you took his place. Please don't let me down.'

Henry softened. 'I would never let you down, Ells.' He took a moment to absorb how much it meant to her. 'Of course I'll do it. I'd be honoured to.'

'Thank you, thank you, thank you. You are the best.' She blew a kiss down the phone. 'When are you coming home by the way? Are you still holed up with some poor misled female?'

Henry looked over at Deborah who was looking gorgeous, wrapped in her sheets and licking Marmite off her fingers. 'At a mate's. Actually, Ella, I think we should invite Deborah Palmer – you know, the solicitor? She can keep Mum in order.'

'Good idea,' said Sennen, writing Deborah's name on the list. 'I'm posting invitations today so that people get them on Monday. Have a good weekend and see you soon? I'm cooking leg of lamb for Sunday lunch if you are about.'

'I'm not sure if I'll be back in time for that, but I will come over later. Need to find my suit and get it to the cleaners.'

Sennen, still sitting in her bed at White Water, was chasing all sorts of thoughts around in her head. The wedding was going to be tricky but she would do everything in her power to make her children happy and to make good memories of it. The one person she wanted to be there, standing next to her, though, was Kafir. She couldn't bear to allow her mind to go near the thought that her marriage may be ended. No, she must hope that he would love her enough to get over this painful bridge and put it behind them. She had texted him twice over the last couple of days, telling him her news as she got it, but he hadn't replied. She picked her phone up. Should she text again or take the plunge and ring him?

Several times she put the phone down, only to pick it up again, but finally she picked it up and, with determined, shaking fingers, dialled his number.

It went to voicemail.

'Kafir, it's me. I know this sounds mad, but the other day, I had a vision of my mother. A sort of visitation I suppose. Anyway, she was saying she was with me and all is well. Kept saying it over and over. And since then a lot has happened. Ella is getting married, two weeks today in Pendruggan church at Midday. Henry is giving her away, and I need you by my side. Please come. Bring Aali and Sabu . . . We'll be doing it together. You and I. I want Henry and Ella to meet you and know how good you are. Why I love you. It's so hard here without you. I know it's all my own fault, but I feel as if Mum is with us and all will be well, as she told me. Mad. Mad, but please come. It's the only way we can find out what the future holds for all of us. I will fight hard for you. The pain of losing you is actually physical. It's real. It hurts. I miss you. Please, please come. I love you, Kafir. And I am so very sorry for my lies. I am not lying now. I need you. Please, please . . . call me.'

Kit was on the phone to Adam, talking about best man duties, while Ella finished writing the invitations. Addressing the last envelope and gathering them all together into a neat pile, she signalled to Kit that she was nipping up to Queenie's to get them posted and, pulling on her waterproof, headed off through the rain that had been falling all day to the village store.

Queenie was ensconced again in her chair in front of an electric fire. 'That rain's brought some cold,' she said.

Ella closed the shop door against the downpour. 'I hope the weather will be all right for the wedding. My dress isn't exactly thermal or waterproof.'

'Never rains on the bride,' wheezed Queenie, hoisting herself up. 'You'll be okay. What do you want? Stamps?'

'Yes. Thank you.'

Queenie got out her antique stamp book with its well-thumbed tabs. 'First or second?'

'Twenty first-class.'

'Righty ho.' Queenie pushed her enormous glasses up her nose and began searching. 'So, where's the hen do?' she asked.

'I hadn't thought of having one,' said Ella.

'You have to have an 'en do. Tradition. Your last chance of a proper knees-up as a single girl.'

'I don't know.' Ella looked doubtful. 'I shouldn't think Kit will have a stag party.'

'Well, he should.'

'Should he?'

'Oh dear, yes. Bad luck for you both not to be given a proper send off.'

'I'll talk to Kit. How much do I owe you for the stamps?'

Queenie was not to be fobbed off. 'A nice Chinese meal is what you want. The Chinese are experts at bringing good luck.'

'Are they?'

'You don't want to risk bad luck do you. That'll be £13, please.'

Ella handed over the money. 'I suppose a meal is better

than getting drunk in a nightclub with an L plate tied round my head.'

'I wouldn't be able to come if it was a nightclub do.' Queenie shook her head. 'It's me legs.'

'Would you want to come for a Chinese supper?'

'Oh, that is kind of you. Yes please. When are you having it?'

Ella laughed at how easily the wily old lady had manipulated her. 'What day suits you?'

'The wedding is on a Saturday so you don't want to go out on the Friday night – how about the Thursday before?'

'Okay, Thursday week it is. Do you have a favourite restaurant?'

'The Fighting Duck, the back of Fore Street in Trevay. They do a lovely sweet-and-sour pork there.'

'I'll book it. And I'll organise a taxi to pick us both up. Say seven o'clock?'

Queenie made her way back to her chair. 'That'd be fine dear. I don't want to be home too late, neither.'

'A stag night?' Kit scratched his chin, 'I hadn't thought about it. Who would I invite?'

'Adam, Simon, Piran and Henry to start with. It's part of Adam's duties as best man to organise it, isn't it?'

'Good point. So, who's going to your hen party? Apart from Queenie?'

'Mum, Penny, Helen. I think Mum would like her friend Rosemary too.'

'Nice.'

'It's all so unreal, isn't it. Can you believe this is happening?'

'It definitely is happening.' He rattled his car keys. 'Shall I tell you how I know?'

'Tell me.'

'I am going to drive the woman I love to the jeweller's and buy her the best engagement ring I can afford.'

Ella caught her breath. 'OMG! I'd almost forgotten!'

'And wedding rings.'

'Oh yes! Oh gosh.' She put her arms around him and smooched. 'I am so lucky to have you. I can't wait to be Mrs Beauchamp. Could things get any better?'

34

The Hen Party

The Chinese restaurant was pleasantly busy, enough for the waiting staff to give Ella's party plenty of attention. The food was excellent and kept on coming, as did the drinks. Queenie was on her fourth Tia Maria and lemonade when she decided to make a speech. Penny and Helen, on either side of her, helped her up and readjusted the veiled hat she had insisted on wearing.

'I just want to wish young Ella 'ere, all the best for her big day and also a big welcome home to her mum, Sennen.' Queenie turned to Sennen, who was plucking at her napkin, 'Sennen scarpered many years ago leaving two little 'uns with her parents. We all thought she was dead, but here she is, right as rain. Sadly, her parents died before she got home to see them.'

Ella's toes were curling and could see that Sennen was screwing her napkin into a tight ball.

Penny saw all this and shot to her feet to save Queenie

345

from embarrassing herself further. 'That's enough, you can sit down now, Queenie.'

'I need to make the toast.' Queenie was adamant.

'Okay then, just a short one, wishing Ella well.'

'I know what I'm doing. I'm not doolally.' Queenie pushed her hat to the back of her head whilst pulling her arm from Penny's crossly. She returned her attention to the table, 'So please raise your glasses to those no longer with us, to absent friends.'

Penny shouted over her quickly, 'To Ella.'

'To Ella,' repeated everyone.

Queenie sat down and knocked her hat into the remains of her banana fritter syrup. 'Now look what you made me do,' she said to Penny. 'That's me best 'at. I'm going to wear that at the wedding.'

Penny removed the hat from the pudding, and put Queenie's Tia Maria to one side. 'Coffees, anyone?'

When the coffees and After Eights arrived, Rosemary tapped her cup with a teaspoon. 'Ladies, what a wonderful evening this has been and I am honoured to have been invited. Thank you, Ella.'

Ella smiled. 'Thank you for looking after Mum.'

'As you know, Sennen and I met as teenagers. She looked just like you, Ella, and I see in you the funny, kind, adventurous girl who loved you and Henry very much. To come back and face the music now is brave, particularly having to leave her family in India to do so. So my toast tonight is to: the Mother of the Bride, Sennen.'

Sennen was overcome and however hard she tried, the tears flowed.

She mouthed to Rosemary, 'Thank you.' Then Ella came next to her and hugged her. 'Thank you, Mum. For coming back. Everything will be all right now.'

Penny and Helen raised their glasses again, all except Queenie who was talking to a tall pot plant. 'Who's in India, then? Nobody bloody tells me anything.'

Coffees finished, chocolate mints eaten, the evening began to wind up. Rosemary was looking at her watch. 'Jools is just coming off shift. Anyone want to come back to mine for a nightcap?'

Ella shook her head. 'I'm up early tomorrow. Kit and I are making quiches for the reception.'

Sennen, who had quietly paid the bill, tucked her arm through Ella's. 'Thank you for including me tonight. You had every right not to.'

Ella looked into her mother's face and said in all sincerity, 'Mum, I love you.'

Everyone was up now and finding coats and bags, all except Queenie who was licking the banana syrup off her hat and still talking to the plant. 'Lovely food tonight. Did you have the pudding? Try some.' She offered her hat to the plant. 'Go on. Have a lick. Delicious, innit.'

Penny leant down and said, 'Queenie. You're hammered. I think it's time for bed.'

'Let me just say goodbye to this gentleman first.'

'Queenie, it's a plastic pot plant.'

'Oh Gawd. Is it?' Queenie peered at the plant and laughed wheezily. 'Bloody hell, it is an all. Lovely fella though.'

Penny called to Helen, 'Help me with Queenie, would you? She's off her head.'

'I'm perfectly sober, if you don't mind.'

Helen and Penny pulled her to her feet. 'You need to get home.'

'I tell you what I need.'

'What's that?' asked Helen, plonking Queenie's hat back on her head.

'I need a pint to sort me out or else I'll have an 'eadache in the morning.'

'I think you would have a worse one if you had a pint,' said Penny, hauling Queenie out onto the pavement.

A collection of wolf whistles sounded behind them. Penny refused to look back but was nonetheless absurdly gratified, until running footsteps came towards her and someone pinched her bottom. She spun around, ready to confront her attacker.

It was her husband, Simon, who was swaying slightly and had a dozy grin on his face. 'It's me,' he said.

Behind him were Kit, Adam, Henry and a couple of local lads, all sniggering.

Helen saw her partner Piran amongst them. 'Hello.' He smiled, fidgeting with the gold hoop in his ear. 'Spotted your arse a mile off.'

Queenie took advantage of the distraction and broke free. ''Ello fellas. Who wants a pint?'

She tottered towards them and before she knew what had happened she was hoisted up in a fireman's lift across Piran's shoulder.

She cackled loudly. 'Oh, Piran, I 'aven't been slung over a bloke's shoulder for a long time.'

Penny and Helen rolled their eyes and watched as Queenie was carried off with her skirt over her head and her bloomers on show.

'She's going to feel so ill in the morning,' giggled Penny.

'Oh, leave her to it. The boys will look after her. Actually, I feel almost jealous,' smiled Helen. 'Almost.'

35

Bill died just a couple of months short of his sixtieth birthday. He and Adela had been sharing a peaceful life.

Occasionally they still took in students who sat rapt as Bill told them about his apprenticeship with the great potter Bernard Leach, teaching them all he knew, and Adela cooked enormous breakfasts and suppers for them, as she always had, and took them to interesting spots around Trevay where they would set up their easels and paint, with her looking over their shoulders and offering generous advice.

Adela was worried about Bill's health. It was hard to put a finger on it but he was lacking the vitality he'd once had.

'Darling,' she said gently, knowing his suspicion of the medical profession, 'I think we should both go to the doctor for an MOT. Blood pressure, cholesterol, that sort of thing.'

'Why?' he asked gruffly. 'What's wrong with you?'

She hadn't been prepared for that and said rather lamely, 'I think it's sensible, that's all.'

They didn't go.

Adela told herself that it was natural for a man of his age

to enjoy long naps in the afternoon – she often did so herself – and, although he was losing weight, he still enjoyed her cooking.

Ella and Henry would visit when they could and the last time they had come Bill seemed rejuvenated.

However, Adela confided in Ella. 'How does Poppa look to you?'

'Really good,' Ella said breezily. 'He's lost a bit of weight and I think it suits him.'

When the children had returned to London, Bill was full of Henry's success in his new job. 'Where did he get such a good business brain? Not from us that's for sure.'

Adela thinking about their father's identity said. 'We'll never know now will we.'

Bill sipped his tea. 'Ella is definitely a chip off the old block, though. Did she show you her illustrations for the book she's writing?'

'Yes. Her line drawings in particular are very good.'

Bill smiled. 'I think we did okay with Henry and Ella.'

'Better than with Sennen?' They rarely talked about their daughter, and to hear her name spoken out loud created a crackling tension in the air.

Bill looked at Adela steadily. 'Yes.'

'Maybe we did too much for her?'

'Possibly.'

'She was so bright. Doing well enough at school. And funny and kind. She'll be thirty-seven now.'

'Well, wherever she is I hope she's happy.' He tapped his fingers on the arm of his chair. 'How the hell could she not come back and see the children?'

'She did,' said Adela simply.

'*What*? When?'

'When you were feeling so wretched and upset.'

Anger flared. 'Why didn't you tell me?'

'I'm sorry. I should have. But she just turned up and you were so ill and Henry and Ella were just getting settled. I couldn't face having her back and creating all that turmoil again. I told her to go away.'

'How – how was she?'

'Grown up. She was only twenty but she seemed, I don't know, a seasoned adult. She had been working in Spain and France and had come here with some actors, to Edinburgh, I think, and decided to come and see us and Henry and Ella.'

'Why the hell didn't you tell me?'

'I was so angry. She was standing there, right as rain, while I had picked up her mess and I was so worried about you. You had burnt all her photos, eradicated her from our lives, and I honestly thought that seeing her would make you ill again. So I told her to go away. My decision. I made the choice for *you*, not for her. I couldn't bear to see you so unhappy and ill again.'

'Did you let her see the children?'

Adela shook her head in regret. 'No. I asked if she was going to stay. And she couldn't promise, so I didn't let her see them.'

Bill softened. 'It must have killed you.'

'Yes. I said some very unkind things to her.'

'We all say and do unkind things in anger. Can you imagine how I felt as soon as I burnt her photographs?'

'I know how I felt.'

'She hurt us, we hurt her. Not very clever.'

'She hates me because I told her to go away.'

'She'll hate herself more.' He smiled. 'Do you remember when she tipped my birthday cake onto the floor because she was so cross that it was my birthday and not hers?'

'It had taken me all morning to make. I wonder if she married and has a new family.'

'Possibly. But she would be so proud of Henry and Ella. We must pity her for not knowing them.'

'I'm so relieved to have told you.'

'That she came back?'

Adela nodded.

'Come on, old girl. No one's life is a piece of cake. We have both done things we regret but we have each other and we have Henry and Ella.'

'I love you, William Tallon.'

'I know – and I love you very much, Mrs Tallon.'

Bill died just a few weeks later. Leukaemia. It had been too late to offer treatment. Adela thanked God that they had no more secrets between them.

36

It was Friday afternoon. The wedding was less than twenty-four hours away, and Ella was getting fractious.

'Kit, I asked you *not* to put anything on top of the trifles.'

'I haven't.'

'Then what are the salmon pinwheels doing?'

'Oh that. Well, the trifles are clingfilmed and there was no other room in the fridge, so I put the salmon things on top.'

Ella noisily banged about in the fridge, moving salads and quiches and cheese before admitting to herself, but not to him, that Kit had been right. There was nowhere else to put the bloody salmon.

'How about a cup of tea?' asked Kit helpfully.

'The dishwasher needs emptying first.'

'Right. Well, I'll pop the kettle on, empty the dishwasher, and then we'll have a cuppa. Yes?'

Ella reversed out of the fridge and closed the door carefully. 'What time is Adam due.'

'About seven, if the traffic isn't too bad.'

Ella was irritated. 'He'll expect me to cook for him, I suppose.'

'No. I'll take him to the pub, with Henry,' Kit said patiently. 'How about a biscuit with your tea? A nice digestive?'

'I don't want to look fat in my wedding dress,' she snapped.

He took her in his arms and kissed her passionately.

'What was that for?' she asked, slightly more mellowed.

'To shut you up. Now sit down because you and I are going to have a cup of tea and a biscuit.'

A couple of hours later Ella finally sat down and went through her check list. Food? Tick. Cutlery, crockery and glasses? Tick. Flowers? Tick. Sheets changed, loos cleaned, toenails painted? Tick.

Kit was upstairs gathering his suit and toiletries ready to take over to the vicarage where he was going to spend the night. He came downstairs and put the suit bag and a smaller bag on the hall floor.

'Ready?' asked Ella coming out of the kitchen.

'I think so.'

'Rings?'

'Yes.'

'Sorry I got a bit Bridezilla earlier.'

'Forgiven.'

The doorbell rang, making them both jump.

'Hi,' said Henry on the doorstep. 'Here I am and I have got something for you. My present to you both.'

Ella was excited. 'What, what?'

'I need to get it from the car. Hang on.'

They watched as he opened the boot and pulled out a large picture frame. All they could see was the back of the canvas, but Ella gasped and whispered to Kit, 'I think I know what this is.'

Henry carried it down the short path and into the house. 'No peeking. Close your eyes and let me take this through to the lounge to set it up properly.'

Ella and Kit stayed where they were until Henry called, 'Okay. Come on in.'

Ella couldn't believe her eyes. 'It's me,' she shrilled, delighted. 'The one Poppa painted of me. Kit, look it's me when I was about five, paddling at Shellsand.'

The painting was large and beautiful. Against the golden pinks of a sandy beach, and the wild blue of the sea beyond, a small girl in an old-fashioned scarlet swimsuit was paddling. Her back was to the viewer, but the long red ringlets rippling down her shoulders were definitely Ella's.

Kit stood for a while, admiring it. 'It's amazing. But I thought it was your granny who painted.'

'Poppa was a very good painter, but he knew that Granny was better so he usually left it up to her. I haven't seen this for a long time. Where was it, Henry?'

'I had it on the wall at Mandalay Road. When Granny died I found it in Poppa's studio. It was behind all sorts of things, hidden really well. I snaffled it hoping that when some idiot married you, not you obviously, Kit, you are the opposite of idiot, I could give it to you on your wedding eve.'

Ella's eyes shone, 'Oh, Henry, you are the best brother.'

'I am your only brother.' He stopped and frowned. 'Actually, I'm not, am I?'

Kit was keen to steer off the subject of the half-brother and sister in India and said, 'Ella, do you remember him painting this?'

'No. I don't. But then I was only little.'

'Well, it's lovely.' Kit gave Henry a man hug. 'Thanks, mate.' They heard a car draw up. 'That'll be Adam,' said Kit walking into the hall to let his cousin and best man in and was surprised to find Sennen on the doorstep.

'Hello, Kit.' She kissed him, her warm Indian fragrance enveloping him. 'Everything ready for tomorrow?'

'Yep. Henry's here. Come into the lounge.'

Walking into the room Sennen immediately saw the painting. She shivered as if someone had walked over her grave. 'I haven't seen that for years,' she almost whispered.

Ella bounced on her toes. 'Henry gave it to me and Kit. Wedding present. Isn't it lovely? The only picture that Poppa painted of me.'

Sennen was quiet. 'Of you?'

'Yes.'

Sennen walked towards the picture and read her father's neat signature. 'Is there a date on it?'

'I haven't looked,' said Henry.

'I had a red costume like that,' said Sennen.

Realisation hit Ella. 'It's you?'

'I think so.'

Henry began to work it out. 'When Granny died, we didn't find any pictures of you. No photographs or school reports or anything. Which I thought was odd because they took photos of Ella and me all the time. I have rows of photo albums in London, as well as our school books and art and stuff.'

'I would like to see those, one day,' Sennen said.

'Yes, okay. But there are no pictures of you. Ella and I never knew what you looked like.

'But he kept this?' asked Sennen, getting closer to the picture.

'Yes, he did.'

Henry picked the picture and turned it over. He scanned the canvas carefully then found something. 'Let's get a light on this.'

Ella angled a table lamp on to it and they crowded round. On the bottom right-hand corner, in faded pencil, Poppa's hand had written. S. Shellsand summer '81.' He looked sharply at Sennen. 'How old were you in 1981?'

'About five. The same age as that little girl in the picture.'.

'You must have it,' Ella said immediately, pushing it to Sennen.

Sennen smiled but waved it away. 'No, my love. If you give it to me I will give it straight back to you. It's yours.' She looked at Henry. 'I'm so glad you had it. It makes me feel that Poppa did still want to keep a bit of me.'

Henry was appalled to find his throat tightening against tears. He grabbed his glass and drank.

'By the way,' said Sennen, 'I've not properly thanked you for the headstones, Henry.'

Her words were sincere.

'But mostly, thank you for adding my name. When I saw it, it made me feel a bit less invisible.'

Henry coughed, embarrassed. 'Yes, well . . . Got to get the facts right. Good. Drink anyone?'

Much later, when Sennen had gone back to Trevay and Kit and Adam had retreated to the vicarage, Henry poured Ella one last gin and tonic. 'To you, my lovely little sister.'

'Aw, thanks. And thank you again for the painting. Did you have any idea?'

'No. If I believed in the occult I'd say Granny and Poppa had a hand in all that tonight.'

'Maybe. It was nice of Mum to let me have it.'

'It was never hers to have. I kept it for you.'

'I know. But still . . . And you did the right thing when you added her to the gravestones.'

'Yeah, well, you know . . .'

'Be honest with me, aren't you glad Mum's back?'

Henry was surprised by the question. 'Blimey. Why do you ask that? I don't know.'

'I think that you *are* glad. You wouldn't be so emotional if you didn't care.'

'Emotional? What are you talking about?'

'You were pleased when she thanked you for the inscription, and you sounded funny when she thanked you for keeping the painting of her.'

'I didn't know it was her though, did I?'

'No, but when you did, I saw your face. You were glad it was her and that we'd had that picture up on the wall when we were little, that Poppa had kept one thing of her to watch over us.'

Henry stood up. 'Come on. It's my duty to make sure you arrive in a fit state at your wedding tomorrow. You need your beauty sleep.'

She took his hand and he hauled her to her feet. 'Henry, beneath your bad-tempered façade, you really have a good heart, don't you?'

He turned off the lights so that she couldn't see his face. 'Bed,' he said. 'Now.'

37

The Wedding Day, White Water

The drill of rain on her bedroom window woke Sennen, like the sound of gravel being thrown onto to the glass.

She got up and looked out at the lowering clouds, blossoming dense and grey. A strong wind was bending the palm trees in the garden below and beyond the wet rooftops she saw the plumes of spray crash onto the harbour wall. Poor Ella. What a terrible day for a wedding.

She thought about sending her an uplifting text on the lines of 'It never rains on the bride, trust me'. But she thought better of it.

There was a knock on the door. It was Amy, the landlady, carrying an unordered tray of coffee and unwanted concern. 'Morning. What a terrible day. I thought you'd like an early coffee, what with getting ready for the wedding and everything.' She went to the window and looked out. 'Terrible, isn't it. Your poor daughter.'

Sennen couldn't help but think the woman was revelling

in the awfulness and was unstoppable. 'The photographs will look terrible. Everyone under umbrellas. The bride's dress will be ruined with the mud. And her hair. Shame.' She turned from the window and shone a pitying smile over Sennen. 'Have you got a raincoat?'

Sennen refused to be martyred. 'It's going to clear up in an hour or two.'

'Is it?' asked Amy, frowning. 'I checked my App and it said it was set for the day.'

'It's an Indian thing. We can smell weather changes,' lied Sennen.

'Really?'

Sennen nodded and drank some coffee. 'Thank you so much for this. Just what I needed. Now, I must get ready.'

Once Amy had gone, Sennen turned her television on in time to catch the weather forecast. 'This belt of rain, coming in from the Atlantic, is producing heavy downpours across the south west and will continue throughout the day . . .' Sennen switched it off and then turned on the main bedroom light.

She opened her wardrobe door and took out her wedding outfit. She had known exactly what she would wear. She had packed very little when she had left India, but she had brought something that had been lying in a drawer for many years. Something she had bought for her mother. Always she had expected to meet her mother again and give her this one thing that she knew the bohemian in Adela would love. Now it was too late but she would wear it for her daughter's wedding. She would wear it so Adela could be there on the day.

It was carefully wrapped in two tissue packets. She opened the smaller one first and shook it onto the bed. The navy-blue silk bodice gleamed under the overhead light. The second packet was heavier. She ran her fingers around the taped edges of the tissue and gently revealed the rich claret and gold silk of the skirt. She rubbed the finely woven fabric between her thumb and forefinger.

She was anxious not to embarrass Ella on her wedding day, but, if by a miracle Kafir did come, she, Sennen Tallon-Singh would be seen as her true self: an Indian wife in a traditional sari.

Marguerite Cottage

Henry barged into Ella's room and farted. Ella stuck her head under her duvet. 'You're disgusting. Go away.'

'I have tea for you. And Jammie Dodgers. Oh, and it's raining.'

Ella's head popped up, her hair tousled, freckles scattered perfectly across her lovely face. '*What?*'

'You look really very pretty. I can almost see why Kit wants to marry you. Budge up.' He settled himself on Kit's side of the bed.

'Is it really raining?' she asked.

'Yep.'

'Have you seen the forecast?'

'Yep.'

'Stop being so irritating. Is it going to stop?'

'Doesn't look good, I'm afraid.'

Ella ran her hand through her hair in despair. 'My shoes.'

'I'll carry you.'

'You'll drop me.'

'If you want.'

'Oh, shut up.'

'Eat a Jammie Dodger – you'll feel better.'

The Vicarage

In the vicarage, Penny was boiling an egg with toast soldiers for Jenna. 'Put fower dress on, Mummy?'

'After breakfast, and then we'll have a bath and then you can put your dress on.'

'Want put it on now!'

'I know, but you don't want tappy egg all down it, do you?'

'Ella put her dress on now?'

'No. She'll be having her tappy egg, then she'll get ready.'

'She like tappy eggs?'

'They are her favourites, and it's lucky for the bride and her flower girl to have the same breakfast as each other, so eat up.' Penny popped the egg into an egg cup and the toast next to it. 'There you are.'

Simon came in, fresh from the shower. He kissed the top of Jenna's head and then smooched Penny. 'Good morning to my favourite girls. I hear that there's a flower girl in the house today.'

Jenna bounced up and down. 'Me is!'

'You? And what do you have to do?'

'Walk front of Ella, not stop till get to Daddy.'

'And what else mustn't you do?'

'Be naughty.'

'Good girl. And what will you do with the petals in your basket?'

'Frow on floor for Jenna walk on.'

'Perfect.' Simon kissed his daughter again.

Penny got up to rinse her cup and looked over the sink into the garden. 'Do you think it'll stop raining?'

'I have faith,' smiled Simon.

'Well, have a word with The Boss.'

'I already have.'

White Water

After a quick breakfast downstairs, Sennen escaped Amy and retreated back to her room. She checked her phone. Kafir had not responded to her voicemail or bothered to text. She sat on the edge of her bed, feeling lonelier than she had ever felt. The want for him was vast and tormenting. She took a deep breath and told herself that today was not about her or her unhappiness, it was about Ella and her happiness.

Her phone buzzed with a text. Her heart bounced. But it wasn't Kafir, it was Ella.

Morning Mum, are you as excited as I am? Can't wait to see you. I'm back from the hairdressers at about 11.30 if you want to come over. I need help getting my dress on. What would I do without you? Love you, Ella xx

Sennen reread the message and her sorry heart soared again.

She typed back,

See you at 11.30. So excited and happy for you. Can't wait. I love you too, Mum xx

She checked it to make sure it wasn't too much too soon, then pressed send.

Three seconds later a line of heart emojis were her answer.

The Vicarage

Kit wrapped a bath towel round his waist and crossed the vicarage landing to Adam's room. 'Morning, best man. Sleep well?'

363

'Very.' Adam stretched and sat up. 'How's the groom?'

'Worryingly fine and looking forward to getting married to the future Mrs Beauchamp.'

'I thought I had to give you the obligatory speech about it not being too late to back out and to only do this if you were absolutely certain?'

'I *am* absolutely certain.'

'Well, that's that done. Is it raining?'

Ocean View Hotel

Kafir had no idea if he was doing the right thing or not, but instinct told him that he had to get on a flight to Heathrow and be with Sennen. He was her husband still and a husband supports his wife where family is involved. And curiosity had got the better of him. He needed to see what she had left behind, had denied and lied about, to truly be able to make the right choice about his marriage. That, and Aali and Sabu who were missing their mother and begging everyday to know why they couldn't see her or speak to her. When he told them that they were coming to England to see her they started packing their little bags straight away.

They had arrived at Heathrow on Thursday. Standing in the long immigration queue, Kafir pulled out his phone and switched it on. Sabu snatched it from him and started playing with it. 'Give it back Sabu, please,' he said impatiently.

Sabu was jumping up and down just out of his father's reach. 'I want it.'

'Give it to me, I need it back now, Sabu.'

'No.'

The phone began to ring and Sabu dropped it in surprise. Aali rescued it and dutifully handed it to her father.

'Who is it, Daddy?'

'A message. Shh.' He dialled into his voicemail and listened to Sennen's voice.

'WHO IS IT,' shouted Sabu, spinning around in a circle.

'Shh, it's Mummy.'

Aali caught hold of Sabu and held his hand. 'Shh, Sabu, Daddy is talking to Mummy.'

'Mummy?'

'Yes.'

'I'm going to see her.'

'We all are,' she whispered.

Kafir put the phone back in his pocket. 'That was Mummy. We are going to give her a big surprise because she really is missing us.'

The journey from the airport to Cornwall was long but the train was comfortable with enough space for Kafir to lie the children across the seats to sleep.

He couldn't sleep. What was he doing coming over on the spur of the moment? Arriving in time for an English family wedding had not been on his agenda at all. He had hoped that he would be able to assess his wife's situation and be able to decide what he needed to do. But now he was on the back foot. What on earth was he walking into?

At last the train pulled into Truro station and the weary three caught a cab to their hotel, the Ocean View, just two miles down the coast from Trevay.

It was evening, and after a simple supper, Kafir got them washed and ready for bed, but blighted with over excitement and jetlag, they barely slept until it was morning when they fell into deep sleeps.

Letting them rest, Kafir made some tea from the array of

hot drink choices set out on a little tray. He didn't like the taste of the milk from the tiny plastic tubs much, but he enjoyed the biscuits and munched steadily through the two tiny packets. He could have done with some proper breakfast but was too afraid to leave Aali and Sabu on their own. Instead, he lay on his bed and watched the television news until he too fell asleep.

At lunchtime, Aali and Sabu woke up grizzly, thirsty and hungry. Kafir had the solution. 'Who wants to see the sea?'

'Me me me,' sang Aali. 'I've never seen the sea.'

'Have I seen the sea?' Sabu asked. 'What does it look like?'

'Look out of the window.' Kafir pulled the curtains open. 'Are there fishes in it?'

'Yes.'

'Can we see them?'

'I don't know, but we can eat fish and chips. Mummy told me all about them. They are her favourite.'

The day became a very jolly one: fish and chips sitting in a shelter on the beach, a little paddling but not for too long as none of them had experienced water as cold, and then an ice cream.

'When will we see Mummy?' asked Aali later, yawning as she cleaned her teeth.

'Tomorrow,' said Kafir, helping Sabu with his pyjamas.

'Good,' shouted Sabu, jumping up onto his bed. 'I have missed her.'

Kafir tucked them both in. 'We all have.'

White Water

Sennen looked at herself in the wardrobe mirror. Tanvi had taught her how to wear a sari years ago and Sennen hoped she had done a good enough job. She had kohled her eyes heavily and added a red bindi between her brows. On her wrists she wore many rows of golden sparkly bracelets and on her feet she wore her favourite Indian sandals. Outside, the rain was still coming down so she put the only warm jacket she had on, and her scarf over her head. She would do.

Ella

The hairdresser had dressed Ella's hair simply and beautifully. She had allowed her natural curls to do their own thing while adding shine and extra bounce.

'You scrub up all right,' said Henry, who had waited at the salon to drive her back to Marguerite Cottage.

'You're so funny, not.' Ella watched the windscreen wipers as they valiantly cleared the persistent rain. 'How much time do we have before we need to leave the house?'

Henry looked at his watch and calculated. 'I reckon about an hour and a half?'

'That's perfect. Mum's coming over to help me into my dress.' She saw, out of the corner of her eye, Henry's lips tighten. 'Don't be like that.'

'Like what?'

'You know like what.'

He changed the subject. 'Do you mind that the painting is her and not you?'

'No. Would you?'

'Probably.'

'Oh, Henry. Get over yourself. We thought we were the last of the Tallons but it turns out we're not and that's exciting, isn't it?' She closed her hand on Henry's knee.

'I suppose.'

'That's a start.'

The Vicarage

'Jenna, would you please put your crayons down and come and get dressed,' said Penny impatiently.

'Not want to.'

'Yes, you do.' Penny was gritting her teeth. 'Come along.'

'Daddy do. Mummy nails scratchy.'

Penny looked at her freshly gelled nails and could only agree with her. 'I think it's the glitter,' she said.

'Did I hear my name?' asked Simon coming in to Jenna's bedroom wearing his full clerical garb.

'Daddy dess me?'

Penny flashed him a look that screamed *help me.*

'Okay. Righto. Now, shall we put the felt-tips away and find your tights and then we'll put your lovely new dress on . . .' Penny slunk out of the room and took sanctuary in her bathroom. She touched up her powder and lipstick and gave herself a last squirt of Tom Ford's perfume Mandorino Di Amalfi. Hellishly expensive, she knew, but so worth it.

Adam, dressed and ready in the hall, called up the vicarage stairs, 'Penny? Simon? Kit and I are going over to the church. See you there?'

'Yes . . .' Simon sounded a little distracted. 'I won't be long. See you there. Jenna, I think we've got this on back to front.'

Ocean View

Kafir had been watching for the taxi through the rain-streaked windows of the hotel reception, tapping the tip of his borrowed umbrella nervously on the floor. As it drew up he called to the children who were swinging on the impressive banister of the wide Victorian staircase. 'Aali, Sabu, Mummy is waiting. Come on.'

He had been thinking a lot about how he would greet Sennen. She had turned their marriage upside down with the revelation of her true story, and he had been angry. Which he now regretted. He had missed her. They had a long road ahead of them, and much to discuss, but he missed her. Could he trust her again, though?

He shepherded the children into the back of the cab and settled himself in the front.

The taxi driver was a chatty one.

'Fancy-dress party, is it?'

'We are going to a wedding,' said Kafir with dignity.

'Is that what you lot wear to weddings?'

'No, in India I would normally wear something more elaborate.'

'Must be hot over there.'

'It can be.'

'I love a curry, me.'

'As do I.'

The driver looked in his mirror at Aali and Sabu on the back seat. 'Do the little'uns eat curry an' all?'

'They do.'

'Not the really hot ones? The vindaloos?'

'If they like it, yes.'

'God love 'em. Have your nippers tried a pasty yet?'

'Yes, my wife has made them before.'

'Not proper Cornish, though.'

'My wife is Cornish.'

'Is she? Where did you meet?'

Kafir told him the story briefly.

'I met *my* wife in Magaluf. She's Spanish. Lovely girl,' the taxi driver chipped in.

'And do you eat paella?'

'No. Can't stand fish.'

'But you are a Cornish man?'

'Funny, isn't it? By the way, have you got any confetti? For the nippers? All kids like confetti to throw over the bride.' He thought for a minute. 'Or do you throw rice?'

Kafir's good manners prevented him from saying anything unpleasant. 'Perhaps you would stop at a shop that sells confetti?'

'There's a shop in the village where I'm taking you. She sells everything in there. Not too far now.'

The taxi drove them to Queenie's shop and the driver pointed out the church just a couple of hundred yards away. Kafir thanked him and handed him the fare with a generous tip.

As the children hopped out of the car, Kafir steered them around the puddles and then realised the rain had stopped.

Queenie's Village Store

Queenie was behind her counter applying dark purple lipstick to her spidery mouth. When the bell on the door jangled she looked up, expecting it to be the postman for parcel collection. But it wasn't. The person who walked in was dressed as a Bollywood film star and twice as handsome.

Tall, strong and wearing a pink turban, he smiled at her. 'Good morning. My children would like to buy some confetti.'

Queenie looked down at the two adorable faces looking up at her in happy anticipation.

'Oh my good Gawd. You're the bloke what's married to Ella's mum.'

'I am Kafir Singh. Pleased to meet you.'

'I'm Queenie. Pleased to meet you too. Oh, you do look a treat. I love your jacket. Is it what you'd call brocade?'

'I believe so.'

'And the kiddies! Pretty as a picture.'

'Thank you. I hope their mother will agree.'

'Oh yes, Sennen Tallon. I remember when she went missing you know. Poor girl. What with having her babies so young, and all them tongues wagging, it was no wonder she ran away. It was hard on her mum and dad but they were always a bit hippyish, if you know what I mean. They never talked about her after she went. I felt sorry for Ella and Henry. Not that I knew them then, only what I read in the paper, but they're lovely now. And Ella's marrying a smashing young man, Kit. They're both artists. But I expect you know all about it.'

Kafir was absorbing all this fresh information. 'Not all of it. Now, the confetti?'

Queenie dug out several packets and showed them to the children. 'There's some with bells and doves, some what's coloured pink and blue – and hang on . . .' She dug about in another box. 'These 'ere, they're rose petals. I think the vicar prefers these because they biodissolvable.'

Aali grabbed a packet. 'Can we have these please, Daddy?'

Queenie clutched her bosom, 'Lovely manners. Don't see so much of that these days. Would the little boy want some too?'

Sabu nodded shyly and took the packet she offered him.

'That's three pounds twenty-five please. And would you like a sweetie from old Queenie because you've been so good?'

Aali and Sabu's eyes were saucers as she showed them the rows of sweet jars on her shelves. 'You point at what you fancy and I'll get it out for you.'

Aali chose a jelly snake and Sabu a lollipop.

''Ere look at that,' said Queenie looking out of the shop's windows, 'that's sunshine, that is. Looks like the rain has blown through. Now, I'll just get me 'at and me fur coat and then I'll close the shop. Would you mind escorting me over to the church?'

The Churchyard

Upstairs in Marguerite Cottage, Ella was staring at her reflection. She had to start on her eye make-up but her hands were shaking too much. She pulled nervously at the opening of her old dressing gown and saw her engagement ring catch the light. She had fallen for it the moment the jeweller had pulled the tray of antique rings out from under the counter. A circle of alternating tiny aquamarine and diamond stones. When Kit had put it on her finger it had fitted perfectly.

'Aquamarines are said to be lucky for couples and travellers,' the jeweller had said brightly. 'This one is dated from the 1920s and is very special.'

'I love it,' said Ella running her fingers over it gently and letting it twinkle.

'How much is it?' enquired Kit crossing his fingers.

When he was told the price, Ella swiftly took it off. 'It's lovely but too much.'

Kit stopped her. 'Do you like it?'

'It's beautiful.'

'Then it's yours.'

There was a gentle knock at the bedroom door. 'Come in,' called Ella.

It was Sennen still in her coat and carrying the box which

she put gently on the bed. 'Hello, darling, Henry said you were up here.'

'Oh, Mum. I'm so glad to see you.'

Sennen heard the catch in Ella's throat, 'Darling? Are you okay?'

Ella nodded her eyes filling with tears. 'Yes.'

'Then why the tears? Are you having doubts?'

'No . . . but, it's all so overwhelming.' Ella got up and went to Sennen who put her arms around her.

'Of course it is. I felt the same on my wedding day.'

'Did you?' Ella snuffled.

'Yes. It wasn't that I didn't want to marry him, it was just such a huge thing to do.'

'That's how I feel. I love Kit. He's kind and gentle and funny and I don't want anyone else but . . .'

Sennen stood back and held her daughter at arm's length. 'I think this is all perfectly normal. He's probably got the jitters too. Right now he's wondering how someone as wonderful as you would want to marry him.'

'Do you think so?'

'I know so. Now, let's get you ready.' Sennen unbuttoned her coat and chucked it onto the bed.

'Mum!'

'What?' Sennen turned and saw her reflection in the dressing table mirror.

Ella was beaming, 'You're wearing a sari!'

Henry popped his head round the door, 'Mother, how do you take your tea?' He eyed her sari, 'Blimey. You won't have to worry about anyone else wearing the same as you today, will you?'

'It's fabulous!' exclaimed Ella, wide-eyed. 'I love it! Granny always said she wanted to wear a sari. Now here you are in one.'

'This was meant for Granny,' said Sennen. 'I bought it years ago. Too late now.'

'God, she would have loved it. Can I try it on later?'

'Let's get you ready for this wedding first.'

'Tell you what,' said Henry, still loitering, 'forget the tea, I've got a bottle of Krug downstairs.'

Getting Ella dressed was the gift Sennen had given up hope of ever earning. But here she was helping with shoes and blusher, hairspray and buttons.

'Let me look at you.' Sennen drank in the vision in front of her. 'You are lovely.'

'Thanks, Mum.'

'Just one more thing.' Sennen collected the small box from the bed and gave it to her daughter. 'For you, from me,' she said simply.

Ella opened it and gently lifted the gossamer veil from its safe keeping.

'Oh, Mum. It's perfect. Help me put it on?'

As light as thistledown, its crystal dewdrops spinning rainbows around the room, Sennen placed it carefully on Ella's hair.

'There.'

Henry was waiting for them at the bottom of the stairs, three glasses of Krug on a tray, and his phone ready to take photos.

'Ells, you look really beautiful,' he said, taking her hand to help her down the last two stairs. 'We'd better do a selfie of the three of us.'

Putting his free arm around Sennen's waist he crammed the three of them into half a dozen laughing selfies.

'Now let me take one of Mum and daughter. Smile . . . gorgeous.'

'Let me take one of you and the bride,' said Sennen. Henry took Ella's hand proudly and smiled broadly as Sennen took the shots.

'Let me see them,' asked Ella. They all crowded around the small screen and for the first time saw photographs of them all together.

'My children and me.' Sennen wiped her eyes. 'It's a miracle.'

Henry pulled his mother to him and kissed her hair. 'Don't go wobbly now, Mother, we've got a whole day to get through.'

He solemnly handed out the glasses of champagne. 'This is a very special day. Not just for Ella but for all of us. It's a day to enjoy ourselves as a family. The Three Tallons.' He lifted his glass: 'To us.'

'Thank you, Henry,' Sennen said softly. 'Thank you.'

Sennen knew she wouldn't be able to keep her emotions at bay much longer so she swallowed some champagne and said briskly, 'Right, I'm off. Henry, don't forget to help Ella pull the veil over her face before you leave the house.'

'Yes, Mother.'

'Good. Right. Let me have a last look at you both. Oh, I love you so much.' She stepped towards her children to give them one last hug, but Henry stopped her.

'Now, no more crying, and no more hugging. We can't get all creased up at this stage!'

'Love you, Mum,' said Ella.

'See you in church.'

She blew a final kiss and left.

Now, with a deep breath, shoulders down, head up, she walked towards the church.

She heard the squeak of children's voices and saw two

young children running at her across the churchyard. She stopped dead in her tracks, unbelieving as Aali and Sabu ran gleefully towards her.

'Mummy! Mummy!' they shouted.

She felt her stomach lurch and her pulse quicken as she tried to take in what was happening. They were with her now, clinging on to her legs, Aali kissing her hand, Sabu with his arms up, pleading to be carried. She bent down and drew them to her, kissing them and saying their names over and over again.

Then she heard Kafir's voice and looked up.

He was coming towards her, controlled and calm and so very handsome.

'Hello, Sennen.'

She stood up quickly and black dots swam in front of her eyes. Her breath came in short pants. She knew she was going to faint but as she faltered he caught her. 'Are you okay?'

'Yes. Yes. It's you. You came. You got my message?'

'Only when I got to London. I was already on my way. Here, you need to sit down.' He led her to a long bench next to an ancient yew tree.

'Sit,' he ordered.

She sat, Aali and Sabu climbing up next to her. 'We've come to surprise you.' Aali said.

'Well, y-you have,' Sennen managed. She looked up at Kafir. 'You all look so lovely.'

'I like your sari,' Kafir said.

'Thank you. I thought I'd be the only one in Indian dress but now . . .'

'We look like a family,' Kafir finished for her.

'Yes.' Sennen held her hand out to him. 'Oh, I have missed you. Thank you for being here.'

'Can we open the carfetti now?' asked Sabu.

'Not yet.' Sennen kissed him. 'We have to wait until the bride and groom are married.'

Queenie came breathlessly to join them. 'I've asked the vicar to save some seats for us. Front row.'

The church was filling up but as the splendidly dressed Kafir Singh walked down the aisle with his wife and children the chatter muted as all eyes turned to them. Kit and Adam were waiting nervously by the pulpit, eyes front, but sensing something unusual was happening, turned and saw them.

Kit beamed at Sennen. She looked so exotic and so happy and he came to greet her with a kiss and then shook hands with Kafir. 'Hello, sir,' he said respectfully, 'Kit Beauchamp. I'm the groom and this is Adam, my cousin and best man.'

Kafir bowed his head. 'It is a pleasure to meet you. I hope you don't mind me joining you without notice?'

'Not at all. You are very welcome.'

The congregation watched the drama unfold in front of them, and as this new and exotic family took their seats, the babble of conversation rose higher than before.

The organist had been playing a medley of classical background themes but on a hidden signal struck up Mendelsohn's 'Wedding March' and the congregation stood as one, their heads swivelled to the main door.

Ella, proudly supported by Henry, began the long walk down the aisle.

Jenna toddled ahead, chucking handfuls of petals at everyone she knew, shouting, 'Hello, hello, hello.'

38

The 'Wedding March' finished on a flourish, its final notes ricocheting around the church's vaulted roof.

Kit felt Ella come to his side and dared to glance at her. Her red curls were muted by her veil, but he could see the light in her eyes.

Jenna turned her flower basket upside down and banged it on the bottom to make sure it was empty before Ella gently nudged her and reminded her to take her bridal bouquet to Penny, who would look after it. Ella watched her go and then looked for her mother. There she was, surrounded by Kafir, Aali and Sabu.

Sennen gave her a look of, 'I know, I know!' and a shaky thumbs up. Ella almost giggled but returned the thumbs up. And whispered to Kit, 'You see who is here?'

'Yes. I met them earlier. Really nice. And by the way, you look amazing.'

Simon, dignified in collar and stole, coughed. 'Please be seated. We are gathered here today in the sight of God . . .'

The wedding was simple and all the more emotional for it.

As Simon pronounced them man and wife and said, 'You may kiss the bride . . .' the congregation applauded loudly. If euphoria is contagious it would explain why Ella and Kit floated down the aisle on a raft of joy.

The sun was shining brightly as they stood for pictures of every permutation. Ella, being drowned in confetti by Aali, Sabu and Jenna, had only the briefest of moments to say hello to Kafir and welcome him.

When the pictures were eventually done, the guests trooped after the bride and groom and into the garden of Marguerite Cottage where trestle tables sagged under the weight of food.

A local lad, who ran a mobile disco, played 'Isn't She Lovely' and the prosecco began to flow.

Henry introduced himself to Kafir. 'I'm Henry – Sennen's first son,' he said rather pointedly, if not a little proprietorially.

Kafir inclined his head in respect. 'I am very happy to meet you. I am Kafir Singh, Sennen's first husband.'

Sennen disengaged herself from Queenie and hurried to Kafir's side. 'You have made your own introductions?'

'We have,' said Henry. 'But I should like to meet my half-brother and -sister too.'

'Oh, they are with Ella. Sabu has fallen in love with her. He thinks she is a Royal Princess and Aali won't let go of her hand.'

'You didn't tell us they were coming,' Henry said to Sennen, pointedly.

'I didn't know. It's a wonderful surprise and a bit of a shock too.' Sennen began to feel anxious. 'It's okay, isn't it?'

Henry ignored her and addressed himself to Kafir. 'But

how did you know there was a wedding today? You got to the church at just the right time. Someone must have told you? Or was it an extraordinarily lucky coincidence.'

Kafir replied calmly, 'Sennen asked me to come.'

Henry looked at his mother in false surprise. 'Did you? But you said you didn't?'

Sennen said awkwardly, 'I didn't think he would come.'

Henry turned back to Kafir. 'To quote Mrs Merton, when were you first attracted to the soon to be wealthy Sennen Tallon?'

'Stop it!' hissed Sennen.

Kafir stood between mother and son. 'That is enough. This is the wedding of your sister. Do not speak to your mother in that way.'

Henry smirked. 'Mother, didn't it even cross your mind? Is he here for you or the money he thinks you've been left?'

Kafir was thunderous and took a step closer to Henry.

'Okay, okay!' Henry backed off. 'Keep your turban on. I'm was going to find another drink anyway.'

'I am so sorry,' Sennen said, watching Henry retreating, 'I-I don't know what to say.'

'Maybe I shouldn't have come after all.'

She put her hand on Kafir's arm. 'Thank God you're here. I can never thank you enough for coming. I have missed you so much.'

He placed his hand over hers.

'Can you forgive me?' asked Sennen. 'Am I still your wife?'

'Let us talk later. For now, I would like you to introduce me to everybody.'

Henry had topped up his glass and was now searching for Deborah amongst the familiar faces. He found her being chatted up by Adam and, walking up behind her, pinched her bottom.

'Ow.' She spun round. 'Oh, it's you. Henry, this is Adam, he's Kit's cousin.'

'I know. He's also the best man.' Henry glowered at Adam. 'Debs is my girlfriend,' he said.

'Am I?' asked Deborah. 'News to me. Since when?'

'Now.'

She held her hand to her throat. 'This is all so sudden. And so romantic buuut . . .'

'What?'

She turned to Adam. 'Would you care to dance?'

'I'd love to.' Adam took Deborah's hand and guided her to the patch of lawn designated as the dance floor, while throwing a wink over his shoulder to Henry.

Henry seethed and went in search of another bottle of prosecco. Rosemary found him sitting in a heap under a tree as the sun started to go down.

'You all right?'

'Tip top,' he said acidly.

'Then why aren't you dancing with Deborah? I know you're seeing her.'

'How?' he sneered. 'Private detective, are you?'

'No, but my partner is in the police force and . . . well, let's say that you have been seen coming and going from Miss Palmer's house.'

'It's a free country, isn't it?'

'Of course, but Trevay likes a gossip.'

Henry crumpled. 'She's dancing with the bloody best man.'

'And you're jealous.'

'Pah. Not a jealous bone in my body.'

Rosemary raised her eyebrows. 'Really? Then why were you so rude to your mother's husband?'

He frowned. 'I don't know what you're talking about.'

'No need to lie to me. Sennen told me what you said.'

Henry looked small. 'I worry about her, you know? Who is this bloke and why is he here?'

'He's her husband and he's come to support her and, I think to confront their marriage problems head on. Like adults.'

'I don't want her going back to India with him.'

'Why not?'

'Because,' his voice trembled, 'because she'll go again, like before.'

'When you were young?'

Henry dashed a tear away with his fist. 'Uh huh.'

'Did you know she came back to see you, when you were little?'

'No she didn't.'

'Your grandmother sent her away. Wouldn't let her see you or Ella or your grandfather.'

'Granny would never have done that,' Henry said, picking at a knuckle.

'But she did. For good reasons, I think. Your grandmother had been left with two tiny children and a husband who had a nervous breakdown. She was angry. I think she must have regretted rejecting her only daughter every day after.'

'I don't believe you.'

'Maybe you should ask your mother.'

Henry stood up. 'That's exactly what I'm going to do.'

'Not now.' Rosemary stood up too. 'Tomorrow.' She tried to stop him but he threw her arm off him and strode off to find Sennen.

Deborah saw him and stopped him. 'Henry, where have you been? I've been looking for you.'

'Really?'

'Yes, really.'

'I thought you were having a lovely time dancing with dreamboat Adam.'

Deborah laughed. 'He's very nice but too smarmy for me.' She stepped closer to Henry and pouted. 'I wanted my caveman Henry to come back to me.' She slid her arms around his waist and spanked one of his buttocks. 'Or is naughty Henry sulking?'

'No.' He felt his resistance lowering.

'I think he is and I think I will have to punish him.'

He pushed himself closer to her. 'You are a naughty girl.'

Their passionate kiss was interrupted by Adam with a microphone, ready to deliver his best man's speech.

Henry took Debs' hand and dragged her off into the bushes.

It had got a lot darker when they returned and the fairy lights in the trees transformed the garden into something magical.

Brushing off their clothes they arrived just as Adam and Kit had finished their speeches and the applause was dying down.

A small section of the crowd started calling, 'We want the bride, we want the bride.'

Ella blushed and waved her hands to say no, but eventually she gave in and took the mic.

'Hello, everyone.' She was clearly a bit tiddly. 'I just want to say how happy I am to be married to Kit and to be Mrs Ella Beauchamp.' She gave a small, breathy laugh that bounced from the sound system. 'Mrs Beauchamp. Who'd have thought it? And I know the wedding was a bit quick, but it's not because I'm expecting or anything . . . No, It's because my mum is here and I wanted her to be here when I got married, so she is here and it's FANTASTIC. Stand up, Mum.'

Sennen cringed, but stood up anyway and waved, then sat down quickly.

'And she's brought a new step-dad for me and Henry. Woo yeah. He's the tall handsome one in the turban.' She waved at Kafir who bowed his head and acknowledged the other guests. 'And, she's brought us a half-brother and sister who are adorable, so cheers to them.' Jenna and Sabu tried to get up to wave and show off but Aali pulled them down and did a little dance instead.

Ella laughed and continued, 'But, I just want to ask you all now, to stand up and make a toast to Granny and Poppa who can't be here tonight because . . . because they are in heaven. Granny and Poppa!' She spilt most of her prosecco down the front of her dress as she missed her mouth but she was incapable of noticing and took her bow to whistles and cheers.

Henry raised his glass and watched as Ella sat down with some help from Kit. He dipped his head and said to Deborah, 'Excuse me. I just need a word with someone.'

He had seen Sennen and Kafir sitting under a garland of bunting, but now Sennen was on her own. Henry walked over and joined her.

'Hello, Henry.' She smiled at him. 'Are you okay?'

'Not really. Rosemary has just told me that you came back to see Ella and me years ago and that Granny told you to go away. Is that true?'

Sennen looked at her hands. 'Yes.'

'So you left us twice?'

'Granny was very clear that she didn't want me here.'

'And you couldn't be arsed to fight and stay? For the sake of Ella and me?'

'It wasn't like that. She said that it would upset you both

too much and that I had made Poppa ill and that if I stayed it could kill him.'

'Granny would never say a thing like that.'

'I am afraid she did, and it hurt me deeply but I did as she said because I couldn't bear the thought of you and Ella being hurt and confused again.'

'You're saying that to cover your own back.'

Kafir, who had returned, was standing behind mother and son and had heard the exchange. He stepped into their vision. 'Your mother is telling the truth.'

'Oh, fuck off,' said Henry.

'I don't mind you using that language in front of me,' Kafir said firmly, 'but not in front of your mother, please.'

'What about me and Ella? What about us?' Henry was red with anger and drink. 'She left us. She's going to leave us again as soon as she can.'

'Look at it another way, Henry,' Kafir's voice was low and grave, 'your grandmother's actions were cruel. Yes. But what did that do to both of them? And how courageous is your mother in coming back to make amends?'

Henry's anger was fading and a small, lost boy emerged. 'Why did you go? Was it me? What did I do? Was it my fault you left us? Did I do something wrong? Did you go away because you didn't want me? Why did you stop loving us?'

Sennen took Henry in her arms and held him, whispering maternal words of comfort.

39

She led him into Marguerite Cottage and found a small study where son and mother could speak without being overheard.

'Henry, I was so stupid and so clueless, I didn't know what else to do. I was ashamed of who I was. Pointed and stared at. Held up as an example to other stupid young girls. I loved you and Ella so much. It was why I left. I went to find your father and to tell him about you both. I told you, I took you to see him when you were just a baby. But he had gone. I would have run away with you, and gone to find him, but it wasn't long before I found out I was expecting Ella so I had to stay. Then, as soon as I thought you were both able to be left with Granny and Poppa, I persuaded Rosemary to come with me. I was so cowardly. Running away has no valour attached to it. I even left Rosemary to face the music alone. I ran and ran from you, from myself, from Granny and Poppa.' She put her head in her hands. 'Not brave at all. And when I came back I was terrified. But I had no idea about the extent of the damage I had done. Granny stood on the doorstep, wouldn't let me in, and made me understand I was not welcome.'

'So why did you come back this time?' Henry asked.

'The letter that found me almost killed me. How could my parents be dead? Both not yet sixty. And I had felt nothing. No sign or premonition that they had died years ago. I thought I'd be able to *know* if anything bad happened and get home in time to be with them, but the threads had been burnt and I had noticed nothing.'

Her voice was breaking. 'I had pictured them hale and hearty and enjoying life. Proud of their two grandchildren, taking time to paint and potter. While I . . .' She laughed bitterly. 'I was gratefully living my new life, selfishly happy with my second chance.'

Henry rubbed his eyes. 'And what about my father?'

Sennen didn't know what to say. 'Do you mind if we leave that to another time? I don't know what that would bring up. I didn't really know him. I was a fool really. I can't honestly tell if he was a bad man or just the wrong man. And I want to protect you from that.'

Henry shuffled his feet and cleared his throat. 'What are you going to do with Granny and Grandad's money?'

'I promise you I did not come back for that. God's truth. I came back only for you and Ella. I thought, naively, that I could explain what happened and rebuild the family I have dreamed about these past twenty-five years. But I see it's not that easy. There's a lot of work to do on my part, if you'd let me.'

'We have come this far without you.'

'Of course.' Sennen was quiet. Thinking. 'Ella's an amazing young woman. And you, you are brave. You always were. When you fell over or banged your knee you never made a fuss.'

Henry swallowed hard. 'I remember being on the beach,

and I think it was you, but, do you remember me getting stung by a bee?'

She nodded. 'Oh yes. Horrible. It had got in the crook of your knee and as you bent down it was crushed and stung you. You screamed so loudly.'

'It *was* you then. I remember you holding me close to you while Poppa sucked the sting out.'

Sennen leant forward and rubbed his head. 'That was me. I feel your hugs even now. You won't make the same mistakes I made. I have been so lucky to be given a child who is the opposite of me. If you were like me I wouldn't like you at all.' She smiled.

'So it wasn't my fault?'

'None of it was your fault. It was me all the time.'

They stood at the same time and faced each other. 'May I hold you again?' asked Sennen.

Henry didn't wait to give his answer. They embraced with mutual affection and a new trust.

Breaking apart, Sennen hitched the scarf from her sari, back onto her shoulder and said, 'Now, do you want to come back to the party? Meet Kafir properly?'

'Maybe tomorrow? Go out for a coffee?'

'That sounds good.' She stroked his cheek. 'See you tomorrow.'

In the garden the wedding party was in full swing. The DJ had pumped up the volume and the disco lights were flashing their colours all over the dark garden. Sennen couldn't find Ella or Kit but she spotted Kafir sitting on a garden bench with two sleepy children leaning against him.

'I'm sorry I disappeared,' she began.

But Kafir understood. 'How did it go?'

She sat down and stroked Aali's hair. 'He'd like to meet you all properly tomorrow.'

'I should be delighted,' said Kafir.

'Always the gentleman.' She looked into Kafir's eyes. 'Would you all come home with me tonight? I need to be with my family.'

Kafir kissed her gently, on the cheek. 'I think we would like that very much.'

Back at White Water, Kafir and Sennen each carried a sleeping child up into her bedroom.

'This was my parents' room when I was little,' Sennen whispered.

'Do you think they would be shocked to see a man in a turban here?'

Sennen giggled softly. 'Not at all. Very egalitarian, my parents.'

'But not always kind?'

'Not always. No.' She shrugged. 'But I did push them beyond their limits.' She smothered a little laugh. 'In fact, seeing you wouldn't surprise them at all!'

They laid Aali and Sabu in her big bed and pulled the covers over them. Sennen stood nervously in front of Kafir, alone, with him for the first time since she had told him the truth about her past.

'Well. Here we are,' he said.

'Indeed.'

He looked around. 'I shall take the little sofa.'

'No. You are six foot two, you can't do that. Have the bed.'

'But you are five foot eleven.' He smiled at her and put his hand to her hair, stroking it. 'You can't do that either.'

'So what shall we do?' she asked.

'We shall sleep on the floor. Together.'

40

Kafir found two blankets on the top shelf of the wardrobe and spread those on the carpeted floor.

Sennen took the top cover from her big bed and two pillows and laid those down too.

In the bathroom they cleaned their teeth, padding around each other softly so as not to disturb the children.

Kafir unwound his turban and let his slightly greying but still glossy hair fall to below his shoulders. Sennen ran her hands through it and then hugged him.

'I love you so. I need to explain so much to you.'

He pulled her chin towards him and kissed her slowly. 'We have the rest of our lives to talk. If you want to stay?'

'Yes,' she said. 'Yes. I'd like to stay.'

He took her hand and led her back into the bedroom.

Lying in just their underwear on the makeshift bed on the floor, they held each other, warm and loving. They slept better than either of them had slept since they had been apart.

*

Kafir woke to the sound of an American cartoon on the television and his children laughing. He twisted his head and saw Sennen coming out of the bathroom, dressed and ready for the day.

'Morning, sleepyhead.' She knelt down to kiss him. 'I'll tell Amy, the landlady, that you are all here, and to bring breakfast up for you. I have to nip out. I'll be back in the hour.'

He caught her arm as she rose. 'You're not leaving me again?'

'Never.' She smiled at him. 'Never ever. But I do have something I need to do.

'What? No secrets please.'

Sennen looked at the children to check they weren't listening then whispered her plan.

'That is good.' Kafir said, when she finished telling him. 'That is right.'

It took only ten minutes to drive from Trevay to Pendruggan and Marguerite Cottage.

Ella opened the door with a hangover. 'I know I look awful. I couldn't be bothered to take my make-up off last night.'

Sennen gazed at her daughter. Her mascara still looked fresh and her cheeks had the bloom of a happy woman. She was wearing an oversized shirt of Kit's which exaggerated her long, slim legs. 'You look like the front cover of a glossy magazine.'

Ella threw her arms around her mother. 'Ohh, Muuuum. Come in.'

Sennen stepped over several pairs of shoes, discarded jackets, a plastic box full of empty prosecco bottles, and a pile of wedding presents on the hall table. ''Scuse the mess.' Ella flapped a hand airily.

'How are you feeling, darling?' Sennen asked, following Ella into the kitchen.

'Fine. Well. No, not totally fine but . . .' She twirled with her arms out wide. 'I'm soooo happy.'

'Shall I make you a coffee?'

'I've had one. I'm thinking of going back to bed. My husband – that sounds funny, doesn't it? – my husband is still sparko. Sit down. I'll make you a coffee.'

'I've only just popped in to make sure you're all right, but I will be back later and I'll cook breakfast and clear up for you. Is Henry here?'

'Yes, he's here somewhere, maybe the sofa? With Deborah. Did you know they had got it together?'

'Yes, Rosemary mentioned it.'

'Oh, Mum, I have something for you.' Ella opened the back door, and disappeared into the garden. Sennen saw her from the window, skipping across the wet grass. She returned clutching her bridal bouquet. 'I left it in the garden overnight to stay cool. I didn't want to throw it to anyone. I want you to have it.'

Sennen was speechless. 'I'm going to cry again.'

'That's all right.' Ella gave the flowers to her mum and cuddled her.

'What have I done to deserve you and Henry?'

'You've come back. That's enough.'

'We still have lots to say to each other,' said Sennen, cradling the precious flowers.

'I think it would be too much to take it all in in one hit,' laughed Ella. 'There's no hurry. Are you sure I can't make you coffee?'

'No thank you. I have something to do but I will be back later, if that's okay with you?'

'Bloody hell, yes!'

As the two women walked to the front door, Ella popped

her head through the lounge door to check if Henry was there. Momentarily unchecked, Sennen achieved her reason for being there and slipped two white envelopes from her pocket amidst the pile of wedding presents. One addressed to Ella, the other to Henry.

Ella came back. 'Yep, Henry is in there, snoring like a little pig.'

Sennen smiled. 'Bless him. Now you go back and get some sleep.'

'I will. Thanks, Mum.'

Sennen was soon back in Trevay and walking up the hill towards St Peter's Church carrying Ella's bouquet. The sun was bright that morning but an onshore breeze ran a coolness through it. She opened the creaky gate, the rusty spring cata-pulting it back to its latch, and walked up the path that took her behind the church to the furthest corner of the graveyard.

She found her parents' graves and sat between them as she had done just a few weeks before.

'Hello, Mum. Hello, Poppa.' The wind was blowing her hair into her eyes, and she brushed it away. 'It's a bit blowy today, Poppa. Good for the drying though, eh Mum? Remember how you used to have to nag me to put the washing out? I hated that job. I love doing it now. In India, everything dries so quickly and smells of sunshine. Funny how we change, isn't it?'

The church bell began to clang, calling the early risers to the first service of the day.

Sennen lifted Ella's flowers to her nose and smelt the sweet freesias and roses. 'Ella got married yesterday and these are her flowers. She was a truly beautiful bride and I think she and Kit will be happy. He's a lovely boy. You have done a good job with her. She's so kind and full of life. What was she like as a teenager? Not as bad as me, I hope.

'I suspect Henry may have been a handful. He's been very tough on me, and rightly so, but underneath he's so gentle. I want to thank you properly for doing the job that I should have done. You have done it better than I ever could at the age I was. Aali and Sabu have a much better me than the one I was. I know I robbed you of the chance to see me grow up, but then again, you had had enough of me, hadn't you, Mum? I ask for your forgiveness – and I forgive you for turning me away when I so wanted to come home.'

She placed the flowers on her mother's grave. 'These are for you both, but I think Mum will appreciate them more than you, Poppa. And by the way, thank you for guiding me, Mum. I think everything will be okay now. Oh, and I've decided what to do with your legacy. I think you'll be pleased. I love you both very much.'

When Sennen had gone, Ella couldn't rest and so brewed a pot of coffee, the smell of which soon lured Kit, Henry and Debs into the kitchen.

'What a wonderful wedding.' Debs gave Ella a hug. 'And you were the most lovely bride I have ever seen. Don't you think, Henry?'

Henry put four mugs on the table and took the milk from the fridge, 'As sisters go, she looked all right.'

'Gee thanks,' said Ella sticking her tongue out.

Kit swung her into his arms and snuggled up to her. 'Morning Mrs Beauchamp.'

Ella raked her hands through his hair and kissed his neck. 'Good morning, Mr Beauchamp.'

'Yeuch,' said Henry. 'Not before breakfast!'

Ella and Kit giggled.

'How about a fry-up?' suggested Debs.

'Sausages, eggs, bacon in the fridge,' Ella said. 'If you don't mind doing that, Kit and I shall open our wedding presents.'

Kit and Henry carried in the exciting parcels and cards and Ella armed herself with notepad and pen to make a thank you list.

Much laughter and excitement was had as wrapping paper was eagerly ripped apart revealing presents that ranged from the good, the quirky and the ridiculous.

Ella was now sorting through the envelopes addressed to Mr and Mrs Beauchamp, her new name giving her little butterflies in her stomach every time she saw it. But then she saw two that were addressed differently. Simply, one said Henry, the other, Ella.

She passed Henry his and together they opened and read the contents.

Ella read hers.

Dear Ella,

I need nothing. I have everything I could ever want. I have found you and you are so precious to me.

I know Mum and Poppa will be happy knowing you are financially secure. Please do whatever you want with the enclosed cheque.

I shall be going back to India with Kafir soon. He is to me what Kit is to you. I do hope you will come and see us as often as you like. I'll teach you how to wrap a sari.

Thank you for letting me back into your lives.

Love

Mum x

Henry read his.

Dear Henry, my son.

I made such a big mistake years ago. Leaving you was so wrong, but I never stopped thinking about you and loving you. Seeing you walk your sister down the aisle yesterday was the proudest day of my life.

The enclosed cheque is for you. I realise now it's not my choice but yours.

I love you very much and always have.

Mum x

A Year Later

It was a stiflingly hot day in Agra. Sennen had the ceiling fans in the house doing their best to stir the turgid air, and outside she had set a small table under the shade of a Plumbago tree. She leant back in her chair and took a sip of the iced lemonade she had made that morning.

Kafir came out to join her. 'Post from Cornwall,' he said, handing her the letter.

She pulled her reading glasses from her head. 'Thank you. Have some lemonade?'

She opened the envelope as Kafir helped himself.

Her new reading glasses brought Ella's handwriting into sharp focus. 'It's an invitation.' She smiled. 'To Billie's Christening.'

Little Billie Beauchamp, named after her great-grandfather and just eight weeks old, blinked and gurgled as the Reverend Simon Canter sprinkled holy water from the font on to her head. He blessed her and kissed her and handed her back to her mother, Ella, who beamed. Her grin could not have stretched further.

Sennen took a photograph on her phone and then asked Simon anxiously, 'Sorry. Is it okay to take pictures in the church?'

'Of course. A joyous occasion such as this must be recorded. How about I take one of you and Grandfather Kafir with Billie and her parents?' Aali and Sabu barged in. 'Oh, yes, and you two. Goodness. Can't forget the uncles and aunts can we?' Simon took several pictures before turning his attention to Deborah and Henry. 'And what about the godparents! Come on, everyone, squeeze in.'

Henry put one arm around Ella and another around Deborah whose pregnant bump was clear.

With all the pictures done, Kit said, 'Right, time for tea. Simon, you and your wife are very welcome. Pencil House is tiny but we'll all squeeze in I'm sure.'

'That's very kind, I'll go and collect Penny and we'll follow on. I have always wanted to see inside Pencil House. It was Ella's grandparents' home, wasn't it?'

'Yes. Their first house. I think Sennen may even have been born there. When it went up for sale, Ella insisted we put an offer in.'

Ella, cradling Billie, touched Kit's arm, 'Your daughter will be hungry in a minute and your wife needs a cup of tea. Mum and Kafir are so looking forward to seeing the house.'

Debs was desperate to take her shoes off. 'Henry, I need to sit down, your son is kicking the hell out of me.'

'Oh, darling. Sorry. I just want a word with the vicar before he goes. Sit on the pew here.'

Henry caught Simon as he was on his way to the vestry. 'Excuse me,' he said.

'Yes, Henry?' Simon replied, smiling.

'I'm not much of a churchgoer, but would you – would we be able to ask you to baptise our baby?'

'Of course. I'd be delighted. May I ask, have you been baptised?'

Henry hung his head, 'No, if that means we can't . . .'

'Not at all, in fact, I could always do a double baptism? Father and child?'

'I don't think that's really . . .'

'Well, maybe a wedding and a baptism?'

Henry chewed his lip. 'Ah well, I haven't asked Debs . . .'

Simon patted him on the shoulder. 'Then I suggest you do.'

The little front garden of Pencil House was bright with pots of dahlias and hydrangeas. Kit had hung pink bunting around the windows and front door and outside was a hand-painted sign saying:

BILLIE BEACHAMP'S CHRISTENING GUESTS WELCOME

The tall thin house gathered the day's joy within its walls and passed that happiness to the people within. Guests left full of sandwiches cake and tea, safe in the certainty that Billie would grow up loved and secure.

The star of the show herself, had not let anyone down and was now sleeping blissfully in her upstairs cot.

Sennen and Ella crept in to look at her. 'She's been a good girl, hasn't she,' doted Sennen. 'And she looks so like you.'

'Does she?' Ella asked, surprised that Sennen would remember.

'Oh yes. And I think she will have your temperament too.'

Sennen stroked the sleeping face with the back of her hand. 'So wonderful. Three generations in the same room. The room where I suppose my cot was and where Mum and Poppa would stand like this looking at me.'

'Four generations if they were here,' sighed Ella.

'I believe they are here,' said Sennen, 'in our hearts and minds.'

Much later, they heard a noise on the stairs and Kafir appeared at the door.

Sennen put her finger to her lips, 'Shh.'

'I've come to tell you that Sabu and Aali are very tired so if it's okay, I shall take them back to the hotel,' he whispered.

'I won't be long,' she whispered back.

Ella hugged him. 'Thank you for coming, Kafir. Billie is lucky to have an Indian grandfather. Think of all those summer holidays.'

'I am proud to have a granddaughter. In India, I would be called Nannaa I believe.'

'Nannaa?'

'Nani, I think.'

Ella looked from Kafir to Sennen, 'Well, from now on, you are Nannaa and Nanni.'

'Thank you.' Kafir bent to kiss Sennen. 'See you later.'

When Ella and Sennen got downstairs, Kit was setting off the dishwasher and Debs was on the sofa, her swollen legs on Henry's knee. He was rubbing her ankles.

'Drink anyone?' called Kit from the kitchen. 'I have a bottle of good red that I have hidden away. And an orange juice for pregnant and breastfeeding women.'

Debs groaned. 'I could murder a glass of Pinot Grigio.'

'Patience my love, patience,' smiled Henry.

Kit came from the kitchen with a corkscrew and three glasses.

Sennen fetched the orange juice. When she came back Ella, Kit, Henry and Debs were all looking at her. 'What?' she said, handing over the orange juice.

Ella looked at Henry. 'Go on Henry. You first.'

Henry stopped massaging Debs' ankles and cleared his throat. 'Over the last few months we've all been talking and, well, I have decided to leave my job in London, sell the house in Clapham and . . .'

'Not Mandalay Road? I thought you loved it?' interjected Sennen.

'Yes, well it seems I love Debs and our baby enough to leave all that behind and buy something here, in Trevay.'

Sennen was amazed. 'Really?'

'Yes, and to erm . . .'

Ella was fidgety with excitement, 'You know the old Chandlers shop up by the boat sheds?'

'Yes.' Sennen was puzzled.

'We've bought it.'

Sennen clapped her hands. 'Whatever for?'

'For Granny and Poppa's art school.'

Sennen's jaw dropped. 'Really?'

'Really.' Henry nodded. He continued. 'It'll give us all a job. Debs has done the conveyancing. Kit and Ella will run the courses and teach, and I'll mop up everything else.'

'But, this is wonderful.' Sennen's tears came suddenly. 'Wonderful. A dream come true. I don't know want to say.'

Henry put his hand in his pocket and threw her a freshly laundered handkerchief, 'Sorry I can't stand up. I'm pinned by these galumphing fat ankles.'

Sennen began to laugh, 'Are you sure about him, Deborah?'

'As sure as I'll ever be,' she sighed.

'So,' said Ella, picking up her glass of wine, 'Let's raise our glasses to the Adela and William Tallon School of Art.'

'To Granny and Poppa,' cheered Henry.

'And,' said Sennen, 'to coming home.'